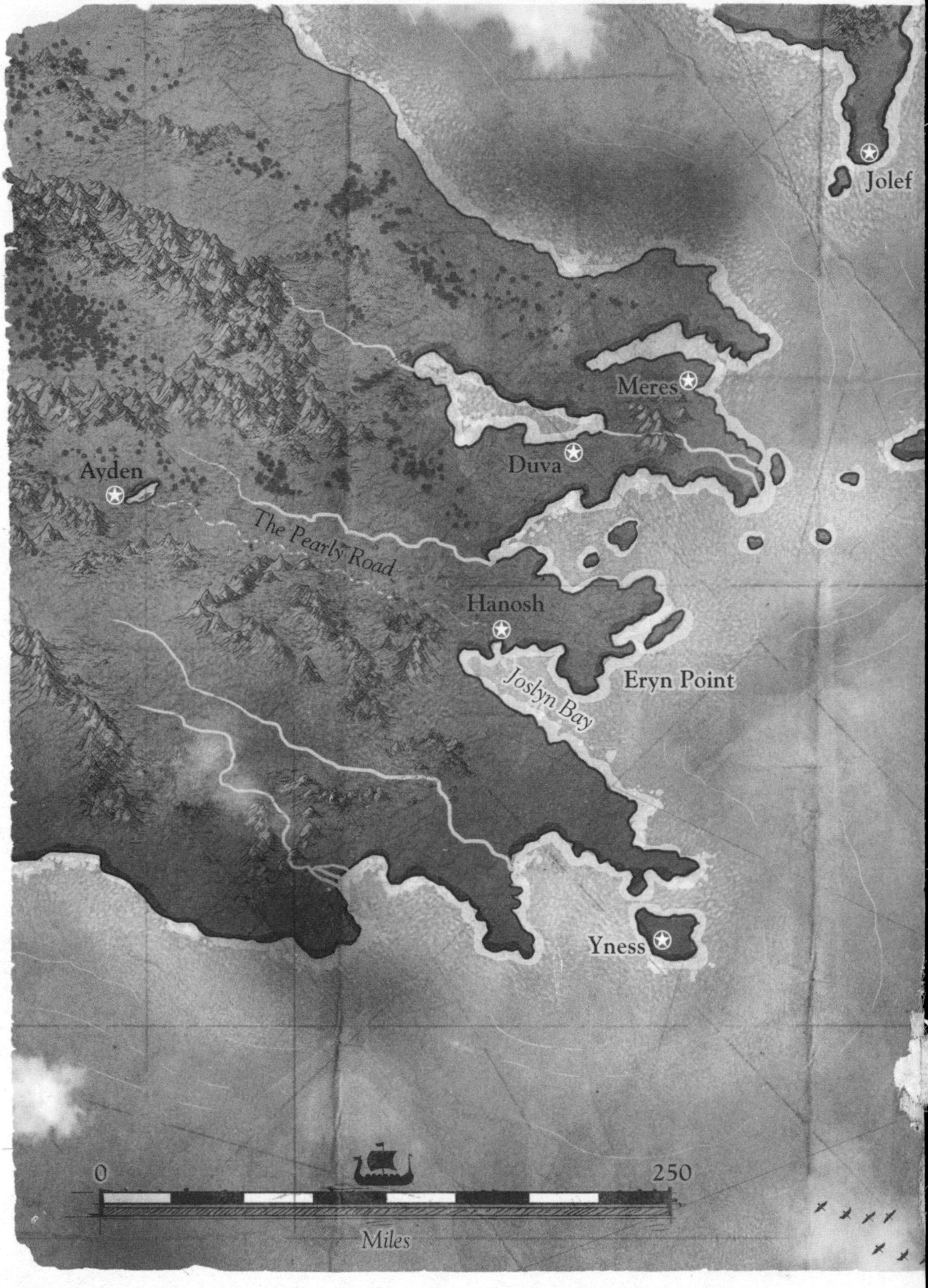
Jolef
Meres
Duva
Ayden
The Pearly Road
Hanosh
Eryn Point
Joslyn Bay
Yness
0
250
Miles

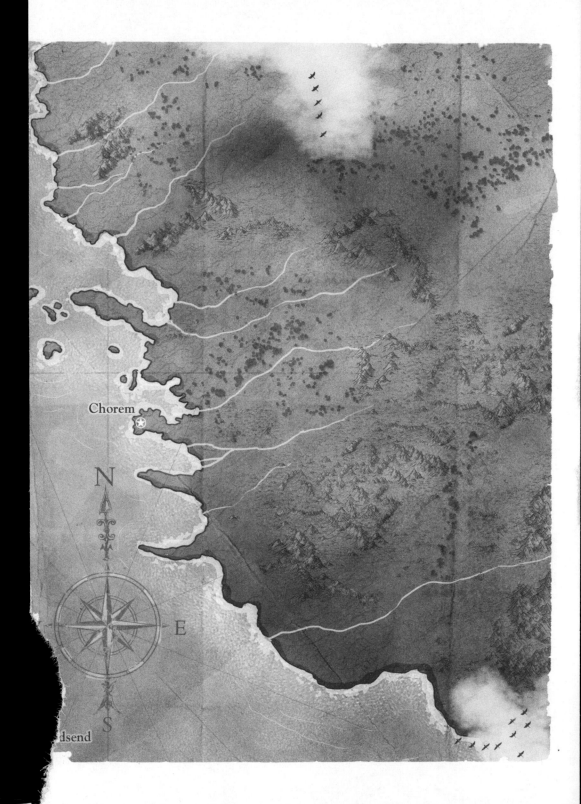

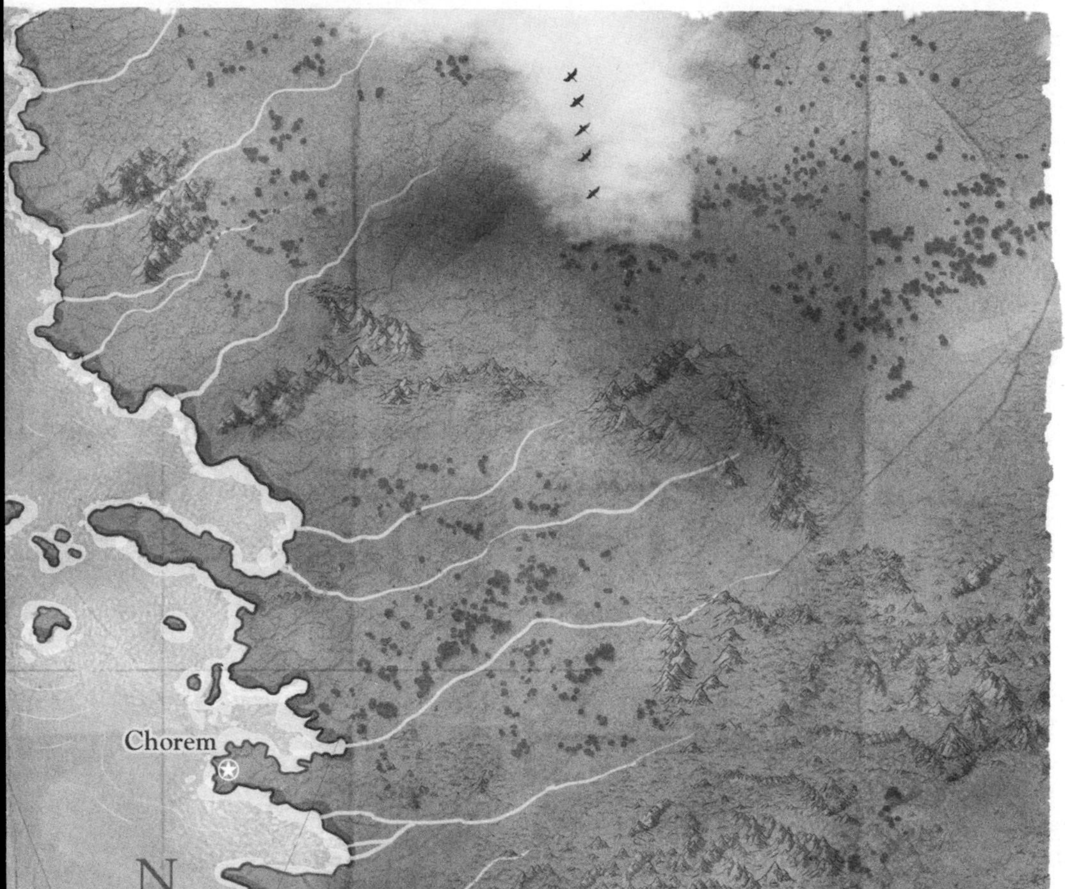
Chorem
N
E
S
dsend

THE DRAGON ROUND

Stephen S. Power

SIMON & SCHUSTER
New York London Toronto Sydney New Delhi

Simon & Schuster
1230 Avenue of the Americas
New York, NY 10020

First Simon & Schuster hardcover edition July 2016

Interior design by Lewelin Polanco
Map design by Robert Lazzaretti

Manufactured in the United States of America

Library of Congress Cataloging-in-Publication Data is available.

ISBN 978-1-5011-3320-6
ISBN 978-1-4767-9461-7 (ebook)

For my father

Contents

Dramatis Personae

COMBER

Jeryon, the captain
Livion, the first mate
Solet, the second mate, an Ynessi
Tuse, the third mate and oarmaster
Everlyn, the apothecary, an Aydeni
Hume, a guilded rower
Bearclaw, a contract rower
Beale, a harpooner
Topp, a sailor

HOPPER

Press, the first mate
Edral, the second mate
Igen, an harpooner
Rowan, the ship's boy

THE WOLF PACK

Jos, the first mate
Mylla and *Barad*, lamps
Bodger and *Gibbery*, harpooners
Mulcent and *Sumpt*, owners
Kley, an oarmaster
Blass, a shoveler

HANOSH

Chelson, an owner
Tristaban, his daughter
Holestar, *Skite*, and *Derc*, his guards
Felic, his office boy
Sivarts, one of his captains
Kathi, one of his remora
Ophardt, his footman
Asper, "the White Widow," a fellow owner
Omer, a trade rider

Herse, the army's general
Rego, his adjutant
Birming and *Pashing*, sergeants

Ject, the city guard's general
Ravis, his first guard
Oftly, new guard of his retinue
Husting, a sergeant of the city guard
Chevron, sergeant of the Tower Guards
Isco and *Bern*, guards

Eles, an owner and leader of the City Council
Prieve, the sea general
Strig, a tanner
Almond, a proprietor
Fakkin Tawmy, a fixer
Mags, a customs official

Assorted sailors and rowers, prisoners and proprietors, traders and whores, workers and servants, guards, soldiers, and citizens.

And several dragons.

THE
DRAGON
ROUND

PART ONE

Jeryon

CHAPTER ONE

The Captain's Chance

1

Just before dawn and still eight hours from Hanosh, the captain of the penteconter *Comber* feels the rowers start to flag. They're pulling together, but behind the drummer's beat, and if he lets them get away with it, they'll fall apart. He can't afford that. However exhausted they are, having rowed for seventeen hours, he brings his galleys in on time.

Jeryon's about to leave his cabin and go below when a whip cracks and he hears his oarmaster, Tuse, call for twenty big ones. The galley lurches forward, and by the seventh heave the rowers are tight again.

Tuse has some promise. Jeryon likes that call. Not twenty for Hanosh. Not twenty to save the sick. Just twenty. Tuse focuses on the job he has, not the one he wants, unlike his other mates.

The first and second mates are on the stern deck above, two whispers through the wood. Jeryon closes his eyes to listen. So far they've only said what all mates say: to advance they have to earn another captain's ship. They're getting bolder, though. It's a short trip from earn to take.

If Jeryon didn't need them for the next eight hours, he'd put them off, maybe before they reached Hanosh. As it is, let them think he would sleep. Once the medicine's unloaded, he'll wake them to reality.

Livion, the first mate, soft-cheeked and slight, leans against the stern rail. Solet, the second, stands to starboard with the rudder trapped between his thick chest and hairy arm. They have the wind, which fills the galley's sail and muffles the crack of Tuse's whip.

"I wish she'd left the city," Livion says over the wind.

"Why?" Solet says. "The flox was in the Harbor. It'd barely touched the Hill. Without some moon-eyed sailor to carry it all the way up to the Crest—"

"Plagues don't care what lane you live on."

"Apparently your woman doesn't either." Livion's eyes narrow, but Solet ignores him and goes on. "And if her father cared before we set out, he won't after we dock and save the city. A father might not want a sailor in his family, but what owner doesn't want a hero in his business?"

"I'm not using her to get to him."

Solet snorts, and Livion stiffens. Sometimes Solet oversteps himself. Hanoshi don't discuss their private lives, which makes an Ynessi like Solet want to pry all the more. The first mate finds it easier to give in a bit and get it over with than to resist. It's his fault, anyway, for trading a long look with Tristaban as they were casting off.

"I want him to find me worthy of command," Livion says.

"Worthy?" Solet says. "You sound like the captain. You sound like my grandfather. There's no worthy anymore, just worth." Solet taps the rudder with the blade he wears in place of half his right forefinger. "Get your woman. Get your command. Get your fortune. That makes you worthy. Money is money to her father, to all the owners. You don't want to end up like Jeryon, do you?" Solet taps the deck with his foot.

"I could do worse," Livion says. "He's been captain for years."

"Decades," Solet says, "which makes him—"

"Reliable?"

"Stalled. He doesn't reach. He's captain of a monoreme. Has been. Always will be. He might as well push a milk cart."

"That milkman," Livion says, "is the real person who'll save the city."

"And he'll give the Trust all the credit for sending him. They'll give him a pat on the head and a perk for being on time. There's a whole city waiting to cheer us, the purest coin there is, and he won't want any of it. Wouldn't you want a taste of that? Wouldn't your woman? She won't settle for nothing, anyone can see that. You shouldn't either." He half closes his eyes. "We'll have triremes." His eyes shine. "What I could do with a trireme."

Livion says, "I'm starting to understand the Ynessi reputation for piracy."

"You wound me," Solet says. "I'm no pirate. But I do need a ship to start, so once you have your woman, you could put a word in her father's ear and see the captain rewarded with a desk while I get *Comber*. That I would settle for."

Sunlight bubbles on the horizon, then erupts and flows along it. The sky is filled with blood and gold and the palest blue. The mates smile at each other.

The whip cracks again. "What about Tuse?" Livion says.

"He'll get all the wine he can drink," Solet says.

The portholes glow, and the cabin has gone from dark to dim. Jeryon can't disagree with Solet. *I am a plodder. I'm also fairly rewarded and content. In a city like Hanosh, where one eats well, four eat poorly, and five don't eat at all, it's better to be hardtack than an empty plate dreaming of steak.*

He feels sorry for Livion. The boy had promise before he started listening to Solet, and probably this woman. If she's as manipulative as

Jeryon thinks, Livion will count himself lucky after the Trust learns of his plotting. He won't get another Hanoshi ship, but he'll be rid of her.

Solet will have to return to Yness, likely a little bruised, where he'll be welcomed with open arms and, knowing the Ynessi, open legs. Jeryon doesn't understand why the Trust puts up with them. A wild people. A wasteful people. At least the Aydeni on board has proven trustworthy.

The door to the adjacent cabin opens. He hears the Aydeni enter, slam the door, rattle through a box of phials and slam out again. He can imagine why she's rattling and slamming. As an apothecary, in addition to making medicine, she has to treat the rowers, and she doesn't approve of the Trust's new tonic. So be it. She was only contracted for this trip. In eight hours she'll be gone too.

As the oarmaster cracks his whip again, Everlyn climbs the aft ladder from the rowers' deck to her cabin. Dawn does its best to cheer her, but fails. The captain won't light the lamps, worried about Aydeni privateers, as if there were any. This makes for a gloomy ship and a gloomier rowers' deck, however much moonlight comes through the half deck above. Gloominess suits the Hanoshi, though.

Theirs is a seafaring city that has largely traded its fishing fleet for trading galleys and its nets for coin purses, whereas Ayden has always trusted the endless bounty of its mountains: the stone and ore, the trees and game. Even the ancient shadows long to be shaped into stories featuring wondrous beasts and secret caves. Hanoshi stories are about the joy of riches and the pain of their loss. They would only shape the shadows on *Comber* if they could be boxed for sale.

Everlyn looks around her cabin. The small room is packed with barrels of golden shield, a curative herb they bought across the Tallan Sea. She's spent every spare moment of the last three days turning it into medicine. The Hanoshi council will give it away for free to employed citizens. The Trust, which owns *Comber*, is charging the city just a nominal coin for the voyage, but this is not a selfless act. The Trust wants to become a ruling company, and ruling companies realize that if the city perishes of the plague, there will be no one left to rule or employ.

Everlyn lifts the lid of a pot simmering on the small iron stove at one end of her spattered worktable. She has spent so much of the past three days in here reducing the shield to medicine, she hardly smells it anymore. This disturbs her. Fresh, the shield smells like liver. As medicine, it smells like rotten liver. Oh, what she must smell like.

It's a small sacrifice, though, compared to the effects of the flox, which bubbles the skin as if boiled from within, then cools into a cracking black crust. The luckiest die, and most are that lucky.

Everlyn rattles through a wooden box under the table, pulls out a clear bottle of fine red powder and pockets it. From a different box she removes a larger green bottle with a skull painted on the label and takes a long pull. She swallows a belch, chases it with another, longer pull, then puts the bottle back and goes below, slamming the door behind her. Let the privateers hear that.

Tuse stalks the alley between the rowers' benches, so tall he shifts from hunching to squatting to both beneath the overhead. He coils and uncoils a white whip. "Fifty-seven strokes that took."

"I'll say it again: They've had too much," Everlyn says.

"I haven't," one rower says, grinning wildly. A bear-claw brand glistens on his shoulder. A cut from Tuse's lash bloodies his cheek.

"Especially you," she says.

"You're worried about my health?" Bearclaw says. He shakes his leg shackle. "I'm not one of them. I'll die down here. Might as well be fired up."

"I won't have it," the rower behind him says. "None of us will." Having no shackles, he looks around. Unlike Bearclaw and the other five prisoners leased from the jail in Hanosh, the rest of the rowers wear a sodden armband with the crest of their guild, the Brothers of the Oar. "Brothers don't cheat. Look to Hume."

Hume is a silent mountain. His eyes are closed. He may be asleep. Yet he pulls true. The brothers have looked at him in admiration before. They aren't as inspired now.

"I need some," a brother says. "To get the job done."

"And me," another says.

"Oarmaster," Bearclaw says, "I asked first."

"You'll die," Everlyn says. "And I won't give you the means. Or let anyone else."

"It's not your choice," Tuse says. "Should I tell the Trust an Aydeni tried to sabotage the trip? How many more would you be risking then?"

Everlyn chokes on her fury. The math is easy. She's done it with every dose of powder she's administered: How many will she save in Hanosh for each rower she might doom on the *Comber*?

She takes out the bottle of red powder and a spoon. Everlyn starts aft with a prisoner, who shakes his head. Some brothers cheer until one of their own takes a huge snort.

"I said it's to get the job done," the brother says and stares at his oar.

Tuse grunts. Bearclaw laughs. Hume pumps the oar. The drum beats on.

Once she's done, Everlyn tucks a stray lock of hair behind her ear, holds her chin up, and says, "I have pots to tend." Tuse ignores her. She marches past him, climbs the aft ladder, and sees the other mates staring abaft. They look concerned. Maybe there *are* privateers out here.

Livion eclipses the sun with his hand and peers around it. "Do you see that? On top of the mist."

"Too high for a sail," Solet says. "Oh." He squeezes the rudder tighter. "Could we outrun it?"

"It might not see us," Livion says.

"It won't have to. The stench of the shield will lead it right to us."

Solet curses. "Why couldn't *Comber* be a trireme? We'd have marines. More weapons. Better defenses. The same speed."

"At ten times the expense," Livion says. "I'll wake the captain."

Jeryon rubs his face awake. The mates weary him, and he needs a shave too. As a man's chin goes, so goes the man, and his will be impeccable. He puts a small towel and clay pot of soap on a shelf beneath a porthole and takes his razor, a circular copper blade, from its ivory case. It would be a ridiculous indulgence if not so useful.

Maybe Livion is worth saving, he thinks, *if he could shave away the bad influences. It would also be indulgent, but he should give his mate that chance. Why should someone suffer for another man's wrongs?*

Jeryon hears Solet say, "Oh." Through the porthole, he sees it: a tiny shadow creeping on the verge of dawn. He holds his hand at arm's length. The shadow's a quarter-thumb wide, no bigger than a fire ant. His stomach churns. The math is easy. If the shadow reaches the *Comber*, it'll cover the entire ship.

As Livion runs overhead to the stern deck ladder, Jeryon fits the razor into its case and pockets it.

2

Everlyn dodges Livion as he slides down the ladder from the stern deck and bangs on the captain's door. He sticks his head in briefly, then walks past her onto the causeway over the rowers' deck. He says to Tuse below, "Silent drumming, double-time."

Tuse glances up. "Aye."

"And shutter the ports," Livion says.

Tuse nods to the drummer stationed by the mast, who plays a

little roll to signal the change, then taps his heavy sticks to keep the beat.

The relative silence is astounding. Everlyn is almost dizzied by the absence of pounding, as if someone had pulled her feet out from under her. She grabs Livion's arm and says, "What is it?"

Before he can answer her, Jeryon emerges from his cabin. His black jacket emphasizes his bony frame, his red three-quarter pants reveal it, and his yellow cotton blouse, regardless of the rank its color designates, does nothing good for his pallor. His clothes have been fiercely brushed and pressed, though. His only informality is a pair of old sandals cut square in the back, Hanoshi-style. Boots are encouraged for officers on Hanoshi ships, but in his mind only Aydeni wear boots.

Jeryon tells Livion, "Break out the crossbows. Eight men to fire, two to load, and I want all sixteen loaded to start. And get the harpooners on their guns."

Livion says, "We're not going to run?"

"We're running already," Jeryon says. "It won't make any difference if we're seen."

Livion knows better than to say they can't possibly win. Jeryon admires his restraint. "I have a plan," he says. "I hope we don't have to use it."

Everlyn says, "Will you tell me—"

"You'll be told what you need to be told, when you need to be told," Jeryon says.

She screws up her mouth and nods. He sounds like one of the Hanoshi ladies on the Crest, with their "I'll tell you what's wrong with me" and "I know what medicine's best."

"Livion, task two sailors with bringing an extra sailcloth to the poth's cabin and a few casks of water. Now," he turns to the poth, "cover the barrels and crates with the sailcloth and keep it drenched. If the *Comber*'s just a smoking hull when it reaches port, our cargo will still survive."

"Might not be fire," Livion says.

"Always prepare for the worst," Jeryon says. "Makes all other outcomes seem less terrible."

Jeryon climbs the stern deck ladder. When Everlyn turns to Livion, he's already beyond the mast. Every word he says springs a sailor into action like a ball scattering skittles.

Everlyn scans the horizon. No privateers. Sailors pass her with the sailcloth. As they go into her cabin, she bends over the larboard rail to look past her cabin to stern. Except for a single far-off gull haunting their wake, they're all alone.

On the stern deck Jeryon asks Solet, "Gliding or flapping?"

"Gliding. It dove a few times, then floated up again."

"Good," Jeryon says. "Flapping means it's interested."

He rubs his chin and considers the sail, a triangle the same yellow as his blouse, and the three banners dangling from the yard of the galley's fore-and-aft rig: company, city, captain. Jeryon's, striped blue and white, is the smallest. It's also set at the bottom, the most easily replaced.

Jeryon says, "Steady as she goes." He slides down the stern ladder and orders the sail and banners brought down, as he would before a storm. They'll slow, but their profile will be smaller. Better to lose an hour from their schedule than to be seen and lose their schedule entirely.

Livion stands on the foredeck between the galley's two harpoon cannons, bulbous iron vases mounted on steel tripods bolted to the deck. A dozen single-flue irons are stacked beside each, and a metal barrel with powder sits on the main deck, given some cover by the foredeck. Trust ships can whale if it won't affect their schedules, which means Jeryon rarely allows it. But on this trip the cannons are meant only for defense.

When they'd set out, Livion told the crew that the Trust believed

Aydeni privateers would attack them. The sailors had thought that far-fetched, regardless of the rumors spreading through the Harbor. None had imagined this alternative.

Beale, a harpooner with arms as thick as his weapon, says, "Will we fight?"

"If we do, we'll be ready," Livion says. "I'll take the larboard cannon." Beale nods.

Topp, a crossbow loader, says, "It would make a rich prize."

"For one ship in a hundred," Livion says. "And the one in a hundred men on it who survives. You know what happens to the other ninety-nine. Let's not push our luck." He heads for the stern deck.

Beale says, "I can't think of a ship that's done it."

"So someone's due, right?" Topp says. "One good shot, and you could get promoted to mate."

"And I'd make you a harpooner so you can see how hard it is," Beale says. "It would be an interesting shot though." He swivels the starboard cannon, aiming over the horizon. "A whale's a cow compared to that." When Topp doesn't respond, he realizes the captain is coming toward them. Topp is already pulling crossbows from compartments under the foredeck. Beale loads the cannon, but the captain takes no notice of either of them.

Solet and Livion watch Jeryon pace fore and aft to the beat of the oars. It's maddening, his precision, but it's better than watching the shadow slowly approach.

Solet says, "You've been through this before, haven't you?"

"Yes, but not with one so big," Livion says. "We still lost the ship." He glances back. "Twenty-five minutes. Could be twenty."

"If we could beat it, though," Solet says, "would we render it? No one's getting a share this trip. Only the captain gets a bonus. But we'd all get a taste of the render."

"We can't beat that," Livion says.

"What if we did beat it?"

"We couldn't render it," Livion says. "Not with our schedule."

"What's a few extra hours?"

"The flox kills quickly. Maybe ten people the first hour, twenty the second, and so on."

"Maybe so," Solet says. "Maybe not. What's a few people you've never met against a fortune you'll never see again?" he says.

"I'd be happy just to keep my life," Livion says. "Again."

"And what's your life now against what it could be?" He looks at Livion. "Stop thinking like him," Solet says. "Think like the owners. The Trust would also get a share of the render. An immense share. The dragon's share. Your woman's father wouldn't just bring you into the family business then. He'd give you a piece of it."

"The only way to get it, though," Livion says, "would be to betray the captain. And mutiny never pays out in the end."

"Not mutiny," Solet says. "Opportunity."

Livion steps away. He should have Solet broken down to sailor. He would if what he said didn't ring true. His monthly would never satisfy Trist, and to her father anyone below captain is a ship's boy. And would the flox spread so quickly? People had been staying indoors. The city guard had been keeping the streets clear. Victims had been isolated. And all the tales he's heard about the plague's virulence, they could be just that, tales. Tristaban, though, she's real.

Did he just see a flap? A grue clutches his spine.

While pacing, Jeryon keeps his head down and his eyes up so he can read Solet's big mouth and expressive lips. He'll deal with the second mate in a moment.

He enters the poth's cabin. Drenched sailcloth cloaks the barrels and crates, many of which are under the table, and it's anchored by the casks of water. He nods and notices the packets in a crate by the door. Another crate holds various tinctures and pills.

"Bandages," Everlyn says. "I never travel without some. And medicine. I could prepare better if I knew what we were facing."

Jeryon says, "Burns."

She plucks some bottles from the table. "Salves."

"And you'll need a saw," he says. "The carpenter will bring you one. And some cord and pins for tourniquets. Ever performed an amputation?"

Some color drains from her face. "No," she says. "My skills are herblore and midwifery."

Jeryon smirks. "It's not hard. Except for the bone. And the screaming."

Everlyn draws herself up. Color pumps into her cheeks. "I've pulled dead children from the living, and living ones from the dead. I'm not afraid of a little screaming."

"We'll see," he says. "Stay here."

"I think I could better serve the ship on deck."

"How many lives have you saved while you were dead?" Jeryon says. "Stay here."

He starts out, but turns in the doorway. He surveys the table and crates of cured shield. "All that you've done," he says. "I won't let it go to waste." Then he leaves.

And that's the limit of Hanoshi gratitude, she thinks. *It's not about you. It's about what you've done for me*.

Everlyn takes out the skull bottle and toasts the closed door. Wine shouldn't go to waste either.

On the stern deck Jeryon says, "Where did it go?"

"Into the sun," Livion says.

"Let's give it a moment. You're on the oar. If we're seen, use your whistle to direct Tuse. It won't matter how much noise we make at that point."

"What about me?" Solet says.

"Larboard cannon," Jeryon says. "A good commander leads from the front. If you want a ship of your own, you'll need that experience."

Jeryon sees fear flicker in Solet's eyes. *Good*, Jeryon thinks, *let him wonder why I'm putting him on the cannon. Solet has his faults, but everyone knows he's better at the oar than Livion, who's the better harpooner.*

After Solet heads forward, Livion says, "Should I drop the rowers to regular time?"

"No," Jeryon says. "That was the mistake your last captain made, thinking the danger had passed."

Solet passes through the rows of crossbowmen lined up against the foredeck as he mounts to his cannon. They fidget. Their fingers flex. "Keep your fingers off the triggers," Solet says. "I don't want anyone shooting his own foot. Or mine."

He looks past the stern deck. How long can it hide inside the glare of the sun? Could it be that smart? Or has it turned away?

Beale gestures at his cannon with his firing rod. The bent tip glows red. "Should we unload?" he says.

"You'll know when it's time." Solet swivels his gun absently, its harpoon loaded and wadded well, and he thinks about how he'll bring it down if he gets the chance. He has to get the chance. A dragon's like a flying treasure ship. He takes his firing rod from a small steel cage containing a lump of burning charcoal to make sure it's also fired, and he gets an idea.

As he puts the rod back in the brazier, he stabs a pebble of charcoal with his finger blade and hides it behind his wrist the way a street magician tucks away a coin. He steps over to Beale and says quietly, "Nervous?"

Beale says, "No."

Instead, he's terrified. They all are, but none will admit it.

Solet says, "Good. Turn around. Look at these men." Beale does so. Solet puts an arm on the cannon behind him, and whispers, "They will look up to us when the time comes, just as we look to the captain." He scrapes the pebble onto the touch hole of Beale's cannon and says, "We have to be worthy, whatever comes. Are you with me?"

"Yes," Beale says.

Solet steps to the edge of the foredeck to address the crossbowmen while waiting for the pebble to burn down. "The old man has a plan, and he sees his plans through, isn't that right?" The crossbowmen nod. "He said we'd cross the sea in record time. And we did. He said we'd get what we needed quick. And we did. We're nearly back in record time too"—he pauses for effect—"but for some possible unpleasantness." The men actually grin. He'd be impressed with the captain too, if the captain were making this speech.

"We may be safe," he says, "but if we fight, we will have a chance." More nods. He pats Beale on the back and glances at the pebble. It's shrunk enough to slip halfway into the touch hole. "And we will win, do you understand me?" he says. "We will bring this boat in on time, and we will complete our contract. The city needs us to." The crossbows quiver less. "Let's keep it down, so let me see your hands." They pump their fists. "Let the captain." They turn and salute him. "And if it's still back there watching, let it too."

The pebble burns down small enough so that when the bow smacks a large wave, it falls all the way into the touch hole. A boom roars across the waves, chased by the harpoon, which splashes uselessly into the sea.

Jeryon's about to risk calling out from the stern deck when Solet turns on Beale. "Do you know what you've done?"

Beale looks from Solet to Topp to the crossbowmen and back to Topp. "I don't know how it could have gone off," he says. Topp's look is especially withering. "Maybe it didn't notice."

They're a hundred feet from the stern deck. Nevertheless, they all hear Livion yell, "Captain."

The shadow rises over the sun, half a thumb wide, still so small, but coming on fast. Its wings reap the sky in twin arcs. Its sinuous neck pumps. Its claws and teeth glint like swords. Even at a mile and a half, its black scales shimmer red in the dawn.

Solet can't see the dragon's eyes, but it feels like the beast is staring at him.

Livion says, "Fifteen minutes, Captain. At most."

3

Jeryon calls his mates into his cabin. They gather around a small slate-topped table. With chalk Jeryon draws an idiot's map of the *Comber*: a long cigar, a triangle at one end for the foredeck, a square at the other for the sterncastle. In the center he draws a circle for the mast, surrounded by four long rectangles where the deck is open. From a shelf he grabs the only decorative thing in the otherwise sparsely furnished room: a whale tooth two hands long. It's covered in a beautifully detailed, blue ink rendering of the *Comber*. Jeryon holds it behind the stern deck and says, "This is the dragon."

Handsome piece, Solet thinks.

"It won't attack immediately," Jeryon says. "It'll pass us first and maybe circle us." He runs the tooth around the picture. "If it doesn't find us interesting, it'll fly away. If it stays"—he sets the tooth behind the stern deck—"we have to make it uninterested. We'll strike first."

"Punch it in the nose," Tuse says. "Like a shark. I've used that strategy in bars." He flexes his scarred fingers.

"Yes, but the shark punch is a myth. They'll just eat your fist. Dragons, though—I've read more than a dozen reports on dragon attacks from the last decade. In the few cases in which ships have struck first, most of the time the dragons left them alone."

"How many is 'most'?" Solet says.

"Two out of three," Jeryon says.

"That's about my record in the bars," Tuse says.

"As first mate," Livion says, "I must remind you—"

Of course you must, Solet thinks.

"That in the event of a dragon attack at sea, company policy dictates that a galley run or otherwise avoid a fight. The insurers won't pay out if we fight. The attack, in their eyes, would become a confrontation, not an act of nature."

"Shall I remind you what's happened to every ship that's waited to fight?" Jeryon says. "Or would you care to present the report you wrote about your previous ship?"

Centered in the porthole, the dragon is as wide as Livion's thumb. It's diving to the wavetops to pick up speed then soaring up.

"No," Livion says.

"How many survived?" Jeryon says.

"Eighteen, not counting me."

"Right," Jeryon says. "You know that I do things by the book. I trust the book. I trust the people who wrote the book. And I expect my crew to abide by the book. In this one case, though, the book is wrong. We will have to rewrite it."

"The Trust will not be pleased," Livion says.

"Their ship will be afloat," Jeryon says. "Their cargo will be safe. Their city will survive. Here's what we'll do." He holds the tooth a few feet over the table and flies it athwart the larboard side. "As the dragon passes, we will veer across its path." Jeryon kicks a table leg so the table slides and the mates jump. "And startle it."

Solet says, "Show it our side?"

"We're not being rammed," Jeryon says. "We want it to think we're tough to catch. Just like a rabbit veers. Unlike a rabbit, though, when the dragon's momentum carries it over us, we will bite its belly with a load of crossbow bolts."

Solet smiles. "This is Ynessi." It's his highest compliment. Perhaps the captain *can* reach.

"What happens if it doesn't lose interest?" Livion says.

"Then we turn and face it head on."

Solet's smile disappears. He'll be on the foredeck, the galley's face.

"We won't get another shot at its belly," Jeryon says. "The soft flesh of its face is its next most vulnerable region. The eyes. The mouth. The nostrils. Besides, there's no room for it to land on the foredeck."

On Livion's last ship, a bireme called *Wanderlust*, a great yellow dragon lit on her stern deck and levered the prow out of the water. He remembers his captain hacking at its foot with an axe, screaming, "To me! To me!" and the creature biting him in two. His legs remained standing before the dragon licked them up, then tore the ship to pieces.

"Livion," Jeryon says, "tell the sailors without crossbows that they're on fire duty. They should have buckets of water and sand at the ready. Put some on each rail and some on the rowers' deck. Then get on the oar again. Solet, you have the foredeck. Tuse, put us at regular time. We'll conserve what energy the rowers have left. And keep the turns sharp. Quickly now." He nods to dismiss them.

As they're leaving, he grabs Solet's arm. The door closes. Jeryon says, "Who fired that cannon?"

"Beale," Solet says. "Poor gun maintenance." He doesn't say that he's overheard Topp trying to get Beale to stand out so they'll get promoted. A captain doesn't play all his cards at once.

"And poor supervision," Jeryon says. "A pity. I was going to report to the Trust that he could be a mate someday. And you could be a captain." He pats Solet on the shoulder blade. "We may have to celebrate our survival with some floggings." He nudges Solet to the door.

Jeryon checks the porthole and does some quick calculating. The dragon's only a mile away.

Topp says, "They have the right idea."

Scores of fins, an enormous school of hammerhead sharks, flow around the galley and past the bow.

"Wish I could swim that fast," Beale says.

"Thanks to you, we might have to try," Topp says.

"I didn't do anything, Topp. Or nothing. And if I did, I don't know how I did it."

Topp shakes his head. His look softens. "You do know how to use that cannon, Beale," he says. "Make it up to us. Make your shots count."

The drumbeats drop by half and the ship slows to what feels like a dead stop. The dragon springs toward them.

On the stern deck Jeryon can smell the dragon now: old earth thrown on a fire to smother it. And he can hear its wings snap. A sail could only dream of such command over the wind. The *Comber* feels like a piece of driftwood.

He watches the sailors perform their various tasks and those who have completed them are checking their buckets, their weapons, even their oars. *Simply having a plan*, he thinks, *is sometimes the best plan. It lets people concentrate on the present instead of dwelling on the future.*

Livion, having nothing to check except his grip on the oar and whether his silver whistle is still hanging around his neck, makes awkward conversation. "How do you know so much about dragons?" he says.

"I read your report after you were assigned to the *Comber*," Jeryon says, "which pointed me to others. I was impressed with how detailed yours was, although you didn't elaborate on what you'd done."

"I just led the survivors back to shore, but everyone did their part. I couldn't take credit for it all."

"The modesty of a second mate who suddenly finds himself in command?"

Livion shrugs. The modesty of one who lived.

"You're lucky those men spoke up for you," Jeryon says. "They're the ones who put you on the *Comber*. You'll never get anywhere by

leaving yourself out of your reports." He adds, "I hope I can speak up for you in mine."

"I'll do my best," Livion says.

Jeryon sees he means it. There's a chance for him yet.

The dragon's now a hand long. "It'll pass us to larboard," Jeryon says. "Pipe Tuse: Larboard turn on my mark."

Livion blows the alert.

Jeryon raises his fist to Solet, who's little more than a thumb's width tall at this distance. Solet says something to Beale and the crossbowmen, whom he's spread across the front of the ship. Each has a weapon in hand, another loaded at his feet. They shout as one, "Aye!" Solet raises his fist too.

The dragon blooms into enormity in what feels like seconds. Its shadow passes them first, a black mass wider on the water than the *Comber* is long. Its wings come next, the color of night wine and just as fluid, but strangely delicate. When the sun catches their membranes, they glow like polished rosewood.

That was probably its original color, Jeryon thinks. *Dragons blacken with age. This one's getting on in years. It'll know its business.*

It comes abeam of the stern deck, flying twice as high as the mast, tail gently whipping behind. The dragon turns its head to better appraise Jeryon and, chillingly, so Jeryon can appraise it: wide mouth, teeth longer and sharper than a whale's, the acrid smell of phlogiston burning through the stench of the poth's medicine. There's something gray lodged between its teeth and gum. Half a shark.

Its head is bigger than me, Jeryon thinks. *Rain barrels could fit in its bulging eye sockets. The two skinny claws on its wing digits would make for decent short bows.*

His hands, hardened by decades at sea, would make for decent hammers, though. He pounds his fist on the rail and shouts, "Larboard!"

Livion pipes the command and pushes the steering oar to starboard. The larboard oars freeze at the end of their pull, the rowers straining, the oar handles locked to their chest, as the starboard oars push forward. The *Comber* pivots beautifully, and the dragon lifts its wing in alarm. It drifts left to avoid them.

The galley slashes through the dragon's shadow, and the foredeck slides under its belly like an assassin's blade. Solet cries, "Fire!" The crossbowmen don't even have to aim. It's tough to miss the sky.

Eight bolts twang and thunk home at once. The dragon bucks and roars. Its tail flails down, seeking balance, and its tip, flared like a diamond, nearly flicks Topp off the boat. A thin rain of blood spatters the deck. The dragon flaps so hard that the wind from its wings presses the ship into the sea. Water convulses over the rails and washes the blood into the rowers' deck. As the dragon passes over the starboard bow, Beale gets down on one knee, aims the cannon as high as it will go, and holds his firing rod over the touch hole.

Beale mutters, "Up, down, up," and on the next downstroke of the massive wings, when the dragon lifts its tail and he's just about to lose the angle, he fires. The harpoon sinks deep into its groin. The dragon roars louder, and now it's the one beating away double-time.

The crossbowmen and sailors cheer. Topp would've jumped onto the foredeck to clasp Beale's hand, but Solet orders, "Reload!"

A furlong off the starboard quarter, the dragon starts to circle the *Comber*.

4

As the dragon passes the sun and puts one wing to the southern horizon, Solet admires Livion's oarwork. He didn't think the first mate was that skilled. Steering and piping, Livion pivots the galley farther to larboard to point the prow at the dragon, then reverses the pivot to keep it dead ahead. *Of course,* Solet thinks, *it's in his best interests to keep the length of the* Comber *between himself and the dragon.*

He sees what the beast is doing. A pirate ship plays games like this with traders, wondering whether they're worth attacking. Usually, they decide yes. Ynessi can't stand not knowing what's inside a chest. Unfortunately, dragons also have a reputation for curiosity.

True to form, the dragon veers toward them, twice as high as the mast, its neck stretched out like a harpoon, rigid and determined.

Solet hears Livion pipe, and the drummer beat double-time, and the rowers groan, reaching the outskirts of their endurance. The crossbowmen aim over his head, and he kneels to avoid taking a bolt in the nape of the neck.

We've picked the lock, Solet thinks. *Time to lift the lid*. "No wasted shots," he calls out.

The rowers' deck responds with a scream and another. They sound like pirates trying to terrify a prize.

Solet counts off the yards: four hundred, three hundred . . . At two hundred the dragon drops to the height of the stern deck, wingtips skipping off the water. Its eyes slit. Solet avoids its gaze. He hears Livion piping. The galley swings to larboard. At fifty yards the dragon rears its head. It drops its jaw impossibly wide. Its teeth shimmer.

"Fire!" Solet cries.

The cannons boom. Bolts shriek. Beale's harpoon only pricks the dragon's thickly scaled right shoulder before spinning away. Solet's rips through the membrane at its wingtip and keeps on going. All but one of the bolts misses the dragon's head, glancing off its cheek or neck, but the one pins the dragon's tongue to the floor of its mouth. The dragon half chokes on a gout of flame. Drops of fire spatter the deck and men as the dragon roars over the foredeck like an avalanche, scrambling for lift.

Jeryon stands at the front of the stern deck as Solet calls out "No wasted shots." He's considering whether to put up the sail again to protect the deck from its breath—could they cut away the flaming sail and let the wind blow it overboard before the mast and yard were damaged?—when the dragon drops. Jeryon sees where its line of attack will take it and thinks, *The rigging.* "Livion!" he yells. "Larboard! Again. Now!"

Livion sees the danger too and pipes insistently. He pushes the oar as far as it will go. The prow slides off the dragon's line of attack. He watches Solet and Beale swivel their cannons to compensate, intent on their target. The oars don't respond, then only Tuse is screaming and the *Comber* turns more sharply.

The dragon's jaw drops, and Solet cries, "Fire!"

The dragon's face jerks to the side, a bolt buried in its tongue. Flames spurt from the corners of its mouth. It blasts over the deck, and that's when it sees the mast and yard. It bucks, trying to heave itself over them, but its shoulder strikes them where they meet, and catches. For half a heartbeat, the mast bends, lines groan, and the prow rears up as this great fly tries to escape the ship's web, then the top of the mast snaps off and the dragon hurdles the stern deck. The wind from its wings crumples Jeryon and folds Livion over the steering oar, which levers its blade into the air.

On the rowers' deck, Tuse hears Solet call out, "No wasted shots!" and he calls out himself, "You hear that? Pull harder! Ram her down its throat!"

Bearclaw screams, and the other prisoners take up the cry, an ululation born of exhaustion and blood fevered with powder. The brothers, as one, suck in a huge breath and let out their own barbaric yawp. Tuse, caught up in the moment, himself hollers. Somehow, through this, he hears Livion piping, and yells, "Quiet! Larboard! Hard! Hard!!" The rowers recover themselves and dig in. The *Comber* turns, then the dragon's shadow swamps the rowers' deck. When it smacks the mast, Tuse is flung over the drummer. The ship is wrenched to a stop.

Half a heartbeat later Tuse hears a snapping as horrible as a skull being crushed. The top half of the mast crashes through the open deck onto the rowers in the larboard quarter. One man kicks as his legs refuse to admit his torso has been crushed.

On the stern deck Jeryon looks up as the top of the mast falls into the rowers' deck, dragging the yard behind it and toward him like a cleaver. It slices into the stern deck, grinding to a stop just before it reaches his head. He spits splinters off his lips.

The dragon is rising away. Jeryon gets up and yells to Solet, "Reload!" He looks down at the carnage in the rowers' deck. He hears the moans of pain. "Tuse!" No answer.

Bearclaw cranes his head from under the walkway and says, "Captain. Hey. Your whipper's conked out on the deck." A hand emerges from the shadows and slaps Bearclaw's bloody face. Tuse follows, the top of his head sticking out of the deck.

"We have to maneuver," Jeryon says.

Tuse makes a quick accounting. "We've lost a dozen oars. Don't know how many men. I have at least another dozen, though, to larboard. We'll make do."

The starboard quarter oars rise out of the water to keep the boat balanced. *He'll use them to make sharper turns when the time comes*, Jeryon thinks. *Smart.*

"It's coming around," Livion says.

"Same as before," Jeryon says. "To start."

He stamps on the stern deck and yells, "Poth! Poth!" Her cabin door rattles, wedged shut. Jeryon calls again. The door bursts open, and Everlyn tumbles out. Jeryon says, "The medicine?"

"Good," she says. "Me too."

"They need you below," Jeryon says. He points to where the mast fell.

She looks into the rowers' deck. "I'll get my supplies," she says.

"And the saw," Jeryon says.

The prow traces the dragon's trail across the sky. It's flying much higher now. Two hundred yards, three, four. It comes around west and heads north. Jeryon pulls in his gaze to look over the galley. "This is going to cost us another hour," he says, "but we can make it up."

Livion pipes an accidental note of shock.

"Never forget your schedule, Livion. Any idiot can captain a ship. It takes a real captain to bring her home on time."

The dragon turns toward the sun and tightens the circle. Jeryon signals to Solet. Solet nods and confers with Beale and the crossbowmen. Jeryon sees Solet laugh. *He's either very confident we're going to win or very confident we're going to die spectacularly. That's Ynessi.*

The dragon curls in closer and closer until it's nearly above the galley. The captain gives Livion alternate orders and has him keep the *Comber* in a slow larboard pivot. He watches Solet give up trying to raise the cannon high enough to target the dragon and grab a stray crossbow. *That should even up the odds*, Jeryon thinks.

With that the dragon tips forward, stiffens its wings, and dives.

5

The poth leaves her cabin with the crate of medicinal packets to find the dragon plunging directly at her. She clenches her butt to hold her pee, looks at the ladder, looks at the dragon, and jumps into the rowing deck.

When the dragon is three hundred yards above the galley, Jeryon says, "Now."

Livion pipes. The galley backrows to starboard and out from under the dragon. The dragon adjusts, bearing down on the foredeck.

The crossbowmen aim as best they can, bolt points bobbing with the ship and their racing hearts. "Steady," Solet says. The dragon extends its claws. *It's going to snatch me*, he thinks. *Please don't let it take me to its nest.*

Jeryon says, "Double-time." Livion pipes. The ship jerks away again, leaving only blue water beneath the dragon.

As Jeryon had hoped, the dragon pulls up, thirty yards dead ahead and thirty yards off the waves, flinging out its huge wings and blocking the sun. It hangs there a moment, beating the air with quick, short thrusts. Solet drops the crossbow and yanks the firing rod of his cannon out of its brazier. The dragon's head rears. Its jaw drops.

"Fire!" Solet yells. Steel rips toward the dragon's right elbow. Liquid fire splashes behind Solet and washes three crossbowmen into the rowers' deck on the larboard bow; the drumming stops again. Half the bolts fly high. The other half stick in the membrane of its wing. Beale's harpoon clanks off its humerus, but Solet's finds the mark, bearing into the joint. The dragon flinches and flaps, and the joint snaps. The outer half of the wing collapses, and the dragon falls toward the *Comber*. It breathes again, but the flames miss the galley, mixing a huge plume of steam with the smoke billowing from the ship. To Solet's alarm, the fire floats, spreading around them.

The dragon's foot reaches for the foredeck. Beale leaps off it and lands on Topp. In a tangle, they crawl along the starboard rail as the foot crushes Beale's cannon. The ship's bow sinks sharply and Solet is knocked down by the waves coursing over the foredeck. His crossbow is pushed toward the edge of the foredeck. Solet dives for it, slides it around to point at the dragon, and fires while on his belly.

The bolt deflects off a claw and under the cuticle, a tender spot for any creature, however immense. The dragon roars and springs from the boat, which forces the foredeck down again. Waves carry a scrabbling Solet into the sea. The dragon's right wing flaps uselessly, and the creature lands with one foot on the forward walkway, which somehow doesn't shatter, and the other on the starboard rail, splintering it. When it tries to grab the larboard rail with its right wing hand, the limb doesn't respond, and the dragon topples onto the remains of the main mast and impales itself.

Jeryon watches the whole ship get swamped by the dragon's

weight. Water surges over the gunwales and into the rowers' deck, which smothers the fires, but pours salt over the wounds of the injured. The screams below achieve a higher pitch.

The *Comber* bobs back up and bounces the dragon off the mast, an immense hole in its breast. It flaps once and flings itself off the galley, one wing full of air, the other full of sailors swept up by it. The dragon makes two more desperate flaps before collapsing into the sea to starboard and driving the *Comber* away with a huge wave. An umbilicus of blood stretches between them.

Jeryon orders, "Backrow! Larboard."

Livion pipes. He doesn't know what's become of Tuse and all the larboard oars dangle lifeless from their oar holes, but there are enough brothers left on the starboard oars to respond. Unlike the inexperienced, untrained prisoners, they know the piping. The stroke is erratic to start, but after a few pulls the *Comber* moves farther away from the dragon—and the men in the water.

The two men floating motionless closest to the dragon appear to be dead until it picks them up. Resurrected, they flail and cry as it bites through their torsos, dribbling their heads and lower legs from the sides of its mouth.

Beale, Topp, and two others struggle to stay afloat. Like most sailors, they can't swim. Like most drowning people, they can't scream. Livion can't spot Solet.

Lest they circle around, Jeryon orders, "Oars up." Livion pipes and the ship drifts to a stop, the dragon dead ahead again. "You have the ship," Jeryon says. "Don't get us any closer." He slides to the deck.

Livion sees the dragon breathe again. Flame arcs toward the captain as he runs forward. It bursts on the starboard bow an instant after he passes by, incinerating a sailor trying to throw a line to his fellows in the water. A pool of flame forms around the burning gunwale. Drops splatter Jeryon's black coat and Livion watches him doff the smoldering garment before leaping onto the foredeck and reloading the remaining cannon.

The poth clambers onto deck, drenched, her long black hair trailing from her ravaged bun, her gray streaks tinted with blood. She needs more bandages, but the flames creeping along the starboard rail and walk are a more pressing concern. As she reaches for a bucket of sand beside the rail to put them out, a hand grasps her wrist through the rail. She starts and pulls back. The hand won't let her go. Another appears on the rail. She's readying the bucket to hold off the boarder when the rest of Solet appears, standing atop the ladder on the hull.

She says, "I thought sailors couldn't swim."

"I'm Ynessi," he says, climbing over the rail. "We're like tadpoles. Born in the water." He spots the bucket and says, "That won't work. Not for this fire."

She reconsiders the flames and says, "I know what we can use."

The Comber has no whale line on this voyage, so Jeryon takes up a coil of sail line and a block meant for the emergency rig. He ties the block onto the line like a fishing float then attaches the line to the harpoon through a hole near its head. He ties the other end of the line to the harpoon's tripod.

He aims the cannon at the dragon and considers what a prize it would make. There are enough men aboard who have rendered whales that they could dummy their way through a dragon. All that bone, teeth, and claw which can be flaked into peerless blades. All that skin, so tough it can be used for armor, but light enough to wear every day. And the phlogiston, the oil secreted from glands behind its jaw that fuels its fire. With Hanosh edging toward war with Ayden it would make a devastating weapon—or it could be sold for a fortune as lamp oil. The dragon rears its head and bares its neck. Then Beale manages to cry out. Jeryon changes his mind, swivels the cannon, and fires the harpoon and its line toward the men.

The iron splashes into a wave beyond them. The block and line are just buoyant enough to keep the latter afloat despite the harpoon sinking. But the men don't move toward it. They might not even see it. Their arms are out. They stare empty eyed at the sun, heads back, mouths open. Only Beale moves, treading water incidentally while trying to climb out of the sea. Jeryon, whose fisherman father taught him to swim before he could tie a bowline, kicks off his sandals, dives off the prow, and swims down the line.

The dragon's wings are spread across the water, keeping it afloat, but they won't hold it up for long. It thrashes and finds that it can drag itself toward the ship. A meal's a meal, especially a last one. Jeryon, seeing this, swims faster.

In the poth's cabin, she and Solet wrestle the drenched sailcloth off the tumbled crates and barrels. It's no easy thing to drag it forward, and two firemen help. They unfold it so two can take the starboard walk and two can take the middle. When the shadow of the sailcloth passes over the rowers, they snap their heads up, worried.

The heat is tremendous, and the stench of burning oil grates at the corners of their eyes. They flap the cloth atop the flames, driving out more smoke. The sailcloth sizzles. Two more firemen bring water casks. Solet tells them to pour it over the cloth, not the flames; it'll be easier to smother them. The flames on the walk are soon out. They hang the cloth over the gunwales, and the waves catch the end and help beat out the flames. Solet listens to the ship. He feels it through his feet. The hull still seems sound.

The poth says, "Where's the captain?" One of the sailors points out toward the harpoon line, then to the dragon.

Solet says, "Has he forgotten his precious book?"

The poth says, "You have to help him. You can swim."

"I lied," Solet says. "Can't swim a stroke. I worked my way along the side to the ladder."

The poth looks at him in disbelief.

"What can I say?" he says. "I wanted to impress you."

She should push him overboard, but that would only compound their problems. She grew up on a lake. She can swim well. But she knows she can't go in after the captain. If she were lost in the water, too many aboard would die without her healing.

"He's going to tie them to the line," the poth says. "We'll haul them in."

Solet follows her and the firemen to the foredeck. *The dragon won't last much longer*, he thinks. *Nor will the captain*. He needs to keep the former from sinking.

Jeryon considers which sailor to save first. The waves decide for him. They drift Beale and Topp farther away while pushing together the other two. As their hands touch, instead of holding on to each other, each tries to get onto the other's shoulders. One goes under, then the next. Their backs and flailing arms appear. It's unclear whose is whose. They disappear again. A moment later Jeryon swims through the spot. He ducks his face into the water. He only sees the murk and matter of the sea. He swims on.

Jeryon reaches Topp first. He tries to talk to him, but waves flood his mouth. Topp doesn't respond anyway. Warily, Jeryon swims behind the sailor, a fist at the ready, then he grabs Topp around his chest. He puts up no resistance, and with a few scissor kicks Jeryon drags him to the line. He slips it under Topp's arm. This Topp understands, and he comes to, as if from sleep.

"Go," Jeryon says. "Climb to safety."

"No. Beale. I have to save him."

"Then haul us in," Jeryon says.

Topp says "Aye," and he pulls for the ship. A cheer goes up on board.

Jeryon swims to where the block is nearly submerged by the weight of the harpoon. Beale is ten yards away. His flailing is getting more frantic. *He'll pull me under if I get close*, Jeryon thinks.

Livion watches the dragon beat toward the *Comber*. It either has no fire left, or it's so intent on swimming that it can't muster a breath. With only starboard oars, any attempt to go forward will carry the *Comber* dangerously close to the dragon. But, if he backrows any farther, Jeryon's lifeline will get pulled away. Company policy dictates: Never risk the ship for a sailor. But he can't let the captain die. And he doesn't have to use all his oars. He pipes for just the forward three to pull, steers to larboard, and the *Comber,* balanced, edges toward the men in the water.

The harpoon line folds before the prow. Everlyn and the sailors, relieved that the ship is moving, take up the slack. With the dragon closing in, Solet hears Livion pipe "to arms." But, instead of gathering the scattered crossbows and men to wield them he runs to the stern deck. Livion pipes again. Solet won't be deterred.

Jeryon holds his hands out as best he can, trying to calm Beale. "I'm going to push you to the rope," he says, circling the harpooner. "Don't do anything. Look at the rope." Beale's eyes follow him, though. He spots the dragon beyond Jeryon, and all the fire goes out of him. He pulls in his arms, exhales, and sinks.

Saving him for a flogging, Jeryon thinks. He dives.

While Topp is being lifted onto the galley Livion searches the water for the captain. He hasn't emerged.

Solet climbs to the stern deck. Livion says, "I have the ship, and I gave you an order!"

"Then I am acting first officer," Solet says, "and it's my duty to remind you—"

"I know the book," Livion says.

"And I know the captain would have ordered you to stay away from the dragon," Solet says.

Livion stares at him coldly. "You want him dead. Then you'll want the dragon as a prize."

Solet has the audacity to appear surprised. He says, "The captain and Beale may already be gone. We aren't."

Jeryon still hasn't emerged. The poth, Topp, and the firemen hold the line, waiting. A few other sailors have taken up crossbows to shoot the dragon. Two bolts stick in its face. The dragon isn't discouraged.

"Crossbows aren't going to kill that thing," Solet says. "We have to back water. We can watch it die from a distance. It can't have long."

Livion has to agree, however insolent and manipulative Solet is. Even if the captain emerges, by the time they could reel him in, the dragon would be climbing over the rail. He pipes again. The remaining rowers lift as one and pull the ship away from the dragon. The harpoon line is dragged through the water. The poth throws the slack out, leaps up, and looks pleadingly at Livion. She points at the line. There's nothing there.

Livion tells Solet, "I want a report on the damage below in five minutes and one on the wounded in ten."

6

As the *Comber* accelerates, the block at the end of the harpoon line rises to the surface. Water streams over it, more than there should be, creating a bright wake. The poth yells, "There!" A head breaks through the overflow, and another. Jeryon holds the block, and Beale holds him. The poth says, "Help me," to two sailors nearby. Topp is already heaving at the line. The others join in. The drag is considerable, though, with the ship moving. They make little progress. And the *Comber* is turning, drawing the line directly across the path of the dragon.

Livion pipes double-time to get them clear. He hopes the captain and Beale can hang on. They look like bait.

Solet sees what he must do. As two more sailors take hold of the line, he sprints to the cannon. The galley is turning into the dragon's field of fire. He grabs a powder packet from its metal storage chest, stuffs it in, tamps it down, and pulls an iron out from under the feet of the poth and Topp. As they move aside, he slams the harpoon home, grabs the firing rod, and sights, conveniently, straight down the harpoon line.

The dragon is only ten yards behind Beale, its head just above the water, its body largely submerged, which doesn't give Solet much of an angle. For a moment he finds the harpoon aimed straight at Jeryon. *No one could blame me*, he thinks. *It'd be like a hunting accident*. Jeryon looks Solet in the eye, clearly thinking the same thing. Solet feels for the touch hole with the rod. Then Beale, exhausted, lets go of the line.

Jeryon rolls over and reaches out to grasp him, but the lightened line is easier to pull in, and Jeryon is jerked forward by the poth and the sailors. He almost loses his own grip and rolls back to dig his fingers into the block. The dragon's head rears and its jaw drops, not for a breath, but for a big downward bite. Beale scrambles in the water. The dragon's wings throw spray over him. It's one stroke away from the men.

Solet has a clear shot. Topp says, "What are you waiting for?" The dragon's head comes down. Solet fires.

The harpoon narrowly clears Beale's head and sinks deep into the dragon's neck. Its head snaps aside. Its neck thrashes in agony, blood spewing from its mouth. The dragon makes one last heave, glides forward, and covers Beale with its wing, trapping him under water.

Livion pipes. The oars drag the *Comber* to a stop. The harpoon line is pulled in and Jeryon is lifted onto the foredeck. He spits water and rolls onto his shoulder to consider the dragon. "Dead?" Jeryon says.

Solet says, "I think so."

"Beale?"

"I don't know."

The dragon's head rolls on its side, its eye open to the sun. Waves fan over the wings. A hand shoots through one of the rents in the membrane made by a bolt. Topp yells, "Beale!" The hand slips under the waves. Topp yells again, "Beale!" Now fingers appear on either side of the rent. They push it apart.

Solet says, "I cannot be seeing this."

Beale's head crowns then pops through. He turns and says to Topp, "What?"

Jeryon stands by the mast, sandals on again, and confers with Tuse on the rowers' deck. The oarmaster is bruised and burned, and he's lost a large clump of dirty, matted hair.

"All but one of our larboard rowers are dead or too injured to row," Tuse says. "And if it weren't for the poth—" he flicks his eyes forward to where she's treating someone and he lowers his voice, "we'd be much worse off. Once the rigging and casualties are removed half the benches should be usable, which matches the number of oars we have left. I'll put twelve on a side and we can get underway."

Jeryon notices Tuse's expression and asks, "Anything else?"

Tuse glances forward again. "More powder won't get another stroke out of these men," he says. "We might manage regular time, nothing more."

Jeryon says, "We'll spell them with sailors."

"The guild would object," Tuse says, "and the brothers."

"Then they can keep their seats," Jeryon says. "And if they can't pull, I'll object to the guild. But we'll be underway in half an hour."

"Half an hour!" Tuse says.

"We have a schedule," Jeryon says.

Solet, who is overseeing the removal of the yard, overhears. As do several sailors watching the school of hammerheads return to attack the dragon. Its hide is tough, and they haven't been able to do much damage, but each bite feels like a full purse gone and they still hope Jeryon will let them take it. That its wings have kept it afloat and the waves have kept it near the galley encourages them.

Jeryon considers addressing the crew on the matter and decides against it. Instead he bets himself that Solet will run to Livion as soon as the yard clears the deck. He'll give Solet this: the second mate knows how to complain up the chain of command. And he's smart enough not to harpoon someone in front of the crew. Fortunately, Livion is weak, but not feebleminded. He thinks like Jeryon. Livion will push Solet off, maybe relieve him. A good test of his quality.

Jeryon doesn't know which galls him more: that he's lost four hours from his schedule or that he needs Solet so he doesn't lose any more.

Then again, maybe he doesn't need Solet that much. He can't get the image of the harpoon pointed at his head out of his mind. A different employment for Solet occurs to him.

Solet feels Jeryon's eyes on him. He knows, he thinks. *He has to know what Livion and I have been talking about. But he can't do anything until we get to port.*

On the stern deck he tells Livion, "He's not going to render the dragon." From up here he can see just how many sharks are roiling the water and banging against the hull. "That'd pay for all this damage ten times over. A hundred times."

"We have to get back to Hanosh," Livion says. "Shall I relieve you of your post? Your insolence—"

"My insolence?" Solet says. "You're the one who left the captain to die."

Livion struggles to keep his jaw from dropping. "You said—"

"Here's how it will sound to the Trust at the inquiry. First, you took the ship into danger against orders, then you saw a way to confirm your new command. Who else would get the *Comber* but the man who brought her valuable cargo in after the ship was damaged and the captain died?"

"I'll tell you what will go in my report," Livion says. "How you tried to undermine the captain—"

"The captain who disobeyed the Trust's clear rules?" Solet says. "Who attacked the dragon, who left his post to save a couple of *sailors*, and who risked its cargo? That's the definition of unfit."

"They'll understand," Livion says. "The city will understand."

Solet laughs. "You're as foolish as him, trusting up. That attitude will ruin you. We'll all be heroes whenever we get in, however many die in the meantime, but to let a fortune slide off the rail into the sea: the Trust won't consider that heroic. *Poor judgment*, they'll say. *Hardly command material*, they'll say. What would your woman's father think?"

Livion says through grinding teeth, "Your sailors are waiting for you to remove the mast."

"Tristaban will think you threw her away along with your career."

Jeryon mounts the stern deck. Behind him are two sailors. He says, "This conference has gone on long enough. Solet, the rowers are exhausted. If we're going to get in as soon as possible, the sailors will have to take a turn at the oars. As a good example, you will lead them."

Solet says, "But I'm a mate."

Jeryon says, "Then I won't need to chain you to a bench." He tells the sailors, "Take Solet to his new station."

Solet says, "Livion."

Whining, Livion thinks, *is not Ynessi. Deception, though, is very Hanoshi. Has the captain overheard them? Has he divined Solet's scheming? It would surely leave its stench on him. And it's better to fire a maid, Trist once said, before the jewelry's gone. If Solet is put in chains once he's below, how long until I am too? If we don't hang together now, we could hang separately later.*

"Livion," Solet says.

Livion curses Jeryon under his breath. "Belay that order," Livion says to the sailors. "As first mate I am declaring the captain unfit for command: for disobeying the rules of engagement, for endangering the ship and her cargo, for putting us behind schedule, for abandoning his post, for doing so during an emergency, and for failing to seek reliable profit by not rendering the dragon."

"As second mate," Solet says, "I concur."

"Ha!" Jeryon says. "Using the book against me. The Trust will see through that."

"Lock him in the hold," Livion says.

"You can't hold me," Jeryon says as two sailors grab his arms.

"Wait," Solet says. He pushes out Jeryon's arms and runs his hands over his torso and hips. Solet smiles, digs out the razor case from the captain's pocket, and flips it into the sea. "Now we can hold you," he says.

Whatever confusion and anger the sailors feel as the captain is dragged below is quickly replaced with the joy of avarice and potential advancement as Solet gathers a rendering crew. An Ynessi could expect nothing less from a Hanoshi crew.

"This is wrong," Beale says. "He saved us. They're relieving him because he saved us."

"What could we do?" Topp says. "We just float on the waves. The mates, they are the waves."

"At least the shares will buy us a better boat," Beale says.

Tuse says, "Your charges are true. Your motives are nonsense. This is mutiny, plain and simple."

Livion says, "So you'll oppose us."

"Yes," Tuse says. He tightens a seeping bandage. "You can't deal me into a game I won't play. I won't have him killed."

"No one said anything about—" Livion said.

"Are you soft-hearted or soft-headed?" Tuse says, holding up a burned hand. "Do you think you can just take him to Hanosh and make your case at the inquiry? Sort this whole thing out? Have everything be normal?"

Livion says, "We're going by the book."

"You're holding it upside down," Tuse says. "Let me explain something to you: When you punch a man, you put him down. Otherwise, he'll put you down." He jerks his thumb at Solet. "He'd agree with me."

Solet guides the half-completed rendering. The dragon has been tied to the galley, and, not having a cutting stage, sailors work on it from the starboard rail and the ship's dinghy. Its head, feet, and wing claws have been hacked off with axes, wrapped in canvas, and put in the captain's cabin. The dragon's body is tied to the starboard rail, and is being spun so the skin can be stripped off in great sheets. This work is easier. The trick was flaking some vertebrae into blades, attaching them to handles, and using these shards, incredibly sharp and difficult to dull, to cut the skin and flay it from the meat.

Meanwhile the sharks work on the meat, exposing more bone, which they'll harvest next.

Livion wishes he had more spit in his mouth. He says, "If we have to kill him, Tuse, we have to kill you. He'd agree with that too."

"You don't have the stones," Tuse says.

"I don't need them. See that bolt of skin?" Livion says. A sailor carries one to the captain's cabin. "It's worth more than the *Comber*. You don't think that sailor would flay you as well if you do something to take it away?"

"You're a good man, Livion," Tuse says. "I like serving under you. But what you're doing here, it'll destroy you. The rot's already setting in."

Livion keeps all expression from his face. He wants to admit he's only saying what he imagines Solet would say, but that would prove Tuse's point. Instead he says, "Are you with us? Or him?"

Tuse slumps into his rowers' deck posture. "My chances are better with you. But here's my price: We give him the captain's chance. We let the sea decide."

"And confirm this was a mutiny," Livion says, "not a legal action."

"Only if he gets back," Tuse says, "and that's the chance we take. We'll say he was lost overboard saving Beale. A hero's end. Who's to complain that it was improper? And our hands are clean." He can see this appeals to Livion.

Livion says, "What about your rowers? Can we count on them?"

"I think so," Tuse says. "They'll need the money soon. The guild is finished. Soon the only rowers will be prisoners. They're half as effective as brothers, but half the cost. And you can whip them."

"Will they keep quiet?" Livion says.

"And risk the gibbet?" Tuse says. "Sure. But the poth won't."

On the rowers' deck the poth wishes she had another bottle of wine and a sharper saw. She's treated those who needed her help the most, and now she can consider those she thought would live regardless. She starts with a brother slumped over his oar.

Sleep is usually the best medicine. Nonetheless, Everlyn clears her throat. He doesn't stir. Everlyn pats his shoulder. He topples slightly. She puts two fingers on his neck. It's warm and wet and without a pulse. She raises his head. His eyes are wide and red; his lips and nostrils covered with sizzling foam the color of fire powder. Everlyn lowers his head then lowers herself to the edge of his bench.

When she looks up, Tuse is standing over her. "Livion's waiting to see you."

"I know," she says. She stands up, her chin thrust at his chest. He slides aside to let her get to the ladder. "No," she says, and heads forward again. "Let him wait. These men shouldn't have to any longer."

As she passes him, Tuse looks at the slumped-over rower. "This one all right?"

"He got the job done," she says. *So did I.*

7

Livion orders Jeryon brought up and the dragon cut loose. They've rendered all they can, stuffing the captain's cabin with bones, bolts of skin, and sheets of wing membrane. The dragon's head has been carefully packed to ensure the phlogiston doesn't escape, and so that it could later be made into a trophy. Crates stacked on deck are moved to the hold as soon as Jeryon emerges. Some people prize dragon meat as an aphrodisiac, but little could be taken that wasn't ruined by the water, a dozen astounded sharks, the sandals of the renderers, and that bit which is being cooked over a brazier by the foredeck.

"Tastes like chicken," Beale says.

"*Fire* chicken," Topp says.

The rest of the carcass sinks quickly. The sharks follow it, and by the time Jeryon is marched the length of the ship past piles of stray flesh to the stern deck, the sea is empty but for the dinghy, now tied to the starboard rail.

Jeryon surveys the *Comber* and his crew without comment. He sees the poth in the rowers' deck, hurrying aft. He says nothing to her either.

The mates stand together by the unmanned steering oar. The poth climbs up behind Jeryon and his escort.

"Have you come to your senses?" Jeryon asks.

Livion says, "We've decided to give you the captain's chance."

Jeryon tsks. "*We've*, Captain? There is no *we* in captain. Only *I*."

The poth says, "What's the captain's chance?"

"A practice old as pirates," Jeryon says without turning around. "The judgment of cowards."

Livion says, "You will be set adrift without food or water, sail or oar, and the waves will decide your fate."

The poth says, "That's monstrous."

"That's prerogative," Livion says.

"He could have me executed," Jeryon says, "but he's too weak." He looks at Solet. "Pliable."

"And you're too rigid," Livion says. "Four hours. That's how long it took to render the dragon. The rowers needed the rest, too. Four hours. And a fortune. That's what you traded for this."

The poth pushes past the escort to stand between the mates and their captain. "And what have you traded?" She looks at them in turn.

"Four hours. How many more got sick in Hanosh? How many more are dead? A body must seem awfully light when it's weighed against a full purse."

"I wanted to explain things earlier," Livion says. "This isn't your business."

She shoots a look at Tuse. "It became mine when I signed on, but not for this. I won't be a party to it. I've got enough blood on my hands."

"Then you can take the same chance we're giving him," Livion says.

Jeryon says, "I didn't want some Aydeni landlubber on this ship. I don't want one in the dinghy either."

"Think of her as provisions then," Solet says. Several sailors, still armed with their gory tools, laugh.

"Stay with us," Tuse tells the poth. "The men need you. Hanosh needs you. And you'll get your share. You've earned it."

"I don't heal for money," she says. "I won't kill for it either. I'll take the chance."

Jeryon says to Tuse, "You don't like this, do you?"

"It's not the choice I would have made," Tuse said.

"Did make, Tuse," Jeryon says. "Putting me in a boat is one thing. Putting her in one is another. You didn't think of that, but you can't stop, can you?" Jeryon shakes off the escort and stands beside the poth. "She'll be the one you see at night, not me. As for you two, if anyone cracks, if anyone lets slip what he's done while he's drunk in a bar, it'll be Tuse. Then I won't need to tell the Trust my side of the story."

Livion and Solet give Tuse a warning look. He returns it.

The poth says, "I'd like to put on a fresh smock."

"No," Solet says. "And let's check those pockets."

"I'm going freely," Everlyn says. "I will not be searched."

"I could take the whole dress," Solet says, "and give you to the sea in whatever's under there."

She tightens her lips and pulls from the deep hip pockets several bottles of lotion and powders. From those in the folds around her legs emerge bandages, small tools, and, improbably, two limes. From the pockets inside her sleeves come bandage ties, a pot of unguent, and packets of medicinal herbs. She drops it all in a clatter.

Solet says, "Is that it?"

"Yes," the poth says.

"Let's check one more place," Solet says, "just in case." He reaches for the thick floral brocade that extends from the deep vee of her collar. She covers her breasts. He taps her wrists. Resigned, she lowers her arms. He reaches behind the brocade and pulls from a pocket there a flat knife with a bone handle. He admires it. It's like the full-size version of his finger blade. He pockets it.

"Is that it?" Solet says.

Again the poth says, "Yes."

"Fool me once," Solet says. "Hold her." Two sailors stretch her by her arms and Solet runs his hands up each arm, over her back, belly, breasts, and broad, heavy hips, then from her crotch to her ankles. He finds no contraband. He and the crew might have taken a greater thrill from the search had her furious dignity not stiffened their hearts. The sailors let her go.

He says to Jeryon, "Pick up anything in the hold?" Jeryon yanks out his two pants pockets. They flap as uselessly as a spaniel's ears.

Solet looks to Livion, who orders, "Put them in the dinghy."

They're led down to the starboard rail. The dinghy's thwarts have been removed, as well as the collapsible mast, the rigging, and the rudder.

It seems so much larger, Jeryon thinks.

"It seems so small," the poth mutters.

Jeryon offers the poth his hand. She refuses it, jumps into the dinghy, and kneels by the transom as he climbs in after her. He remains standing, the cords in his arms and his neck tensed. A sailor unties the painter and tosses it into the dinghy. It drifts away from the *Comber*.

Everlyn gets up, rocking the boat as little as possible, and stands behind Jeryon.

Jeryon says, "Livion, remember this. I don't take chances. I plot a course, and I bring my boat in."

"If you did take chances," Livion says, "you wouldn't have that one to bring in."

Tuse descends to the rowers' deck, Solet takes the oar, and Livion pipes. The oars extend from the galley like the legs of a crab. The ports have been reopened, but none of the rowers look at the dinghy. Livion pipes again. As the oars stroke for Hanosh, Beale comes to the rail. He can't help it. He waves.

Jeryon calls out, "I still would have saved you."

CHAPTER TWO

The Poth

1

I shouldn't have saved him, Jeryon thinks. *Now I'll have to destroy him too.*

Solet would happily kill for revenge. Ynessi love revenge so much they have songs celebrating it. They feature the most brutal and cunning slaughters, people and places, times and events. Children are taught the songs as much to learn about the city's history as to learn about its mores. And you can dance to them. Because revenge leads to more revenge, songs are often parts of a cycle, and these are the basis for daylong, sometimes weeklong, parties.

Tuse would kill for revenge if he were drunk and angry enough.

Not Livion. He would take a slight as his due until someone told him what to do.

I'll get my revenge the old-fashioned way, Jeryon thinks. Nothing threatens trade like mutiny, and trade is all the Trust and the city care about. The Trust will be his hammer and the law his anvil. He looks forward to seeing the fear in his mates' eyes as they're condemned. He looks forward to watching them struggle or, better, sit stunned as mullets while they're carted through town and rowed to the gibbets, then listening to them scream as thirst gets its claws into them. It'll take three days for them to die. Such is the essence of justice.

The poth settles against the transom, her knees pulled up, her smock tucked around them, her arms shrunken into her sleeves and wrapped around her calves. She feels unmoored in such an empty smock. And it will be a long, hot afternoon. She's already thirsty. Who decided poths must wear dark green?

When the *Comber* is far enough away that Jeryon can no longer make out the crew on deck, he says, "There are two things you need to know, poth."

"Sit," Everlyn says.

"What?"

"Sit," she says. "I like your shade, but not you looming over me like some shipowner on his parlor throne."

He sits, pressing his spine as far into the bow as possible. *If that's how it's going to be, let her squint*, he thinks. She does.

"One," Jeryon says, "here's what stands between us and Hanosh. The nearest land is Eryn Point at the mouth of Joslin Bay, eighty nautical miles away. Hanosh is twenty beyond that. If we had oars, half a barrel of water, and the stamina of guilded rowers, we could make the trip in three days and see my mates tucked into their gibbets in four. Instead, we have the Tallan River."

"What's that?" she says.

He looks as if she'd asked, *What's air?* "It's a current. The current. How can you live in Hanosh and—"

"I'm not Hanoshi," Everlyn says. "I'm Aydeni."

"I know," he says. "It's the fault of you Aydeni that we're here in the first place."

She nearly stands. The dinghy rocks severely. She doesn't care. "I'm here because I wouldn't have a hand in your death."

"You're here," Jeryon says, "because Ayden wouldn't sell us its store of shield. At any price."

"I wouldn't have a hand in Hanoshi deaths either," she says. "Your Trust didn't come to me. I went to them. I said I could help."

"They trusted you?" he says.

Ayden, deep in the mountains west of Hanosh, has been the city's chief rival in the Six Cities Trading League since it was allowed to join. Their admission ended a ruinous war and ushered in four decades of mutual prosperity, but for the last several years they've been taking baby steps toward another conflict. There's not enough money to go around. Pirates who've plundered Hanoshi ships are rumored to have been Aydeni privateers. Bandits who've attacked Hanoshi caravans are suspected of being backed by Ayden. Not that Hanosh doesn't have its own agents in Ayden to steal their trade secrets. Not that they aren't rumored to have attacked Aydeni traders too. Denying Hanosh the golden shield it needed to fight the flox was the first adult step, even if Ayden claims they only took it because two years ago Hanosh gouged them on the price of grain after a drought doomed their crops.

"Of course they didn't trust me," Everlyn says. "They thought I was a saboteur, maybe a venomist. But my patients, the shipowners' wives, they vouched for me."

Owners aren't easily swayed, and their wives don't sway lightly: Where's the profit? Jeryon figures her advocates still consider it fashionable to have an Aydeni apothecary, just as some still wear boots and plain smocks instead of returning to sandals and embroidered chitons and mantles. To get her on the *Comber* would signal their power.

"Which brings us back to the Tallan River," he says. "An actual agent probably would have been briefed on it." He lays his arms over the gunwales. "The sea is shaped like the bow of a boat pointing north. That—" he points to the starboard oarlock, "is Chorem. And this—" he points to the larboard oarlock, "is Yness. Eryn Point is a couple hands forward, where the center thwart would go. Everything aft of the oarlocks is ocean: trackless, empty ocean. Now—"

As he scoots forward, Everlyn tucks her knees tighter.

Jeryon puts his left foot on the bottom beneath the starboard oarlock. "The current is fifty miles wide," he says, "a bit wider than my sandal in boat scale. It leaves the ocean here, runs up my left leg, around my back, and down my right leg into the sea here." He plants his right foot under the larboard oarlock. "And we are here." He puts his finger on the bottom between his knees, amidships, and too close to his crotch, in Everlyn's opinion. "Do you see our problem?"

The poth had hated her loremasters. When she was twelve her father discovered that she was running away from them to tramp through the woods with a forest warden. The warden convinced him that Everlyn, whatever her talent for sums, had a real devotion to herblore and healing. So her father gave Everlyn to her for schooling. She broke her slate in joy.

"How fast does the current run?" she asks.

"Correct," Jeryon says. "Six knots. The *Comber* could cross it in four or five hours under full sail and oar, entering the river north of Eryn Point and letting it carry the galley down to the mouth of the bay. If we had oars to reach it, we would cross more slowly and be carried much farther south. Hopefully we'd make it to Yness before being swept to sea."

"But we have no oars," she says.

"Or water, which makes the issue moot. We'll be dead of thirst before we make it across."

"So we have no chance?"

"Not according to my mates' calculations," Jeryon says.

2

"Which brings us," Jeryon continues, "to the second thing you need to know. I will get you to Hanosh so you can testify against my crew."

"I could write it down," she says, "and save you the trouble of saving me too."

"We don't have anything to write with," he says. Jeryon reads her like a manifest: "Smock. Boots. Presumably undergarments." She scowls. "Those sticks in your hair, let me see them," he says. She looks skeptical. He says, "I won't run off," and holds out his hand.

She draws the pair of long steel pins from her bun. Her hair unfurls. Her neck sweats. "Why do you need them?" she says.

He tests their points, which are oddly sharp, and taps them together. Their surfaces are mottled like flowing water. "Gift from one of your company ladies?" he says. "These aren't cheap."

"Not everything has a price," she says.

"In Hanosh it does." He crosses his right leg and with one of the pins worries the seam of his pant leg. He says, "I bet someone came to you for help and discovered afterward that she was also suffering from a touch of embarrassment. So she paid you with these. Her husband's going to be very upset when he finds out. What did you palm while Solet was searching you?"

Startled, the poth says, "You saw that?"

"Never lose sight of a person's hand," he says. "That's Solet's weakness. He's easily distracted."

The poth reaches into her pocket and removes a purple phial. "For cuts and burns."

"Handy, if we live long enough to be cut." He looks at the sun. "We will be burned. Especially you." Her upland skin is more golden than his, what the Hanoshi described in better times as "tea with honey" and now call "milky."

"There we go." A stitch pops and he yanks out the thread with the pin. He opens the seam and removes a steel blade, one edge straight, the other serrated, and a thin envelope the length of her pinky.

"Aren't you full of surprises," she says.

Jeryon has such a bland face, like dough too dry and hard to be pounded, that she's shocked to see a bit of mischief dart through his eyes.

"Trust your sails, but not the wind," Jeryon says. "And I've been thinking the wind was about to turn."

"Do you have an aphorism for everything?" she says. "Any port in a storm? Nodding the head won't row the boat?"

"Simple rules prevent complex problems," he says.

She humphs. "What's in the envelope?"

He unfolds it carefully. In it sits a bone needle and some red thread.

"What's that for? Sutures?"

"Do I look like a surgeon?" he says. "It's for fixing my pants. I can't run around with my pants falling to pieces, can I?"

Everlyn stifles a laugh at his serious expression.

He threads the needle and goes to work. "While I do this," he says, "crawl to the bow and untie the painter." Everlyn looks confused. "The line. The rope." *Landlubber*, he thinks.

She nods and slips past him. She doesn't ask why he needs the rope and lets the mystery of it burnish the next five minutes of life adrift.

The knot is hard as steel, hammered by a thousand waves. She wonders if this is a test of patience. Her fingers are powerful from yanking roots and nimble from untangling vines, but the knot gives only the tiniest bit with each tug. She develops a rhythm after a while, which lets her look into the water.

The sea is lifeless compared to the lake at Ayden, whose shallows are covered in nests. She splashed and shrieked in summer, especially when a mother fish nipped at her for stepping on a nest, and she slid in winter until her friend went through the ice and drowned, then it wasn't so much fun. The lake was huge to her as a child. It could fit in the dinghy compared to the sea.

Everlyn gets the painter free. Having fixed his pants—all sailors can sew—Jeryon rewraps and pockets the needle, then trades her pins for the painter and cuts off a piece as long as his blade. This he slices longitudinally a third of the way through. He fits the straight edge into the rope and saws experimentally at the starboard gunwale forward of the oarlock. The rope guards his finger satisfactorily. He keeps sawing.

"First, we're going to remove the gunwales section by section," Jeryon says.

The poth says, "Won't that make the boat fall apart?"

"Were this a new dinghy, maybe," he says. "Nowadays, every bit of wood is minimized to keep costs down. Boats don't last more than a couple years. Some galleys don't even carry them anymore. But this dinghy is pre-League and overdesigned. It'll last." He taps the gunwale with his blade. "Two boards. We'll just take the top one." He shakes his head. "I even got her cheap, for being ancient."

He cuts through the top board, pushes past the poth, and saws the end by the breasthook.

"If it eases your mind," he said, "the boat only has to stay afloat for three days. We'll be dead of thirst after that. Actually we'll probably be too weak for work after two."

"Once a child got lost in the woods around Ayden," she says. "He lasted six days without water before he was found."

"He wasn't in this sun. But you could be right. Maybe we could go a week. Let's plan for three days, though."

He cuts through the board and wedges it up with the blade. "Take the pin," he says, "and slide it underneath the gunwale so it doesn't sit back down." She does so. "Don't lever it. You'll bend the pin. Just slide it aft as I do the levering."

They work it free slowly and steadily until Jeryon can get his fingers under it and yank it up nails and all. His rope handle has been nearly worn through, so he makes an inch-long slice up one end of the piece of gunwale, cuts off the end to make two opposing pieces, makes a quarter-inch cut in their opposing faces, and clasps the pieces together tight around half the blade to create a handle. He folds the rest of his rope to make a new fingerguard. "Now, let's take up the rest."

It doesn't take her much longer to realize that he doesn't really need her to help. "You're just giving me something to do," she says, "so I don't panic."

"Yes," he says.

"I don't panic," she says.

He gives her a long look and says, "Reduce the painter to its strands. I'll need those soon."

After a while she says, "We could be found by another galley."

"We won't be," he says. "Galleys don't often cross Tallan. They row north in the gutter between the coast and the river, where they can trade and stop ashore for water and game." He yanks the larboard bow gunwale free. "Ships from the Dawn Lands ride the river north to Jolef to trade with us, then work their way home down the coast. There's no profit in the sea itself. Besides, there were no other ships at Chorem planning to cross." He gets to work on the starboard quarter gunwale.

"What about whalers?" she says.

"What about needles in haystacks?"

"Pirates?"

"Now pirates are more likely. Then we'd have the pleasure of being violated before we died."

"We?" she says.

"The Ynessi don't discriminate. Any Aydeni ships out here that you know of?"

"That's just propaganda," she says. "Fear-mongering. Ayden has no navy, unless you count trade wagons. And if we did, we still wouldn't attack Hanosh. Where's the profit, as you say?"

"We?" he says. "You can take the woman out of Ayden . . ."

"I'm not ashamed of being Aydeni," Everlyn says. "I'm ashamed of Ayden, at least when it comes to the golden shield."

"The luxury of principles is fading as quickly as that of good boat building," he says. "That's why I'm here."

As the sun falls toward the west and the small moon, Med, appears in the east, Jeryon pulls free the last piece of gunwale from the starboard transom. He surveys Everlyn's neatly tied coils of painter strands. "Where did you learn that hitch?"

"We have knots on land too, you know."

He shrugs and saws the gunwale pieces in half. Once this is done he flips them over, takes off a sandal and uses it to bang out a nail. A muffled clang follows each blow.

"How can you hammer with leather?" she says.

"It's leather on the outside," he says. "There's a thick steel plate in each heel. They give me a heavy tread on deck. Sailors don't like a sneaky captain. They like to know where he is, and he likes them to know where he is."

"And that's not sneaky?" she says.

"That's command," he says. "Collect the nails as I bang them out. We'll need them."

The big moon, Ah, is up when he arranges the forward pieces of gunwale into a rough rectangle, the aft pieces into a smaller, neater one, and lays across each two pieces of transom gunwale. Then he nails them together.

"There. Paddles," he says. "Or something approaching paddles. And to make sure we don't lose them . . ." He enlarges two nail holes in the end of each with a hair pin and threads a strand of painter through them. He ties the forward assemblage to his right wrist, motions for her to hold up her left wrist and ties the other to it. She doesn't know the knot, and he makes it too quickly for her to follow.

He kneels amidships, she kneels beside him, and facing the horizon they paddle in easy tandem for the League. The spare nails jingle pleasantly in her pocket.

After a few dozen strokes he waits until the poth's not looking and changes his grip to match hers. It's more comfortable and efficient.

3

Jeryon jerks awake: Where's his paddle? His right arm dangles over the starboard gunwale. His fist is full of water. He digs into the sea with both hands until he remembers the strand of painter. He clasps his wrist and draws the paddle to him from where it had been drifting astern. He sits on his heels, catching his breath.

The poth is slumped over her gunwale. Her arm and paddle aren't in the boat either. Just looking for them makes him feel so dizzy he has to lean a hand on the bottom. He rolls his head slowly to match the spinning inside. He lays the back of his forefinger on her neck. It's very dry. He fishes around beneath her hand, finds the strand from her wrist, and pulls her oar in. He leans it against the gunwale. This dislodges her and she stirs enough to slap some hair off her face. Her cheek would normally look gray in the moonlight. It's grayer than it should be.

It's not long after midnight, and the small moon, Med, has a five-length lead on Ah. Their position is the first thing Jeryon's father checked when they went to their boat a few hours before dawn. He had a theory about them. If Med beat Ah across the sky, the nets would be full that day. If Ah beat Med, they'd be empty. If they rose and set together, anything could happen. Jeryon used to check the theory. The nets were mostly empty wherever the moons happened to be, but telling his father this made no difference. He couldn't be convinced.

Jeryon was convinced, though, that steady work for a shipowner was more secure than rolling the dice with your own boat's net.

He paddles, however ineffectually, too tired to sleep. They couldn't have made more than seven or eight miles, although the poth was steady and strong. Maybe she's not as much of a landlubber as he thought.

When Everlyn awakes it's nearly dawn. Her paddle lies in the boat. He must have put it there. He's slumped over the gunwale, his paddle still gripped in his hand. How long had he kept rowing before passing out? Jeryon's flushed. She touches his neck. His pulse remains steady, and they're both sweating. The cool night might have bought them a few more hours.

A silver flicker kicks at the water. She thinks a wave reflected off the boat, then sees another one and another, like the stars swimming up to greet them. She pushes Jeryon's shoulder and, as he rouses, points over the side. She tries to say, "Look," but the word skids to a halt on her dry tongue.

He says, "Some dragon meat must have caught on the hull."

The pearly-silver fish spill across the surface as they take a chance at the meat. Neither fish nor castaways can believe their good luck.

Jeryon slams his paddle at a fish. He succeeds only in scattering the school. The fish come back, and he tries again. Same result.

"Silly way to fish anyway," he mutters.

On the other side of the boat, the poth tries and clips one. It floats, stunned, a coin waiting to be plucked from the mud. She slams it again for good measure. It turns belly up and its schoolmates consider it for their own breakfast. She grabs its tail, lifts it up, and cries, "Aha!" Jeryon turns just in time to see a longtom as big as her arm jump out of the water and tear her prize from her hand with its needlelike jaws. She tucks her hand against her belly as the fish vanishes, the school evaporating in its wake.

"We could eat the dragon meat," Jeryon says, "but it's probably too salty at this point."

The thought of eating makes her thirstier, which makes her hungrier. She had some rice and fish at midday yesterday, followed by a handful of figs. She doesn't recall Jeryon eating at all. "Give me your blade," she says.

"Why?"

She puts out her palm. "We shouldn't speak too much," she says. "Need to save our energy."

He takes the blade and handle from his pocket, assembles them, and gives her the knife. *How long until we turn on each other?* he thinks. *A person could survive a long time on the sack of meat and water that is the poth.*

She undoes a tie in the brocade on her smock. It flops aside to reveal a panel with two bone buttons white as the moons. She cuts them off and hands him one along with the blade. "Put it beneath your tongue," she says. "It'll encourage spit."

He rubs it between his fingers then rubs it with a clean patch of shirt. She rolls her eyes and holds hers up. "To your health," she says. He returns the toast, and they pop the buttons.

Steak is rarely this wonderfully juicy. They savor and smack. As she pulls her smock closed, he swallows carefully and says, "Save that spare thread."

She plucks two tufts from where the buttons had been and puts them in his hand. He looks at them and laughs. She laughs too.

"That'll save us," she says.

"Two more," he says, "and we could weave a sail."

When they stop laughing, they paddle on.

Four hours after sunrise, Jeryon watches his hands shift his paddle to one side. He's curious as to what they plan to do. There's a silver flash in the water, and the hands bash it with the paddle. The school has returned. Once he realizes what his hands have done, he nearly leaps overboard to scoop the stunned fish into the boat.

It's as big as his sandal and twice as thick. It flops a few times on the bottom. Its gills yawn.

Jeryon is beginning to think his father was on to something, although he's so light-headed the thought keeps slipping away.

"It's a meagre," he says.

"Big enough for us," she says.

"No," he says, "it's a type of—never mind." He cleans and fillets the fish. In the splashes pooled in the boat, threads of blood and stray gore wind around their knees. He combs up the guts with the fish's skeleton and puts the remains on his paddle. He hands one fillet to her. They take out their buttons, toast, and bite.

The fish's juices make him gag. His eyes seep and burn. His mouth fills with acid. Swallowing feels like he's sucking a cork down his throat. He takes a smaller bite. It's barely more palatable. And he feels thirstier than ever.

The poth slurps the fish, but she's having the same problem. And her hands are shivering.

His are too. Gripping the paddle disguised it.

He swallows the acid then puts the button in his mouth again. When his tongue is glazed with spit, he trades the button for a tiny bite of fish. He still doesn't want to swallow, but he can. His hands shiver a little less.

She does the same thing. She smiles encouragingly. Then they eat in unison: button, bite, button, bite. When the fillets are done, he presents her with half the skin draped over the knife. They gnaw the flakes of meat remaining. He gives her the fish head to suck.

Given the circumstances, Everlyn thinks it's the nicest gift she's ever received. She licks out the eyes with relish.

They use the guts and tail as chum to attract more fish. With their paddles raised they watch for hours. It seems like weeks. The school is gone again. The chum dissipates.

They return to paddling. After a few strokes, Jeryon pokes at his teeth with this tongue, then stops and picks at them with his finger. A scale is lodged there. He can't get it out. He puts the blade between his teeth, but Everlyn grabs his hand before he can scrape. She pushes his hand down and holds it, tilts his head with her other hand so that his jaw drops wide, and works the scale free with her shield-stained nails. He lacks the will to resist.

She shows it to him, a translucent gray blade, and flicks it overboard. He nods in appreciation, rubs his teeth with this tongue, and takes up his paddle.

At dusk, he still feels the scale between his teeth. Or is that her nail? He can't remember the last time he let a woman touch him. No sense in it.

After star-rise he adjusts their course. It gives him something to do and gives her some hope. They don't mention how thirsty they are. The first rule of thirst: don't mention thirst. The buttons have long stopped working except as token comfort. Neither has mentioned a need to urinate or defecate, an alarming situation mitigated only slightly by their mutual relief at not having to do so before the other.

They haven't spoken since the fish, so Jeryon has to scrape the roof of his mouth and bite his tongue to work up the spit to say, "We made good time. Should be in the river tomorrow. Won't have to row. Just steer. If we get two miles west for every six south, we'll reach Yness."

She'll be happy not to row. Her hands are blistered on both sides, the palms from the paddle, the backs from the sun. Blood is smeared across the rough-edged ends of the wood. Her hands are so numb she can barely hold her paddle, and her arms are so numb she can barely hold them out.

She digs for the phial of lotion. "No sense in letting it go to waste," she says. She puts a few dabs on her hands, then, after some initial reluctance, on his. Rubbing it into her fingers is like donning mittens in winter.

He sniffs his hands. They smell like some flower. He flexes them and reaches for his paddle. "We still need to row now, though," he says.

"Let's keep going then," Everlyn says and puts the phial away.

She's tough. If someone has to put fingers in his mouth, it might as well be her.

4

The world is cellar black when the poth awakes. Thick clouds obliterate the sky. For a moment she thinks she's dead. She can't see him. She can't see the boat. She can't feel anything. She's beyond pain. She's not sweating. She would be sweating if she were alive. She's happy the darkness is a floating, not a falling. The soft breeze, though, wafting across her face, suggests there's little difference between the two when there is no ground, no up or down.

Did she work herself to death? Did he coax her into it, playing on her willfulness? He wanted to keep paddling, even though they didn't have to anymore. Or did he slit her throat after she collapsed? Has he already started to devour her?

One winter a pair of trappers was lost for months above Ayden. They weren't found until spring, holed up in a cave, one woman fat and happy, the other gnawed and cracked to release her marrow. Her rescuers, appalled, bludgeoned the survivor with her own walking stick. Everlyn still wonders if the devoured woman knew what was in store for her. Did she fight her partner? Or did she surrender herself with pleasure?

Everlyn sees him crawling up her legs, gnashing with his scaly teeth. She kicks. She'll fight. She slams her boot heel into his belly. He wheezes. How did he get over there? She kicks him again. She hears him roll onto his side. Her heart rate slows. She rubs her neck. No slits, no blood. She's alive. She must be.

She could kill him first. He wants her to testify. She could steer down the river like he said and race from Yness to Hanosh. It would be her tribute to him. She would carry him inside her belly. They would testify together with one voice and one mind.

She's skinned game. She's a fair butcher. She doesn't want to slaughter him, though. She wants him to keep. She has to savor him. She needs the knife. She'll make a little prick in his wrist and suck his blood slowly. She doesn't even need to kill him. She smiles. He doesn't have to die. She'll drink a little whenever he's not looking. A sip here, a sip there. He'll never know. He's so exhausted. His hands are cut up like hers. What's another cut?

Her eyes adjust to the darkness. Everything glows green. She's like a cat. She waves her paws around him. He's slumped over the pocket with the knife. She can't get to it. Wait. She should wash her hands. Always wash your hands before working with food, Everlyn

She pads on her knees to her side of the boat. The sea is licking it. It's like a cat too. A thousand black cats in little white caps make little tiny laps. She pets the cats. So warm. So soft. Their fur is so deep. She smells them on her fingers. More like kitties than cats. She takes a little taste. Delicious! Why would she eat bony old him when she could eat these kitties? Don't eat kitties, Everlyn. There's so many, though. No one would miss a couple or six. She lifts one yowling to her lips.

He yanks her backward with his claw. It slides beneath her smock. It burns her bare shoulder. She screams a trickle of bile. He falls on top of her. Her smock slides up. Where's his other hand? Where's the knife? She lets the kitty go, it flees to the bow, and she grabs at him.

He locks her wrists in his fists and crushes them between their chests. His head falls on her shoulder. He sniffs at her ear. She tucks her chin against her chest and folds her head over so he can't bite her neck.

He whispers, "No. No water."

She says, "It's kitties!"

He doesn't respond. He may have fainted. He doesn't let go. His hands are tight as a painter knot. She can't get him off her. Dawn comes as a surprise to her. She must have fainted too. He lifts his head. He says, "I want you—" and coughs. He lifts himself. He helps her sit up. He releases her hands, kicks her paddle at her, and says, "I want you alive. One more day." His voice sounds like wind in a tunnel.

She puts her paddle in the water. It bobs. It bobs. The strand has rubbed her wrist raw. "Which way?" she says.

He looks at the sky. The cloud cover is so thick, he can't tell where the sun rose. The uniform gray makes him strain his eyes. "Pin," he says.

She takes a pin from her bun, where he graciously lets her store them. His hands are shaking terribly. He stabs himself in the crotch twice before the stick finds its real target: a tiny catch on the back of his top pants button, a tacky golden globe. He holds the button and works the stick around until the front of the button opens like a locket. A yellow-green gem is set inside. He holds it against the sky.

The gem gathers light from somewhere, and a line appears inside it. He turns the boat at a right angle to it.

"Magic?" she says.

"Yolite."

They paddle. The air leans on their shoulders until a following wind erupts from the night's breeze. It's cool and encouraging. They paddle faster, although each stroke is like pushing through an angry mob.

At some point, the water changes color. "River," Jeryon says.

The sky darkens behind them. Night is still a long way ahead. "Storm," she says. "Water."

"Too much." He motions for her wrist. He cuts the cord with a jittery slash. He cuts his own strand in a way that nearly costs him his thumb. Then he tries to pull the crosspieces off her paddle. He can't get the blade under them. His fingers refuse to obey. He hacks the wood uselessly. She reaches for the paddle. He pushes her away and tears at the crosspieces with his fingers. She reaches for the paddle again. He jabs at her with the knife. She returns his glare. His features slacken, and he pushes the paddle and knife at her. He hangs his head.

It takes her awhile, but the poth finds the same rhythm she did with the painter and the paddle comes undone. His spirit returns. He nails two pieces of her paddle along either side of the top of his, his sandal hammer broad enough to accommodate his fluctuating aim. He wedges another piece between them to lengthen the extension, nails it in place securely, and ties it to his wrist.

"Rudder," he says.

He puts the paddle portion behind the transom and slots the tiller in the sculling notch. It doesn't fit.

He shakes his head, unties the rudder, and drags the serrated edge of the knife across the transom's gunwale to enlarge the notch. He barely scratches the wood at first. The sky grows darker. The sea grumbles. The blade catches. In a few minutes or hours he's cut half-way through. He falls aside and the poth takes a turn

She squeezes the jury-rigged knife handle so hard her hands regain enough feeling to ache. The metal chips away the wood. She counts the flakes to keep her focused. The horizon collapses toward them. She cuts horizontally from the bottom of the notch, yanking the blade. The gunwale grips, the handle gives, and the blade flips free across the boat.

Jeryon crawls on top of it then roots for it beneath his chest. He looks at her as if he really might eat her if he had the strength. She looks sadly at the well-worn handle. It wasn't her fault. He puts the knife together again, considers the notch, and hands it to her. This cheers her.

In a moment she pries free the bit of gunwale. Now the tiller fits and turns. He nails a former paddle crosspiece over it loosely as a guide.

He sits against the transom and pulls the tiller across his chest. He puts his arms over it, spreads his knees, and points between them. Reluctantly, she sits. He spins his finger. She pivots until he can pull her back against his chest, anchoring the rudder in place. He flops his arms over her. She can remember the last time she let a man lie on top of her, but not the last time one put his arms around her. So be it. She pulls her smock down then holds his wrists with the opposite hands. They knot together and let the river take them.

Jeryon whispers, "Swallowed my button" and passes out.

Everlyn realizes she has the knife now. She strokes the veins in his wrists with her thumbnails.

5

The Hanoshi harbor has two notable features. The most useful is its long, broad piers. At Yness, Jolef, and Meres, galleys beach themselves, making these cities no more than up-jumped versions of coastal towns. At Hanosh, the galleys tie up, shipowners come aboard on Tower-blue gangplanks, and cranes handle cargo day and night.

Its more arresting feature is the line of gibbets, also painted blue, a hundred yards beyond the docks. Four consist of tall posts with single beams pointing at inbound ships as a warning. The Great Gibbet in the center, reserved for the most celebrated or vicious criminals, looks like a cross-staff. From its two transoms four prisoners can either swing in iron cages or, if banded, hang by chains directly.

Jeryon stands at the end of Hanosh's main pier with the leaders of the Trust arrayed behind him. They are silent. The wind picks up. Tuse sways in his cage, pleading for Jeryon to understand. He sticks one bare foot through the bars. It dangles well above the tide. In time flesh will drip beneath it to be eaten by crabs. Livion and Solet snap and sway in their bands like broken pendulums. They can't speak with the bits in their mouths, but they can moan. Their spit has dried up. Thirst scrapes in their throats like mice in a wall.

The wind gusts harder. A gale is moving in, strange for this season. The Great Gibbet twists, while the tide bursts over the pier. Its spray wails with the prisoners' despair. Jeryon bathes in it, and he feels beautiful.

He turns to ask the Trust where the poth is, and he finds himself staring at the gibbet again with the Trust behind him. He turns the other way. The world turns with him. He can't face the Trust. He can't see their faces. He can hear them laughing.

Then he's in the dinghy, filthy and contorted, clutching the tiller against a heaving sea. He closes his eyes again.

Something smacks his face. His eyes grind open. The poth holds a heavy bulb of smock above his lips. A wave makes her fall, and the bulb dives into his mouth. He sucks. Rainwater flows into the cracks in his tongue. It's warm and sweet, and he's drowning in it. He spits out the cloth and water. She sops more water from the bottom of the boat with her hem, braces herself, and wrings the water into his mouth. His head droops over the transom so the rain can fall down his throat while she sops up a third drink

This time he grabs the bulb and takes it into his mouth himself. She tugs the bulb free, touches it to his lips, and squeezes. "Slowly," she says.

As she resops, so slowly, a frenzy takes him. Shaking, he works free the crosspiece guide and hauls in the rudder. It splashes in nearly an inch of water. It can't all be fresh, but enough is, and the rain is picking up. He wrenches his shirt off, mops it across the bottom, and squeezes the water over his face. Still too slow. He flings himself down and drinks directly from the dinghy. He slurps and waits for her to pull him away, except she's beside him on all fours now, lapping and gagging, the frenzy in her too. Once the boat is empty, he will suck her long hair dry.

The rain falls in great fans faster than they can drink it, and the sea rises high enough to stuff it back into the clouds. Only the drops lancing their skin let them know which way is up.

A wave nearly jounces them from the boat. Jeryon yells in the poth's ear, "Blade!" She stares at him. He yells again. She searches through her pockets for it. Did she lose it? Jeryon feels around in the boat. She finds it in the pocket behind her smock's brocade and gives it to him. He saws through the strand attaching his wrist to the rudder, pockets the blade, and ties the strand to her left wrist with a child's knot. "Float," he says.

He notices something odd on his left wrist. A tiny cut seeps blood. A bruise blooms around it. He wonders how it got there.

A wave rolls the dinghy mere seconds from the righting moment, pushing her on top of him, before it settles back. She grabs his wrists. A wave flips them the other way. Another gushes over the gunwale, half filling the dinghy. Jeryon slips under the poth so she can keep her head above the water. The rudder floats beside them, clacking against the remaining pieces of her paddle.

Something scrapes the hull, the dinghy shudders, and a strake cracks. Water spits through the hull then disappears as more waves fill the boat, and the poth lets go of his wrists. Splashing for purchase, she floats away from him. The rudder is tossed overboard, dragging her half over the gunwale. He grabs her collar and hauls her back in. She hooks her free arm around his neck. He folds her smock's brocade into his fist and tucks her against his body. They're more afloat than the dinghy. He wraps a leg around her thigh to weigh her down. A huge wave rises astern, dawning black above the transom.

His eyes tell her what's coming. Hers plead, *Don't die*. His say, *You can't*.

A mat of fresh palm leaves sloshes by and vanishes. In disbelief they look around for it, and obligingly it returns to moor in the lagoon between their chests. A tiny white horned crab shakes its claws at them and scuttles off its raft into the dinghy. The wave crest bubbles white and reaches for them.

The dinghy rises slowly, stern first. Jeryon throws out his feet to catch his sandals on the boat's ribs. Water pours over the bow, pulling them forward toward the sea. The remains of the poth's paddle slide past them and disappear into the sea. The toes of Jeryon's sandals slip to the next rib, then the next.

The crest curls over them like his father's hand. It rises, strikes, holds them inside its fist, squeezes, and shoots the dinghy through its foamy fingers across the sea.

Everlyn screams because she knows they're going to live until the bow is stoved in. Water blasts through it like a gout of dragon flame. It slices her from Jeryon's grasp, and the boat pitches over their heads. The last thing Everlyn sees is him reaching for her as they soar into a sky of water.

CHAPTER THREE

The Beach

1

Jeryon tumbles through the gray, getting nowhere. Sometimes his face is thrust into a huge bubble, and he gobbles air before he's pulled out. He sees a flash of pale skin and kicks for it. His hands grab only sand.

Jeryon pushes off the sandy ridge, his head breaks the surface, and he sees a beach before a wave drives him under again. When his feet hit the bottom, he springs forward with what strength he has. He bobs up. He flings his arms, trying to ride a wave in, but an undertow holds him in place. He can't stay on the surface much longer. He drops under again and lunges to his right. There's another ridge there. Rich sand. Jagged rocks. Coral.

He grabs it and presses his knees beneath himself. That's enough for him to poke his face above the waves before the next wave drives him again into the gray.

Desire leaves his body: for food, for water, for breath. His will uncoils. His body relaxes. All sounds fade. His shoulder scrapes against the bottom. He's pushed along it until he can't rise anymore. One last roll and he's on his back, anchored by his outstretched arms and legs, sucking air, drinking the rain. Waves flood his ear. The darkness just is.

Then it's not. The tide has receded, but not the rain. Where is the poth? A line of black rocks extends from the shore, ending at three skinny stacks, which the dinghy must have hit. Is that an arm waving? Something is floating beside them. Jeryon lifts his arm.

He floats awake, engulfed in blue; a rich, unchanging, endless blue. Somehow that's more terrifying than black. A gull flies overhead, and his weight returns. Sand skitters across his cheeks and pushes at his back. His lips are so parched he wants to chew them off. Something is touching his foot.

A white horned crab a foot wide with legs three feet long and a split mouth as big as his face stands over his foot. It holds his big toe lightly with a broad, toothy claw. Its eyestalks sway around the toe, its split mouth ruminating, as if the crab is measuring his toe with calipers. The crab brings out its other, thinner claw, which has needlelike teeth. It taps the end of his toe here, there, then snips the pad. Jeryon jerks his foot, but his foot ignores him. The crab snips again. Blood appears.

More crabs sidle over, curious, their claws clicking. The beach is covered with them. A few dart into the waves to drag fish onto shore. A dozen are stripping the skeleton of what looks like a dolphin thrown up by the storm. One crab, not two feet from Jeryon's face, looks out to sea, claws upraised. Splatters of meat and bloody sand stain its shell.

Snip. Jeryon stifles a cry. He tries to sit up, but he's so stiff he has to grab his legs and fold himself into a sitting position. The crab doesn't notice him until Jeryon grabs its claws and wrenches the large one off.

All clicking ceases. The crabs scuttle back. One clicks tentatively.

The toesnipper is appalled. It snips, its other legs flail and its eyestalks stare at him, daring him to do that again. Off comes the skinny claw. It joins the first in Jeryon's lap. He presses the toesnipper against the sand with his foot, and makes it watch him suck the meat from its claws. Shards stick to his throat. He chokes them down.

The other crabs develop a sudden interest in the dolphin. The ocean challenger charges the waves. The toesnipper waggles its eyes at them.

Jeryon flips the toesnipper to pry up its bell-shaped apron with his fingers, but it would be easier to pry a brick from a wall. His father told him, "Never mallet a crab," but his shaking fingers couldn't lever the blade either. He looks for a rock. The only one he finds within crawling distance is a black boulder poking through the sand, so the crab becomes the mallet. After several blows, the apron shatters and its legs stop flailing. He peels it away, then its carapace, scrapes off the dead man's fingers, and sucks the meat out. The butter helps him swallow.

It's gamier than Joslin crabs, but the mustard and roe are tasty, even if his father, who always put the roe in a soup, would mock him for eating it like an owner: raw off a blade.

When the meat hits his stomach, it rebounds with a gush. His throat flames. He hopes the mustard didn't poison him. He crawls away from the puddle in the sand, and eats the rest of the crab flake by flake.

Refreshed, Jeryon manages to stand and cross the beach to a tree line of oak, bamboo, and pitcher trees. From the latter's deep vessel-like leaves he drinks the collected rainwater, heeding the poth's advice to drink slowly, however glorious the water tastes. Thinking of her leads him to look at the stacks. There's nothing there, and no place for anyone to cling if there were. He doesn't know what he saw during the storm. He spots bits of wood sticking out of the sand farther up the beach: the remnants of the dinghy. If he were kicked up here, where is the poth? He takes another drink and steadies himself to approach the dolphin carcass.

The crabs battle for the choicest bits, but they won't give up their meal to him. They envelop it to hide the bones. They'll snip his hands off if he tries to move them, so Jeryon trudges a ways up the beach and returns with a pointed length of gunwale from his tiller, the broken painter strand still attached. With this he weakly bats the crabs off the bones. When one attacks him, he manages to whack it hard enough to change its mind. The last he flicks off so it lands upside down. Before it can roll over, he stakes it to the beach. While its legs kick at the sky, he examines the carcass.

It's half-buried in the sand; a rib cage, shoulder blades, and skull scratched and nearly free of flesh. It isn't the poth's. It might have been her, though, and Jeryon takes out his elation on the staked crab.

Most of the crabs give him a wide berth now. The few that don't seem resigned to whatever fate this terrible avenger has for them. One soon finds out.

Jeryon stretches. He's regaining strength and sensation, the latter mostly agony. He plots a survey of the island. It's the first act of any prisoner: pacing one's cell. And he has to find a better source of water. It's approaching noon, and the water in the leaves of the pitcher trees won't last much longer in this heat.

As far as he can tell, he's at the northwest corner of an island surrounded by low cliffs rising from the sea. Thick forest rambles uphill some five hundred feet to ring a flat-topped column of gray rock another two hundred feet high. This beach is the only place he can see where the land ramps up to the island's interior. If the poth didn't land here, she'll have been in more trouble than not having landed at all.

Jeryon pushes himself from tree to tree until he finds a fallen branch he can use as a walking stick. He tosses aside the piece of gunwale.

After such a storm, it isn't hard to find a stream. Grasses, bright flowers of every hue, and thick bushes race alongside it. It's so loud it drowns out the constant buzz and whirr of insects, which also drowns out the thought that those insects would make a good source of nutrition should the crabs run out.

He follows the stream a few hundred yards southwest toward the column to where it cuts through a bamboo grove. Using the folds of his shirt to guard the straight edge of the blade, he saws through a wide culm just beneath a node with his blade, then through the internode just beneath the next node. He checks inside the hollow for bugs, rinses it a few times in the stream, fills it to the brink, and drinks heartily. The water is cold and rich and tastes like a new life just begun.

Beyond the bamboo the stream enters a meadow that ends to the north at a cliff overlooking the sea. A single tree in its center guards a broadening of the stream. Jeryon can't believe his luck. It's a shega tree. The fruit is his secret vice. He would treat himself to one at the end of every voyage when they were in season, and to a big slice of fresh bread with shega preserves when they weren't. He figures he's deserving now.

Most of the fruit aren't ripe yet, shega won't be in season for another month, but a few are close enough, and Jeryon picks the biggest he can reach. He slices it in half and sucks from the white pulp a purple jewel of flesh with a seed inside. It may be the best shega he's ever eaten, and not just because the shega are reserved for shipowners back in Hanosh. He eats another jewel and admires the ocean's beautiful nothing.

He has water. He has meat and fruit. He has all the materials to build a shelter. He could survive here, day after endless day, until the crabs enjoy their final triumph. There's no point leaving without the poth. The Trust won't believe his testimony alone.

He walks toward the cliff. Would it be worth giving the crabs their meal now? The cliff is high enough, fifty or sixty feet. He eats another jewel. Even shega will get boring in time. So will time on the island. Just sunrise and noontime, star-rise and midnight, being awake and being asleep, one after the other after the other. What kind of life is that? Waves pound the cliff. He could live a hundred years and the waves would pound the cliff and the cliff wouldn't change. He spits the shega seed over the edge. It vanishes from sight long before it reaches the water.

I've already vanished from sight, he thinks. He eats another jewel. *These are tasty, though*. Maybe he'll wait until the season ends.

To the east he spies a trail through the meadow from the stream to the cliff. It's much wider than his own, the grasses and underbrush beaten down. He walks along the cliff's edge to where it meets the trail. He stands as if thunderstruck by what he finds. There, in the dirt: a single footprint, massive, four-toed, and clawed.

2

Standing alone on the clifftop, Jeryon has never felt so exposed. He ducks behind a fragrant shrub and scans the surrounding forest. A landscape that had been almost welcoming a moment ago is now full of waving blades of underbrush and the shaking limbs of trees. Every boulder resolves into a head, and the shadows of clouds become those of wings. He listens. He hears nothing. He takes a longer look at the track.

The print is worn around the edges. The lowest points are puddled. It was made before the storm, but what made it may still be on the island. He has to know. Jeryon follows the creature's trail to the stream then upstream into the forest again, where it fades away.

The stream widens into a pond full of fat black frogs. He'll gig some when he gets the chance and hope they're edible. He eats more shega. The sweetness is intoxicating. As he chews he considers the trees: a variety of oaks, a few ulmus and chinkapins with their spiky nuts, amid the ubiquitous bamboo and many stands of palm. He could make a good raft from this forest. He strips some threads from a fallen palm leaf. How long would it take him to weave a sail?

Beyond the frog pond the forest opens into another meadow. The land is rising more noticeably, and he's high enough to see more of the island. It could be eight or ten miles around. He doesn't see any other approaches besides his beach, and it's guarded for hundreds of yards by sandbars, coral, and jagged rocks. It's remarkable that the dinghy made it as close to the island as it did.

He sees no smoke, no fire, no movement, no sign of the poth. *I should blaze my trails*, he thinks, *to lead her to me*. He'll light a fire too. He needs to find her, and no longer just to testify. However rich the island is, he's just one infection or injury away from death, and she can heal. The endless leaves and weeds, roots and blooms that surround him: He can't understand their language.

On the high side of the meadow end he finds more tracks, older, barely visible in the underbrush, the toes lost in the stream. Whatever made them must drink here often. He fills his own cup and washes down the last of the jewels.

Again in the woods, he makes a blaze every thirty paces. After twenty blazes, the stream turns south between two steep rises. On one the trees are blackened from fire and the underbrush has barely returned. In the ashen dirt Jeryon sees another footprint, heading over the crest. The earthy smell of dragon wafts toward him, deeper and uglier than the one he smelled on the *Comber*. He crouches behind a tree.

He sets the cup down and pulls himself up the rise. He lays on the edge of the crest. Beyond is a clearing not made by nature.

In a broad hollow scoured by fire, trees have been shattered and others toppled so their root mouths yawn at the world like wooden octopi reaching for prey. Sunlight fingers great furrows in the earth. Blood stains exposed wood and tattered leaves. Jeryon sees in the midst of the destruction a line of short jagged spines atop an enormous black back.

This isn't the maturing black of the *Comber* dragon, but the abysmal black of a very old one. Its wings are folded neatly, soft and floppy. Jeryon feels the urge to touch them until he thinks that each is probably bigger than the *Comber*. The dragon is withered with age. Its ribs and spine show through its skin, which rises in strange bursts like the chest of a person struggling for breath.

Jeryon inches over the crest. He's moving as silently as possible, but sounds, he thinks, like a sword on a grindstone. Before he peeks over the edge he pictures himself staring straight down the creature's throat. He hopes it's sleeping. Its head must be the size of the dinghy. Its back alone looks nearly as long as the *Comber* dragon.

What he finds is carnage. The dragon's neck is ripped in half. Its empty eye sockets bloom with nerve tendrils. Half its rotting tongue is clamped between its teeth; the other half has been chewed away. Its sides are rent, its tail, thicker than a man, is broken like a carpenter's square, and the neck left on the body, wide enough to push a barrow down, has been cored of meat and bone. The remaining skin partially drapes it.

Jeryon sighs with relief. He could render the dragon for himself. A dragon bone blade is better than steel, and mounted in a bamboo culm it would make a spear or a knife far easier to wield than his tiny blade and far sharper than a bamboo blade. The skin would be too heavy for a sail, but it would be a great tarp. If the phlogiston hasn't leaked away, he would have a precious source of fuel for light and fire.

If he could bring the renderings to Hanosh, he would have the wealth to ruin his mates, their families, and everyone they ever knew. He could go in disguise under an assumed name so they wouldn't suspect anything. He could befriend them so they would also feel betrayed when he finally revealed his identity. And being close to them would make his revenge more exquisite. Such a complex plan, though, would have too many potential pitfalls. Better to trust the Trust and the law.

It occurs to him: How can the dragon be breathing?

Its skin doesn't rise so much as it bulges in places. And the bulges are moving. The skin draping the neck billows out. Something is inside. The skin flips up. A broad blue claw, leaf-shaped and smiling with sharp white teeth, emerges. A thinner claw, as long and as toothy, tests the air, followed by two eyes the size of shegas on stalks. They peer in every direction before settling on Jeryon. He doesn't move. The front legs come next, a darker blue and as long as hand-and-a-half swords, followed by the body, blue with white smears and big as a buckler. Whereas the crabs on the beach had stubby white horns, this crab has a crown of them.

It scuttles out of the neck toward Jeryon. He dares to slide an inch down the rise. The crab takes a few more steps forward. Jeryon snakes away until he can barely see over the crest. The crab's eyes bend from side to side, as if it can't see him anymore, and it clicks its claws. Jeryon smiles at the crab's frustration. He'll return with a bamboo spear, he will kill and eat that crab, and he will take this dragon for his own.

A few answering clicks come from inside the neck. Then a few more. Another claw appears. And another. The watch crab clacks once decisively, and Jeryon would swear it's pointing its skinny claw at him. A chorus of clicks erupts from the neck, followed by dozens of the huge blue crabs, which charge across the hollow, claws raised.

Jeryon slides down the rise and flees downstream.

The crabs spread across the water and the banks. They leap from tree trunk to tree trunk. A few get into the canopy and leap along the branches like spiders until they dive at him, but miss and crack open on the rocks in the stream.

He counts the blazes. When he gets to the grassland, he thinks he'll be able to lose them in the brush. This is their island, though, and as he veers into the underbrush it trips him up. Ship life makes for strong bodies, but not fleet runners. He returns to the stream and hurtles downhill.

His salvation is the pond, where the fat black frogs prove a more tempting meal than the bounding brown man. The frogs dive deep, the crabs plunge in, the frogs hop out, and soon his pursuers are scattering through the forest while he races past the shega tree. That's enough exploring for one day.

For the rest of the afternoon he weaves bamboo and vines into a lean-to, periodically feasting on the increasingly fatalistic white crabs. He also makes himself three spears, a bamboo handle for his blade, and a set of cups to replace the one he left at the dragon hollow. He sets the lean-to against a spur of cliff at the edge of the beach and puts the spears inside. Then he makes a bow drill out of vine and bamboo, gathers firewood, scrapes himself a pile of tinder, and gets a blaze going in pits on either side of the lean-to. If a ship sees his fire, if the poth sees its smoke, so be it. They're meant to keep the white crabs at bay. The spears are for the blue ones, although he doubts they stray far from the dragon.

A few more crab claws and legs grilled on bamboo skewers, several more cups of water, and the shega, then Jeryon lets himself fall asleep long before star-rise.

Nevertheless he bolts up in the middle of the night. The pits glow red. Shadows seethe in the lean-to. The sand is skillet hard. The sea will not stop sizzling on the beach. Knowing that no one can hear him, that no one might ever hear him again, Jeryon screams and screams and sobs and screams.

3

Four days later, Jeryon jiggles a blue crab's shell above a fire, using two wet palm leaves folded into squares as pot holders. The crab's body meat falls off skewers too easily, so he begins frying a mix of blue and white with the paste of crushed olives. The bitterness is worth the oil. With his other hand he pours water from a broad bamboo culm into a cup. As someone who lives from berth to berth, port to port, he knows that wherever your plate and cup are, that's your home.

Having a detailed schedule is as good as having oars tick his way through the day, so he plans his next assault on the blue crabs. His system is simple: get them to chase him, run to the frog pond, and once they scatter spear them one by one.

With a bamboo spatula he transfers the cooked meat to another blue crab shell, his plate. He wishes he had a pot to make soup. His sister made an excellent one, but after she left, Jeryon couldn't stomach crab for a long time. Then he ate it to remind himself of her. At some point it lost the quality of remembrance and became just another bland seafood. His taste for it is returning, he's surprised to find.

He banks the fire, no longer trying to maintain a steady stream of smoke to attract ships or the poth. It breaks up too quickly in the ever-present breeze, barely reaching the tops of the trees, let alone the tops of the adjoining cliffs. As for the light attracting ships, there's little point in bothering. His second night on the island he built a cross-staff to confirm what he already suspected from the star's positions: the island is deep in the ocean, well south of any route a ship from the League might take to the Dawn Lands. The dinghy must have reached the river a day or two after they were set adrift. All the time he was telling the poth he could get them to Yness, they were probably passing it, heading into oblivion.

He thinks he might be on Gladsend, an island that shows up on few maps because few are sure where it is and fewer believe it exists. It was supposedly a pirate refuge long ago, but why refuge here when prey is so far away and Yness so accommodating?

He cleans his pan and dish, making a weak soap of some ash, water, and the hot olive oil, and rests them against the lean-to to dry. He overturns the cup and pitcher on little posts. He rakes his house with a leafy frond. When all is in order, he tucks in his shirt and rubs his chin. He hates his stubble. His knife isn't up to the task of shaving, preferring to slice instead. Hopefully a dragonbone blade will do a better job. He picks up a spear and his knife and sets out.

Along the stream he's erected stakes to hold bamboo cups. There are also supplies of spears in case the blue crabs decide they're sick of frogs.

When he reaches the dragon hollow, the crabs are swarming over the hill beyond it and heading toward the gray column of rock to the south. Have they given up on the dragon? Are they chasing something?

If the poth found the stakes and blazes along the path, he realizes, they might not lead her to the beach. They might lead her here.

Jeryon slides down the hill and shadows the crabs up the wooded slopes surrounding the column, a wide green collar around a headless stone neck. The crabs climb at an angle and Jeryon moves to their side so he can see what they're pursuing. He hears it bounding and breaking through the brush, sounds drowned in the furious clacking of crab claws, but he can't see what it is.

The crabs slow. Do they have their quarry trapped? Did they catch it and kill it? If so, it didn't put up much of a struggle. With a spear in each hand he edges closer. Just a glimpse is all he needs. He hopes it's not her, as much as he wants it to be her. The crabs eddy in a pool of shell and claw, several clicks responding to each interrogative clack, as if they're discussing what to do. Some are looking his way. Jeryon hides behind an oak. If he climbed it, he might be able to see, but if they saw him, he would be trapped. He has to chance it.

He leans his spears against the tree, pulls himself onto a low branch, and it snaps. He falls on his face. The spears clatter over him.

Dozens of eyestalks waggle as one in his direction.

Jeryon jumps up, grabs the spears, and leaps away like a fat black frog.

Halfway to the next hill he realizes he won't be able to climb the slope quickly enough to stay ahead of the crabs, so he veers north. The trees grow thicker. All he has to do is pace the crabs and eventually they'll forget about him, just as they've forgotten about their original quarry. He might even be able to spear a few in the end.

They're catching up, though. The crabs, large as they are, can slip between the trees more easily than him, and a few are jumping over branches and bushes he has to avoid. Three leap at him just as he bursts between two trees into a meadow—except there is no meadow. The sky he saw through the trees heralds a fifty-foot drop where the wind has stripped the hill down to its rock, a cliff above the cliffs.

Jeryon grabs a branch, swinging it aside like a door on a hinge as two crabs fly past him. They and his spear plummet to the scree below. One foot follows them while the other scrambles for purchase. His hand slips down the branch. His knee finds the edge, he finds his balance on it, and his other spear comes up just in time to find the belly of a third leaping crab, catapulting it over his head. It slides off the spear, scrabbles at his shirt, caroms off his heel and falls.

The rest of the crabs spread out as he stands so he can't escape. Their split mouths ruminate. One in the center darts at him. He jabs. It scuttles back. Two dart from either side. He swings the spear in an arc. They scuttle back. When three come, he has no good response. He jabs at the middle one, which lets the outside two get close enough to snip before he swings and they retreat. They missed, but hitting him wasn't the point. Now four edge closer. The others click to goad them. One scrapes a pointed blue foot against the dirt. Then Jeryon hears something much larger crashing through the woods. He pictures the Crab King coming to finish him off.

A half-dozen crabs investigate. They disappear beyond a bamboo grove, where they're met with cries of fury and steel clanking through shell. The bamboo waves. Only one returns to tell the tale. It scuttles toward the swarm, clicking frantically, the poth in pursuit, swinging a rusty broad sword with a cat's head pommel. She cries again and hacks the crab in half, the creature running all the way to its comrades before it realizes that it's dead, and its legs topple in opposite directions.

The blue crabs scatter. She starts to sheathe her sword in a steel sheath before thinking better of it.

Jeryon says, "How are you?"

"For one," she says, "I'm sick of eating crab."

Jeryon takes a step toward her, and a crab leaps from under the cliff's edge onto his shoulder. Its broad claw bites into his arm. Its split mouth gnashes his head. Jeryon hollers and twists to get it off and stumbles toward the cliff's edge.

Everlyn reaches out to him with the sword. He clutches the blade as his heels tip over the edge, which jerks her forward. Her sword opens his palm as he slowly topples backward, the crab riding him over the edge with its skinny claw raised in victory.

She rushes to the edge. The cliff isn't perfectly vertical, and he slid for twenty feet before his sandals caught on a blade of rock. He's pressed against the cliff face, clinging to cracks, while the crab worries his right arm. Blood seeps through his tattering sleeves.

She lies on her belly and swings her sword at the crab. She misses by a wide margin. The crab comes at her again, she swings again, and it turns aside to skitter along the cliff face. It disappears behind an outcrop.

She leaps up and faces the woods; the other crabs might come back. She holds her sword before her, sturdy but flexible, moving without moving, the way her father taught her when she was a girl. A trader has to be a duelist, he said, in case his guards are absent or traitorous. And swordsmanship offered a profitable worldview. Although she deplored the taking of life, he was right. Knowing intimately that every thrust could be her last had taught her anticipation, poise, intimidation, and planning. Still, her lessons would have been more interesting had she been armed with a cleaver like this broad sword instead of a foil.

The crab doesn't appear, nor do the others. Is it waiting for her to reach for him and make herself vulnerable? Is it skulking through the bushes to flank her? Jeryon barks, "Poth." She turns and flattens herself along the edge. He points to his right with his eyes. She swings. The sword sweeps the crab's legs out from under it, and it falls. It skips off the cliff face, breaking off its legs and pieces of its shell.

"Hold on," she says. She gets up and sees exactly what she needs near the edge: a thick vine dangling from a chinkapin. It's lined with withering yellow flowers and small purple fruit like plums. She works it loose in stages and pushes it to Jeryon. He grabs hold and climbs it while she holds it over her shoulder, facing the roots to keep it from tearing out of the ground.

When he's nearly up, she hears clicking in the brush. She left her sword by the chinkapin. Ten feet away, it feels like ten miles. "I have to drop the vine," she says.

"No," he says, "I'm almost there."

The crabs come closer. "I'm going to try something," she says. "Don't let go."

Everlyn hugs the vine tight and charges toward her sword and the crabs, drawing him up behind her. The crabs rush her. The vine goes slack. She hopes he's on top of the cliff. She kneels to grab her sword and a crab flies at her. She comes up quickly to stab it between its eyes. Two more leap on her. Their claws have her hair and her smock, trying to find her arms. A third snips at her ankle, putting her into a fighting retreat, and she screams as she cuts through one claw, then the other.

She waves her sword in an arc to keep the rest at bay while Jeryon wrenches one crab off her back and tosses it over the cliff, then does the same to the other. Its broad claw comes off in his hand, and Jeryon shakes it at the other crabs.

That and the sword convince the crabs they've lost the day. They leave the field sideways, each with one eye curled over its shoulders like an upraised finger.

When he can't hear their clicking anymore, Jeryon says, "I'm sick of crab too."

4

Jeryon tries to line up the rips in his sleeve. "I don't think I can mend this."

"Good. Tear it off. I need it for a bandage."

"It's just a flesh wound."

"You can live without a sleeve, not without an arm."

"I've known plenty of one-armed sailors," he says. Nonetheless, he tears off the sleeve while she hacks off a long piece of the vine with her sword. Then he cuts off the other sleeve with his blade. "Balance," he says.

Everlyn upends the vine over his arm and hand. Water trickles out to clean his wounds and wash away the seeping blood.

"A water vine?" he says.

"Exactly." *Lubber*. She takes a swallow and hands him the vine. "You can eat the fruit too."

He twists one off, bites it, and makes a face.

"Too bitter?" she says.

"Looks like a plum. Thought it would taste like one."

She takes a big bite of one herself. "I like bitter."

"I like tart."

"Then we'll get along just dandy," she says.

"What choice do we have?" he says.

Everlyn takes a roll of thick aloe leaves from her smock. With his blade she scores them to release their medicinal juices, then uses the sleeves to bind the leaves to the wounds. "I'll disinfect them with seawater after they've clotted," she says.

He wipes his blade on his pants and pockets it. "Where are your hair pins?"

"Lost at sea. But this island more than makes up for it." She produces a sprig of leaves with a blue flower. "Boneset. It's a pain reliever. Chew it."

After a moment he says, "I feel pretty good. Kind of invincible."

"That's just what it's like not to hurt after so long." She chews a wad herself.

He looks at the bandages. "These, and back there: How can I repay you?"

"Make me lunch. Then get me off this island."

At the beach, Jeryon kills two crabs. While he piles their meat on one of their carapaces, Everlyn pulls up her smock and sits with her bare legs

stretched out on the sand. A misshapen target, dark purple ringing yellow, covers her ankle. She scratches it with the ornate brass cap on her sword sheath. He asks, "Where did you get the sword?"

"Not, 'Where did you get the bruise?'"

"Where did you get the bruise?"

"I twisted my ankle badly when I washed up. If I hadn't found the boneset by the pond where I made camp, you might have found me by my screaming. I couldn't walk until this morning."

"That's when you found the sword?" He feeds the fire, crushes olives into his cooking shell, and sets it to warm.

"Yes." There's more to her story, but why should she bother? "On the south side of the island beneath a large patch of yellow asphodel."

He looks at her blankly.

"King's spear. Cousin of aloe."

"Ah." Jeryon lays crab meat in the oil to sizzle. "What's that got to do with the sword?"

"It only grows in patches when it's planted on an Ynessi grave or where one of them died."

"Right. Yes," Jeryon says. "That's piss blossom. They use it like dogs to mark their territory. The streets of Yness are covered with it. So you dug?"

Everlyn waggles her filthy, ragged fingernails. "You said Ynessi pirates might work these waters. Perhaps one had been buried there with something useful."

"The Ynessi are sentimental that way," Jeryon says. "Probably shrouded him in sailcloth too."

"It would've been sad if they hadn't," she says. "I'm hardly sentimental, but I want my shroud."

"Waste of cloth. And the time spent digging. If it comes to that, give my body back to the waves." He flips the meat. "Make the crabs work for their vengeance."

Everlyn rolls the sheathed sword over her lap. She doesn't want to think about that. Or what a Hanoshi might do with her body.

"Of course, their waste is our reward," Jeryon says.

She draws the blade. "It would've been a waste had they buried it without its scabbard. The leather rotted away, but the metal sheath has an oiled fur lining that kept the blade sharp." She holds it so the sun glares on the spider rust. "I think it's from the far north. It's bigger than a spatha."

"I didn't think pothing required a knowledge of swords."

"A tool's a tool. I would've preferred a kopis. Or an axe. Beggars and choosers, though."

Jeryon snorts in agreement and adds just a touch more olive.

"After I found it, I was feeling pretty good—I've practically been living on boneset—so I decided to explore the peak. And you know the rest." She resheaths the sword and rubs her ankle. It's swelling again. Too much running and walking today. Thinking about trudging to her pond makes it ache more. "I think I should stay here," she says.

"Your pond would make for a better camp," Jeryon says, flipping the crab. "Water, probably shade, certainly no crabs. And the ground has to be softer."

"I meant for tonight," she says. "So I don't have to walk back."

"Yes, of course," he says. "We should stay close, though. And pool our resources."

"A Hanoshi sharing? We are in desperate straits."

"Given the circumstances, it's rational. Provided we each do our part."

"I'm sure you'll keep track." She looks out to sea. "Someone should be here when a boat comes by."

Jeryon pours some crab onto a clean shell for her and gives her two freshly cut bamboo shards to eat with. "A smart captain would give this island a wide berth. Too many rocks and sandbars. He'd never get close enough to see us."

"Then let's make a sign that could be seen. After all, ships came here once. They could come again." She eats some crab. It's tastier

than she gave him credit for. She could probably find some herbs and spices to complement it. "This is good," she says.

"You make do," he says. He serves himself the rest and sits across the fire from her.

She points at the cross-staff propped against the lean-to. "What's that?"

"A failed experiment."

"It's perfect, though, for a signal," she says. Her shoulders straighten. She likes a project. "It's unnatural. The eye would pick it up. Someone would want to investigate. If we put some on the peak, larger ones, they could be seen far out to sea. We could build a fire, too, as a beacon."

"A beacon could cause a ship to wreck," he says. "And something like that would be unstable in the wind."

"Then we can prop up big X-frames." She puts down her bamboo shards. "Start saying 'yes.' 'No' just gets you nowhere."

He stares at her plate. She won't eat.

"Let's see what's up there first," Jeryon says, "then maybe. If your ankle's better, we can go tomorrow. In the meantime, we'll build you a lean-to and dig another fire pit to keep the crabs away."

That night, after Jeryon falls asleep, Everlyn remembers when she was fourteen and her father sent her around the League with one of his caravans. He described it as a chance to see not just the cities, but also the world in between: the plants and the landscape, the husbandry and agriculture. This was a compelling argument, and she loved him for it even though the real reason for the trip was obvious: She was the caravan's chief trade good.

For every useless son she met, for every dreary nephew and lonely old man, there was a bloom beside the road she had to investigate. She hated to sit in her red-wheeled box and would have demanded to walk the entire route had her father not predicted this attitude and filled her wagon with books on plants from around the League, boxes and bottles for samples, and blank journals for her notes. Thus she was kept busy, the caravan was kept on schedule, and she understood why her father was respected as a trader.

She filled every journal and bought more on the way. She had to find room in another wagon for her samples. And she wrote her father scores of letters describing what she'd found, seeing as none of her suitors cared half a whit.

But one night on this island had been worth the hundred on the trip. The fragrance of so many strange flowers was intoxicating. For every plant she knew, there were ten she didn't. She could spend endless days learning about the flora, just as she had with her herb master in the forests around Ayden, not to mention naming the birds and bugs she'd never seen. Everlyn should have been indescribably happy, but lying there in her lean-to she couldn't help thinking, *What's the point of learning something if you can't teach it to someone else?* Knowledge must propagate, her herb master would say. It dies in isolation. And so might she. Everlyn knew she could survive on the island. She didn't think she could survive being alone.

She'd bet the captain could. On the *Comber* he'd rarely spoken except to give commands. He'd kept to his cabin when he had no duty, even in Chorem with all its wonders, and when he ate he ate alone. His only pleasure seemed to be in routine. That afternoon, after they'd attended to all their tasks, he'd retreated to his lean-to without a word to her. He'd barely spoken during dinner. Everlyn can't imagine what that must be like. Dreary. Lonely.

How her father would laugh. At the end of her tour, he lauded her research and bound three copies of her notes and letters: one for her, one for her herb master, and one for his library. He was less congratulatory about her suitoring. He said if she didn't find a partner soon, she'd likely be left with the last man in the League.

And there he is, Everlyn thinks. "At least he's not useless," she whispers.

That night, after the poth falls asleep, Jeryon wonders if he should have told her that his calculations had been wrong. There was no hope of rescue. What purpose would that have served, though? He might as well humor her. A hopeful crew's a happy crew, even when trapped in a maelstrom.

He hears the poth whisper something in her sleep, and Jeryon realizes he can't have his scream, not with her five feet away. He also realizes he doesn't need it. Getting comfortable with her around: *that's not a productive attitude*, he tells himself.

5

Everlyn is woken up by Jeryon scraping the cliff face with a sharp stone.

"What are you doing?" she says.

"Day seven," he says. He touches up the first two of the slashes he's made.

"I've been keeping track too," she says. She picks up a spear and digs a long furrow in the sand. "One," she says, then rubs it out with her foot. "Now what's for breakfast?"

Her ankle feels stronger, so Jeryon shows her how to clean a crab with her sword instead of hacking it to pieces: flip it over, cleave it halfway through, lop off its limbs, and pry free its carapace. His father gave him the same lecture. Jeryon points out one for her to practice on while he gathers firewood and fills cups at the stream. When he returns the job is done "mostly competently," and she says she'll do the cooking today. She crushes some of his store of wild olives into a paste, but before she adds the crab to the cooking shell she puts in some herbs she gathered before he returned. A wonderful smell rises over the beach. The olives' bitterness lingers, though.

After he tidies his camp and she changes his dressings, they set out for the island's peak. He has a spear in each hand and his knife in his pocket, and she has her sword, but they take a long detour south around the blue crabs. They can clear them out later.

The slope surrounding the column of gray rock is gentler to the south, which makes hiking easier, but they aren't making good time. The fifth time the poth stops to examine some plant, Jeryon snaps, "Can we eat that? Can it cure us? Will it kill a blue crab?"

"Not that I know of," she says.

"Then let's go."

"Maybe it could."

"Look," he says, "when you see something interesting, I'll add a mark to the next blaze so you can find it later."

"Are we late?" she says. "Is there something up there waiting for us?"

He looks toward the dragon hollow. "I hope not."

"No reason to hurry then. Besides," she says, "my ankle is acting up again."

"I'm sure it is," he says. He slows to her excruciating pace, though, and gives her a spear to use as a walking stick.

At the tree line around the column, they spot no trails or ledges they can use to climb it. They circle to the east and observe that half of the island. Disappointingly, it is much the same as the rest. There don't appear to be any other beaches. They see more streams, several ponds, and meadows. Nothing breaks the horizon.

"No dragons, at least," she says.

When they find a water vine, they take a break to drink and eat. The poth sits on a slab of fallen rock. There isn't a place for Jeryon to sit except the ground, and he's wearied of that. Another slab has fallen behind and above her seat. There's a third higher up the column. Jeryon slides into the tree line, looking up.

"What is it?" the poth asks.

He says, "You're sitting on a step."

She looks up too and sees the shelves of rock climbing around the peak. The stairway is cleverly made, blending into the stone and sturdy despite ages of weathering.

"Who do you think built it?" she says. "I've seen stairs like this in the mountains. My herb master said they were made by giants or maybe dwarves, and once there were great castles at the top to defend against hobgoblins."

Jeryon says, "Given the rise between steps, I'd say everyday men, albeit taller." He points at her ankle. "Are you up for this?"

"Says the sailor, king of flat water. I'm mostly mountain goat." She springs up the first few steps, trying not to wince, and is amused that he can't keep up. The stairs are wider than they look from below and slightly canted toward the column, so she feels comfortable setting a brutal pace.

In a few minutes she peeks over the top step to make sure something horrible isn't lying in wait, then steps onto the plateau. She says, "See? Castles!"

The plateau is three acres of bare stone, cracked and depressed in places, punctuated by tall spikes of gray rock. The wind and rain have filled many with curious holes. "Where?" he huffs.

"Well, they aren't here anymore. But these were once columns for the halls of the Giant Kings. Or the Dwarf Kings. Their shadow birds would roost in the nooks."

"No. They're spread too unevenly. Looks more like—"

"Why are Hanoshi so stiff?" she says. "Where's your imagination?"

"Make-believe doesn't put food on the table," he says.

Seeing the looks she makes, Jeryon adds, "Give me some proof a castle was actually here, then I'll be filled with wonder. Isn't it more exciting to find a use for a plant than to imagine it has some magical property? Isn't it magical enough that boneset alleviates pain?"

"If I didn't imagine what a plant could do," she says, "I'd never figure out what it actually does."

They cross the plateau. The sun has dried out the weeds growing in the cracks. Mosses and lichen scab the surface. The spikes cast shadows like sweeping black blades.

Jeryon stops and says, "Where are the birds?"

"What do you mean?"

"This is an ideal roost. It should be covered with larus. Sea crows. Shag. And guano. Acres of guano. Birds are all over the island, but the plateau's clean."

"If something's scared them off," she says, "wouldn't we see signs of it? Like its guano?"

"Perhaps."

They head to the northern edge. Everlyn dangles her legs over the cliff, leans forward, and spits. He sits farther away and resists the urge to pull her to safety.

"I bet we can see thirty miles," he says. "Of course, this must be just a hill to you."

"No," she says. Tears shimmer atop her cheek.

"I'll get you home," he says.

"That's not it," she says. "I can see the curve of the world. I could see the horizon from the ship. I could see half the League from the mountains. But the view wasn't like this. The curve's so pronounced. As if it were drawn."

"I know," he says.

It's her turn to look skeptical.

"When I was a boy," he hears himself say, "I left my father in the Harbor and snuck into the Upper City, then climbed to the top of the Blue Tower. I couldn't see this far, maybe twenty-five miles, but I'd never been more than five miles from home. I could see towns I didn't know existed, hills and forests beyond them, the tips of your mountains, and, most of all, the bay. I could see the other side. I could see Eryn Point and the Tallan Sea. I watched a galley head for them. That, I decided right then, is where I would go. I wanted to touch the curve of the world. And here I am."

She smiles. "So you do have imagination," she says.

"I picked a port," he says, "and plotted a course. The next day the Trust took me in as a ship's boy."

Took him in, Everlyn thinks, *as if he were a foundling*.

"What if we called the plateau the Crown? These spikes remind me of radiates."

"That'll do," she says. It's nice of him to try. "We could tie the bamboo Xs to them. We could probably make them even bigger if they aren't freestanding. How big would they have to be to be seen thirty miles away?"

Something scrapes behind them. They scramble away from the edge. Jeryon brings up his spears. She draws her sword. They don't see anything. He whispers, "Stay close."

She says, "Not too close. I don't want to hit you."

He points at a nearby spike. Each one is wide enough for a man to hide behind. Jeryon didn't think there were that many spikes until now. They're outnumbered. And the plateau's edge feels exceedingly close. He survived a cliff fall yesterday. He doesn't want to make a habit of it.

"This way," he says. They edge to their right to look around the spike. Nothing's there. More noise echoes off the spikes so he can't tell where it's coming from.

Everlyn closes her eyes. It sounds like a boot on gravel, digging in, waiting to spring. She points the sword at one of the larger spikes. She motions left. He nods and slides right. They charge the last few steps around and half swing at themselves. The scraping comes from above.

There's a large hole near the top of the spike. "Boost me up," she says. She sheathes her sword and leans it against the spike.

He holds his clasped hands for her to step in and pushes her up to where she can step on one outcropping, pivot, and sit on another. She looks into the hole and smiles broadly.

"What is it?" he says. "A bird's nest?"

"You have to see this."

Something in the hole scrapes insistently.

He looks for a foothold. She hugs the spike tight to her hip, pulls her foot off the outcropping, and holds out her hand. "Step where I did," she says.

She's stronger than he imagined, and her hands are big and useful.

He stands on the outcrop and hugs the spike opposite her. She puts her foot on his to steady herself. They start to let go of each other's hand, but can't. Both could fall.

The scraping changes to the sound of tiny dishes breaking. But all that's in the hole are two large charcoal stones. "Rocks?" he says. "I'm up here for rocks?"

One of the rocks wobbles, scraping against the floor of the hole, then cracks down the middle. A tiny white claw reaches out to scratch the air.

CHAPTER FOUR

The Gray

1

Two more claws widen the crack. A whole foot appears, as white as surf, then a two-clawed hand. A snout pokes out. Its nostrils huff as its horn chips at the crack.

The other egg wobbles and tips over. A white horn bursts through its bottom and thrashes side to side to make a wider hole. The first snout answers by hacking at its own crack faster.

"It's a race," the poth says.

"We have to be the first people to see this," Jeryon says. "No one's written anything about dragons being born white. It makes sense, with them turning black as they age."

"Shhh!" she says.

The first snout retreats and a red eye appears to check its progress. Its pupil is shaped like a keyhole and its iris is covered in a lace of black veins. It stares at Jeryon, then Everlyn. They hear tiny jaws snap.

The second snout resolves into the face of a white wyrmling with black eyes shot with gold. One more push and its head is through. It's the size of a walnut, but its mouth is already full of needle-sharp teeth. Its forked tongue lashes the egg as it beats its shoulders against its shell. It can't get any leverage, though. The egg rocks futilely.

The red-eyed wyrmling works more deliberately. Another hand appears, and the wyrmling pulls bits of shell inside instead of pushing them out. Its escape route widens considerably while the other wyrmling rolls its shell over in its struggles. When red eye can get its shoulders through the hole, it clutches either side and flexes its impossibly skinny arms. The shell snaps in two. The wyrmling tumbles out, tangled in the limp, translucent wings stretching beneath its arms. Fastidiously, it orders itself then plays its tongue over its lips at the sight of its clutchmate.

Black eye's head rears, its jaw drops, but it only releases a panicked squeal. Red eye crawls toward it. Its pupils tighten.

Jeryon yanks his hand out of the poth's, which nearly topples them both. She clutches his shirt. He puts his hand like a wall between the two wyrmlings.

"What are you doing?" the poth says.

Red snaps at his hand. He doesn't move it. It bites his hand. He stifles a yelp, but doesn't move it. The wyrmling squeals at him. The hand remains undaunted.

The poth says, "I wish we could keep them both. I've seen this before with raptors, but you have to let that one—"

"Watch," Jeryon says.

Red tries to crawl around his hand, then over it; he pushes the wyrmling back. Black, sensing an opportunity, resumes freeing itself, which makes red more frantic. Jeryon still won't let it at its clutchmate. Finally, the wyrmling sits in frustration. Jeryon doesn't move his hand. Red looks at him. Now he does.

"Did you just teach it to sit?" the poth says.

"No, I taught it to ask permission," Jeryon says.

Red leaps onto its clutchmate's egg. Black snaps at Red's face and rolls the egg, which knocks Red off, so Red spreads its wings over the egg to keep it in place. Its tongue flicks over Black's eyes. It nips at Black's snout. Its head rears, and Black ducks into its shell.

"I don't know, poth," Jeryon says, "Black's either very smart or very dumb."

Red considers its options: storm the castle or siege it. The wyrmling hisses a challenge. No response. It looks into the hole, and a claw darts out, nearly slicing Red's eyeball. Red reaches inside, there's a snap, and Red jerks out its hand and shakes it. A pinprick of blood spatters Jeryon's shirt.

The egg wobbles again. Then it rocks. It develops a rhythm. Red scurries around the egg, trying to decide what Black is doing. A crack forms on its underside, where the egg beats against a small, sharp stone.

Jeryon says, "It's trying to break a new way out."

"No," says the poth, "it's trying to rock the egg out of the hole." One more push and the egg rolls over the chock and toward the hole's mouth. It gets to the edge and teeters on the lip. Red claws at the egg, trying to keep it in the hole.

The poth lets go of Jeryon's shirt and cups her hand under the lip to catch Black's egg. "I thought we weren't playing favorites," he says.

"Maybe I was wrong," she says. "Maybe this is a form of play, not population control."

"From what I've read about dragons, there's no distinction."

Red slaps at the egg, which spins a little. The wyrmling squeals in delight, having found a solution. Red stands up and turns the egg around so Black rolls the egg back into the hole. When the egg lodges against the back of the hole, Black realizes how it's been fooled and lunges out of its egg, teeth snapping, one claw grasping. Red dances backward, squealing in terror, and falls on its back. The wyrmling kicks and flings up its wings to ward off its clutchmate until it realizes that Black has wedged itself in the crack in its egg. Trapped, Black dips its head and mewls.

"This is no longer cute," Jeryon says.

Red sits up and licks its wounded hand. It picks at a scale on its belly and eats whatever it found there. It flaps its wings, which are starting to stiffen, folds them, and snaps its tail. Ordered again, it crawls to Black.

Red sniffs Black's snout, strokes it, licks it, the gracious victor, then claws out an eye. Red holds it up, bites it in half, and chews it thoughtfully. Red likes it. It eats the other half. As Black hisses and flails, Jeryon lowers his hand between them. Snap. Bite. Sit. Glower. Look. And the hand goes up. Red slides its claws around Black's remaining eye and plucks it like a shega. Black spits and mewls as Red eats it, then, appetized, moves in for the feast.

Again the hand, the sitting, the glare, the raising.

"I didn't think a dragon could be trained," the poth says.

"Neither did I," Jeryon says, "but who's had the chance? Dragons hide their eggs in remote locations and move them at the slightest sign of a threat. Few have ever been seen, let alone taken."

They can't look as Red devours Black's tongue, then tears off a piece of Black's face, which finally kills the wyrmling. This doesn't suit Red, so it climbs over Black's ruined head and uses its horn to crack the shell.

"So where's its mother?" the poth says as Red breaks through the top of the shell and digs heartily into Black's shoulders. "Is that her down there?"

"I'm hoping she's the one the *Comber* killed," Jeryon says.

The dragon slurps and chomps. When it's done, it slides out of the shell, a sticky mass of pride and gore, and wipes its face with a claw. It does a terrible job. Jeryon holds out his hand, and the wyrmling climbs onto it, curls up, and falls asleep. Blood puddles around it.

"Has anything been written," the poth says, "about how big a dragon would have to be to fly us away?"

The issue of whether they'll stay at Jeryon's camp or the poth's is settled by the need to keep the wyrmling safe. The white crabs would treat a wyrmling penned on the beach the same as they would a fish head handed into a crab pot: like bait.

Before heading for Everlyn's pond, they retrieve his collection of blue crab carapaces, his stash of wild olives and shega, his bow drill, and a few spears tied in a bundle with bamboo thread. He leaves the rest. It won't take long to re-create them.

While Jeryon gathers his stuff, the poth kills a crab for the wyrmling, which is hungry again. It sits quietly as Jeryon cleans it, glancing at him. He still makes it go through the hand dance before letting it have some meat.

Jeryon says, "It's already growing."

"I hope we don't run out of crab," the poth says. "It probably eats faster than they can breed."

The wyrmling rides to the pond in Everlyn's hip pocket, sometimes poking its head up to look around, sometimes falling to the bottom to sleep. It alternates about every thirty steps by Jeryon's count. When she brushes past a branch, she knocks an enormous red rhino beetle off a leaf into her pocket. A furious battle ensues in the depths of her smock. Peace comes with a muffled crunching.

Jeryon wants to say something, but as the poth tries to settle her smock and collect herself he decides to save it for later. Beetles, at least, could solve the crab problem. There's no end of beetles.

Oaks shade the pond and shatter the wind into gentle breezes. Jeryon feels refreshed until he sees a bow drill beside the neat fire ring that puts his own to shame. "Where do you sleep?" he says.

She points to a patch of spongy orange moss near the ring. He chooses a spot farther away and separated from hers by a tangle of branches.

"I don't need a screen," she says. "I'm not that modest."

"I am," he says. "I'll put the pen by the fire."

The poth pulls the wyrmling out of her pocket by its scruff. "It could stay with me," she says. "It likes my pocket."

"It's not a kitten. It needs a proper enclosure so we can contain it and train it."

"I don't think it's going to like that." The wyrmling kicks and squrims.

"It'll have to get used to it." Jeryon scuffs a square into the dirt and holds out his hand. "I need to cut some bamboo. Let me have the sword."

"My sword," Everlyn says after he disappears into the woods. She looks at the square and for the first time notices how the trees box in the camp.

"What do you think?" she says and puts the wyrmling in the square. It promptly scuttles away. "I agree. We're going to need a lot of walks to make this place bearable."

When the wyrmling reaches the pond, it snaps at its reflection. It gets a mouthful of water instead. It smacks its lips. It likes water. It drinks lustily.

"The box won't be so bad with you, though," she says.

Jeryon returns with a twenty-foot-long culm of green bamboo, then he drags in a ten-foot piece that's older, browner, and thicker.

"What should we call it?" she says. "We can't keep calling it 'it.'"

"Why?" He cuts off the brown culm's branches and reduces it to five two-foot logs.

"This could be a legendary dragon," she says. "The first trained. The first ridden. It needs a legendary name." She holds the dragon in front of her face. "Sea Blight. Cloudbreaker. The Chiefest and Greatest of Calamities." The wyrmling shakes its head. "No, you're right. You're a good dragon. Another first."

"We better hope so." With one log Jeryon mallets the others into the ground to serve as corner posts.

"Why not Hope?"

"Why not Desperation?" He surveys his work. "It needs a practical name. Something easy to say." He gives a post a whack, and a splinter flies off. The wyrmling leaps out of the poth's grasp to pounce on it. "Like that."

"Splinter?"

"No, Gray, like those spots appearing on its spine."

"Actually," the poth says, "that's not terrible." Jeryon shrugs his shoulders. He whacks another post, trying to get them even, and a larger splinter flies off.

She looks at it and says, "Huh. Let me check something."

Everlyn picks up the splinter, then the wyrmling, which she lays on its back across her hand. It spreads its arms so its wings flop over her fingers and wrist like two washcloths. Its head and legs loll as if broken. It's asleep. She prods the base of its tail with the splinter.

"What are you doing?" He comes over to watch.

"Sexing it," she says. "My sister kept emperor snakes. She showed me how. It's sort of a snake, isn't it?" She probes some more. "I think our wyrmling's female."

"Gray works either way," he says.

She flips the wyrmling back over and sets her on her palm. The wyrmling wakes up, and Everlyn says, "Gray." The wyrmling shakes her wings, revealing a few faint gray streaks in the white.

"That settles it then." Jeryon smiles slightly, but enough for her to see.

"Wait, you *did* mean Splinter, didn't you?"

Jeryon says nothing and goes to the green culm. The poth laughs. And Jeryon thinks their prospects are about as good as the wyrmling's color. They might escape. They might not.

2

They spend the rest of the afternoon finishing the pen. After splitting the green culm into slats, they use some as uprights between the corners and weave the rest through them and into slits in the posts. They reinforce the connections with bamboo threads. For hours they speak only with their work, which pleases them both.

The waste bamboo they use to light a fire for dinner and, to the wyrmling's delight, to warm some rocks for her pen. Energized by sitting on one, she runs along the walls so fervently they threaten to topple. Seeing this, Jeryon starts weaving slats for a lid.

"Where did you learn to do that?" the poth says. "Make pens and all?"

"You pick things up," Jeryon says. "How much did she eat?"

"Two whole whites," she says. "As much as me. I don't know where it went, especially after all she ate earlier."

The wyrmling stops, looks up at them, and takes an enormous dump. It has to waddle forward to let it all out, as if the dump were having her. The gentle breezes by the pond suddenly become a liability, too weak to carry off such a heavy stench.

"I'll get some leaves to pick it up," she says.

"I can make a trowel," he says.

"No, that's all right." Her altruism is undermined by how quickly she runs from the pen and how slowly she returns.

While waiting, Jeryon parses the smell. Lye, with a hint of old stable and older man.

After the poth disposes of the scat downwind west of the pond, they watch the wyrmling mount a rock and wrap her wings around it. Her head flops to the side and slowly rolls over, twisting her neck nearly all the way around.

"Is that normal?" Jeryon says.

"She may be part cat," the poth says.

The wyrmling falls asleep. Everlyn strokes between her wings. The wyrmling's mouth flops open. The poth plucks a firefly out of the air and feeds it to her.

"Don't do that," he says. "She has to ask."

"It's just a little bedtime snack." The wyrmling chews herself back to sleep, the firefly's glowing posterior sticking out of her mouth.

"She doesn't get to snack," he says. "You can't just let her have every beetle that falls into your pocket."

"That was an accident," she says.

"She has to do something for it," he says. "She has to learn that we control her food. Otherwise, she'll never obey, and we'll never get off this island."

"What, by riding her?" she says. "I was just kidding earlier. It'll take years for her to be big enough to ride, if she even could be. We'll be found long before then."

The wyrmling wakes up, chokes on the firefly, swallows it, and falls asleep again with a sigh.

"We should let her sleep," Jeryon says. "Big day and all. First day."

The poth grabs his wrist. "We will be found before then, right? How far south could we be? We weren't in the river that long."

He sits back. "Remember when you asked how big the Xs would have to be?"

"Yes." Her nails bite into his wrist.

"Half a mile," he says. "A mile would be better."

She throws his wrist away. "How far south are we?"

"We really should be thinking about—"

"Plotting a course?" she says. "How far?"

"More than a hundred miles," he whispers. "Maybe two. My cross-staff isn't precise."

She nods. "Your failed experiment." She nods some more. "You knew. And you lied to me. No one is coming."

"We're too far south," he says, "which is why I can't let you inhibit her training."

"Don't turn this around on me." She stands up. Her plate falls off her lap. "I never should have trusted you. This is what Hanoshi do: You lie to get what you want. Your mates did. Your whole crew did. You did in Chorem, not telling them there was plague in Hanosh. How many sailors went to Hanosh and risked catching the flox so you could keep the price of shield down?"

"I wanted to give you hope."

"While you hoped I wouldn't notice we're still here?" She snorts. "I see what you meant by desperation."

He stands up and takes her arm. "I didn't lie. It'll just take longer than I thought to get you home."

"Not me." She pulls away. "My testimony. And for what? Justice?"

"Yes. The Trust will make things right."

"Years from now? They've got their share of the dragon. They've probably forgotten you already." She mimics washing her hands.

"Never," he says. "I've given them everything. They must be searching. If they can't find me, it's my fault. I got our position wrong. I got us lost. It's my fault, not theirs."

He grabs at her arm again. She steps back. He nearly falls like a man whose cane has slipped.

"Believe with me," he says.

She steps forward. She lets him clutch her sleeve.

"I can't," she says.

He steadies himself. He lets go. "I won't lie to you again."

"I won't forget that."

Gray wakes and opens her mouth. Everlyn reaches out and grabs another firefly. She holds it in front of the wyrmling. When she sits, the poth lets it go. The wyrmling snaps it out of the air.

"At least you're not Ynessi," she says. "They'd want to butcher your mates in their beds. I didn't refuse a part in your murder to take one in theirs." She looks at him. "That's not justice. I'd sooner stay here than help you do that."

"I do things by the book," Jeryon says. "I trust the book. I trust the people who wrote the book."

Everlyn goes to her orange moss bed, lies down facing away from him, and wraps herself around her sword. Gray climbs atop a corner post to watch her before turning to Jeryon.

He finishes assembling the lid. It's a difficult task with shaking hands. What would he do if he found his mates helpless in bed? What if the book is wrong again? Jeryon flicks Gray into the pen, sits the lid, and weighs it down with rocks.

For a long while Gray squeals inside while he stirs the fire. He can't get it to burn exactly as he would like it.

Jeryon wakes before dawn to a crunching near camp. He grabs a spear and crouches, but doesn't see anyone. He peers through the screen of branches. The poth is asleep.

The lid is on the pen, but he checks anyway. The wyrmling is gone, as is the bottom of a slat, chewed to flinders. *Why*, Jeryon thinks, *do I permit myself to sleep?*

More crunching draws him to the pond, where a long line of beetles troops across dead leaves. He follows.

Where the poth buried Gray's scat, the wyrmling's created more, a formidable mound of it, drawing the beetles. The wyrmling stands beside it, plucking the beetles as they approach the mound, twisting them in two, then popping the halves into her mouth. When she sees Jeryon, Gray sits and looks at him. He's hardly placated, especially when the poth appears behind him.

"Apparently she wants to control her own food," the poth says.

"She'll have to learn," he says, picks the wyrmling up by its scruff, and carries it kicking to camp. He puts her in the pen and piles stones around it to prevent any more breakouts.

The next night Jeryon sleeps beside the pen. He's worn out from spending the day killing blue crabs, gathering with the poth, and constructing a box to keep beetles as training treats. When he wakes up, he finds a hole scratched through the lid of the pen and another through the beetle box. Fortunately, the wyrmling has created enough dung in the beetle box that more training treats are already crawling toward it.

"I think she's mocking you," the poth says.

"You were a willful child, weren't you?"

"And you didn't get anything you wanted," she says. "Don't treat her the same way. A leash only reminds a dog that it could run away."

Some like a leash, he's not foolish enough to say.

For lunch Gray eats two crabs. The wyrmling sits and looks at him before receiving each one, Jeryon's relieved to see.

The wyrmling's filled out so much her legs barely keep her belly off the ground. The poth suggests they track its growth with a culm. Jeryon cuts a ten-foot-long piece and scores a line around it to act as a base. She stretches out the dragon, and he makes a mark at its snout before scoring a connecting line. The poth also measures her wingspan and, with a piece of palm leaf fiber, her girth. She records these on the culm, and he notes the day: day nine. They'll measure again in three days, rotating the culm to create comparison lines.

That night Jeryon puts the dragon down and lays heavy brown bamboo logs atop the lid of its pen. He hangs the repaired beetle box from a tree.

Jeryon prods the poth awake with the butt of his spear. "She's gone again. I don't know where."

His trying not to look concerned is very disconcerting.

"The beetle box hasn't been rummaged," he says. "I don't smell new scat."

"Have you—"

"I've walked all around the pond."

She notes that the slat that replaced the one the wyrmling had chewed earlier has also been chewed to flinders, and the surrounding rocks have been moved. She kneels and puts her cheek to the ground to see if the dragon left a trail.

"You can track?" he says.

"You have waves. I have leaves."

She was never good at tracking, but a few leaves have been overturned nearby, bits of beetle lie beyond them, and tail carvings and footprints mark the soft dirt beyond the fire.

"She's left the camp," the poth says.

They hurry beyond the oaks. Gray crouches in the trail between the stream and the beach. Her head is down, her butt raised, her tail poised.

"Don't spook her," Jeryon says. He takes a slow step toward the wyrmling, flexing the fingers of his free hand.

The poth blocks him. "She's hunting something," she says.

"I hope it's not a blue crab," Jeryon says. Now he readies his spear.

The wind is stiffer here, and when it gusts the wyrmling lifts her snout to smell it, shakes her hindquarters, flings out her wings like wispy sails, and catches it. She's picked up and flung with a high-pitched "Eeee!" over their heads.

"She can fly!" the poth says.

"But can she land?" Jeryon says.

They watch the wyrmling float like a kite all the way to the center of the pond, where the wind gives out. It squeals and falls, flapping frantically, and disappears.

They run to the edge and wait for Gray to emerge. She doesn't. They wade in tentatively then push toward where she went under. The bottom is soft, and their steps quickly muddy the water.

Jeryon crouches down and slides forward, dragging the bottom with his fingers.

"Don't!" the poth says. "You might step on her."

"You have a better idea?"

She shakes her head, stands an arm's length away, and searches in a parallel line. They reach the other side. Nothing.

Jeryon turns to her. "I hate losing things," he says.

"We'll find her," she says.

A gust of wind cuts through the oaks, and they hear "Eeee!" again. Jeryon drops his spear and catches Gray with a smack just as the wind gives out. He hands her to the poth.

"It's the pocket for you," she says.

"If she won't stay," Jeryon says, "we can at least work on 'Come.'"

The poth spends much of the next week gathering with Gray poking out of her pocket. She finds spreads of oyster grass, whose roots and greens make a good salad; patches of haveet, whose purple taproot is sweet, if woody, and whose seeds and greens can be made into an anti-poison; and a pulse bush, whose beans will make a fine soup if she can make a pot. She's also delighted to find some golden shield, which she replants around the camp.

The abundance and diversity of plants surprise her. If she didn't know better, Everlyn would think they were the vestiges of a once great garden.

Meanwhile, Jeryon spends hours reinforcing the pen, standing guard, rebuilding the pen, standing guard, and redesigning the pen's elements. All he succeeds in doing is driving the poth away from camp.

Finally, Everlyn says, "She could just sleep in my pocket. I'd feel her trying to escape. For one night, let's try it."

Jeryon throws down his tools. "Fine. I could use the sleep."

When the poth holds up a beetle in the morning as a reward, and Gray sits and looks at the poth just as the wyrmling looks at him, Jeryon is surprised at how upset he is that she was right. The crabs will suffer for this, and, he thinks for the first time, so will his mates.

3

In two weeks the wyrmling doubles in size to more than a foot, and her wingspan stretches to eighteen inches. She looks like the most ungainly of butterflies.

Although she still plays Wind Catcher, her new favorite game is

Beetle Pole, which has enabled Jeryon to teach her some commands. He lances a beetle with a bamboo needle to which he's tied a long thread of palm leaf fibers, wraps the beetle a few times, and lances it again to hold the beetle tight. He whistles twice for Gray to come to him and sit, then he casts the beetle like a lure. She can't attack, however, until he whistles three times quickly; otherwise, he pulls the beetle away.

Gray digs her little claws into the ground in anticipation of the whistles, and she digs them into him when she wants to play.

She's a ferocious pouncer, spreading her wings to cover a wide area should the beetle try to escape, and she's getting the hang of flying and striking while in the air, though her aim needs work. Jeryon is now on his fourth pole.

He's impressed by the thread, which the poth has been hand-spinning around bamboo spindles. Early versions frayed or snapped at the slightest tug, but she's continually improving her design. The poth says she'd be much better at spinning had she paid any attention to her lessons as a girl. Nonetheless, the wyrmling can chew off the beetle and the thread remains usable.

Her goal is to spin a thread thin enough for use with Jeryon's needle, and still strong enough to fix the rips in her smock and underclothes. At least they're clean. She made a crude olive press out of mats woven from thin strips of bamboo and a large stone, then turned some of the resulting oil into a stronger version of Jeryon's campfire soap. Another pond nearby has become their washbasin. There's even a nice flat rock for each of them to sit on while their clothes lie around them drying.

She made a flower out of palm fronds that, when mounted on a bamboo post, indicates a desire for privacy. Sometimes it's her freedom rock. Sometimes it's her weeping one.

Jeryon doesn't waste much time bathing and less time drying. He spends more time agonizing over his stubble, which he has, on several occasions, attacked nearly fatally with his blade.

One night, when it's her turn to cook, she sits him down while her meal sizzles to check his latest shaving wounds. "You could just grow out your beard," she says. "It would look nice."

"I like a clean face," he says.

"By 'clean' you must mean 'laced with scars.'" She dabs his cheek with a medicinal lotion she's made. "I'll trim it for you, if you'd like. I used to do my father's."

"Will you take away the lotion if I don't?"

"No," she says. "Who would do such a thing?"

Anyone in Hanosh. If a game's going against you, take the ball. "Fine," he says and turns away.

"Good," she says. She fills a plate and holds it out. When he looks at her, she hands it to him.

A bite later he thinks, *Hey, wait a minute.*

After a month, Jeryon says Gray is big enough to learn a new game, Crab Fight. The pen is too small for what he has in mind, so he builds a six-foot-wide, three-foot-high bamboo arena out of logs piled between stakes. Into it will go a white crab and the wyrmling. Jeryon calls it the Hanoshi Sandbox.

"She'll be so small in there," the poth says.

"She'll be fine," Jeryon says. "Toss a kid off the dock, he learns how to swim."

"Is that how you learned?" she says.

"Actually, I was thrown over the transom," he says. "If it makes you feel better, you can stand in one corner and I'll stand in the other and we'll pull the combatants apart at the first sign of trouble."

This placates her. They get into the arena.

Jeryon sets a crab in the pit. The poth hauls the wyrmling from her pocket. Gray struggles, but she isn't scared. She smells her opponent. She knows what crab is for. The poth sets her down and whistles twice. She sits, staring at the crab.

The crab raises its claws and clacks once.

Jeryon whistles three times: Fight!

Gray crawls forward cautiously on her wing hands, assessing the crab, which circles sideways around the wyrmling. She turns, following its waggling eyes. The crab opens its claws as wide as they can go, then snaps them shut. Each is bigger than the wyrmling's head. They could easily break her neck. She stands and stretches her wings and flaps a few times. The crab snips at them. Her head rears, her jaw drops, and she squeals at the crab. It snips at her face, gauging the distance between them.

The poth holds her sword, sheathed, ready to bat the crab away. Jeryon makes little feints with his fists.

Gray readies a pounce. The crab raises a claw to discourage her. She isn't and springs into flight. She floats around the crab in tight circles, the crab scuttling around to follow her eyes. She darts at its back. She makes a grab for its claws to lift it up and drop it. She snaps at its face. The crab won't let her get close. Its claws are a waving, clicking wall. Finally, frustrated, the wyrmling lands in a neutral corner and sits with her tail swishing at the crab.

"What's she doing?" Jeryon says.

The crabs wonders too. It edges closer. *Swish*. Closer still. *Swish*. The crab reaches for her tail. The poth bites her lip. The wyrmling flicks its tail and snaps the crab right in the eye. It bows in pain as the wyrmling spins, slides her wing under the crab's left legs, then lifts. The crab's broad claw clamps down on the wing. Gray hisses. The crab's legs come off the ground. It readies its other claw to strike. Gray heaves the crab over.

The crab lets go of the wyrmling's bleeding wing and flings out its claws to press off the ground and right itself. Gray stands on one claw and bites off the other, then gnashes off the first. The crab waggles its stumps and legs, trying to rock itself right-side up. Gray studies the crab a moment before sitting on its apron and biting off its legs, one by one. The crab's split mouth shouts silently.

Jeryon and Everlyn cheer.

Gray drags the body to Everlyn, who's touched.

Before she can pick Gray up to tend her wing, the wyrmling pounces on the broad claw and tries to crack it open with her mouth. Jeryon whistles twice. She doesn't come, so he yanks the wyrmling away from the claw by her scruff. She hisses at him, flaps her wings, and breaks free. Jeryon grabs the claw, and she dives on his hand, biting him. He flings her off and shakes the blood from his hand.

The poth yells and steps toward the wyrmling. Jeryon says, "No!"

"You'll hurt her," the poth says. "She earned that claw. Let her have it."

He steps between her and Gray. "On my terms," he says. Then he drops the claw and puts his foot in front of it.

The wyrmling hisses, she squeals, she snaps at his foot, but he won't let her have it. Finally, she sits and looks at him. He moves his foot. Gray attacks the claw.

"Now you may," Jeryon says and steps aside so the poth can reach the wyrmling. He kicks the crab's body out of the arena and stalks off, clutching his hand.

Everlyn finds him on the rock at the washbasin, probably the last place he thought she'd look for him. She has a packet of aloe leaves and one of his sleeves, now clean, to tie them on.

"I put the flower up," he says.

"You could get a disease," she says. "Do you want to be the first person to die from dragon spit?" She takes the ointment from the *Comber* out of her pocket. "Give me your hand." He grudgingly sticks it out. She dabs some ointment on his wound, two matching semicircles of needle-thin punctures.

"You're scaring me," she says. She scores an aloe leaf with a bamboo splinter and wraps the leaf over his wound. "I know angry. I understand angry. That's why I spend so much time on this rock. Not just to get away from you. I have to get away from me. Hold that there." He does. "So I can live with angry. What I can't live with is controlling. And I have to live with you if we're going to survive."

"I will not be undermined," he says. "She's bad enough."

The wyrmling has poked out of her pocket. There's a little bandage on its wing. It ducks into the depths.

"I've been around enough shipowners—and their wives—to understand that attitude," she says. She puts one end of the sleeve on the leaf, he holds it with his finger, and she neatly wraps his hand. "What you misunderstand is, you're not in charge. Flex your fingers." He does. She knots the sleeve end to the last round. "And I will not obey. I'm not your mate. Those are my terms."

He doesn't know what to say. The captain commands. The rowers row. That's the Hanoshi way. There is no middle ground. There isn't even a term for middle ground, except perhaps "at crossed oars."

She surveys his hand. "I used more bandage than the wound calls for, but I don't want to cut the sleeve down in case we need a longer bandage at some point—or a tourniquet." She stows the rest of the leaves and the ointment.

She wouldn't deny him medical care, Jeryon thinks. She didn't bring her sword. She can't leave the island. What does she have to bargain with? "Then who controls the wyrmling?" he says.

"She does," the poth says. "It's clear she'll do what we want, but only if she also wants to do it."

"What about when we get back?"

"Let's worry about that when we get back."

He doesn't see that he has a choice. He rubs his chin. He should cut off his beard to spite her, but he's starting to like it.

4

Another month passes. The wyrmling is nearly two feet long now, and it's getting perceptibly longer and broader each day. They have to start a new measuring culm to keep track of its growth, and they're at risk of running out of white crabs to fuel it. Only a handful are left on the beach and flats where the poth washed up, while those at the base of cliffs elsewhere are largely inaccessible. Jeryon's worried that if they kill any more the population in those areas won't recover, so he says they need to attack the blue crabs. He and the poth can only kill a few a day, given the effort it takes, and that'd be barely enough to feed them. The wyrmling will have to hold up her end.

Also, it's getting cooler. Winter, however mild, is coming, and the rainy season after that. They need the dead dragon's renderings to make it through. The wyrmling's molt has proven a terrible cloth, even for patches, and Jeryon's attempts at making a net out of the poth's thread were failures. The skin will serve for coats and tarps, and Jeryon can make fishhooks out of the bone. He can also make adzes, axes, and knives. The poth's sword is becoming blunt from its use as a universal blade, and they're concerned it will break.

More importantly, they need the distraction. They've built up their camp as much as they can. The poth has planted herbs and small vegetables. She surrounded it with so many replanted flowers of such variety and color that it looks like an island on the island, a wondrous and magical refuge. Their days have settled into a routine that he finds comfortable; every chore completed another galley brought into port, but which drives her crazy—as does his comfort in routine. Apparently there is a limit to how long she can study plants each day. She's mapped the island and found no other signs of civilization—man, giant, or dwarf. She's found many more blue crabs and black frogs. She would have tried to build a sundial if it weren't for all the hour lines having to be labeled YOU ARE ON AN ISLAND. She's been spending more time at the basin rock.

However well they've worked together, however curious that has been for him, the lack of novelty has led to her sniping at him and to him returning fire. It's made the days unpleasant, the nights more so, and the wyrmling sullen.

So they're looking forward to an adventure with Gray, whose

wings have begun turning gray and who increasingly uses them instead of walking. There's nothing worse than being dive-bombed by a wyrmling who thinks you've slept long enough.

The poth emerges from behind the bamboo screen he built between their sleeping areas after too many leaves fell. Her hair is wet and held in a loose bun by two bamboo spikes. Her skin is bright and tight from the lotion she made out of her soap, and she smells minty from the nepeta she put in it. Her smock, faded and worn thin in places, but deftly repaired in others, swishes from a fresh washing. She wears her sword on a shoulder belt made of cloth from the hem of her smock and reinforced with palm thread. She's even put in some rudimentary embroidery.

Jeryon feels underdressed. There's dirt between his toes.

She greets him with bright eyes. "Let's go!" she says. "Where's Gray?"

He points up. The dragon is sitting on a high branch, her elbows held up to arch her wings, her neck bent low. A black vulture found its way to the island recently. The wyrmling took to imitating its looming posture before they killed and ate it.

Jeryon whistles twice. The mighty vulture raises her snout and considers the call of carrion ripe on the forest floor. It opens its wings to declare to the world, *The kill is mine*. She steps off her mountain perch. Let the hawk dive. Let the larus plummet. The mighty vulture spirals lazily, the stench of rot and blood making her buoyant. She is surprised, though. The kill still walks and whistles. The mighty vulture flicks its tongue at it and thinks it needs a bath.

Jeryon says, "Put your tongue away." The wyrmling sits and looks at him. He shakes his head. "I want you hungry."

The mighty vulture lowers her gaze. She is displeased.

They set off for the dragon hollow. The path is well worn, the leaves and underbrush giving way to packed dirt. They walk side by side, with the dragon flying from tree to tree and sometimes disappearing above the canopy. Everlyn bumps Jeryon with her shoulder, he steps aside to avoid crowding her and she bumps him again. He looks at her, wondering why she can't keep to her side of the path, and finds her smiling. She moves her head as if looking around, but keeps her eyes on him. He looks around. The sky is bright. The air is light. *Yes*, he thinks, *it is a nice day for a walk*.

Of its own volition, his elbow sticks out. She takes it. Jeryon spends the next ten minutes wondering how he can get it back.

They drink from the stream. They stop at the shega meadow to look over the ocean toward home, and the wyrmling lands and nuzzles between them to wonder what is so interesting. Everlyn rubs the wyrmling's neck.

"Not even big enough for a child to ride yet," the poth says.

"Perhaps she'll grow quickly," he says. "No one sees wyrmlings."

"It'll be another year, I think. Maybe two." She takes her hand off the wyrmling.

The wyrmling wonders what she's done wrong. She looks at the poth and Jeryon, but they won't stop staring at the ocean. She drags her head into the brush to look for beetles.

There are no beetles in the brush.

A few moments later Jeryon whistles twice, and they head out again.

They stop at the frog pond, where Jeryon takes another spear from his cache there. The population of black frogs has suffered as much as that of the white crabs. It's quiet. They see no frogs at all, in fact.

Jeryon repeats their plan: He'll lead the blue crabs here, yelling when he's close. When the crabs scatter to chase the frogs, they'll release Gray to attack one, the smallest if possible. They'll follow behind in case she gets in trouble. The woods are dense, so her maneuverability will be hampered, which will make for a better test.

The poth draws her sword in agreement. The wyrmling flicks her tongue and flaps her wings. The sword usually means food. Or bamboo. Food often enough.

They toast with sword and spear, and the wyrmling watches Jeryon leave. She follows. The poth whistles her back. The wyrmling turns her head as if to say, *Why aren't you coming?* The poth whistles again more insistently. The wyrmling's neck droops and she crawls to the poth's side. She puts away her sword.

The mighty vulture is having no fun.

As he walks to the hollow, Jeryon plans the cabin he wants to build: square, three rooms, a common one in front and two bedrooms behind it, big windows to let in air with shutters to keep out bugs, a peaked roof thatched with palm fronds, maybe a porch. For interior doors they could use dragon-skin drapes. He'd like to elevate the cabin on stilts for better circulation and storage below.

When his father couldn't find fish or he lost his boat or position, he would rent Jeryon to various makers and tradesmen for the coin it could bring in. He most enjoyed building. There was something about transforming lumber into homes and boats that he found fascinating. His only engineering lore, though, came from actually putting things together and asking why they went that way. He sometimes wishes he'd stayed with building.

He'll put the house on the other side of the path to make sure the pond stays pristine and just in case it floods. They could also use the old camp for planting. The poth has been gathering seeds and experimenting with what she can grow in the wicker pots she's woven. He'll have to build a place for those on the porch so she can check on them more easily.

He wonders what it will be like to live in a house of his own. His family never did. They moved from room to room. One year they slept in tents at a dog farm beyond Hanoshi Town. His father let him to the owner, who taught him how to train dogs for the pits—and how to butcher those who failed. Another time, they lived above a stable, where he learned to ride and break horses. The best year they slept on his father's boat, a real fishing boat for once, not just a dory. Then came the Trust, and it was berth to berth for him. He still had everything he owned in one bag, but he no longer had to worry about where he would sleep. It'll be a shame leaving the cabin, even after a couple years.

The thought surprises him, missing something that doesn't exist yet.

Maybe he should stick with his sleeping panel. A tarp would keep the rain off, and he wouldn't have to stagger down a ladder in the middle of the night when the urge comes. Why would he need a whole cabin to put storage underneath? A few crates would be more useful, and he could move them around. They cook outside and eat outside, so why do they need a common room? How would they keep it lit safely? The poth has been trying to make candles, but he might as well set fire to the place before they do. As for her pots, everything will just go in the ground eventually. So why bother? He could spend his time more profitably by training Gray.

At the rise before the dragon hollow, he readies his spear and looks over the top of the rise. He doesn't see any crabs, nor does he see the telltale bulges moving on the dragon's skin. The bones are more pronounced now that the crabs have eaten away most of the muscle and fat. He flings a rock at the severed neck. There's no response. He throws another, bigger rock at the dragon's side. Nothing. He whistles. He clacks his spear against a tree. He throws a rock into the trees across from the rise to see if they've migrated. Nothing. Far less has motivated the crabs to chase him previously. Have they finally moved on? Jeryon doesn't want to get any closer in case they're lying in wait, so he works his way around and above the hollow.

Jeryon is walking to the frog pond when he hears branches shattering and the poth yelling. Gray bursts through the canopy, circles once, drops something wide and round, and dives, claws outstretched.

He sprints down the path. The crabs were at the pond the whole time. It was an ambush.

5

When he was ten, Jeryon's father took him to a crab boil where a host of Hanoshi fishermen were joined by a fleet of Ynessi who'd worked their way up the coast. They didn't fish the bay, more out of self-preservation than respect, but ill feelings resulted from the encroachment nonetheless, and the boil was called to relieve them. It was held on the wide beach of Ba Isle, whose name came either from the wild sheep that lived there before falling prey to fishermen or from the frequent comment of sailors when passing by it, "Bah, that's hardly an isle." It could accommodate many boats, making it convenient for the fishermen, and it was far from any guards who might have had a problem if a fight broke out, which many expected and some hoped for.

The Ynessi have a saying, "Every Ynessi has a thousand brothers": fight one and you fight them all. Plenty of Hanoshi fishermen were willing to show them that the Hanoshi saying "You're on your own" isn't a weakness when a hundred men fight individually for the same thing at the same time, and that thing is their livelihoods.

There were no fights, though, besides the usual argument over whether crabs should be put in the pot or steamed over it. (Both sides agreed to not even broach the issue of spices.) And by midnight everyone was singing songs about their real enemy, those landlubbers up at Ayden. It was such a wonderful boil that ten times the number of people who attended later claimed to have been there. Jeryon remembers only one thing clearly: the enormous tower of cooked crabs that was served. His father stood him against it, having bet a penny that his boy was taller than the tower. He wasn't. His father was furious, but

Jeryon didn't care. He'd never seen so much food in one place. And he could have as much as he wanted.

He recalls this when he gets to the frog pond, spear raised, and sees the stack of rent and ruined blue crabs the wyrmling is building. Many are still alive, clawless, legless, their eyes waggling in desperate attempts to orient themselves. Other crabs have been cleaved in two and three. A few lie shattered where the wyrmling dropped them. Two are stuck in trees. The poth is crab-splattered, glazed with sweat, and showing skin through rents in her smock.

She watches him walk over to one rocking on its back beside the pond. He gores it, picks it up with his spear, and adds it to the pile.

"There," he says. "That should do it."

Gray stands for a pat on the head, and Jeryon gives it to her, but he can't stop looking at the poth. She's serene.

Another force gathers around them: birds. When one darts at a crab, the wyrmling chases it off, which lets two more dart at the crabs. One gets an eyestalk. The mighty vulture hisses.

They can't carry all the crabs to camp, so Everlyn suggests a picnic at the cliff with shega for dessert. Jeryon's not sure he deserves shega, having done almost no work, but it's a fine idea otherwise. He weaves a mat of branches that they pile high with the choicest crabs. Gray has no patience for this operation and licks empty half a dozen halves while glaring at the birds. They have to practically drag her away.

The crab meat is tough, but made more succulent by grilling it with pieces of wild cherry peppers the poth found nearby. Gray prefers the crab raw, and she would prefer even more to return to her pile. More birds gather to feast and call others to join them. "Hey, vulture, we've got your food, vulture," they say. Each time she sneaks away, though, Jeryon whistles her back, and the crab in his hand is worth two in the bush.

Sitting atop the cliff, they watch the whitecaps and suck on shega jewels. The big moon watches them from above the Dawn Lands while the little moon tries to catch up.

"It's a double high spring," he says, "a good sign. Best tide to come in on."

Gray crawls to the edge and looks at the ocean too. Jeryon whistles to get her attention and waves her aside; she's in his view. She hunkers down and hangs her face over the edge.

"What would the tides be like if there were only one moon?" she asks.

"Boring," he says. "A high and low tide a day maybe. The world would feel slack."

She spits a seed into a leaf and sets it aside. "My forest warden said there used to be only one moon," she says. "Ages and ages ago."

"How could she know then? And where does a moon just come from?"

"She was told by her warden and her warden was told by hers and so on. She said the moons were sisters who had lost their home and were forced to wander among the stars."

"More make-believe?" he says.

"You told me about the tides."

He lays back. "Tell me about the sisters."

She crosses her legs and draws herself up. "One day they lost each other. The oldest, Ah, searched everywhere for Med. She asked this star and that. She asked the Abyss and the White Bridge that crosses it. She asked the Crab and the Dragon."

Gray sees something. She bolts upright and flares her wings. She peers off the cliff, neck outstretched, tail slowly rising.

Jeryon says, "I could see asking a single star, but constellations—"

"Quiet," the poth says. "When Ah reached the sun, the sun said it hadn't seen Med either. So she asked the worlds. Ours said, 'What if you stayed in one place? It might be easy to find each other if one of you isn't moving. Besides, you look tired.' Ah agreed and the world put out its arm and hugged her tight."

"What if Med had—"

She pokes him with a skewer. "And the world was right. Med flew by, and the sisters didn't think they could be any happier until the world said, 'Please don't leave me. All the other worlds have sisters except me. I can be your new home.' And she put out her other arm. Med remembered the ages she'd spent wandering alone and fell into the world's embrace. And the tides are the sisters hugging and releasing the world, who's still so happy."

"Huh," he says, rolling onto an elbow. "That fits with something I heard from an old rower."

"What?" She leans forward.

"I don't know where he was from," Jeryon says, "but he claimed that once he'd been a stargazer, and he could prove that dragons first came from Med. Maybe she picked them up during her wandering."

The poth's eyes get big then shrink to a squint. "You made that up."

"Yep. Dragons are giant newts with arm flaps."

She pokes him again, looks at the waves, then closer at hand. "Where's Gray?" she says.

"I bet she went to the crabs," Jeryon says.

"No." The poth points north over the ocean. "There."

The wyrmling is barely discernible, a gray nick in the blue. Jeryon stands beside her and whistles; Gray doesn't respond. The poth puts two fingers in her mouth and whistles loud enough to make the bushes tremble. Either the wyrmling can't hear her or she's ignoring her.

"We weren't paying enough attention to her," Jeryon says.

"She'll come back," the poth says.

"Birds don't," Jeryon says.

The dragon shrinks to a point and vanishes.

They stand for a while then they sit. The wind shifts, and the birdcalls come more clearly, as does the smell of the crab rotting. The tide goes slack.

"How far could she go?" Jeryon says. "If she rested in the water, could she take off again?"

"I don't know," she says. "She was bound to do this, stretch her wings. She's not a bird. We couldn't put her in a cage."

"I tried."

The poth doesn't rise to the bait. "She has to come back. This is her home. You have to trust her."

"Having to trust isn't trust," he says.

Her face wrinkles around her eyes.

"And everyone runs off eventually," Jeryon says. "I'm going to the hollow. I might as well start rendering." He gets up and grabs his spears. He scatters the wood in the ring they made, but the fire's long out. He doesn't ask if she wants to help.

"What about us?" she calls to him. Her voice is thick. "What if she doesn't return?"

"They win."

Dinner is a somber affair: nuts, berries, greens, plus an herb tea the poth brews in an exceptionally concave blue crab carapace. The birds ate the rest of the crab, and what was left wouldn't have been worth eating anyway. They sit on logs around the fire and pick at their food.

The poth waited in the meadow until Jeryon came down from the hollow. He carried a ragged, uneven strip of dragon skin and a few vertebrae whose spikes he planned to knap into cutting tools.

He would have walked right past their picnic site, but couldn't, not the way she sat there with her arms around her knees just as she'd done when they were first put in the dinghy. He waited for her to catch up to him, and they left the meadow side by side.

After they eat he works on the vertebrae while she spins palm thread, her best spool yet. The bone's harder than he expected. He tries a variety of hammerstones, none of which works well. Then he snaps off a spike entirely. He flings the vertebrae into the pond, followed by the spike.

As he rears back to throw the hammerstone, the poth takes one of the other vertebrae and lobs it into the pond. He stares at her. She stares at the hammerstone. When he doesn't drop it, she palms her spool and brings her arm back. He drops the rock and grabs her wrist. She glares at him. He sucks his lips, nods, and releases her. They sit, and he goes back to work on his last vertebrae.

After a while he says, "Can you fish?"

"Ayden's on a lake," she said. "I caught sixteen silver carp the first time I touched a pole. I was three."

"I'll make us both hooks then," he says, running his finger along the curve where the spike meets the backbone. "Your thread will make a fine line. I've also been thinking about a cabin we can build." She touches his leg. "And a raft."

There's a rustling in the treetops, and something huge drops in front of them, scattering the edge of the fire and sending up a plume of sparks. They fall backward off the log and scramble away on their knees. The attacker doesn't move. It's not a blue crab. It's long, thick, and silver with a band of white. It slowly arches its face and tail, slaps the ground with both and does it again.

The poth says, "It's a fish! A huge fish!"

"A robalo," Jeryon says. "Not known for flight."

There's more rustling in the canopy. They cover their heads, and the wyrmling dives through the treetops to stand over the fish. She squeals and noses it toward them.

"I guess she's sick of crab too," the poth says.

CHAPTER FIVE

The Cabin

1

Jeryon gets out of bed and a creak works itself from his bed to the cabin's wall, where his tools sway faintly on their pegs. The poth decorated her room with flowers, ink drawings on bamboo slats, and little bamboo sculptures, many of which also hold plants. Her room smells like their garden; his, like its dirt. She calls his room the storehouse, but he likes being surrounded by useful things, and tools, if they're properly crafted, are an artwork all their own. He's proud of his hoe, made from the dragon's complex shoulder blade and sinew; his axe, made from its other shoulder blade; as well as his razor, made from a flake of the dragon's tooth so sharp he wouldn't need soap to shave if she tired of his beard.

He opens his shutters, then uses a dragonbone stylus to mark a skinny bamboo tube hanging beneath the window. It's the fourteenth tube for their fourteenth month, not counting the shorter tube for the five days of Jubilee at the turn of the year. When he drops it, the tubes rattle like bones.

He puts on his dragonskin trousers and tunic over his uniform. They're hot, the material doesn't breathe at all, but the skin is remarkably resilient. It won't wear or tear easily, even though he didn't tan it. However crudely made his outfit—all sailors can sew, but few can design—it would be the richest in Hanosh. A mere captain wouldn't be allowed to wear dragonskin, except by special dispensation from the City Council.

In the common room he loads a woven plate with vegetables and fruit picked yesterday. He's never felt better. Still, what he wouldn't give for a yank of bread.

He listens at the poth's door. She snorts and rolls over. He grabs the bridle from a peg by the front door and leaves to work with Gray. He's glad she's comfortable. It was worth it, building the cabin, then building it again.

Everlyn hears him listen at her door. He always does before leaving, as if she might have disappeared in the night. She rolls over to let him know she's awake. The fresh straw beneath its dragonskin cover crunches as she does, and the skin and bed squeak. She means to yawn, but accidentally snorts. When she hears him close the cabin door, she decides to go back to sleep. She'll get up when he and Gray take a break, and she'll make them some tea. What she wouldn't give for toast with butter and honey.

Outside Gray suns her wings, which are as wide as Jeryon is tall. Like the larger squaluses, the wyrm's turned a cool blue-gray on top, and will probably get darker, while her underside remains platinum. When she hears him, she furls her wings, rolls on her side, and lifts her leg for a morning scratch. He lays the bridle quietly on the porch where she can't see it and jumps down. He would use his hand, but her hide's so tough it's no longer effective. He pulls a bamboo rake from underneath the porch and goes to work on her belly. She falls asleep. He stops. She heaves as if stabbed. More rake. She falls asleep again.

Jeryon retrieves the bridle and steps behind her head. He rakes her neck, which arches, and she yawns. With a practiced swoop, he slips the dragonbone bit past her teeth, catches the rising neck between his thighs, and sets the dragonskin strap in the bamboo buckle beneath her throat.

He holds her in place, getting her used to being straddled. It makes her skittish. Lots of things do. She's constantly charging at things that aren't there or chomping the air. He figures she's just at an age for dragons. Gray's four feet long, much of that neck and tail. As broad as her body is, riding her would still be like riding a racing hound or snap dog. They have a long way to go. If you don't want to ride a horse until it's at least two, how old would a dragon have to be?

Gray relaxes. He steps aside and whistles her to sit. She does, gnashing at the bit. She chewed straight through rope and bamboo, but in dragonbone she's met her match. He unbars a woven crate lined with a dragonwing membrane pouch and filled with water, and he pulls out a white crab. It shakes its bound claws. He tosses it to the wyrm, who swallows it in a few bites. He takes a coil of rope from a peg on a stilt and ties it to the bit. For letting him, she gets another crab.

Jeryon releases Gray to lead her around the pond so she can get further used to the bridle. She smells more dragony than usual, which reminds him of the *Comber*. Jeryon realizes he hasn't thought about his mates in a while, unlike during their first rainy season.

At first the cabin withstood the season well, then the pond overflowed and flooded it. As he and the poth scrambled to save their possessions, Jeryon pictured his mates dry in his quarters on the *Comber*, laughing at him and the Trust amid their render. When the rain became a torrent that battered the walls, and the wind chewed away the roof thatch, he wanted to tear the *Comber*'s stern deck open to get at his mates before they could reach Hanosh. Whenever he saw the poth drowning in her own hair and trying to keep a fire lit, Jeryon's hands would jerk as if reaching out and flinging his mates into the sea.

Soon he would have the power to do that, he thought. Unfortunately, Gray had little interest in learning a new training game, Snatch the Mutineers.

One day as she was coming down the trail to the beach the poth caught Jeryon yelling a mate's name while hacking a crab.

She looked at the slaughter on the beach and asked, "What are you doing?"

"I'm hungry."

"What a waste," she said. "I've made us lunch already. Let's talk about rebuilding." She held out her hand.

He followed her back to camp. As they made plans for the spring over oyster grass salad, the crab corpses washed away along with thoughts of his mates. He took to eating more fish to keep them out of mind.

After the rainy season ended, they put the cabin on stilts. They reinforced it with timber columns and thatched the roof more thickly. To keep the rain out, they fitted the bamboo in the walls more tightly together, and made the windows smaller and higher in the walls. They also built shutters and planned to daub the walls before the next rainy season if they were still there.

Meanwhile the island yielded a bounty of fruit and vegetables that they struggled to eat before it rotted. For a month, they didn't need Gray to fish for them. They even gained weight. And the camp turned gold as the shield the poth had replanted ran rampant. It was like living in a field of treasure.

Jeryon sniffs. For some reason the shield doesn't smell so terrible anymore. He could stay here forever, he thinks. No one in Hanosh except the shipowners eats so well. The cabin is more sturdy than most of the places he lived in as a boy. And he has a schedule to keep, one set by the land and the needs of the day without the worry of living hand to mouth. He could almost thank his mates for it.

The poth, though, would want to go home. She talks about touring the League again from Jolef to Yness. As for Hanosh, she's likely had her fill of their people. She gets antsy when they're on the porch together for more than an hour. Then again, she'd be the ideal partner for a captain. She wouldn't mind him being gone for six months at a time, and they'd get along fine for the month before he left again. They wouldn't even have to live in any one place. They could catch up with each other at various cities.

It's a clever arrangement, but not worth considering now. He pats Gray on the head. The wyrm's still puny as dragons go. He and the poth, they have a long way to go too.

2

Everlyn can't lie in bed anymore. She opens the shutters in her room and the common room and watches Jeryon lead the wyrm around the pond. They wave to each other. For the first time, it strikes her: He'll really be able to ride Gray. They're so easy together.

He looks ridiculous in his new clothes, of course, like someone going to a masquerade as a dragon. She shouldn't mock, though. She's shortened her smock considerably and taken off much of the sleeves to use the fabric to fix the rest. Her undergarments are a ruin. Going without them, though, even if he didn't know, is entirely out of the question. Beetles get everywhere.

She joins them as they pass the cabin and walks with them to the pond's outlet stream.

"Tea?" he says.

"Shouldn't be more than a moment," she says.

He loves her tea, especially when she puts a shega jewel in it. Who would have thought that tea would be what could please him? He once told her he didn't think he deserved cooked water.

The wyrm flaps and screeches, "Eeee!"

"None for you," the poth says.

A bird flies by, and the wyrm leaps toward it. Jeryon checks her, and they watch it disappear into the canopy. He gets a look in his eye and says to Gray, "I know a game we could play, but we'll need more crab."

"What is it?" Everlyn says. She relishes that too rare look in his eye. The dragon has a rambunctious effect.

"You'll see," he says and hands her the lead. "Back in a minute." He retrieves an empty crate and hurries downstream to the flats.

Everlyn gets a look in her eye. She waits until he disappears, then whistles twice. Gray sits and licks her. Slowly she straddles the wyrm and puts a little weight on Gray's shoulders. Her tiny dorsal spikes are blunted by her smock. *She's like a rocking horse*, the poth thinks. She settles herself. Gray pushes up. *So much poise*, the poth thinks, *as if she's already in flight*. Everlyn lifts her heels off the ground. She lifts her toes. Gray flips out her wings and takes a step. Everlyn smiles and rolls with her. She always had a good seat. Then the dragon flaps, lifts, and topples the poth. She lands hard on her back, and Gray licks her face.

They have a long way to go.

When Jeryon returns to the cabin, the poth is steeping and Gray is sitting on the roof. He can't decide if he loves her tea because of the steeping or in spite of it. It's a whole operation, putting leaves in hot water and staring at them, as complex as refitting a galley. First the water has to be boiling, not a bit below or it's ruined. Then you have to pour the water in slowly. Too fast, and it's ruined. Then you have to wait a precise number of seconds. Too few or too many, ruined. Pouring the tea out is a whole other operation. That precision appeals to him tremendously. It's not the type of attitude he'd have expected of her. Trouble is, he wants the tea now.

He whistles twice and Gray glides down to sit beside the crate. He grabs a crab between its back legs, extends his arm twice slowly, her eyes following the crab, then he flings it, spinning, high in the air. He whistles three times.

The wyrm leaps into the air after it. The crab tips off her snout and falls to the ground. Before it can get away, Gray picks it up with her mouth. And before she can chomp it, Jeryon whistles twice. She brings it to him for another throw. The crab is completely uninterested in flight. The next time, Gray relieves it of all interests.

He doesn't know what it is about her, but the poth makes him puckish sometimes. It's probably the tea.

Everlyn hears the wyrm whoosh and bang into the cabin. After a particularly solid strike, she leaves her tea, but not her count of how long it's been steeping, to find out what they're doing.

Jeryon makes the catches increasingly difficult by tossing the crabs near branches and close to the cabin. After one throw he watches the poth through a window. Her lips count off every tenth second. She gathers her hair and twists it behind her neck. *I'll make her a comb*, he thinks. Three tines. He'll inlay each with a piece of polished shell.

Gray sits beside him. He throws a crab near the cabin. Her angle to it causes her to clip a corner column. She squeals and flexes her wing. While she retrieves the missed crab, the poth appears in the doorway.

"What are you doing?" she says.

"Crab Skeet. Watch this."

He flings the crab toward the porch rail, and maybe because he's trying to impress her he gets his whole arm into it. The crab flies high and long. Gray gets a good jump, but has to slow to avoid hitting the rail. The wyrm doesn't want to miss in front of the poth, so she rears her head to snap it forward to make up the last bit of distance. She drops her jaw to give her the best chance of catching the crab. And as the crab falls nearly into the poth's hands the wyrm reaches out with her very breath to snatch it, blasting the crab, the poth, and the cabin with a long gout of flame.

The cabin goes up like a brushfire. Culms explode from the steam trapped inside, spraying the porch with shrapnel. The poth screams, falls inside through a wall of smoke, and disappears.

Jeryon rushes to the cabin, but the heat drives him back, air feeding the fire from all sides, turning the cabin into a chimney. His eyebrows singe and the ends of his hair evaporate. Air is sucked from his lungs. He shouts for the poth, but can't hear himself, all sound blown from his ears.

Gray darts for the doorway, which is filled with flame. Jeryon grabs her tail to keep her from destroying herself. Gray can breathe fire. That doesn't mean she can withstand it. Gray snaps her tail, flinging off Jeryon's hand, and slithers inside.

Jeryon runs behind the cabin. The poth is at his window. It's too thin and high for her to crawl out, so she's chopping at the sill with his axe, the same idea he had. Her smock smokes where she's beaten fire off it. Her skin is blistering. Her hair is full of wisps. Her eyes are crazed. Smoke pours out of the window, and she starts coughing too hard to swing the axe.

"Give it to me," he yells. She tumbles it out the window. He hacks at the bottom of the wall. When he strikes horizontally, the bamboo splinters instead of slicing neatly. When he strikes vertically, the axe breaks through the supports, but leaves the slats in place. He has to stop when he sees her fingers pulling at the slats from the other side, her mouth wide open, wanting air, while wind drafts under the deck to pour up through the floor.

"Jeryon," she cries, "I can't get out!"

"I will get you out," he says. He's crying too, but doesn't realize it.

He hears Gray inside. He hits the bottom of the wall with the axe and whistles three times. The wyrm attacks it savagely. An opening appears. Jeryon pulls the slats out, but they're woven so tightly he can only remove one at a time. He gashes his hand on the bamboo splinters, and his blood soothes his own burns. The roof has caught. It's about to collapse. The fire is in the columns too, and the whole cabin lists toward him.

The poth sticks her foot through the hole, but that's all she can get out. He says, "Your arms! Maybe I can pull you out!" She sticks one hand through and her head. They're face-to-face. He pulls. She pushes at the floor of the cabin with her feet. They wedge her shoulder through.

Gray chews at the slats trapping her other shoulder. That's all they need, but they have so far to go. The bamboo frays. It will not break. Gray retreats. Jeryon whistles three times, but she doesn't return. The cabin lists farther.

"Go," the poth says, terribly calm. She folds her body tightly against the wall.

He keeps pulling. The cabin rocks toward him. A corner of the porch collapses sending a wave of fire around his legs.

"Go," she says and releases her grip.

He grabs her hand again. Their blood seems to boil between them. She pulls his hand to her scorched cheek. He combs her hair away from her face with his other hand. Bristled clumps fall out and float away. A hunk of flaming roof thatch flops beside him and shatters. The underbrush around the cabin threatens to catch.

He rubs a tear into her cheek. "Everlyn," he says.

"So you do know my name," she says.

3

Jeryon has hiked to the Crown to watch the sunrise. The spikes look like cenotaphs. Their shadows stab the west. The eastern sky is clear and pale blue where the night before it had been cranberry. A good day to sail.

The wind topples a log on the remains of a large fire near the edge, and a wave of old ash blows over him. Maybe he should have set up a signal fire, he thinks, however difficult it would have been to maintain. Maybe a ship would have come.

The sun crowns the horizon. Jeryon heads for camp.

In the hollow, the dragon is a grove of rib bones too big for him to carry off. He could render them, but there's a lucrative market for long bones provided they're unspoiled. At some point he'll sell them. The skull will be the greatest prize, despite his having removed the teeth to make tools. Mounted with its jaws open, it would make the perfect doorway for a shipowner's home.

The frogs at the pond have recovered. They make for good eating, but tough gigging. They're more shy than they once were.

At the shega meadow he gathers the last of the fruit from the tree and puts them in a dragonskin bag slung over his shoulder. He walks to the cliff's edge. The dragonprint has vanished, worn away or swallowed by the meadow. The sea remains, endlessly wearing.

Jeryon follows the stream to the beach and his salting operation. He puts seawater onto dragon skin stretched loosely in a frame, then uses a bamboo scraper to collect the salt after the water evaporates. He stores it in bamboo tubes for use in salting fish. The frames are empty now, as are the drying racks and salting crates lined with wing membrane. He hauls them into the trees. The salt tubes are already at camp.

The new cabin faces where the last one stood, a mirror image except it's elevated only half as high and the windows are even larger than those of the first cabin. Where the last one stood, asphodel grows.

He sits on the porch. He won't miss this cabin.

He hears a rustling under the porch. Jeryon swings his feet. More rustling. He swings his feet higher and counts. One. Two. On the third upswing, he feints bringing his legs down and a long, wide snout snaps at where his much-repaired sandal would have been. He puts his foot on Gray's head between her new horns. She can't shake it off. Her tongue whips over her nose and licks him between the toes. That does it. He jerks his foot away and she pushes out.

Her breath whips over him too. It smells like charcoal. She's good about her fire now. She won't use it around the camp and rarely uses it when he hasn't commanded her to.

When she does it's usually to torch white crabs. The gelatinous phlogiston, which bursts into flame on contact with air, sticks to their shells, and she likes to watch them run around in a panic. Jeryon douses them before they set fire to the forest, although that, he's come to understand, is one of her fire's purposes: to light the brush and drive game into the open. Doing so once resulted in her discovering a hive of blue crabs, which normally hide when they don't have a dragon to strip.

Disappointingly, her fire also imparts a bad taste to food, like rancid oil, when used to light a cooking fire. So Jeryon trained her to use it on command by having her light a branch he could then use to light his fires. He wishes he could put the raw gel on the ends of small sticks, then coat the gel with a substance that could be rubbed off to set the stock on fire. The Trust would make gobs of money, and he would become the hero of housemaids and sculleries everywhere.

Jeryon had thought that Gray getting her fire signaled the onset of adolescence and a new growth spurt, one that would make her large enough to ride soon, but it hadn't. Perhaps she was traumatized by the fire. She wasn't burned badly. Her skin is indeed largely fireproof. When she charged through the cabin wall just before the roof collapsed, she was more injured by the jagged ends of bamboo.

He spent a week trying to wrap her wounds in healing leaves the way the poth had done for him, but she chewed them off. She was surlier than anything for a month, snapping at him and refusing to obey. Fortunately, the wounds healed well, the scars vanished as her top color hardened, along with her scales, to a slate gray, and six months later she began the growth spurt that's still ongoing.

As her neck emerges, she scrapes it against the bottom of the porch to remove some pale flakes of dead skin left over from her most recent shed. He lined the underside with long wedges of bamboo to help her and, more importantly, to reinforce the porch. They're no use, though, when she has to scratch in the middle of the night and uses the columns, shaking the whole cabin. He's worried she could bring it down, and he's becoming worried she'll grow so much one night she won't be able to get out in the morning.

Next come her shoulders, the forearms of her wings, and her elbows with their hand-long bone spikes. She uses them to hold things, pin crabs, stab beetles, and, most often, scratch her back. When he was breaking her to the saddle, she destroyed the first, a wicker number, with her spikes. And when he was breaking her to his weight by lying across her back, she nearly stabbed him several times. In one respect she's trained him. When she twitches an elbow spike he scratches her back with a small rake. He put a strap to hold the rake on saddle number seven, which has a wooden frame covered in dragonhide.

Now, her torso. Gray flattens like a cat and proceeds with little jerks. The cabin creaks alarmingly as the edge of the porch catches and releases her dorsal spikes like a clock's movement. She finally pops free and reinflates. She's seven feet at the shoulders, a foot taller than the tallest draft horse Jeryon's ever seen, with a body like an aurochs, nineteen feet from snout to tail, with a thirty-five-foot wingspan. She weighs a ton, he estimates.

To get this big, she ate six times a day, and nothing on the island was large enough to satisfy her. One week, when a pod of dolphins was migrating nearby, she ate ten of them, bringing each to Jeryon for his approval. The stink was horrific, especially when a few didn't agree with her and she vomited them up under the cabin. At least she ate them again. Worse was their whistles and squawks and the way they flopped on the ground before she gobbled them.

Her greatest catch was a whale calf bigger than her. To his horror she kept dropping it in the sea while flying to the island, then diving down to retrieve it again. He wasn't sure if she couldn't carry it very far or if she was playing with the poor thing. Eventually she dropped it into camp with such force it left a dent in the packed ground before the cabin.

He takes his saddle, bridle, and other tack from a peg on the edge of the porch and puts them on her. To the saddle he affixes a dozen waterskins made of dragon skin, the bag full of shega, another full of olives boiled with herbs, sprinkled with sea salt and pepper and wrapped in palm leaves, and several spears with dragonbone tips. He figures this will last him several days. Of course if he doesn't reach land, none of his supplies will matter. The dragon, which he's flown in circles around the island to test her range and endurance, should be able to reach the land south of Yness in a day, but he's not sure how far east he is and so could miss the continent entirely.

Jeryon goes inside. He wonders what life will be like with keys. And without bamboo. In the common area he checks the barrel of water, as well as crates full of dried fish, fruit, olives, and spices. These should last at least two months. He evens up the bamboo spears standing beside the door. He ducks into his bedroom. There, beside his bed, is his blade. He puts it in the pocket of his dragonskin pants, a good luck charm now that he has a dragonbone knife with a bamboo handle.

He pauses at the door of the other room. The cabin is silent. He steps in.

4

Everlyn lies facedown on a wide bed beneath a dragonskin coverlid. He's cut her hair close to disguise the places where it didn't grow back, but patches of puckered skin betray them.

She rolls on her side to show him the good half of her face. He kneels beside her. She says, "You're going?" Her voice is raspy from her throat and lungs being burned.

He nods. He glances under the bed. Her sword is there. Somehow it survived the fire. A bamboo spear is easier for her to use, but she won't give in to one. Practicing with the sword, she claims, works her body and eases her mind.

"I'll see you off," she says and sits up.

He puts a hand on her shoulder. "No."

She shakes him off. "I can't spend the week in bed."

"It could be longer. Maybe a month. Or two."

"Then I'll have to get up," she says. The blanket slides off her as she swings her legs over the other side of the bed. She wears only his old yellow shirt, which is long enough to reach her knees and worn soft. Her arms are crosshatched with pale white scars from where he pulled her through the hole Gray made, and they accent her wiry muscles.

"Shall I do your back?" he says.

She shakes her head. "I can do that."

"I want to."

She unbuttons the shirt and lets it drape over her hips. He uncovers a bamboo cup sitting beside the bed. The smell of honey and pepper fills the room. He spreads lotion on his palms and works it into her scars.

He also works in a year of fury at his mates. He sees their names written in wrinkles and puckers. He sees their faces drawn in desperate flesh. *They did this*, he thinks. *They made her choose*. He would trade every minute of their two years together, he would trade their ever having met, if she could be whole again. Even justice will have to wait. Seeing his mates in gibbets won't heal her. He needs a ship to get her off the island.

The dragon isn't big enough to carry them both on her back. He'd tested that proposition by hanging bags of rocks over his saddle. She found it difficult to take off and couldn't balance in the air. Nor is she strong enough to carry one of them all the way to the League with her back claws. He'd tested that with a sling full of rocks. She's fine for short distances, but Gray has to let go after a few miles. The poth is in too much pain to fly so he'll go to Hanosh and bring back a ship.

The Trust, he's sure, will be more than accommodating in exchange for his services with Gray.

He would fly to Yness, which is hundreds of miles closer, but no doubt they would kill him on sight and take the dragon.

When the poth can stretch without feeling like her skin will tear, he lifts his shirt back up over her shoulders, and she rebuttons it. He comes around the bed and offers her his arm. Her feet are sore. She doesn't often wear her boots, and her legs stiffen when she doesn't move for a while. They go outside. He climbs off the porch into the saddle and straps himself to it. He and the dragon move together. They didn't always.

His first effort to ride Gray was comical, the dragon lying down before taxiing him around the pond for the price of a beetle per step. Their first flight was nearly tragic. They were on the beach and she flipped out her wings to toss him off when the wind caught them and threw dragon and rider into the trees. Their first real flight was little more than a hop across the shega meadow, but it was exhilarating for them both. For a moment they were one.

Their next test was a glide from the meadow cliff to the beach. As they yawed and plummeted in the tricky winds, he realized he couldn't steer the dragon the way he would a boat. He had to point out a destination and give Gray her head to figure out the best way to get there. As with a razor, he had to let the dragon do the work.

Everlyn insisted on hearing everything, and he cringed a bit when relating this part. She didn't disguise her glee at being right about this and, by extension, so many other things.

Soon he and Gray were making trips across the island, then circuits around it. They flew out to sea to the point where the island had nearly vanished and soared high enough for the sea to flatten into a smear of blue and white. Jeryon would have screamed with joy as they plunged had vomit not stoppered his throat. A month ago, he felt confident that Gray could stay aloft long enough to reach the League. He began preparations for leaving the poth. She began arguing to take the dragon up.

He was apprehensive, given her pain and limited mobility, as well as her unfamiliarity with the actual process. She recited from memory every lesson he had learned. She said she wasn't going to watch the first broken dragon in history fly away without having a chance in the saddle. Gray sensed her desire and would lower her neck beside Everlyn to let her sit on her shoulders. Jeryon couldn't refuse in the face of joint opposition. And he had no right to, she reminded him.

He would have called it a mutiny, but that would have spoiled the moment. Instead, he asked that she ride the next day. He wanted to prepare a surprise for her.

The next morning he lotioned her thoroughly, she ate a fair quantity of boneset and golden shield, and he led her out to Gray, already saddled. Her seat was good, and the pain slipped out of her. He told her to end her ride by cruising over the Crown. She asked why. He remained clay-faced.

At first the dragon flew close to the ground and so slowly she thought Gray might land. Everlyn couldn't believe the dragon was babying her too. She yanked the dragon up hard. Jeryon's stomach fell to hear her scream, then rose when he realized what a wonderful scream it was. It was the scream of the whole sky greeting the morning. He watched the dragon turn and glide. She was, he would tell her later, a great rider. As she passed by the third time, he could see she was getting fatigued, and he pointed at the Crown.

She cruised north over the beach to come at the Crown from the seaward side, a long dramatic slope. Later she would recall finding Gray's egg, fighting the crabs, rendering the dragon, and many walks up to the Crown with Jeryon, but in the moment she only recalled that she should occasionally breathe. As she came over the top, she discovered Jeryon's surprise: a huge pile of wood in a ring of stones. She brought Gray around, aimed the dragon at the pyre, and dove at it. At the last second she gave the command to fire: "Comber!" The dragon's flames exploded off the wood and roared high enough for Jeryon to see it at camp and cheer. She soared off in a great circle around the pyre, laughing. She couldn't feel her body at all.

Two hours later, Jeryon looks past Gray's slowly waving tail and sees the island sink into the horizon. He rubs his beard. He's let it get long and full. He feels bushier too.

At midday the dragon spots a pod of razorback whales also traveling north by northwest. She bobs toward them. He reins her in. They have no time for hunting. Then he considers: Razorbacks are exceedingly fast for whales, and other galley captains would race them to see if their rowers could keep up. Jeryon never went in for such exercises in ego. The rowers would have to move at double-time, which would exhaust them quickly and cost them more time later. He does wonder, though, just how fast she can go.

Jeryon lets her swoop, which spooks the whales. Gray falls behind, but with a few beats of her wings she catches up. She isn't straining. She's waiting for the order. He gives it, and she fires past the whales like a harpoon from a cannon. As she slows, Jeryon sees another pod ahead and beyond it a galley heading east.

He circles far to larboard. Gray is so close to the water, small and dark, they might not have been seen. Should he just continue past them? He doesn't want to risk getting shot at. He's tempted to show off, confident that when they get to the Dawn Lands no one will believe they saw a man riding a dragon. He decides to fly just close enough to read the galley's flags. Maybe he can persuade the captain to make a detour to the island. He could pay him off with a few dragon bones, more than recompense for the ruin of his schedule.

The galley is Hanoshi. He doesn't recognize the company insignia, a gold circle in a blue field. It must be a new outfit, which is unusual, but not unprecedented. Perhaps a company split or two combined. He does recognize the captain's flag. It bears the insignia of his former third mate, Tuse.

So his mates did fool the Trust. Why isn't this a Trust ship, though? Like all officers, Tuse wouldn't be able to work for another company in the League for five years after leaving the Trust. Who would have made him a captain anyway? No one is that good a mate. Tuse wasn't. Tuse's share might have filled his pockets to bursting, but you can't buy a command, even in Hanosh. So how could he have moved up the ranks so quickly?

A terrible thought strikes him: What if the Trust doesn't exist anymore? Where would that leave him? Who else could he trust? Blue Island, the Trust's main rival? Hanosh Consolidated, the city's most powerful company? The former licks the latter's boots, and the latter would kick him to the curb to confiscate Gray and the island while the other companies fought to wrench them away. Jeryon bends over the saddle. His throat wants to retch, but his stomach feels empty.

Jeryon is directly astern now, and the galley hasn't made any motion that would indicate he's been spotted. They're probably looking at the whales, wondering if they could take a few without falling behind schedule. Jeryon realizes he has to give up his own schedule. He had planned to be over land by star-rise, to hide overnight in the coastal hills north of Yness, and to be in Hanosh a day or two later. He has to be opportunistic, though. What would Solet say? He has to grasp?

How fortunate he is to have found someone he wants to reach out and take hold of. After all, Tuse was the final vote. Tuse put the poth in the boat. She wouldn't care for what he wishes he could do, so he'll just question him. What he'll do with him afterward will depend on his answers.

Jeryon has Gray glide in a slow circle to keep them in place while he surveys the ship. How can he get the yolk without breaking the egg? The stink of sulfur wafts over him downwind from the ship. *And it's a rotten egg at that*, Jeryon thinks. He laughs. He knows what Tuse would do if a dragon attacked. He doesn't have the imagination to do anything except what he saw Jeryon do. His old oarmaster is in for a few surprises.

PART TWO

The Mates

CHAPTER SIX

The Oarmaster

1

Tuse puts his massive foot on the foredeck of the penteconter *Hopper* and flicks some grime off his dragonskin boots. The stitching's worn, the heel should be replaced, and the piping at the tip is coming loose, but the red-tinged black skin looks as fresh and tough as it did the day it was flensed beside the *Comber.* Officers and sailors of Hanoshi companies must all wear sandals of Hanoshi make, but Tuse received these boots from the Shield and the City Council approved their use, which is tantamount to law. They remind his crew of what he had to do to get this ship, which is one reason he doesn't like to wear them.

That they remind him too is the other.

He also doesn't like the blue embroidered pants recently foisted on officers. They pull. They're hot. The cloth won't last. They're only meant to make him look fancier than the Blue Island captains. At least his blouse is light and loose, if more gold than a captain's used to be. He won't wear the blue felt hat, however. Let them dock his monthly.

They're already taking out the rent for his uniform. Nothing with a feather will go on his head.

Standing watch between the harpoon cannons, the ship's boy, Rowan, says in a hush, "Whales. Off the starboard bow."

The kid's as hard and skinny as an iron, and as sharp too, the son of a sergeant, but this is only his third voyage and he's still soft with awe for the sea. Tuse envies him that.

"Do you think you'll scare them?" Tuse says. "Tell the ship, son."

"Whales!" Rowan hollers. "Off the starboard bow!"

Tuse flinches. The boy smiles. Tuse says, "Actually, maybe you will scare them."

Tuse considers the patch of rough water and, beyond it, another. Two pods are coming together. "Tell Press to pipe me some cannons, then bring us close for a calf or two."

"You'll take a cannon?"

"Aye. I'll tell Edral."

Rowan smiles and runs ahead of him to the first mate at the oar. The cannon, Tuse knows, is something Rowan envies him.

He should have the boy trained on it. He's been giving him a taste of every job, something he never got coming through the rowers' deck. If the crew thinks he's playing favorites, let them wonder instead why they aren't his favorite. Besides, the boy's done the job of the two most galleys carry. He wouldn't have thought it of a soldier's son.

The only thing Rowan doesn't like is powdering the rowers. Too many are former soldiers who fell on hard times, then fell into the wrong sort of business. That's a softness Tuse will have to wean him of. He should train the boy with the whip too.

Amidships Tuse flops a hatch and looks down at Edral, his blinking second mate and oarmaster. Around him the rowers are chained to their benches, straining so hard their neck muscles threaten to snap. Sweat courses through their scars and shines on their tattoos. They breathe like a great bellows, mouths wide to mitigate the stench of rotten eggs lingering from their previous cargo. Every trip to Chorem and back is a race against their last. That's why he gets to keep his ship.

"What about our schedule?" Edral says.

"We'll take them in passing," Tuse says. "Besides, the boy could always fix a double ration to make up any time lost."

"Aye, aye!" a rower says. Tuse doesn't have to look to know whom. Bearclaw's trunk is broader than it was on the *Comber* from the years of rowing, but his face is pocked and wasted, and his teeth are gone. The changes in his face are the result of too much powder, the changes in his teeth, too much mouth. "Your boy's good with the spoon," he says, "but I preferred that lady. She had a heavier hand."

Tuse's face reddens. "That one's had enough. If he flags, fix him an old-fashioned ration."

The oarmaster uncoils his whip.

Tuse closes the hatch. Since the *Comber*, he's preferred a covered deck. The rowers get hot, but they need so much water as it is, what's a little more? Let them burn. There's more where they came from.

He tries to close the hatch on his memory of the poth too, but it won't stay battened.

When Rowan reaches the stern deck, the first mate, a man as dour as he is sallow, is already clenching his whistle in his teeth.

"The captain will exercise his privilege?" Press says.

"Yes," Rowan says.

Press's lips curdle. He blows the call for whaling.

Many in the crew leave off their duties to prepare the galley for rendering. The second harpooner, a lank-limbed man with lankier hair named Igen, runs to the foredeck to load the cannons. While the captain is looking into the hatch, Igen holds two fingers downward, then six fingers upward.

The crew looks at Press. Press peers at the whales, considers the distance and roll of the sea, and raises his arm with three fingers down. Igen nods. Other crewmen out of the captain's sight show one or two fingers held downward as well. Igen marks these with a nod, then a disappointed shake of his head. He holds eight fingers up. No one raises an arm. He holds up ten fingers. Still no takers.

Press chuckles. "He's going to take a bath."

"You shouldn't bet on the captain to miss," Rowan says.

"You shouldn't still be standing here." The boy leaves. Who is he to talk to a mate? The captain favors him too much, perhaps because only the boy favors the captain. Some of the old-fashioned ration would bring him down a peg.

Press watches Tuse go forward and bend over a cannon. Press should be the one to shoot, not man the oar. He's far more accurate. So's Edral, probably so's the boy, and neither's ever shot before. Captain Boots says he doesn't need a third mate because two can do the work of three, something the company appreciates, but Press has heard the rumors that something curious happened on the *Comber*. Maybe he thinks he can only control two mates. The joke on the galley is that Boots is in fact the third mate impersonating a captain.

When he gets his galley, he won't run it like Boots. He'll have the proper three mates and two fearful boys, not one little bootlicker. He'll dress the way a captain should. And he won't allow gambling.

Tuse swivels the cannon. The motion relaxes him, like picturing a punch before you throw it. Others are better shots, especially Press, but he has to take any opportunity to prove himself worthy of his shirt. He knows they call him Boots. Maybe a little whale meat for dinner will placate them. And if he can show the other captains that sea foraging will lessen the ration expense, maybe they'll stop calling him "the oarmaster" for skipping first and second mate.

"Do you want me on the other?" Igen says.

"We won't need it," Tuse says.

"Aye." Igen smiles, cautiously optimistic.

On the foredeck stairs, Rowan holds ten fingers upward against his chest.

Igen gives him a look: Where would you get—

Rowan clinks the pouch tucked inside his short pants. Igen, with the grin of a man just pulled from the sea, nods. Rowan goes to stand beside Tuse.

Tuse mutters, "It's nice to get at least one vote of confidence."

"It's your money," Rowan says.

"Not all of it. I only gave you eight pennies to bet."

Rowan says, "'Bet on the man who bets on himself,' my father says. Besides, you're going to hit the whale."

Tuse suppresses a smile.

Press kicks himself. He should have bet five pennies. If the kid is betting, he must know something. Stupid to miss such an easy opportunity. Press makes a mental note: *Vigilance! You'll never be captain if you won't take a chance.*

The first mate hears a strange whooshing astern then something hits him square in the back of the head.

2

The galley closes on the whale pods, which are merging in a great eddy. They're razorbacks, enormous, fast and easy to spook when they're alone, but being in such a large group gives them confidence, and they ignore the galley. It's like a family reunion. Some bob together like old men chatting. Calves jump and race. A few imperious matrons slap them down.

Tuse finds a tubby little calf dead ahead. The other calves swim away from it, and it wallows as it watches them go. Tuse digs in his heels. Other men get dragons. He gets the saddest whale. It figures. He knew kids like that when he was growing up. They didn't last long. He might have been one had he not learned to use his fists.

Tuse considers the range and wind. The calf flops around to look at him with wide, empty eyes. "This'll be a mercy," he says, and he brings the firing rod to the touch hole.

The sail explodes behind him. Heat roars over the foredeck. The sound of lines snapping and the sail whipping loose is lost in the groan and shudder of the galley pulling up short. Tuse, startled, pushes the cannon down and fires the harpoon into the sea. He watches it drag down the whale line. His first thought is, *I'll have to make it up to the boy.*

His next are: *Is that a dragon rising away? Where did it come from? Why didn't it make an exploratory pass?*

"Who's riding it?" Rowan says.

"Riding?" Igen says.

Tuse drifts down the stairs, shadowed by Rowan, watching the dragon and its rider come around astern. Where did he come from? Is he Aydeni? Ynessi? A pirate? How is he staying on the dragon?

A voice pierces the deck. Bearclaw says, "I won't go through it again! No!" Edral's whip cracks. The voice stops. The oars keep moving.

We have to keep moving, Tuse thinks, and he realizes the rest of the crew has been gawking at the dragon rider too. His hand twitches as if he had his whip. "Dragon stations!"

The crew comes to. He's trained them well, and they've repelled two attacks by Aydeni privateers in the last six months. The threat of defense, just putting up your fists, is often the best one. The shutters on the rowers' deck are closed. A four-man fire team assembles to deal with the sail and the mast. Two crossbow teams take their weapons from under the foredeck. Igen reloads the larboard cannon, which he'll man. Press should be coming to take the starboard cannon while another crewman takes the oar. Tuse peers through the smoke to find him, only to see his first mate's head bouncing toward him. Tuse traps it with his foot.

While Press's head stares up at Tuse in horror, he sees Press's replacement stuck on the stern deck ladder, staring at something by the oar, then at the dragon diving astern. Training is one thing; reality, another. The crewman ducks and hugs the ladder, and Tuse realizes the rider's plan.

The dragon's glide path will take it along the water, using the stern deck as a shield, presumably to rake their oars, probably starboard. He'll cripple them, test their aim, then come in for the kill.

Tuse tells Rowan, "Get to the hatch and tell Edral hard larboard, double-time."

"On your mark?"

"Immediately. Then relay from there." He pats Rowan on the back, and the boy springs away. Tuse picks up Press's head, he can't leave it on the deck, and after a second's consideration puts it in the iron powder bin. He mounts the foredeck. "Igen, ten seconds to load that cannon. We'll catch the rider as he comes amidships. We can use the stern deck for cover too."

Igen sees the plan in his head as he wads and packs. If the rider is attacking from the stern, he may know their defenses, which means he may think the cannons can't be fired back over the deck. Tuse, however, had the stays removed after the Shield refused his requisition for a stern deck cannon following the last privateer attack. The rider will be flying right down their barrels. Igen swivels the cannon to aim behind Tuse's and says, "Three–one against."

"Us?" Tuse says.

"Him."

Tuse grunts with satisfaction and swings the starboard cannon around. He glances at the hatch. Rowan half dives into it. Edral yells. The drumming accelerates. The ship veers to larboard and the dragon appears, unable to make the turn with them. It floats away to starboard and the rider makes the mistake Tuse had hoped he would. Instead of curling away for another run, he tries to turn with the galley, unwilling to give up his prey and, as the dragon banks, making himself a better target for them.

Tuse says, "Fire!"

Igen's harpoon nearly takes off an errant crewman's head then gashes the dragon's shoulder. Tuse's harpoon, loosed a heartbeat later, unspools whale line behind it. The crewman, leaping for cover, almost has his head taken off again. The shot looks true and Tuse thinks they could winch the dragon in until the dragon jerks. His harpoon gashes its tail before sailing into the sea.

Now the rider peels away, cuts around the stern deck, and with a shout causes the dragon to enflame the larboard oars. As the oars go slack, the galley curls farther in that direction, and the dragon has to roar over the bow. It's so low that the crossbow teams fling themselves down and Igen flings himself overboard to avoid Press's fate.

Tuse and the rider glare at each other as they pass, and Tuse knows the rider more than he recognizes him. Jeryon doesn't have a beard in his nightmares.

The rider turns the dragon's head and yells, "Comber!" and the dragon enflames the forward oars on the starboard side.

Rowan, standing on the ladder beneath the hatch, watches the dragon fly nearly straight up. The dragon's fire has crept up the oars and through the tholes and unshuttered ports on both sides of the galley to sear the rowers and burn the benches. Smoke fills the rowers' deck. It's laced with yellow tendrils from their last cargo, Dawn Lands sulfur. The hatch becomes a chimney, and Rowan has to lean out of the smoke. The sulfur burns his throat. Chains rattle as the rowers beg to be released, Bearclaw loudest of all.

"Help me, boy," he says. "You're a good boy. Be a good boy."

He has to help the rowers. They're men, whatever the captain says. And as the dragon pivots like a swimmer after a lap and floats high above the ship, he has a moment. What can he do, though? Tuse ordered him here. If the ship can't steer, they're a sitting duck.

"Boy! Are you listening?" Bearclaw says.

The captain wouldn't let them die down there, would he? Rowan could break the chains, but the tools he'd need are in the carpenter's box, which is stored too far away. Besides, that would take too long. He needs the key. The rowers could unlock themselves. The captain has it.

The dragon dives. The crossbowmen drop their weapons and crawl for cover. The fire team working on the sail brings it down just enough to hide behind it. And Tuse is still loading.

"Faster," Rowan mutters.

Flames burst below. Patches of deck darken. The dragon rears its head.

Tuse jams the harpoon home, stops, and scans the galley. Rowan follows his eyes.

The mast is burning like a candle. The sail is about to collapse. The oars are flopping uselessly. Tuse looks at Rowan. He smiles grimly, then hangs the firing rod on its hook, turns to face the dragon, and puts his arms out.

Rowan yells, "What are you doing? Shoot it! Shoot the rider!" Rowan races forward.

Bearclaw says, "Come back, boy!"

He's small, and the captain is huge, but Rowan knows how to tackle. He'll save the captain from his madness and get the key. He runs through the dragon's shadow. Tuse watches it come. The dragon doesn't enflame him, though. Instead, it flips its back legs forward and snatches Tuse off the deck. The captain screams, the dragon lifts and whirls, and they head south.

Rowan leaps onto the foredeck. He quickly finishes loading. He raises the harpoon as high as it will go. The dragon is a hundred yards away and bobbing each time Tuse kicks. Rowan points the cannon more than he aims. A wave lifts the bow and gives him the extra distance he needs. He takes up the firing rod and stabs the touch hole.

The charge sizzles, and the iron bloops into the falling wave.

"Why didn't he fight?" Rowan says. "Why did he leave me?" Then he spots something shiny hanging on the firing rod hook. It's the key. The captain did fight, Rowan realizes, by surrendering himself.

A half-mile away the dragon dives and just above the water drops the tiny speck that is the captain. Rowan is about to yell for someone to get the galley's dinghy so they can save him when the dragon circles, dives again, and plucks Tuse from the water before continuing south.

The fight isn't over, though. Rowan runs to the hatch with the key. He'll free the rowers, even that weasel Bearclaw. They'll help put out the fires. Then he'll persuade Edral to follow the rider. The rest can have the dragon. He wants his captain.

3

Where they're going Tuse has no idea, and he wonders if Jeryon knows himself. The first time he soared to a thousand feet, Tuse grabbed the dragon's ankles in case he were dropped. By the fourth time he decided Jeryon was looking for his destination. The trip isn't so bad except for the uncertainty, the numbness in his shoulders and arms, the vomit covering his blouse, and the frequent dunkings as the dragon rests its claws. Fortunately, Livion made all the Shield's crewmen learn how to swim, and the waves wash away some of the vomit.

During one dunking he looks north. The pillar of smoke from the *Hopper* has dissipated. He hopes his crew and not the sea put out the fires.

When an island comes into view hours later and the dragon settles into a gentle descent, gliding out of exhaustion, that's when Tuse is most frightened. The water's full of rocks, bars, and reefs and shallow where it's not. The dragon flexes its claws to keep its grip. Blood trickles down his chest from the points where it does. He can't lift his arms anymore. He can clench his fists.

He gave up his body to save the boy. He won't give up his life as easily.

The dragon heads for a beach with more crabs than Tuse has ever seen and a well-worn trail leading into the trees. He braces himself. If he can land on his feet he'll race up the trail and try to disappear into the woods. At the last second, though, the dragon veers to larboard along a cliff face, skirts the northern side of the island, and dives for an opening along the rocky eastern shore. He sees no trails. Spray blasts over one side, craggy oaks loom over the other, and the shadow of the island's great column descends like a pestle into a mortar.

The few crabs here scatter as the dragon drops Tuse heavily in the weeds and lands beyond him. He jumps up and bolts for the tree line. The dragon scuttles in front of him, elbow spikes cleating through the scrub. Its quickness defies its ungainliness on the ground. Tuse cuts left, and the dragon corrals him with a wing. He cuts back the other way, and the dragon's tail hooks him so he falls. Jeryon turns the dragon to face Tuse and dismounts.

Jeryon draws a dragonbone knife with a bamboo handle. Why would the captain fly him here just to slit his throat? He's not the throat-slitting type anyway. Tuse is hardly relieved when Jeryon removes a coil of cord from a saddlebag. He might be the strangling type.

"Hands behind your back."

"What are you going to do?" Tuse says as Jeryon slides behind him.

"You should be asking, What is she going to do?"

The dragon says, "Eeee!"

"I just want to talk," Jeryon says.

"You tore off Press's head."

"She did that," Jeryon says, "not me."

The dragon stretches out its neck and licks the tip of Tuse's nose.

Tuse falls on his belly and spreads his arms and legs. Jeryon ties his hands behind his back then he pulls off Tuse's boots and ties his ankles to his hands. Jeryon searches him thoroughly, including, strangely, the hems of his pants. He has nothing.

"You don't have to do this," Tuse says.

Jeryon removes two waterskins from his saddle and pours them down the dragon's throat. The dragon bobs its head and Jeryon gives it some from a third. Then he takes a long pull himself.

"Can I have some water?" Tuse says.

Jeryon takes another long pull, closes the skin, and replaces it on the saddle.

Tuse compresses his lips. He's been arrested. He's had this conversation before.

Jeryon checks the dragon's injuries. The gashes on its tail and shoulder have partially healed already. Jeryon fetches a crude clay pot from a saddlebag, then he spears a couple crabs who have an interest in Tuse. He whistles twice. The dragon, staring at the crabs, sits up. He drops one and whistles three times. The dragon snaps up the crab, and Jeryon quickly smears something from the pot on its shoulder wound. The dragon says, "Eeee!" and looks at him severely. He gives it another crab and tends to its tail, which the dragon lashes angrily. Jeryon points at Tuse. The dragon shifts its gaze.

Tuse won't meet it. "You said you wanted to talk," Tuse says. "Say something."

Jeryon pulls a shega from a saddlebag, sits, and leans against Gray's haunch. He cuts out a seed and sucks it with relish. The dark juice bubbles on his lips.

"Fine," Tuse says. "I can wait." The *Hopper*, if it survived, would have followed him.

Jeryon spits the seed, crosses his legs, and leans back. He closes his eyes. The dragon doesn't. It licks some crab off its lips.

Tuse estimates how far he flew and how long it would take the *Hopper*, damaged with many rowers dead or too injured to work, to reach the island. *Midnight*, he thinks. His crew should see the island in the moonlight. They might not see the rocks surrounding it. He feels an unusual pang: Has he simply postponed the boy's doom?

Tuse works the cord. One hand free is all he needs. The effort is waking up his arms. He'll stab Jeryon with his own knife or spear then he'll take the dragon to warn off the galley. He twists and stretches the cord to no effect. Tuse can't wait to see the look on the shipowners' faces when they see what he brings them. He rolls and yanks. He thinks his right is about to be freed, then his left. He yanks and growls and finally blurts, "What do you want me to say?"

Jeryon opens his eyes. He carves out another jewel.

Tuse grinds his forehead into the scrub. "You were right. It's the poth's face I see. In shadows. In strangers. In glass. I saw it in a roll once." He looks at Jeryon. "Is she all right? Tell me she's all right."

Jeryon sucks.

"I couldn't stop them. I wouldn't have let her get in the boat. I need to see her. To explain."

Jeryon spits the seed.

Tuse ducks his head. "That wasn't the plan. It was only supposed to be you. And me, if I didn't go along. I had to go along."

Jeryon nods to the dragon and flicks some pulp at Tuse. The dragon snaps it out of the air a handsbreadth away from the oarmaster's nose. It swallows, bares its teeth, and slowly withdraws its head.

"I didn't want to," Tuse says. "I was like their hostage. I argued against the whole thing. But they wanted the dragon. It was Solet's plan, and Livion made me go along with it. I didn't do anything. Was I supposed to die too? I couldn't get you out of the boat. Why should I have gone in? They put a knife to my throat."

Jeryon carves another chunk of shega. The dragon rears its head.

"And we had to get the medicine home. Could they have driven the rowers the way I did? We made up nearly an hour! How many people didn't die because I didn't get in the dinghy? I have to have some water. My mouth is so dry."

Jeryon gets up, pulls a skin and a second fruit from his saddle, and sits again. Tuse looks expectantly, but Jeryon returns to slicing his first shega. The dragon sniffs at it. Jeryon waves it off.

"Sure, some people died in Hanosh. A fair amount of the medicine the poth made was destroyed; the pots had cracked. Some of the shield was ruined too. But that's not my fault. It's yours. You should have run. You were supposed to run. We could have gotten away. We had guild rowers back then. And with the powder? We could have made it. But you fought. You endangered the ship. They were right."

Jeryon notices a bit of pulp in his lap and flips it at Tuse. Again the dragon snaps it out of the air. Spittle flecks Tuse's face. Its breath smells like scalded fish oil. Jeryon takes a drink of water. Tuse concentrates on the skin to avoid looking at the dragon.

"You know I'm right," he says. "And what do you have to complain about? You landed here, right? This is where you've been living. It's like a paradise, this island: food, fresh water, no responsibilities, no shipowners breathing down your neck. You had a woman. She was no—"

Jeryon raises an eyebrow.

Tuse takes a different tack. "And you got a dragon. No one has that. You've lucked out. If you'd gone back to Hanosh without the render we took, you'd have been fired. You wouldn't have been able to find a job piloting a skiff. We did you a favor, really, giving you a chance. Don't you know that?"

Jeryon lowers his eyebrow.

"I didn't think their story would hold water, of course. You were a hero. You saved the ship. You saved those men in the water. You saved the city. You killed the dragon. I told everyone how you did that. I wouldn't say you drowned. They did. I wanted you to be remembered well. I thought the Shield should name a galley after you. They didn't care, though. All they did was rename themselves—the Golden Shield Trust—to claim the glory you should have had. They were as wrong as Solet. No justice at all."

Jeryon sits up so sharply the dragon jerks, alarmed. Jeryon holds up a hand to calm it.

Encouraged, Tuse goes on. "We thought they'd ask questions about you and what happened, but they only cared about the dragon. They even off-loaded the render before the medicine. They made a fortune. They bought more boats and more companies. They bought two seats on the City Council. They practically run the city now.

"Blood money. I hinted at what really happened, even if it risked me ending up in a gibbet, but they were only too glad to trade you for the render. Solet and Livion too. Solet sold them on the idea of hunting dragons. They gave him three galleys to do it. And he's been successful. He just set out to bag one roaming the coast between Yness and Hanosh. This one could set him up for life.

"Livion made out best. He married the daughter of a shipowner, Chelson, and that got him his own command. Now he's in the Castle. He was given shares. He's an owner now. He's set. And here we are."

Jeryon nods at Tuse. So does the dragon.

"I never wanted to be silent. I never wanted a command. I'm no good at it, and everyone knows." Tuse widens his eyes. "I got what I deserved."

Jeryon's mouth twists. His knuckles whiten as he grips his knife.

"Listen." Tuse tries to get on his knees. "If you want justice, leave me here. That would be fair. I should have been here with you from the start. You have a dragon. Take the poth and go. Just leave me here. Give me the captain's chance. It's only fair."

Jeryon stands and sets the waterskin in a fountain of seagrass and the shega on the skin. He licks his knife clean and tucks it away. He flips one of Tuse's boots with his toe. "Nice boots," he says. He scratches under the dragon's chin and heads inland.

The dragon watches him go, then turns back to Tuse, its mouth slightly open.

"Don't leave me here! Not with that."

Jeryon pushes into the trees.

Tuse can't help himself. "They're coming," he yells. "They know what a dragon's worth. They're coming, and you'll pay."

Jeryon turns around. "I used to think that too," he says, and dissolves into the greenery.

When he doesn't return, Tuse stares at the waterskin and shega.

The dragon lays its head on the scrub and watches them too, as if daring Tuse to try and grab them before it can. Tuse won't chance it. The dragon waits.

4

In the morning, Tuse's shivering wakes him. Or he thinks he wakes up. He doesn't remember falling asleep. He only remembers the dragon's eyes glowing in the moonlight and not seeing the *Hopper.*

Scrub crunches. He hopes it's not the crabs. They won't come near the dragon, but the way they goggle at his fingers and toes is unnerving.

Jeryon carries a spear across his shoulders. At either end a huge blue crab dangles, their bladelike claws tied together to form a loop. If that's what lives on this island, Tuse isn't sure he wants to be left here.

When the dragon sees Jeryon, it stands up and stretches. It flings out its wings and flaps them to get the grit off. It twists its neck this way and that, then does the same with its tail. Jeryon dumps the crabs before the dragon. It folds its wings and, almost primly, sits. Jeryon whistles three times, and the dragon eats. Not primly.

Tuse hopes that's enough food for its breakfast.

Jeryon looks out to sea. "Any sign of your galley? I didn't think so."

Tuse's hunger turns acid. He's doomed. And he doomed Rowan too. You can't stop a ripple once you've cast your stone. The crew, they knew the risks of the sea. The rowers, they put on their own chains. Rowan did nothing except be his father's son. Tuse ducks his head and clamps his teeth as hard as he can. Something is trying to get out of him, something less physical and more vulgar than vomit, and he can't let it.

Jeryon picks up the waterskin and takes a long pull. He leaves it open and props it on the seagrass again.

Tuse looks at the dragon. When the dragon doesn't move to stop him, he pushes his mouth toward the skin. What does it matter anyway?

"No," Jeryon says, "you look to me."

"What?"

"You don't ask the dragon for permission," Jeryon says and snatches up the waterskin. "You ask me."

"I'm not your dog."

Jeryon replaces the skin on the seagrass. Tuse stares at it. He stares at Jeryon's old and oft-repaired sandals. He stares at the dragon's haunches.

The dragon rips off a crab leg and crunches it.

Tuse cranes his neck to glare at Jeryon.

Jeryon whistles once, long and rising, once short and backs away.

Tuse worms forward, unable to feel his arms and legs. He gets his mouth onto the spout of the skin then rolls on his side to drain the water out.

"Good," Jeryon says. He yanks the skin away. "The poth did survive," he says. "She'd want you to live. She'd bear you no ill will. She'd want me to bear you no ill will. You led her to the wheel, but she put down her own coin."

"If I could have rigged—"

Jeryon holds up his hand. He puts down the skin. He waits. Tuse looks at him. Jeryon whistles and Tuse drinks more water. Tuse tells himself he's training Jeryon to talk.

"You were right," Jeryon says. "I did luck out. She's made me a better man." He checks the dragon's wounds. They're glazed with new tissue. "We share, for instance. It's an old idea. At first we had to help each other to survive, but now we share because there's a joy in it. I think sharing's been out of the world for too long." Jeryon puts some salve on the wounds just in case. "All we have now are contracts. Incentives. Targets."

Tuse sucks out the last of the water. His stomach burns. His heart is full of smoke. His arms and legs contract, and the cord on his left wrist slips and slackens. Pins rush into his fingers.

"She shares a dream of mine," Jeryon says, retrieving the empty skin. "We'd go to Hanosh, tell the Trust our story, and see the three of you gibbeted. Two years, and that's all I've wanted. That was our deal."

"I'll speak for you too," Tuse says. "I'll say anything you want." He rolls onto his left side so his hand can worry the cord unseen.

"They wouldn't listen," Jeryon says. "'No justice at all,' you said."

"They treated you wrong," Tuse says. "Maybe—"

"They'd treat me worse if I returned," Jeryon says. He brushes grit off the dragon and rubs her neck. "The company can't have me walking around, talking about mutiny. I'd be a risk. Worse, a liability. Other owners would use me against them. And they couldn't buy my silence with a ship and fancy shoes. They'd have to kill me. And her."

When I get free, I'll spare the poth, Tuse thinks. He twists his hand. It uncovers a stub of wood, a root, or a buried stump. The cord catches.

"You're dead already," Tuse says, "so you can do anything. You have a dragon. You have the world. Tame the North. Disappear in the Dawn Lands."

"She wants to go home too."

Tuse slowly saws the cord against the stub, the rest of his body dead still.

"Then go to Ayden," Tuse says. "They're nearly at war with Hanosh. They'd open their purses to you."

"And see them make the dragon a weapon against my own city?" Jeryon says. "The poth would clip the dragon's wings before that happened."

The dragon looks at Jeryon.

"It's not your city anymore," Tuse says. "Never was, really, not for people like us. We're just coins passing through the owners' purses. See how they've spent you? Go. Leave me and go. You owe them nothing."

"No," Jeryon says, "they owe me." He grinds his spear into the scrub. "I gave them decades. I gave them trust. And where's my return?"

Jeryon stabs the ground. Tuse saws more vigorously.

"When I washed up here, where were they? When the rainy seasons came, where were they? When the fire—" Jeryon chokes. "Two years here. How could they forsake me?"

The cord frays.

"I deserve more than a monthly. Or a bonus. They owe me your head, and if they won't pay," he points his spear at Tuse, "I'll collect the debt myself."

Tuse jerks away from Jeryon. The cord pops. He rolls on his back to hide his free hand. The spear point circles his chest. Tuse says, "She wouldn't want this."

"No." Jeryon taps Tuse's chest.

"What would she say if you killed me? If you killed them?"

"Nothing. She'd leave. I'd never see her again."

"So leave me. Take her and go." Tuse thinks he couldn't grab the spear before it gored him. Jeryon's leg, though, if he could catch him off balance . . .

"I can't. The dragon's not big enough for two riders yet. You're lucky she made it all the way here with you."

"Then go alone. She'll never know I was here. Or I can help. To make up for what I did. I owe her."

Jeryon shakes his head. "I thought of a better course. Last night while watching you from the trees and thinking about all you told me."

"You didn't spend the night with her?"

"No, I didn't let her know we were here. That's the solution. What she doesn't know can't upset her." Jeryon whistles twice. The dragon sits up. "Naturally, we can't leave any traces," he says.

"Mercy," Tuse says. He wiggles against Jeryon's toes. "Have mercy."

"Where's the profit?" Jeryon says.

Tuse growls and rolls into Jeryon's skinny ankles. Jeryon yelps, falls forward, and jabs the spear into the ground to catch himself. Tuse hammers the back of Jeryon's calf with his free fist, unlocking his knee, then he grabs the top of the calf and collapses Jeryon's lower leg against his own chest. Tuse rolls back. Jeryon twists, trying to skip away before his leg is folded between Tuse and the ground, but the spear loses its grip in the scrub, Jeryon loses his grip on the spear, and he falls on his face.

Tuse pivots and claws his way up Jeryon's back with his free hand. He clenches Jeryon's neck. He straddles him with his free leg spread to one side and the knee of his bound leg dug into the sand on the other. Tuse makes himself heavy.

"Any sign of your poth?" Tuse whispers. "I didn't think so."

Jeryon bucks. Tuse barely moves. Jeryon puckers his lips. The dragon cocks its head. Tuse grinds his mouth into the scrub.

"There was a boy on the *Hopper*," Tuse says, and presses his frying-pan thumb into Jeryon's carotid artery and jugular vein. "He wasn't a part of this. He didn't deserve what he got. He was a good kid. Now you owe me."

"Gray," Jeryon says, his voice already woozy. *"Comber."*

"Those days are—oh." Tuse remembers Jeryon yelling the galley's name while passing over the *Hopper*. He turns and sees the dragon rear its head. Jeryon tucks his head and pulls his left knee up so he's entirely under the larger man. The dragon drops its jaw. Jeryon heaves Tuse toward it. Tuse yells. The dragon spits a gob of fire.

The fire spreads across Tuse's back. He flips over to smother the flames. The dragon spits another gob on his chest. That inspires some flailing. When it stops, Jeryon whistles three times.

CHAPTER SEVEN

The Hunter

1

Solet grinds the heel of his dragonskin boot into the deck of his monoreme *Gamo* as two of the Shield's shipowners push themselves away from a portable mahogany dining table. Their valets swoop in to replace the remains of their grilled quail and okra with a bottle of burnt wine, two snifters, and a silver ceramic narghile for each. As the owners take their respective hoses, Solet thinks, *They'll share their interests, but not their smoke.*

He isn't surprised. They wouldn't share their table with him, despite the fact he wore their ridiculous formal uniform. Pants, on an Ynessi! In Yness they'd never be welcome to eat again.

One must smile at an owner, though, even when one, Mulcent, blows a huge cloud of honeyed smoke at you and says, "We can expect a dragon tonight?"

"Trackers found signs on shore today," Solet says. "They believe it hunts there before returning to the spires, where it lives. When it flies past, we'll engage."

"You've been saying that for a week," Sumpt, the other owner, says.

"Dragons aren't as keen about schedules as are the Shield's compters," Solet says. "We can encourage it, however."

Solet signals for his lamp to flash the *Pyg*, the penteconter to starboard. A girl on *Gamo*'s stern deck wears a candlebox around her neck. She points it at the *Pyg*, opens it once long, once short, and once long. A moment later the *Pyg* begins the dragon march, a rhythm the beasts like best. Ideally, the dragon will be drawn to the *Pyg* then *Gamo* and the monoreme *Kolos*, positioned on the other side of the *Pyg*, will flank the dragon and pounce.

Solet's wolf pack sits a mile off a broad fan of thick woods and hard leaf shrubs that fills the dusk with the scent of pine and oak. It spills toward the sea through a break in the black cliffs that line much of the ragged coast between Hanosh and Yness. Another mile behind them, glittering in the dusklight slipping over the cliffs, are a line of black basalt stacks, the ruins of an ancient cliff. Solet knows how they must feel. The owners are wearing him down too.

Solet taps his foot to the beat. Sumpt withdraws his bald, bulbous head into his rolling shoulders. "That sound," he says. "How do you stand it?"

Solet points to a badge sewn onto his blouse beside his Shield badge. "You see this?" It depicts the rearing head of a black dragon, its jaw dropped. "All my men have them."

"They should be fined for a uniform violation," Mulcent says.

"They'd happily pay it," Solet says. "When other crews are in port, they look for whores. When mine are in port, the whores look for them."

"I'd happily pay a dragon to attack just so I didn't have to listen to that sound again," Sumpt says.

"We are paying," Mulcent says. "Dearly. We can't afford another empty hold." He looks at the *Pyg*, and Solet can tell he's tallying the cost of every man, line, and oar. Despite bagging two dragons already, Solet's had a run of bad luck lately, so Mulcent has come aboard to protect their investment. Sumpt has also, but he's more interested in the adventure.

"You will not only recoup your investment," Solet says. "This dragon will be our most profitable yet." They hold smoke as he steps to the table. "We aren't going to kill this dragon. We're going to capture it."

Sumpt spits his smoke. "Why would we want to do that when there's a ready market for render?"

Mulcent's pale eyes thin. He says, "This is not our arrangement."

They sadden Solet. Their families were traders before the League, men who recognized opportunity in the strange and figured out how to cultivate it. Their grandfathers had formed the League. These men, however, these boys, only know counting books. They haven't traveled to every corner of the Tallan Sea to buy and sell while gripping a knife under the table. They're quill dippers, managing stock and schedules. And they only meet people like themselves, soft, wealthy, usually Hanoshi. It had been hard enough getting them to support his wolf pack, convincing them that killing a dragon was possible only by actually killing one. But capturing a dragon? He understands their minds: It had never been done, which meant it couldn't be done, so where was the profit? That's why he hasn't broached the subject until now, when impatience would help him win the day.

Solet's voice drops to a slow, Hanoshi heaviness as he explains: "What is the biggest expense in hunting dragons?"

"The ships," Sumpt says.

"No," Mulcent says. His needle-like fingers bob as he thinks. "The crew."

"The uncertainty," Solet says, stabbing the tablecloth with his finger blade to emphasize his point. "If we kept a dragon as stock and milked its phlogiston instead of removing it from the dead organ, we could predict supply and costs would be dramatically diminished. Feeding and barning one dragon would be cheaper than maintaining three ships. Perhaps we could catch a second and husband them."

"We?" Mulcent says and sips some smoke. "Wouldn't you be putting yourself out of a job?"

"I think a man who can capture a dragon would be in great demand," Solet says, "if relieved from his position or undercompensated. Markets do thrive when there's competition."

Sumpt sorts. Smoke drifts up from his nose.

Solet doesn't add that his position is already endangered. How many more dragons can there be that his pack could kill easily?

Mulcent is not amused. "How do you plan on accomplishing this?" he says. "Our ships have already incurred significant repair costs from previous excursions, which have diminished expected returns."

"The ships are outfitted with a number of new devices," Solet says, "as you're aware from having paid for them. The *Pyg* has pots that will blast a cloud of pepper into a dragon's face to disorient and possibly blind it. Our harpoons have weighted heads for greater penetration—"

"Much like my own," Sumpt says, waving his snifter to be refilled.

"Plus the harpoons will be attached to chains," Solet says, "and the chains to winches so we can hold the dragon, keep it from flying, and, once it falls into the water, drag it into a position to subdue it."

"How will you do that?" Mulcent says.

"We'll stretch it between the boats, then fire a harpoon through its snout. This iron will have a flange near the end so the dragon can't work it out. It won't be able to open its mouth, saving more phlogiston for us."

"I know some foremen who need that treatment," Sumpt says, and takes a long draft of the burnt wine.

Mulcent holds his hand to his ear. "Curious," he says, "I don't hear the laughter you think you hear."

Sumpt scowls and blows smoke at Mulcent.

A long sharp whistle comes from the *Kolos*. The watches on the foredecks of the *Pyg* and the *Gamo* blow theirs. Sumpt sits up. He points off the *Pyg*'s bow, where a green-blue dragon with broad wings has lifted into the dusk above the black backdrop of the cliffs. It has an enormous red stag in its claws.

"It must be as big as our ship," Sumpt says.

Solet gives a hand signal to the stern deck. A whistle is returned. The *Gamo*'s drum replies with a soft, slow beat, and the oars gently pivot the galley to face the *Pyg*. Another whistle stops them.

"It must be as big as our ship," Sumpt says again.

"Not quite," Solet says. "The one I took on the *Comber* was longer. It'll be no trouble. Now," he motions to stern, "if you'll take your places in your cabins."

"Do they always fly like that?" Mulcent says. The dragon darts and drifts as it flies. It looks agitated, but not in the way a dragon gets when it's considering an attack. "Is it looking for something?"

"Must be the weight of the stag," Solet says, "and the wind against it, throwing it off." He holds out his arm. "Your cabins. We only have a few moments."

A passing crewman, misunderstanding, hands Solet a pair of leather goggles with glass lenses and a bandana to cover his nose and mouth.

Sumpt jiggles to his feet and polishes off his wine, but Mulcent stays in his seat and says, "I've changed my mind. I will remain on deck." He gestures for the valets to clear the table and take it away.

Sumpt grabs the bottle before his valet can and says, "We must get out of the crew's way. The portholes will afford us excellent views." He takes two encouraging steps toward the cabin.

Mulcent sniffs his wine and waves away the valet's tray. "No," he says, "I'm here to observe. I wish to see that none of these devices are merely for show. I may be able to suggest some additional efficiencies. For instance, fewer ships."

Solet half expects Mulcent to demand that he make the decisive blow as well, the way other owners are guided through a wood, handed a loaded crossbow, and told when to fire so they can later call themselves hunters.

The dragon closes. Sumpt drinks straight from the bottle. Mulcent looks at him stonily. Sumpt decides. With his puffy cheeks held as firmly as possible, he follows the valets and their loads of tableware and linen to the cabin that once was Solet's.

Mulcent takes his glass to the mast and says, "I will stay here."

Solet says, "As you wish." He smiles again and gives Mulcent his goggles and bandana. "Because of the pepper," he says.

A sailor gives Solet a replacement pair of goggles as he mounts the stern deck. He hears Sumpt bar the cabin door, as if a four-inch iron peg will protect him. Solet laughs. Sumpt is too scared to act stupid. Mulcent is too stupid to be scared. And if he and his efficiencies are swept overboard in the confusion, there is a precedent for such a tragedy.

2

The first mate, Jos, has the oar. An old bone pipe hangs from his bottom lip like the stump of a cigar. Others might be bothered by that, waiting for the pipe to fall, but Solet finds it amusing. He appreciates insolence when carried off well. Jos would make an excellent match for one of his sisters, but he's from Duva, and they wouldn't have one not truly of the sea. Pity.

Mylla, Solet's cousin and former ship's boy, rests her candlebox on the rail as she reads messages from the other two ships. "The *Kolos* has concerns about the dragon," she says. "Barad's nervous."

Barad, the *Kolos*'s lamp, is always nervous around her, Solet thinks, even when he lets them flash chat during their downtime. Poor kid likes her, and he has zero chance. She keeps her black hair tied up and back. If she liked Barad, she'd grow her bangs long to hide behind them.

Mylla is still on the scrawny side, but carries herself as far larger. Although an obscure regulation would let her wear, as a female, a fustanella, which she would prefer, she nonetheless wears plain blue uniform pants with the white one-button shirt befitting her rank. Solet got his uniformed personnel exempted from wearing the uniform hat—by throwing them all away during their first voyage, then claiming they were lost in the fighting—but she doesn't mind the blue vest, which her own study of the regulations revealed she could cut short and have made of any fabric she wanted. She chose a thick cotton and made a pocket inside for her knife. Trapped in his boots, he envies her sandals, which she despises. They catch on her toe rings.

After her predecessor was devoured, she proved such a quick study with the candlebox that she can identify other lamps by how they flash. He'd be concerned that her expertise would get her transferred to another ship if he didn't know how much the Shield hated girls being aboard in the first place.

"The *Kolos* may be right," Jos says. "That dragon looks rabid."

"Could be injured," Mylla says, "or distressed or diseased."

Solet hates to read, and he hated schooling even more; when did math keep a boy from being incinerated? Fortunately, Mylla loves it, another thing that recommended her to him, and she happily traded her cheap broadsheets full of fanciful tales about dragons for stolid reports about actual ones.

"We might want to give it a wide berth," Jos says. "Or watch it for a bit."

"We can't afford that," Solet says. The dragon jerks and flies a hundred yards south before jerking east again. "Mylla, see if anyone can spot a second dragon. Maybe it's caught the scent of one."

The girl flashes the other two galleys. The *Kolos* responds, then, a moment later, the *Pyg*. "No," Mylla says. "I also told Barad to ask the trackers if they found spoor from more than one dragon, and they said no."

"Good," Solet says.

"Besides, a dragon thinks either food or enemy," Mylla says.

Solet has an idea. "Tell the *Pyg* if the dragon passes without dropping the stag, she should send up some bolts to get its attention." Mylla flashes. "We may have to improvise a bit with this one." That might not be a bad thing. After two successful attacks, then the dry season, the crews may have gotten complacent or bored. *What could happen?* they might be thinking. How many ways could a dragon and a galley fight? If they lost interest, they could lose focus, then real problems would arise.

Solet says, "Oh, and tell them, 'Good luck.'"

Mylla flashes.

Barad responds, "You too, Mylla."

She scowls at Solet. "You're a bad man," Mylla says as he and Jos grin.

By the time the dragon flies over the rocky shore, the crews are prepared: goggles and bandanas on, weapons ready, decks sanded, pails of water and sand at hand. The dragon glides toward them, a hundred yards high, to investigate. Solet stands at the front of the stern deck and says to Jos, "Let's begin."

Jos blows three shrill notes. Mylla flashes. The *Pyg* and the *Kolos* acknowledge. As the *Pyg* backrows, the monoremes row forward, creating a pocket between the ships.

When the dragon reaches the edge of the pocket, the *Pyg* blasts two large packets of pepper into the air. The spicers have charged them well: the packets explode in front of the dragon, and the pepper washes across the beast's face. It chokes and drops, catches itself, and flings the stag, which bounces down the *Pyg*'s deck.

The *Pyg*'s crew comes alive, to Solet's satisfaction.

The dragon swerves down and out of the cloud and straight into a harpoon fired from the *Kolos*. The iron finds the hollow beneath the dragon's left shoulder, and the dragon swerves toward the *Pyg*. The harpoon chain, painted bright red, clatters as it unspools. When the paint changes to white a sailor locks the winch. A harpooner on the *Pyg* buries an iron in its right thigh. Again red chain unspools as the dragon retreats from the pocket, turning the *Kolos*'s bow. The white chain appears, the winch is locked, and the *Pyg*'s deck strains. The galleys backrow at right angles to each other, stretching the dragon between them and too far away for its breath to reach either. Perfect.

The dragon's wings, bigger than sails, gulp huge bowls of air and drag the galleys toward shore. Solet didn't think that was possible. It has to tire soon.

The deck around the winches puckers. The galleys are drawn closer together. Harpooners on each galley fire, landing shots in its left leg and right side, enraging the dragon and holding it more securely. The winches settle. The steersmen lean on their oars and pipe for the galleys to row back and away, which spreads the dragon out again. The galleys are still moving toward shore, though.

Now archers, who aren't sailors doubling as crossbowmen and who can fire more frequently and accurately, move up and shoot at the dragon's eyes. Arrows whisker its snout. The *Pyg*'s pepper pot gives it another whiff.

Mylla winces as the harpoons pull out the dragon's hide, and the creature gags on the pepper. Its roars are horrible. She thinks she hears words, threats promising the worst sort of death. Its head and neck twist wildly. It heaves more furiously and to her horror the bows of the galleys lift a bit and the crews brace themselves. She has to be like Solet, though: However impressive dragons are, and in the old books she's read dragons are spell-weaving, mysterious, and wise, in reality they are just big cows waiting to be slaughtered.

Solet says, "Jos, take us behind it. Mylla, tell our harpooners, on my signal, to pin its wings." *It can't stay up with three galleys on it*, he thinks, *not with three*. Jos pipes and the galley glides around the struggling dragon. Solet raises his fist, and the harpooners raise their firing rods.

When the dragon flings out its wings, he hammers the rail. One iron bursts through the right wing and falls into the water. The dangling chain widens the hole in the membrane with each flap. The second iron catches in the thicker membrane near the dragon's left elbow. Solet orders, "Backrow halftime." The chain unspools. When it turns white, the winch is locked, and the galley pulls the wing back until the dragon can barely stay aloft.

This is almost too easy, Solet thinks. *The shipowners have to be impressed*.

The dragon, desperate for lift, changes tactics and lunges, pulling the *Gamo* and causing the *Pyg* and the *Kolos* to lurch. The *Pyg*'s rowers lose their coordination for a moment, the dragon lunges again, and the chains connecting them slacken considerably. As the *Pyg*'s oars find the water together again, the dragon's head lowers against its chest, its belly heaves, and its head flips up. A huge, yolky gob flies from its mouth and splashes just ahead of the *Pyg*'s bow.

The yolk doesn't splatter. It spreads. Waves sloshing over it burst, and the spray wafts over the harpooners, who frantically rub their hands and faces.

Peering beneath the dragon's wings, Mylla says, "What was that?"

Solet shakes his head. "Vomit?"

"Acid," Jos says. "Same idea, though."

Mulcent says, "Why is it not breathing fire?"

How long he has been standing beside them on the stern deck, still as a piling, Solet doesn't know, but this is no place for him. "To the mast," he says, "or to your cabin."

"We sell phlogiston," Mulcent says. "What use is . . . regurgitation?"

Solet's hand is waving to larboard as Jos maneuvers them directly behind the dragon so they can pull it away from the *Pyg*. He says, "This is hardly—it still has hide and bone."

"The profit is in the phlogiston," Mulcent says. "Hide and bone won't recoup the repair costs you will inevitably incur. Cut it loose."

"It's too late for that," Solet says. "This isn't some gamefish. It's a dragon. It'll swallow you whole if we let it go." The dragon lunges again to make his point, throwing them off balance.

"Cut it loose," Mulcent says, regaining himself, "so we can cut our losses."

"I'm captain of this ship," Solet says. "Mylla, two more harpoons."

"And I own these ships," Mulcent says. "You're just a foreman in fancy pants."

Jos's eyes widen. This is too much for Solet. Before he does anything rash, he shouts down the ladder to two firemen, "Put this man in his cabin. If he tries to leave, put him in a barrel and nail the lid down."

The men scramble up and grab Mulcent, who tries to shake them off. As they pull him down the ladder, he says, "That's the end of the operation. And you."

"Only a fool leaves an Ynessi with nothing to lose," Solet says. This worries Jos even more than Mulcent's comment.

Meanwhile, the dragon turns its head all the way around and peers at Mylla. Its eyes remind her of Solet's when he's up to something.

The dragon's belly heaves again, its head whips around and another gob flies at the *Pyg*. The whip action gives the gob more momentum, it clears the bow and foredeck and breaks on the archers. They're knocked back by its weight, and it spreads over their skin. The *Pyg*'s harpooners dance around the deck to avoid the fumes.

Firemen with pails move in to douse the injured with water, thinking the acid some strange liquid fire, but the water makes their skin boil and spit. Those with shovels scoop up the sand spread on the deck to remove the acid and toss it overboard. The deck is turning black, and all understand if the acid burns through, it'll kill the rowers, then go through the hull and kill the ship.

One shoveler named Blass notices a clump has landed on the powder barrel. It reminds him of a jellyfish stranded on a beach after a tide. He and his sister used to poke them to see if they would move. They never did. Then the clump bubbles and drops through the steel lid.

In the dragon's lee Solet sees a flash make the dragon's wings translucent. He watches shards of wood and metal, bone and Blass, pierce the wings' membranes and rain across the *Gamo*, chased by an immense boom, men's screams, the dragon's roar, the snap of chains, and the groaning of a ship going down by its bow. Somehow above them all he hears a long sharp whistle from the *Kolos*.

Through a rent in the dragon's wing, Mylla sees Barad flash the strangest thing: "He's coming."

3

Bodger, the *Gamo*'s larboard harpooner, reloads. He barely feels the shrapnel embedded in his skin, he's so furious that his first shot went through the wing. After an engagement, the captain, mates, and harpooners discuss every shot, and a miss will cost him part of his monthly. Worse, Gibbery, the starboard harpooner, is offering him smug suggestions for improvement. Gibbery could care less if he hits nor does he care about money, which he gambles away. He loves the hunt, and he'd be just as happy with a shortbow in the woods, waiting for a turkey to waddle by. Bodger doesn't have that luxury. He has family, most too young or too injured to work. He decides he'll shoot the dragon's rump. A cheap shot, but at this point they just have to hold it.

"What is that?" Gibbery says. A thick gray line waves in the sky.

"Another dragon," Bodger says. This one's much smaller than the green, but he bets it will circle around the green and give him a perfect target. He pivots the cannon and readies the firing rod. This prize is all his. And the bonus for taking it.

Mulcent stalks to the porthole, which gives a view of the darkening sea, the dismal shore, and the first glimpses of the southern constellations. The Crow. The Cup. The Water Snake. His brother had known them all. From the time they were boys, all his brother had dreamed about was sailing the world like their grandfather and father. He'd made a list of the cities he would visit, creatures he would see, and tastes and smells he would experience. Mulcent, though, knew the real adventures were in the counting books, plus they offered no chance of drowning the way his brother eventually did.

He puts his goggled eye to the spyhole in the door as an explosion lights up the dragon's wings, then debris shreds them. The *Gamo* jerks back, and Mulcent's nose is mashed against the door. Blood trickles over his top lip. He has to put a stop to this misadventure. He figured Solet's reports underplayed the risks he took, but not by this much.

Sumpt staggers into view, his bottle near empty, debris fluttering around him, pepper getting into his unprotected eyes. Mulcent's guards try to corral him, and Mulcent takes the opportunity to slip out.

"Magnificent!" Sumpt says to the air as Mulcent passes them. "What a creature. I will have its foot for a wastebasket."

Mulcent runs to the foredeck where he sees Bodger bent over his cannon, firing rod in hand. *No more chains*, Mulcent thinks. He rushes the harpooner and grabs his arm.

The harpooner, shorter than him, but solid as an iron, wheels around in confusion, then pushes Mulcent forward. They fall together off the foredeck. Mulcent feels every breath he's ever taken crushed from his body. Over the man's ham of a shoulder he sees a small gray dragon rip past the bow and up the larboard rail. Was someone riding it? This harpooner just saved his life. He should be rewarded in some way. Fortunately Mulcent travels with a sleeve of commemorative coins for just such an occasion.

With the Pyg*'s chains broken by* the explosion, the *Gamo* heaves toward shore, and the green dragon twists between it and the *Kolos*. The *Pyg* emerges from behind the dragon's wing, backrowing and turning sharply in order to drag its shattered bow to shore before the galley goes under.

Mylla flashes Barad, "Who is 'he'?" He doesn't respond with his candlebox. Instead he points behind her.

She turns as the dragon tears over the stern deck. She yells, "Someone's riding it!" It isn't possible. The tales she read often featured people riding dragons, but no one ever had, at least not for long. She would do anything to ride a dragon. She notes the saddle, the packs, the spears, the bearded man in his strange black outfit, the object he drops to the stern deck, before everything speeds up again and the gray heads for the *Pyg*.

"Barad!" Mylla yells, as if the boy could hear her, then flashes, "Look out!"

The gray dragon swathes the *Pyg*'s stern deck with flames. Her captain leaps over the side, nearly incinerated by the time he splashes into the water. Her steersman disappears altogether. Barad leaps to the main deck, but she can't tell if the flames caught him. "No!" she whispers and immediately hopes Solet and Jos didn't hear that.

The *Pyg*'s oarmaster, Kley, unaware of the casualties on the stern deck and not hearing any piping to straighten out the galley, lets the rowers continue turning until the galley's stern is aimed at the *Gamo* and they are headed right for each other. Before Solet can open his mouth, Jos pipes "all stop" as loud as he can, over and over, until both the *Gamo* and the *Pyg* drag oars. The *Pyg* pulls up twenty yards from the *Gamo*'s larboard side.

Solet claps Jos on the back. He doesn't know what he'll say to his sisters, but one of them will have this man. He may not be of the sea, but he certainly owns it.

Through the smoke and confusion Mylla sees flashing from the *Pyg*'s waist: "You all right?" She sighs with relief.

Solet sees the flashing and the sigh. *Well played, Barad.*

One of the *Pyg*'s stern shutters flips up. A face appears: the powder boy. Solet yells, "Kley is captain. And first mate. You're his eyes. Get to shore." The powder boy relays the message to the oarmaster. The *Pyg* pivots and heads inland double-time. *They might actually make it*, Solet thinks, *and I am going to salvage this day.*

"Mylla, flash the *Kolos*. Kill the green. And the rider. I want the gray." Mylla smiles and leans over the rail to flash past the dragon.

With only the *Kolos* pulling, though, the dragon regains some lift, maneuverability, and, worse, heart. It shortens its wings to minimize the effects of the damage they've taken and lunges at the *Kolos*. The chains between them slacken. Its head drops to its chest.

Gibbery pulls Bodger off Mulcent. The harpooner is immediately filled with buyer's remorse. Forget the bonus Mulcent stole from him. Forget his job. He'll be lucky to escape the gibbet for touching an owner. Who will feed his family then?

The gray dragon circles behind the green, heading around the *Kolos*.

"Shoot that little gray," Gibbery whispers to Bodger, "and the owner will forget everything."

"No," Mulcent says. He stands up and adjusts his goggles. "Shoot the rider, and your reward will be even greater. I want that dragon."

Greater? Bodger thinks.

Solet orders, "Backrow, larboard!" Jos pipes. The *Gamo* responds instantly, jerking the dragon. Its gob of acid flies wide right of the *Kolos*, only splattering a few oars and sending up a caustic spray.

A cheer from the other monoreme is cut short when the green sees the gray flying behind her. It loses all sense of itself. It roars and digs through the air toward the gray, dragging the *Gamo* so hard its oars get disordered. The *Kolos* backrows, trying to keep its distance, and its harpooners blast two irons into its belly, but the dragon won't be dissuaded. It lands on the foredeck, crushing the cannons, and crawls down the galley as if it were a bridge, dragging its chains and crushing men and deck with every step.

Solet stamps at the deck of the *Gamo* with his heel and orders again, "Backrow, double-time." Jos pipes. With every step the dragon takes, the *Gamo* is pulled closer to the *Kolos*, which is so low in the water it will act like a ram.

Archers flee to the *Kolos*'s stern deck, and her captain orders them to shoot the rider, but the gray is darting too quickly and the galley is rocking too severely for them to hit it.

The *Gamo*'s aft oars organize themselves and pull. The dragon's foot slips off the side of the *Kolos* and snaps some dangling forward oars, their rowers crushed beneath the smashed deck. Its eyes never leave the gray.

Jos says, "The little one must be in heat."

"We'll cool it down," Solet says. "Bring us wide of the *Kolos*. We'll pull it off her. Mylla, tell the harpooners to kill the dragon. Tell the archers to shoot the rider."

The green grabs onto the *Kolos*'s mast to regain its balance, and a horrible cracking comes from deep within the galley. Her hull has snapped beneath the dragon's weight. Water rushes into the rowers' deck, from beneath, then every side. Dozens of voices cry out in terror and are suddenly silenced.

The dragon tries to escape the sinking ship, but the chains connecting it to the *Kolos* are tangled in wreckage on the deck and it can't get free. It roars in frustration and launches itself over the side, tangling the chains farther on the mast. The galley rolls sidewise. Timbers shatter throughout the ship.

Solet sees Mulcent by the foredeck. He has no idea why he's there or when or how he got there, but it makes his next order all the more painful. "Cut the dragon loose," he says, "before we're pulled under also."

Mylla flashes. The winches are disengaged. Chains unspool and clatter over the side. Mulcent looks at Solet with a miserable smirk and shakes his head.

Freed, the *Gamo* slides into a safer position off the *Kolos*'s starboard beam. Bodger and Gibbery have already undone the chains from their irons. Gibbery fires at the dragon's head, but it moves at the last second, trying to get itself back on deck, and the iron misses. Bodger fires. His iron flies true and catches the dragon in the cheek. Its head collapses on deck. Its wings spread over the water. The *Kolos* settles and somehow stays afloat, now a raft.

Solet says, "Great shot. Mylla, tell the *Kolos* to use the dinghy to bring her survivors to us. Then we'll use it to pick up those in the water. Let's see if they complain now about having to learn to swim. Jos, bring us astern so we can cover them better."

Mylla isn't paying attention, though. She's looking at what the rider dropped onto the stern deck. She holds it up for the others to see: a dragonskin boot.

Jos says, "Looks like one of yours."

Solet sniffs the inside of the boot. "Tuse's," he says. "That's one way to throw down the gauntlet."

Jos says. "He's saving you for last."

Mylla finishes flashing. "Why? Who is it? How did he get the boot?" she asks, and then laughs. "How did he get a *dragon*?"

"No idea," Solet says. "Plenty of people resented Tuse and me jumping up to our commands. Having a dragon would certainly jump him over us, so why bother with all this?" They watch the gray fly in a broad circle. It's becoming more of a ghost with every minute the dusk deepens. "He knows his business: how we're armed, how long our reach is, that we're ready for him. And he didn't cut us from the herd; he used the green to cut the herd away from us."

"So what's he waiting for?" Jos says.

"Night," Solet says. Ah is barely above the horizon and Med is lost again. "Mylla, flash the *Pyg*."

There's no response. She flashes again. Solet reads the concern in her flashing. He doesn't want Barad dead, but if he is, what a song this tragedy will make. Still no response.

"It was a long shot," he tells her. "It might not be dark enough for them to see the flashing at this distance. Jos, as soon as the survivors are on board, get us to shore as fast as possible. I have a plan to deal with the rider there. I will have that gray. In the meantime anchor a buoy and attach it to the dragon so we can dredge it up later and render whatever the crabs don't."

Jos passes Mulcent at the top of the ladder. "Attack the rider," the shipowner says. "I must have that dragon."

Mylla sees the dragon look in Solet's eyes as he takes the oar. "As you indicated, the operation's at an end," he says. "I assumed you were coming to relieve me now that the dragon's been taken. Jos can return us to Hanosh once we've gathered the survivors." He takes off his goggles and bandana.

"Conditions have changed," Mulcent says. "It's a fire-breather."

"We aren't equipped to capture so small a dragon alive," Solet says. "Certainly not one that's being ridden. The risks and costs are unpredictable."

"Forget the risks!" Mulcent says. "Forget the costs!"

Sumpt appears on the ladder. "Did I just hear that?"

"Our arrangement," Solet says, "calls for us to be paid in render or a percentage of its realized value. This dragon would be more useful ridden than as parts or a gland for milking. So where's the profit in my capturing it?"

"We can reorganize our terms later," Mulcent says, "when we have more time."

"Ah, but I am Ynessi," Solet says. "We live for the present. Do you know that the old Ynessi word for 'now' is the same as that for 'forever'?"

No, it's not, Mylla thinks.

"There's paper and ink in your cabin," Solet says. "Let's draw up a new agreement quickly before we're attacked again."

Mulcent shivers with rage, and he leads Sumpt and Solet below.

Mylla is amused. Her cousin has learned to play the Hanoshi game very well. When he was younger, Solet would have simply tossed those men overboard, taken the ship, then claimed the dragon for his own. Of course, he still might, given how the owners have treated him. They haven't learned to play the Ynessi game yet.

4

The trip to shore takes ten minutes and feels like ten hours. Time reasserts itself when a flashing comes from the beach. The *Pyg* made it. Barad made it. Kley has freed his remaining rowers, and hidden them and the surviving crew in the trees. A single archer guards them. Solet has Mylla tell Barad he'll need a dozen men in the surf to unload some cargo quietly.

The wolf pack has been mooring on the beach all week to get fresh water from a nearby stream, hunt small game, and track the dragon, so they know where to land. The partially submerged, partially aflame hulk of the *Pyg* rests nearby.

The gray dragon is nowhere to be seen in the remains of the day. *It can't have left*, Mylla thinks. It must be circling them or watching from a nearby roost. Although Solet often makes the best of a bad lot, this time Mylla can't be as confident as the rest. Unlike most of the crew, she doesn't remove her goggles and bandana.

As soon as the galley grabs sand, two large bundles wrapped in canvas are lowered off the bow into waiting arms, then several more bundles of various sizes, then Jos, who directs the party from the *Pyg*. Sailors and archers slide down after him and pull the *Gamo* farther onto shore. The whole operation lasts five minutes.

Solet retrieves a lantern from his cabin, runs to the bow, and throws one leg over the starboard rail to slide down a line to the beach. He says, "Stay on the *Gamo*, Mylla. Keep the owners in their cabins and the rowers at their benches. And be our eyes."

"What are you going to do?"

"Something stupid." He takes from a pocket a small roll of paper lumpy with a wax seal, and he hands it to her. "Hold on to this for me," he says. "Just in case."

On the beach Solet loads a drop of phlogiston into his lantern's wick. It flames on touching the air and burns brighter and cleaner than any light Mylla has ever seen, illuminating the forty yards of beach between the *Pyg* and the *Gamo*. It gives the beach the warmth of dawn and touches the trees with spring. It shimmers on the galley's wood. Circling the light, Solet seems to glow himself.

Solet calls out to the gray dragon's rider in that voice only a captain has, "You want me. Here I am."

A line of fire erupts thirty yards deep in the forest. Men hidden at the edge leap onto the beach as the trees catch. Mylla sees the dragon cruise above the flames before disappearing down the beach.

Solet turns to watch it. He continues calling, "Here I am. You want me. Here I am."

At the edge of the dragonlight Mylla sees the gray racing back up the beach toward Solet. The Ynessi retreats past the lantern. The gray stretches out its claws. Solet holds out his arms, but when the dragon reaches the lantern, he falls backward. The *Gamo*'s harpoon cannons, planted in the sand at the tree line, fire simultaneously. Their irons spread a cargo net between them that tangles the dragon and rider and sends them crashing to the sand.

Had it not been slowing to snatch Solet, the dragon might have been seriously injured. Had the rider not been strapped to his saddle, he might have been thrown. Instead, the dragon thrashes and rolls while the rider tries to calm it and avoid being crushed. Sailors rush forward with rope and lash different parts of the net together. As the net tightens around the dragon it pulls in its wings and lays still.

Bodger and Gibbery come up to check their work and help Solet to his feet. Relieved he's alive, Solet gives the harpooners immense hugs. The Hanoshi do not hug. Bodger and Gibbery are too impressed with themselves to care.

Mulcent appears. He watched the action from the door of his cabin and slid to shore once it was over. He gives the harpooners a curt nod that says he'll remember their shots when their monthlies are remitted.

Solet turns to the rider, who glares at the toes of his boots, then up at him through the netting. "I don't know what's more shocking," Solet says. "That you're alive, or that you're bearded."

Mulcent says, "Who is he?"

"My former captain."

"It can't be," Mulcent says, peering at him. "He's dead."

"Yes," Solet says. "You have the *Comber* render as proof." Jeryon gives Mulcent a long look at this.

The *Pyg*'s deck collapses and the flames expand. Smoke blots out the stars. Fortunately the fire in the woods is burning inland, thanks to a breeze, and doing so slowly, thanks to a recent storm.

"So how is he here?" Mulcent says.

"A momentary lapse. I'll correct that." Solet raises his finger blade, thinks, and says, "No." He draws a knife from the scabbard inside his boot and holds it out to Mulcent. "You should have the honor."

Mulcent looks at the knife with distaste.

Jeryon says, "Either you're as much of a coward as he is, or you're smart enough to know that you won't be able to ride this dragon without me showing you how."

"How hard could it be?" Solet says. "He did it. It's a horse with wings."

"Horses don't set you on fire if they don't want you on their backs." Jeryon says to Mulcent, "Let me go. Take me on again. I've always been devoted to the company. I'm sure you've calculated the profits of having a dragon rider. I'm your ticket to the Council."

As Mulcent considers the offer, Solet slides between him and the dragon. "This was not our arrangement," he says. "New or old."

"You'll get your bonus," Mulcent says. "You'll all get bonuses. So will the families of those who were lost."

One sailor elbows another, they nod to each other, and they squat over the net. Two others join them in considering how to release Jeryon, but keep the dragon still.

Solet pushes them away and turns on Mulcent. "The gray is mine to ride."

"If you killed the rider," Mulcent says. "You failed."

"I won't let you have it," Solet says.

"It's not yours to let," Mulcent says. "You don't have anything. And don't look to them. They aren't your crew, either. All this is mine."

"You're the bread, Captain," a sailor says, "but he's the butter." After a moment, they slide Jeryon out of the net. One stands him up while the others retie the lashes. Gray squirms her head around to watch.

"First thing you both need to learn about this dragon is," Jeryon says, "nobody owns her. *Comber!*"

He drops as the dragon lashes the sailors with fire. They spring in all directions, crashing into others, setting their clothes and skin alight and scattering them as well.

In the confusion, Jeryon limps toward the tree line. Solet slashes at him with his finger blade, but a flaming sailor gets in his way and gets slashed. Solet gasps as fire spreads to his sleeve. He drops and digs it into the sand. Jeryon vanishes into the woods.

Mulcent is apoplectic. "He's gone!" he says to Solet.

"He'll be back," Solet says, pulling off the remains of his sleeve.

"He won't leave his mount." *Pity we'll be gone by then*, he thinks. *I really should finish him off.*

Solet looks around for someone to bring the dragon aboard the *Gamo*, but they are obviously occupied. Jos, Kley, and the captain of the *Kolos* have triaged the injured and pushed the burning dead into the sea.

Solet shakes his head and squats beside the dragon. A patch of net has burned away, but not enough for the dragon to escape.

Mulcent says, "Are you sure you should get so close?"

Solet says, "I don't think I'm in any danger."

The dragon says, "Eeee!"

Solet shrieks, leaps away, and smiles. He creeps forward again, saying, "Did you hear what Jeryon said?"

"That no one owns her?" Mulcent says. "Nonsense. Everything can be owned."

"No," Solet says. "After that." He straddles the dragon, grabs her neck with his thick fingers, and points her face at Mulcent. "The command. *Comber.*" The dragon enflames Mulcent's chest. Fire splatters up over his cheeks and drips into his crotch. His face starts to melt and his screams evaporate as he draws fire down his throat. He runs across the beach straight at Barad.

The lamp freezes. His eyes are wide open, but not seeing anything. Mulcent's shirtsleeves wick the flames along his arms, which spread as if to grab Barad. His hands drip fire. Mylla charges out of the darkness and bulls her candlebox into Mulcent, knocking him aside.

Barad doesn't see Mulcent stagger past him and, brought to his senses, head for the water. Barad turns to her. His lips pucker. She looks him straight in the eyes as they recall how to focus and says, "No."

Solet and the dragon watch Mulcent collapse into the waves. "We are going to make a great marriage, you and I," Solet says, rubbing its head. "I will call you Thea, after my sister. She is a ferocious woman."

The gray wrenches its neck out of Solet's hands. It sees something huge sliding behind the *Gamo.* It glimmers green in the firelight coming off the *Pyg*. Solet says, "It can't be."

Mylla and Barad hear a splash, a scraping of wood on wood and the rattle of chains as the bulk heaves through the shallows. They swallow their breath and slowly step away from the water.

Bodger and Gibbery bolt for the harpoon cannons.

Another concussion of wood on galley draws Sumpt from his cabin at last. He slams open the door. He coughs, his cheeks bulge, then he staggers to the larboard rail, where he bends deeply and vomits into the eye of the green dragon.

5

The green must have only been stunned by the iron sticking out of its face. Its skin has swollen around it, half-closing one eye. Pus oozes over its snout, dripping off the arrows still stuck there. It's clearly exhausted from paddling to shore with its tattered wings while towing the buoy, its anchor, and an expanse of foredeck from the *Kolos* by the chains still harpooned to it. It gazes at Sumpt with the contempt reserved for clerks presiding over long lines.

Sumpt gapes, attempting to breathe, and vomits again. The dragon grabs the larboard rail with a wing claw to stand in the shallows. The *Gamo* tips alarmingly. Sumpt falls to his knees and hugs the rail. With its free hand the dragon peels him off and carries him onto the beach toward Mylla and Barad. Its eyes are locked on the gray. Barad wants to run, but Mylla grips his wrist. "Don't move," she whispers, "and it won't see us. It's not thinking food or enemy." Barad moves only to slide his hand into hers. A lock of her hair flops free of its binding and drapes her eye. She doesn't dare push it aside.

As the dragon scrapes past them, Sumpt says, "Help me!" Barad bows his head. Mylla shakes hers slowly.

Sumpt looks to Solet, who's abandoned the bucking gray dragon and crawled beside Bodger, Gibbery, and their reloaded cannons. "Shoot it!" Sumpt says. "What are you waiting for?"

The harpooners hold their firing rods to a piece of lit charcoal in the sand and wait for the word. Solet holds up his hand. "Wait," he says. "This operation is about to get infinitely more profitable."

When the harpooners pause, the dragon drops its head to its chest. The men from the *Gamo* scatter. A gob of acid splashes over the cannons. Bodger and Gibbery follow the other men who've decided, despite their officers' orders, to cede the beach to the dragon. Solet crouches behind a tree. Ynessi never cede anything.

The green drops to all fours and slams Sumpt to the beach. There's a horrid snap. Sumpt screams. His head lolls back so he can see Solet. "Shoot me," he sobs.

Solet doesn't move. The gray says, "Eeee!" which captures the other dragon's attention. The green finds its last reserve of strength, lifts Sumpt up to show him to the gray, then chews his head off and lays the body before her.

The gray hisses. *You just can't please some women*, Solet thinks. He slides farther into the woods to give them some privacy. A stick pops behind him. He checks whether the fire is getting closer. It's dying out instead.

Almost tenderly the green bites apart the net around the gray and pulls it off. Half freed, the gray rolls onto her belly, breathing heavily. The green pins her with a hand between her shoulders. With his other he rips away the rest of the net and lifts her tail.

Mylla releases Barad's hand. The gray is small beneath the thrusting, snorting green. Mylla looks to see if Solet's out of harm's way. It takes her a moment to make him out in the woods, then to make out the leaves moving deliberately behind him. She says, "Come on!" and pulls Barad's sleeve. They circle far around the dragon to reach her cousin. In her other hand a small, thin knife appears.

Bodger stops to watch the green from the woods. He says, "We should go back to help. One more shot should do it."

"Help who?" Gibbery says, "Solet? The Shield? I think it's time we took a break from the sea. Let me show you the ways of the woods. I'll start you off with simple snares. Soon you'll be able to feed your whole family." They pick their way around the fire and into the night.

With the green distracted, the Gamo pushes out her oars. The ship digs its blades into the shallows and heaves itself off the beach. Solet is incredulous, the rowers are commanding themselves, and he doesn't hear the leaves whisper behind him. A rock slams down on his head. His knees fold.

A voice says, "You don't deserve to get off so easy."

The rock falls again. Solet falls onto his side. He waves feebly with his finger blade. Another blow goes through his temple and lets the tide into his head. It fills him up and rushes over him.

Solet remembers something his uncle told him when he was a boy. They were watching a huge storm blow in. Solet said he felt bad for the fish. His uncle said the fish didn't care. They wouldn't even know there was a storm. They were safe underwater. That night he dreamed of being a fish, swimming around safe from those above. He swims again now, letting the tide take him farther from shore, plunging ever deeper.

Jeryon caves in Solet's skull with one last blow to make sure he's dead and leaves the rock amid the gore. He shakes the splatter off his hands and arms, face and neck, as the green backs away from Gray, its business quickly done. It rolls onto its side and throws its head back, offering her its neck. Gray leaps on it, tearing and gnashing until tooth grates through bone and the green's head rolls aside.

Then Gray moves to its belly and feasts on its innards. She ignores Sumpt's corpse.

Something settles into the brush off to his side. A branch bends. The leaves behind him whisper. Jeryon rolls aside so only his forearm is slashed by the knife coming at him from the shadows. He pulls himself around a tree. The knife lunges at his knees, but his dragonskin pants stop the blade. Using the tree as both shield and crutch, he stands, but the knife slashes his fingers and a wood and metal box slams his head. He falls on his back. The knife darts at his throat, and he catches the hand bearing it just as it pricks the skin.

A girl straddles him, her eyes as thin and sharp as her blade. He grabs her wrist. She puts her other hand behind her knife and leans on it. He brings up his other hand to hold her off.

The box, a black shadow, hovers above her, but the boy holding it either can't get a clear shot at his face or is ambivalent about smashing someone while he's looking at him. If he rolls the girl and gets on top of her, he'll get the box in the head again.

As the knife inches toward his eye, he realizes he's seen it before. It's a flat fingernail knife with a bone handle. He doesn't want to do this, she's just a girl, he's just a boy, but he has to. He whistles.

Mylla's weight slackens. She knows that tune. It gathers the crew. Why would he whistle it now? She hears a scraping on the sand, then through the underbrush.

Barad takes a step backward and adopts a defensive stance. The gray dragon's head rises over him, and its mouth opens. He quavers, but doesn't break.

Mylla jumps off the man and says, "Call it off! Call it off!"

The man stands and touches the boy on the shoulder without taking his eyes off the girl's knife. The dragon sits and looks at him. The man whispers, "Move away slowly. There you go. Stand beside the girl." He says to her, "I didn't come for you."

Mylla screams at him, "You killed Solet!"

He says, "He killed me a long time ago."

She screams again, "You killed him!" He starts to protest again when her eyes flick toward the beach. He sees this and smiles. He knows what she is doing: letting the others know where he is.

"Clever girl," he says and leaps at her. He grabs her knife hand, spins her around to pin her to his chest and drags her, kicking and screaming, to the gray. He climbs into the saddle and sits her before him.

"They'll put an arrow through me to get to you," she says.

He's unconcerned. "Don't move," he says, "or you'll slide off the saddle and tear open your crotch on her spines. Don't you move either," he says to Barad, "or I'll slide her off the saddle myself."

Barad stops advancing. Mylla stops struggling. As the rider takes her knife, Barad flashes her, "I'll find you."

She says, "I know."

The rider takes the dragon's reins, kicks her flanks, and turns her onto the beach.

Two archers are moving into a position to shoot, directed by some officers armed with discarded bows. He pressures the dragon with his knees and pulls the reins again, and the dragon lifts off. The rider jerks the reins so she veers this way and that. The girl pushes into him and grabs his arms so she doesn't fall. Bits of gore unstick themselves from the dragon's head and spit into their faces. Jeryon easily avoids the arrows shot at them and heads out to sea.

This is not how she imagined her first time riding a dragon. The strange man holds her like a crate waiting to be stacked. He stinks of fish and earth. His beard scratches her skin. His breath is too hot and quick. And she's not in control. Every time the dragon's wings are buffeted, he tightens his grip and she shrinks a bit.

Once she's convinced he's not planning to throw her off the dragon, she asks, "Where are you taking me?"

The rider says nothing.

"Who are you? You're Hanoshi. I heard it in your voice."

The rider starts to say something and stops.

She can't enjoy the view because there isn't much of one, despite Med rising. So she memorizes how he controls the dragon, feeling when his legs tense, watching how he works the reins, and leaning herself when he uses his weight.

A few minutes later she spots the *Gamo*'s wake, milky in the moonlight, and dives. Mylla's scream is clenched by her throat. She tries to grab the reins, but her brain no longer speaks to her arms. As they approach the stern deck, the rider yells, *"Comber!"* and the dragon scours the galley with flame from the steering oar to the foredeck. The rider brings the dragon around twice, setting the shutters on both sides of the rowers' deck alight. The oars collapse like the legs of a man whose neck has been snapped. With the rowers shackled to their benches and the oarmaster and his team trapped below, there's no one to put the fires out. The rider spirals the dragon up to watch the ship become fully engulfed, collapse in on itself, and sink, leaving only a tower of smoke quickly dissipating into the night.

Mylla can't imagine a worse death, and she saw Sumpt die. As the rider returns west, Mylla says, "Why are you doing this?"

The rider says something she can't make out, the wind is so loud.

Nearing the beach where the *Pyg* has burned nearly to the waterline, she says again, "Why are you doing this?"

He says in her ear, "You remind me of someone I know. Can you swim?"

"Of course. I'm Ynessi. Wait!"

The dragon dives again. They skim the water toward the beach. She tries to take control of the dragon. She clings to the dragon with her legs, leans over, and braves the spikes to hold its neck. The dragon slows. First he grabs her goggles, but they come off in his hand and slide over his wrist. Then he grabs her by the back of her pants and slides her half off.

"Don't go to Hanosh," he says.

Turning sharply finishes the job. She skips off the water, flips, half loses her pants, and splashes to a stop.

The officers and archers weren't expecting the dragon to return and so they had gathered in a tight clump in the light to discuss what to do. The dragon blasts them, and they decide to run around burning and screaming.

I don't care, Mylla thinks, I'd rather sink than call Barad for help. She doesn't have to. He sees her, throws off his candlebox, and swims out. He's huffing so hard by the time he reaches her, though, that she has to save him. They collapse in the shallows to avoid being seen. She pulls up her pants, rakes her soggy hair off her face, then rakes his off his face and says, "We have to find him. The dragon rider. We'll go to Hanosh. Are you with me?"

He nods. She had him at "we."

"First, though, we'll go to Yness," she says, "to get Solet's brothers."

Jos, wreathed in flames, runs by and flings himself into the surf. A cloud of steam stinking of burned hair wafts over them.

"And his sister Thea," Mylla says.

6

Midafternoon the next day Jeryon spots the island. The weather's lousy, dank and misty, the sun a mere suggestion. Jeryon's new goggles keep fogging.

The previous night, after flying a mile toward Hanosh, Gray tugged for home, and he gave her his head and they flew down the coast. Hanosh could wait a few more days. After spending the night a few hours south of Solet's beach, Jeryon longs for his lumpy bamboo bed a wall away from the poth.

A week hasn't passed, but it feels much longer as the magnitude of what he's done bleeds through his exhaustion. So many dead. That wasn't the plan. What can he possibly tell her? He doesn't lie. He could argue they worked for the Shield and his former mates, but they weren't soldiers, nor is he. He can't understand how he enjoyed watching Tuse suffer. He can't fathom how he crushed Solet's skull. He tries hard not to admit it thrilled him. Instead he feels released.

He doesn't need Hanosh anymore. Why risk all by going there? What more could he do? He doesn't have to finish the job. He's already cost the company four ships. The reasons why will come out, and the other companies will make sure the Shield suffers further. Livion won't escape. That he can count on.

He only needs a boat. He could buy one outside Yness and tow it to the island. He and the poth could then ride it into the sunrise. He could talk her out of going to Ayden by saying they'd take the dragon. In the Dawn Lands, she'd never find out for sure what's happened.

Jeryon soars over the island to make a more dramatic descent to the cabin and notices a galley on the flats where the poth washed up. At first he thinks it's a pirate ship, then he sees the burned mast and the scorched remnants of deck and knows it's the *Hopper*. He doesn't want to be spotted by the men lounging on the galley and the beach, so he pulls the dragon up until the mist obscures the galley and races for the Crown along the treetops.

If they've done anything to the poth, he doesn't want them to know he's there. His vengeance would be swift. His remorse disintegrates. Having killed before makes it surprisingly easy to consider afterward.

When Gray lands, she becomes very agitated, as if looking for something. He takes two spears and dismounts then stays behind her for cover as she rushes from spire to spire. Men from the *Hopper* may be waiting. He'd prefer that to another dragon.

At the spire where Jeryon and Everlyn found Gray's egg, she curls around it, groaning. He wonders if she's hurt, and she's come here because instinctually it's the place she feels most safe. She rolls on her belly then pushes herself up into a crouch, bent nearly double. Her stomach heaves. Having seen what the green dragon did in a similar posture, Jeryon flees around a spire behind her where he couldn't be drenched with acid. She squeals and her tail whips up. She squeals again as if in pain. Jeryon peeks around the spire and sees the first egg slide onto the bare rock. Another follows and a third, a tiny cairn mortared with strands of gray mucus.

Her head snaps around. She gives him a ferocious look. He ducks behind the spire, presses his back to it, and tucks his spears against his chest. He doesn't have a command, he realizes, that means *Don't eat me*. When he peeks around the other side of the spire, she's putting the eggs in the hole where hers was. *Amazing*, he thinks. He'll keep them apart when they're hatched. They could create an armada.

Gray curls around the spire again and falls asleep. He takes a step toward her to see if she's all right. One eye opens, red-rimmed and slitted. She's all right enough, he decides, and hurries down the steps to find the poth.

Insects swarm the first body a few hundred yards from the dragon corpse. It's a rower from the looks of his shoulders and the number of scars and tattoos on his body beneath the devouring beetles. There's a sword wound in the center of his back.

At the shega meadow, he finds his tree ravaged, the fruit torn off, and many branches broken.

At the stream overlook he finds another rower's body, this one with several sword wounds, a few to the hands and one, the decisive one, to the throat. Jeryon looks at the beach. No one is moving. Can they be asleep? Then he notices the crabs on some of the bodies and more exiting the rowers' deck.

Footprints clutter the trail to the cabin, so he forces himself to take a roundabout route. His leg is stiff and sore from tumbling with Gray, then riding, and a sharp pain cuts from his knees to his hip. He pushes through, using his spears as walking sticks, growing more worried with each agonizing step as he imagines what a boatload of fired-up prisoners would do to a helpless woman.

He comes across a body half-decapitated. Was she lying in wait for them? How did she get around so quickly? Or was this someone else's work?

He can hear the cabin before he can smell it. It's a chittering hive of beetles, insects, and blue crabs. The latter pour through the front door, carrying out pieces of flesh and cloth, which they devour on the porch and beneath the cabin. Jeryon can't get close and he has no desire to clear it out, so he climbs a tree and looks through the window.

Corpses are sitting up, shoulder-to-shoulder, along the walls and back-to-back in the center of the common room. One holds his own head in his hands. Jeryon moves to other trees to look in other windows. There's blood on the poth's bed, which has been moved across the room. The door to her room has been knocked down as has his. His tools have been knocked from the walls and some are impaled in the bodies. He doesn't see her.

He also doesn't see the crates of food, the water barrels, or her sword. She must be alive, perhaps hiding until the danger has passed. He counts the bodies in the cabin and tries to remember how many were on the beach. There couldn't be many left. Then again, how many could she have killed? She could fight one if she took him by surprise, but she couldn't have slaughtered as many as are in the cabin, certainly not if they were together, nor could she have arrayed them the way they are. What purpose did that serve anyway?

He wants to scream, "Where are you? What happened?," when he sees parallel tracks in front of the cabin. Something was dragged, he thinks, but the gouges are too thin and deep to have been heels. He follows the tracks downstream to the flats.

The smell reaches him long before he comes through the trees. They ignore him as he inspects their bounty of sailors and rowers. It's difficult to tell, but all have some sort of wounds: gashes, broken bones, smashed faces. A few have bolts in them. Others were stabbed with what must have been harpoons. At least one was strangled. Did they turn on one another and destroy themselves? If not, where's the faction that did this?

Jeryon checks the galley's transom, sweeping white crabs out of his path with his spears: the dinghy is gone. The tracks end at the tide line. Could she have managed to drag something all the way from her cabin with her injuries? Did she get off the island? Was she taken against her will along with their supplies?

Jeryon can't decide whom he's more furious at: her for not leaving him any sign of where she's gone or himself for letting the *Hopper* go.

He impales several crabs on a spear and runs as best he can to the Crown. He needs the dragon to search the island, but Gray is still unwilling to be approached. She grudgingly accepts the crabs.

Jeryon barely sleeps that night, pacing the expanse of rock and peering across the island for any sign of her or the *Hopper*'s crew. By morning he's worked himself into a lather.

Gray is back to normal. Perhaps she's already forgotten her eggs. She doesn't glance at them and comes at Jeryon's whistle. They search the island in a crisscross pattern. They see nothing except blue crabs that don't realize they're missing an unprecedented feast at the cabin and on the beach.

Jeryon and Gray circle the island in an ever-widening gyre and find the sea as empty. If she had gotten off the island after the *Hopper* arrived, she might already be in the League. Could she sail, though? Could she navigate? Would he have seen her on the way to the island, or did he overlook her in the lousy weather? Is she lost right now?

He can't search the ocean, but he can go to the one place where he knows she would look for him eventually. He'll find her and bring her back to take care of Gray's eggs. In the meantime, he'll deal with

Livion and the owners. No more loose ends. No more counting on others to make things go his way. He brings his boats in on time.

Jeryon tends to Gray's wounds then brings her to the beach so she can fill up on crab before the trip to Hanosh. Disturbingly, she prefers to feed on the corpses.

CHAPTER EIGHT

The Junior

1

Atop the Quiet Tower in Hanosh, a guard named Isco hears a scuffing behind him, then a voice call out, "Who's there?"

Isco can't make out whom it is. The moons have withered to new, the wind off the bay has put out the torches again, and firelight from the city won't bleed past the crenellations. He raises his crossbow and says, "Stand, and show yourself."

The voice says, "Long live the Guard!" Someone not a guard giggles.

"Bern?" Isco says.

"Who else?" Another guard comes forward.

"Indeed," Isco says, "who else?" He waves his crossbow toward the door. The faintest of shadows moves. "You come most carefully," Isco says.

"Bern," the shadow says with a girl's voice. "You said there wouldn't be—"

"Isco," Bern says, "the clock's struck twelve. Go to bed."

Isco lowers his crossbow. "With pleasure. It's bitter cold, and I am sick at heart."

"Aw," the shadow says. "He's a poet."

Bern hushes her. "Have you had a quiet guard?" he says.

"Not a mouse stirring," Isco says. "And if you wish the mice to stay quiet . . ."

"There's a bottle of warm behind my bunk," Bern says. "That should salve your heart."

Isco salutes Bern, then the shadow, which giggles again. Relieved, he goes downstairs.

After the door clicks shut, the shadow pads to Bern and resolves into a maid still wearing her knee-length black chiton. Her bare arms shiver, and she slips beneath his.

"Where's my bottle of warm?" she says.

"I thought I was," Bern says. She hits his chest. He hands her a flask. "Now let me salve you," Bern says. He puts his other arm around her.

She hugs him and pulls away. "You promised to show me something exciting first."

He takes her hand and leads her to the southwest curve of the tower. The Quiet Tower squats at the end of the West Wall, which slopes downhill protecting the homes of deputies and juniors, functionaries and factotums, that is, the Greater and Lesser Silk, until naked cliffs make it unnecessary.

"There's my dorm," she says. The servants' quarter lies below the tower, eventually bleeding into the warehouses, rope houses, closed houses, taverns, and casinos of the Harbor.

"Not down there," Bern says and points west across the cliffs. "There. A shadow climbing, maybe flying."

"I don't see anything," she says. "It's too dark. Have you been putting me on?"

"There was more moon the other night. I heard a strange whooshing too when the shadow came close."

The maid shivers again. "I can't hear anything either," she says. "The wind is too loud." She takes a pull on the bottle and wraps her arms around her chest. "Do you really stand here all night long? By yourself?"

"Yes," he says. "When war comes, I may be the first to know. This is probably where I'll fight too." He pulls on her arms to unwrap her. "We shouldn't waste our last doomed hours."

She twists aside. She wanted to see something wondrous, not think about war. She lifts the bottle then changes her mind. "Can we go inside? Maybe I should go."

Bern says, "Wait. Did you hear that?"

"Now you're just trying to make me stay."

"No," Bern says. "Look, here it comes again." He gets behind her to guide her gaze. A shadow rushes at them.

"I hear it now," she says, "the whooshing." She laughs and presses against him. "You said it was bigger."

The shadow closes. The stars atop the bay are blotted out. Then maid and guard are whooshing upward, claws digging beneath their collarbones. She screams and Bern blows his horn, but they're too far above the city already for anyone to hear.

2

On a small bench beside his front door, Livion sits in his stocking feet while his partner, Tristaban, dresses down their servant girl for leaving a spot of mud on the toe of his dragonskin boots. He can't see it, but he trusts it's there. Nonetheless, he wishes he could save the girl. He knows what it's like to be dressed down in front of another, that's the life of a sailor, and it only got worse as a mate. He didn't grow up in a world of glossy boots and girls who shined them, though, so he leaves the issue to Tristaban and considers the hall tiles.

When did it stop feeling strange to spend his days on unmoving stone?

Tristaban looks like she's conducting musicians, the way she's moving her finger around. It's not like the boots aren't going to get filthy once he gets to the Harbor. He'd rather wear sandals, which are less conspicuous and comfortable. And boots, like the Aydeni who favor them, have gone out of fashion. But "Trist insists." If he wants to solidify his new position in the Shield, he has to remind people constantly how he became a Hero of Hanosh and why her father let them be partnered.

She wasn't so conscientious when they were seeing each other behind her father's back: meeting in artisan taverns where no one would recognize them, finding quiet places alone beyond the walls, even taking a room for a week in Hanoshi Town and playing at living together as if they were common laborers or farmers come to sell their crop. She was coy, adventurous, and lively. Now she is . . . pretty. When she smiles. Thanks to her father, Chelson, he lives far more comfortably than he would have in the stern cabin he pictured for himself as a boy. He does love her. And he can't shake from his memory the looks she used to give him right under her father's nose, even as she orders their girl to wipe his boots again and dismisses her.

Tristaban takes a deep breath and settles back into herself. She brushes the shoulders of his white silk shirt, the latest trend among shipowners. She says, "I hate to trouble you with household affairs. Say hello to my father at Council." She pecks his forehead. Her neck smells like vanilla. It's his favorite scent. And if her neck smells like strawberries tomorrow, that will be his favorite scent.

She goes around the corner toward her chamber. A moment later the girl appears. She silently pushes his boots on. She reminds him of a doll, her cheeks as hard as ceramic, her eyes as cold. She can't be more than twelve.

Livion stands up and turns each boot in the dawnlight coming through the small window beside the door. "Good," he says. "Here, between you and me." He holds up a penny then sets it on the bench.

"I cannot," she says and hurries away. Did she rebuff his guilt? Or, how stupid is he, a perceived advance? Livion shakes his head. He pockets the penny—today's penny is tomorrow's coin, his father-in-law says—and steps outside.

His small whitewashed stucco home is on a skinny lane, Brimurray, just above the servants' district, and halfway up the Hill. It's a respectable height for one of his position, and the sundeck abutting its blue tile roof adds a rare distinction. Nonetheless, Trist has her eye on a house a few lanes higher, one big enough for children. Or live-in servants.

Brimurray leads to a larger, guarded boulevard that connects to one of the switchbacking streets between the weathered Harbor and the blinding white mansions of the Crest at the top of the Hill. The streets are already streaming with barrows and carts bringing goods from the early galleys to the Upper City beyond the Crest, and with people flowing down to offices and jobs in the Harbor. Most are dressed in drab cotton and leather, and he remains surprised when someone darts out of his way. Trist says they dart out of respect—he's a Hero of Hanosh—but he can't believe he's recognized even when people do point him out to their children.

At a switchback he stops at a grill cart to buy an okono, a pancake rolled around pork, cabbage, and a brown sauce. The vendor is Aydeni, a rarity in the city nowadays, and he wouldn't say it out loud, but Livion prefers that city's version of okono to the Hanoshi, which has crab instead of pork. He hates crab. The vendor keeps his secret with a rough finger pressed to his nose, and for that Livion puts an extra penny in his tray.

Livion would make small talk if a voice in his head didn't tell him the man was probably a spy. He should avoid the vendor altogether. But his okono is so good.

Instead, he looks at the galleys docked at Hanosh's three piers. He doesn't see any of Solet's ships, which were due this morning, nor has Tuse's arrived with its cargo of sulfur from the Dawn Lands. It's several days late. This isn't unusual, but he will have to excuse it to Chelson. He calls tardiness a theft of hours. The additional time away from Mulcent and Sumpt should assuage him somewhat.

A towering man blocks his view, his arms like tree trunks, his eyes cold steel, his shock of hair a fiery red. It's not his size that alarms Livion. It's his presence. The trade rider is a day early and obviously looking for him.

"Omer," Livion says, pulling the paper wrapper over his okono. "Let's go down to my office."

Omer grunts, and Livion lets himself be pulled along by the large man's wake.

Decades earlier the Shield built a block of warehouses near the docks, whose stone-walled lower floors, towers, and central courtyard saw it dubbed the Castle. Livion is officed atop the warehouse beside the main gate so he can keep an eye on the movement of goods from one window and the movement of galleys from his other. He precedes Omer into his office, overturning memos, charts, and manifests. Trade riders traffic information. Although Omer's under contract to the Shield for a few more years, there's no reason to reveal something Omer might sell later. Or on the side today. The gibbets that others earn by selling commercial secrets don't deter the Omers of the world.

Omer smirks at Livion's precautions. Even he could fit through one of those windows at night. He nods to a harpoon mounted on the wall with a brass plate of appreciation from the City Council. "That the one?"

"One of them," Livion says, sitting behind his desk. "Solet got the kill shot. Why the rush to see me?"

"Ever hear of Wheaton?" Omer says. "No? Nothing little town a ways off the coastal road to Yness. Doesn't even grow wheat. Last night I found a drunk outside its tavern. He wanted to earn some pennies to get back in and offered me the story of three ships, two dragons, and one dramatic escape."

Livion gestures toward his couch. "Have a seat."

Omer glances at it and remains standing. "He was a rower on your *Pyg*. His bench was a poor vantage point, so some of the details he got secondhand. I'll spare you the belching, confusion, and minor inconsistencies, and summarize."

Livion leans forward, trying not to look concerned, and opens his hand to indicate *Proceed*.

"Several days ago your wolf pack attacked an immense green dragon. The *Pyg* was seriously damaged when her deck was bathed in acid and her powder barrel exploded. The *Pyg* disengaged, then a second, smaller dragon came out of nowhere and fired their stern deck. They lost all their officers except their oarmaster, who got them, barely, to shore."

"The oarmaster released the rowers?"

"Yes," Omer says. "The galley was half-sunk. As you might expect, several took this opportunity to shorten their contracts and scamped into the woods. The drunk struggled up a high, steep slope in the dark. At the top he could see that another one of your galleys, he didn't know the name, had landed nearby. Then a line of fire erupted in the woods, and the little dragon—"

"What color?"

"Dark gray," Omer says, a bit annoyed. "The gray flew at one of the men. He seemed to invite this. He'd put out a lantern with a beautiful light as if to attract the dragon. It was brighter than the flames already engulfing the *Pyg*. A harpoon cannon fired, and the dragon went down. Men ran from the woods, swarmed it, and apparently netted it. It was tough to see details from that height."

"Solet captured a dragon?" Livion says.

"Momentarily," Omer says. "The dragon blasted everyone standing around it, and they scattered. Then the green reappeared, badly injured. It swam—"

"Swam?"

"Did I stutter?" Omer says. "It crawled onto the beach, which sent the first man flying to the woods. It attacked the little dragon, which somehow got the better of it. Or maybe the green just died from its earlier injuries. The gray bit its head off then ate its guts. At this point, our drunk left before the gray could look for more prey."

And that explains why Solet hasn't arrived. The third ship must have been lost at sea, but what happened to the second? Did the dragon destroy it after the drunk left? A predatory dragon is bad enough. One that sinks ships and kills larger dragons is an unprecedented threat. One that kills shipowners exceeds catastrophe. On top of that, the Shield has two galleys about to head to Yness. Other companies have their own. He has to tell his superiors. They have to tell the Council.

He wishes he had more evidence. His superiors aren't likely to accept hearsay from a trade rider. "Where's the drunk now?" Livion says. "I'd like to question him myself and find out exactly where all this took place."

"That will be difficult," Omer says. "I only stopped there because I recognized him as Chalfin, the man who robbed and raped my sister. I figured I'd get his story before I gave him a more fitting punishment than a bench. I rode for Hanosh immediately afterward."

And away from any law in Wheaton. "That was unfortunate. Nevertheless, I'll see that your monthly has a perk for your efforts."

"I could be dead by the end of the month," Omer says, "the roads the way they are these days, Aydeni bandits everywhere."

Livion groans inside. He writes a chit and says, "Give this to Gran. She'll advance the perk."

Omer takes it, considers the number the way he did the couch, and returns it. Livion adds the monthly to it and says, "For your discretion." Omer, grudgingly satisfied, leaves.

There's one thing Livion can check. He takes up his pipe and blows a little tune.

A young man appears in the door. Livion says, "Felic, get me the bench roster for the *Pyg*." A moment later he reappears with several sheets of paper. He hands them over, head bowed, and leaves.

Livion's glad Felic's head is bowed less than it used to be. Like scores of plague children, a black crust covers half his face like a mask, and he lost many family members, in his case, his two sisters. Livion often wonders how many wouldn't have caught the flox had Solet not persuaded him to render the dragon, so he's found homes and places for as many of the plague children as he can, including Felic. Many think he's an even greater hero for this than for what got him the boots: saving the medicine and, by staving off the plague, saving Hanosh from declaring war on Ayden at the time.

Livion scans the list. There: Chalfin. They'd bought only the first six months of his sentence, the usual probationary period for a small or weak man who might not make it on the benches. Another write-off.

Would this be enough? Maybe he jumped ship while the galleys were on shore getting water and wanted a story to sell for drinks. He couldn't let his superiors go to Council, though, without knowing about the rumor.

Livion heads to the Round Dragon, the coffeehouse where the real business of the Shield is done. It's off a small square that's become called, naturally, the Round Square. There, itinerant traders hawk their wares, the financially embarrassed hawk their household goods, and indigents hawk oddments they've scavenged. The latter always present a container into which potential shoppers can throw pennies as down payments on future purchases. Charity is illegal, but commerce is law.

As Livion pushes through the square, one of the indigents calls to him, "Captain! My captain!" He wears black leather pants beneath a ratty black shift tied at the waist with a flaxen cord, old sandals repaired with similar cord, and a poorly tended black beard. Before him on a folded square of sailcloth are several huge blue shells, possibly from crabs. Livion's never seen anything like them. They could have value as decorative goods or maybe platters, but he doesn't have time to ask where they came from.

The man calls after him, "Can you help an old sailor, Captain?" Livion keeps going. There aren't enough berths in the world to help every old sailor.

3

Almond, owner of the Round, ushers Livion through a wide, low-ceilinged hall choked with smoke, chatter, and petty traders, past a curtain and down a corridor to a private room. His father-in-law, Chelson, stands amid several other Shield owners. All have hard eyes, harder cheeks, and the barest hint of lip. There are no seats. Sitting prolongs meetings.

"You've anticipated our call," Chelson says. "Almond." Chelson jabs at the urn on the sideboard. The owner pours Livion a bowl of pit roast, serves it on a matching dish, and leaves with the elevated dignity of one who's been forced to perform a service below his presumed station.

Chelson says, "We've had news from Herse regarding our wolf pack."

"I've had news myself," Livion says, "from one of our trade riders."

Chelson opens his hand. Livion relates what Omer told him. All but Chelson exchange glances when he mentions the second dragon.

Chelson says, "The general says the wolf pack was destroyed by Aydeni ships."

Livion knows what a party line sounds like. The conversation was over before he arrived. Nevertheless, he says, "Our rider's source was on the *Pyg*. I confirmed it."

"Your rider's source," Chelson says, "was a wretch. Now dead."

"He was very specific regarding dragons."

"He saw fire. He heard explosions," Chelson says. "The damage to the wrecks bears that out."

"They've been found?"

"Yes," Chelson says. "A dragon's corpse was not, however. Only evidence of how our officers were treated by the Aydeni. Burned alive, the general said."

"That would mean war," Livion says. "A disaster for trade. For us. And," he adds, "the city."

"Trade knows no disaster," Chelson says. "Only opportunities."

This brings to mind another of Chelson's axioms: "When one wave falls, another must rise."

"The general will report at Council today," Chelson says. "We can't have any wild talk about dragons. As for the city, if there's a war, we would rebuild it."

Livion tallies the construction interests the Shield has assembled the past few years, the raw materials and weapons it's stockpiled, the forests and quarries it's acquired, all in anticipation of a war with Ayden. The markups will be enormous. As will the destruction.

"You look conflicted," Chelson says. "I'm surprised. You've taken the long view before. It's why you're sitting here." Chelson puts his hand on Livion's arm. "I'm sure we can continue to count on you."

Could the rider have been wrong? Livion thinks. If he contradicts the Shield at Council, his career would be over. He would lose Trist. And, if he's wrong, he might leave Hanosh unprepared for an Aydeni attack.

Chelson notices Livion's bowl. "You've barely touched your coffee. It is bitter today. Here." He takes a tiny silver box from his pocket. The spoonful of sugar inside probably cost three of Livion's monthlies. Chelson rubs a pinch into his bowl. "This will make it more palatable."

Livion says, "An Aydeni attack would explain why Tuse's ship hasn't arrived either. It passed through the same area. It might have also been sunk."

Chelson grunts and the owners respond in kind.

As Livion sips his coffee, trying not to scald his tongue, something occurs to him. "What if the other survivors spread the dragon story?"

"The general assures us there are no other survivors."

Herse is playing a friendly game of hip ball against two brothers in a wide Upper City alley. People cheer them from doorways at either end of the alley, and the windows above. They admire the general's ability to lose without seeming to.

His adjutant, Rego, argued that he didn't have time before Council, but Herse can't help himself. Who knows whom he'll inspire? Who knows whom he'll discover? Hip ball gave him his start. It took him from alleys lower than this one to the captaincy of a company team and several League championships. There, in fact, painted on the wall is a faded advert in which a much younger Herse touts Sea Circle olive oil with the slogan WINNERS STAND ALONE. He won't fade himself, though, and pick-up games keep him popular. Besides, by playing he'll distract people from seeing Rego and several soldiers enter a nearby lodging house. They have to deal with a situation.

Herse sends a lob to the older boy, who's playing back. Given the boy's stance, Herse readies himself for a lob in return, but the boy closes his hips and passes the ball to his brother, playing up. Herse, now out of position, says, "Ah!" and leaps to where the up man should send the ball. The younger boy can't handle the pass, though, and costs them the point. The older boy gags in frustration. His brother scowls and sags.

Herse picks up the ball and gathers the boys to him. He says, "That was an excellent pass. You fooled me completely, but you fooled your brother too. Keep an eye on him to make sure he knows what you're doing. And, you, you were playing me well, your position was good, but you have to play with your brother too. Angle your hips toward him to stay ready for a pass. Good?" The boys nod. "Let's call this match point," Herse says. They run to their positions, and he serves another lob.

The older brother crouches, smacks the ball on the short hop, and sends his brother another nice pass. The younger boy turns on it like an oar in its thole. Herse was ready for the return, and the ball still skips off the wall past him. "There it is!" he says. "Work together. Win together." The boys bump their left hips, then right, and the crowd applauds. Of course a few smirk, thinking Herse a grandstander with no business inside the walls, but that's better than jeering or throwing fish.

Herse uses the break to spot Rego looking at him from next to a window across the square outside the alley. Herse nods, Rego points at a door, and the soldiers break it down. The crack is drowned out by the crowd's sudden "oooh!" and laughter.

Herse turns to find a new challenger, a woman nearly his age with hips as formidable as her eyes. She wears a worn tunic carefully repaired and soft leather pants that have been severely brushed. His mother treated her clothes the same way, having nothing else to keep nice. He learned early to sew with a fishbone needle to keep her from crying when he tore holes in his own threadbare outfits. Herse shrugs his shoulders to shift his black sash of rank. It makes him feel like a dandy.

He bows to the woman in a pre-League way, then turns this into a greater sign of respect: a deep stretch to open up his hips and hamstrings.

The woman transforms the curtsey her grandmother might have performed into a long, slow lunge. She doesn't bow her head, though.

They stand. "To five?" she says. The crowd vibrates like a plucked string.

He considers how much time Rego will need. It can't be much. Although the situation is a military matter, Herse's jurisdiction ends at the city gate. Everything inside the walls is under Ject, the city guard's general. He and Herse don't get along as it is, the popinjay, and he would certainly want to take charge, take credit, and take the spoils.

"To nine," Herse says. "That red cobble can be our center line."

"No," she says, "the advert. I want to remember you in your prime."

The crowd "ooohs" again, and Herse laughs. "I want to remember me in my prime too," he says. He moves back and looks around for the ball. Behind him a painter, given the stains on his canvas pants and overshirt, tosses it to him. Herse catches it on his hip, a nifty trick, and says to the woman, "Losers serve first."

She opens her hands to indicate her readiness.

As Herse considers how to serve, he pictures the lovers in the room beyond the broken door. They're half-naked, sweaty with terror, and holding up their hands to ward off Rego and his force. One is his soldier. The other, his soldier's Aydeni and, like all Aydeni, a possible spy.

"Don't let her off easy, General," the painter says. "She's got no use for war. Or you."

"You have to work for every fan," he says, "some harder than others." She doesn't appreciate this. So much for a friendly game.

Herse bounces the ball, a bladder of blackened guayule in a hard leather shell, and fires it with his right hip to her left, thinking her right-handed from how she lunged. She isn't troubled, slides gracefully, and fires it back. They volley a few times before she short hops him and he can't get his hip down quickly enough to return it. He realizes she'd been testing how limber he is. *Well, I'm warmed up now*, he thinks. The painter throws the ball to him and he passes it to her.

"She's not going to let you off easy either," the painter says.

"Good practice for Ayden then," he says. The crowd laughs.

"I'm not Aydeni," she says.

"That's fortunate," he says. "If they had your spirit, we should surrender now."

Herse figures the lovers surrendered immediately. They would know the penalty for consorting and that Rego's force, drawn from the soldier's own squad, couldn't afford to be gentle. The lovers also had to know they'd be discovered. They had to be awaiting this. Their affair's surely been exciting, but also draining. They must be relieved it's over.

He hopes the lovers are resisting, though. The soldier knows his fate. The Aydeni can imagine hers. As a Hanoshi, his first instinct will be to think of himself and turn on her, and if the Aydeni's smart she'll turn on her own people. As a couple, though, they could have the will to fight together. That's what Herse wants most for his men and for his city.

Herse wins the next two volleys, the first on a lob with so much spin she strikes at empty air, the second on a ball low to her right with enough topspin to elude her too. She retaliates with a ball off the wall that has him taking three steps down the alley after it. The painter holds it out to him with a plastic grin. All even at two.

"I'm feeling ambushed," Herse says.

The painter tilts his head as if to say, *Curious*.

Herse hears the woman tapping her foot on the cobblestones. He decides he doesn't like having the painter behind him. The alley feels tighter. But he has to turn and bounce her the ball.

Her serve comes straight at his head. He leaps off a crate beside the wall and flings up his hip so he can return it. It's a spectacular move that leaves him in no position to deal with her return. Three–two.

The crowd sours. The game's getting personal, and he's their man. Herse takes her side, though. He says, "All's fair when the ball's in play."

So after she serves off a quick dribble, he blasts one at her head. She drops to a knee to avoid it and scowls. The crowd laughs. They're still on his side.

When the lovers are brought back to camp, he'll show his men the Aydeni and make her watch the soldier do his final duty: die for his crimes. They'll appreciate that. Nothing brings a group together like a good execution. He won't give her to them, though. He's no Ynessi.

Herse's stomach burbles. *Nevertheless*, he thinks, *this is a disgusting business*. Where did the soldier even find an Aydeni woman? Most Aydeni left the city long ago, encouraged by the interrogations of those the army picked up. And he's no prize. He might have a dozen teeth. Why has he made Herse do this to him?

Herse almost smiles. His soldier couldn't resist.

The general serves.

The woman returns the ball sharply off the wall. His return is weak, and she puts away her fourth point. A half minute later she gets her fifth.

She isn't stopping between points, serving as soon as the returned ball touches her hands. So he slows the game down, volleying not to win the point but to push her increasingly off balance. He won't try to overpower her as she expected. He'll wait until she makes a mistake. He feints to one side, and she gives just enough for him to get the ball past her on her other side. The crowd sees she's lost the advantage. He tries the same ploy again, an insult really, and she counters, but twice more he does it, moving her farther to one side, then practically rolls it past her to the other. With the slightest smile, she appreciates his change in tactics then responds in kind. The crowd leans forward, waiting for one to strike fatally. For a long time, they're tied at five.

As the lovers, tied up and hooded, are dragged through the broken door into the hallway, Herse pictures the soldier begging for her life. Rego, ever measured, responds, "She won't be killed. She'll be questioned." Rego turns to the Aydeni. "And afterward, you'll be released. You aren't a spy, are you?" The bag tips up and shakes. "Good," he says. She's reassured. The soldier doesn't say that "afterward" never has a set date. From that point, they come quietly.

Herse is about to put away his point when the painter cries out, "Ho!" and Herse mishits the ball. The woman charges and fires it past him, and she keeps running at him. Does she have something in her hands? Herse grabs her wrists, locks them together, and swings her around to use her as a shield in case the painter is coming at him from behind. He isn't, and the crowd is preoccupied with the faceless figures being led out of the lodging house to the wagon.

"Don't worry," she says, "I'm not like you. Lots of people aren't."

"Let's see," he says, letting her go.

One of the boys has started to cry. Herse squats beside him. Many are asking, "What have they done?" but the boy puts it more simply, "Are they the bad people?"

"Yes," Herse says. "We try to keep them outside the walls, but they're sneaky. Like rats. Sometimes they get inside, and what do you do when a rat gets inside?"

"Eat it!"

"Exactly," Herse says. "We gobble them up." He makes a chomping motion with one hand. This amuses the boy. Herse clasps the boy's shoulder.

The crowd jeers the lovers. The boy's brother retrieves the ball and winds up to throw it at the soldier. Herse plucks the ball from his hand. "No need for that, though. If you want to help, keep your eyes open. See something. Say something. That's how we caught them, one of our own soldiers ensnared by an Aydeni. Do your duty better than he did."

The boys salute. Herse stands and returns it smartly. He tosses them the ball and they run off as the lovers are locked in the wagon's windowless cabinet.

The woman is still there. She says, "You'd eat your own to survive?"

"No," he says. "I'd eat our own so you'd survive. And everyone here."

The crowd approves and turns its jeering on her. He whispers, "You might run off as well. I'd eat you too, if you were worth eating." He jogs to the wagon, waving good-bye, and climbs up beside Rego on the seat in front of the cabinet. The driver snaps the reins. The other soldiers walk alongside.

Rego scans a side street. "No patrols. Our information was good."

Herse says, "Did they surrender or resist?"

"Neither," Rego says. "That information was bad. The landlord was wrong. They weren't there. Left yesterday. So we grabbed these two, who were squatting." Herse gives him a look. "We had to grab someone," Rego says.

"They'll do," Herse says. "Just keep the bags on. If the other two are smart, and we're lucky, they're already halfway to nowhere." *Good for them*, he thinks. "Let's go over the script for the Council."

The Tripple Inn is notable for three things: cheap rooms, cheaper beer, and the cheapest secrets in the Harbor if, like Omer, you're fluent in drunk.

Having ridden all night, he planned to go straight to sleep, but a man in the common room chooses Omer to tell his tale of woe to, and no one ever went broke trading in woe. He gets the man to tell him about a load of Meresi cinnamon that is stranded on the docks for want of harbor fees. Omer thinks the Shield could pick it up cheap, and that would mean an easy finder's fee for him.

As he pours the man some wine to open the negotiation, the good half of Felic's face slides into the doorway. He locates Omer, one side of his lips moves, and he disappears. A moment later three men take his place. If they haven't spent time at the oars, they will, should their scars testify against them. The one with a half-red eye leads them to a table behind Omer, a hand on the hatchet tucked in his belt.

4

Having spent a half hour staring at manifests, bills, and logs to avoid staring at the galleys leaving for Yness, Livion climbs to the Upper City and the Blue Tower, where Council takes place. Three hundred feet tall, the tower is the most recent magnification of the simple wooden keep around which the city first grew. The previous iteration was called the Raven Tower for the birds that had long roosted on it. The current name comes from the great blue dome that was added when the tower was heightened to mark the League's creation. The ravens now float around the dome's white cupola, their own private tower.

Livion hurries across the plaza in front of the tower, through the tall double doors, and up a wide staircase to a thin vestibule. It's crammed with the aggrieved and desperate waiting for the public pleading later in the meeting. As a guard lets him through the door into the council chamber, Livion wonders how many of them would end up dying if Hanosh went to war. They seem to wonder why, having paid their pleading fee, they can't go in with him.

The semicircular room covers half a floor of the tower. From an elevated banc the councilors face two columns of pews populated by those scheduled to address them. Agents and factotums from the major and minor companies, as well as the few petty companies that can afford it, have standing tables around the room. Each sports a small company flag like those in front of each councilor, except theirs belong to the richest companies in Hanosh.

The largest tables are empty, though, their flagsticks pulled. Over the last six months, the other League cities have called their lead agents home to protest Hanosh's war talk. They still have their sources in the city and their alliances with various companies, so the Council declared the gesture mere pageantry. Livion slows as he passes through them, feeling the weight of their agents' absence, until he notices Chelson staring at him from one end of the banc and he ducks into a back pew.

The Council is dispensing with basic business: decobbling the streets in the workers' district instead of repairing them (backburnered), installing more streetlamps in the servants' district (rejected), adding workhouses in both (heartily approved). It's dreary talk in a dreary room. The walls are bare stone, the ceiling plain wood. The only decoration other than the flags hangs behind the banc: a large pine H. The symbol of the city, its crossbar extends beyond its stems, making it look like either a gallows or, as the Aydeni say, a double cross.

Livion wishes they could meet in the original council chamber beneath the dome. He's heard it's magnificent, with gorgeous murals, stained glass windows, and dominating views, a celebration of all the League aspired to be. But when the councilors discovered how taxing it was to climb so high, they moved Council here to what had been a ballroom and left the old chamber to the rats and dust. The decision makes sense in retrospect. The League is decaying too. And no one has balls anymore. They're a pointless expense.

Eles, leader of the council, gavels the ongoing business closed and opens the speakers' portion of the meeting. Ject, general of the city guard, rises from the front row. He's polished from his boots to his mustache. Given his rank, he's allowed dyed silk for his shirt, which is cut to recall a guardsman's blouse. Its deep green vibrates against his red sash of rank, which glitters with a long matrix of honors. His tight pants are brushed to perfection. A ceremonial dirk completes his outfit.

Before he can say anything, Eles says, "Where is our general of the army? We pushed this meeting up to hear his news. Is it not so alarming that I must sit here squandering minutes?" Eles is so old and desiccated he reminds Livion of a chicken killed, plucked, and forgotten for a week in the sun. His voice, though, retains the sharpness of a beak.

"The general," Ject says, "has been overstepping his bounds, arresting people in the Upper City, an alarming issue in its own right. While the general may conduct certain operations in the city, I ask the Council to remind him that his activities must be coordinated with the guard. For the public's safety."

And for a cut of any prisoner's board, Livion thinks, if Ject can have a prisoner sent to the guard's cells instead of the army's. Ject also gets a piece of a prisoner's service contract with a company after a conviction. Some of this coin trickles down to the guards, who call it the spoils of their daily war.

"I would like the Council to instruct the general," Ject says, "when he deigns to appear—" As if on cue, a guard opens the chamber doors and Herse enters.

Unlike Ject's clothes, Herse's are rumpled, as if he has just returned from an engagement in the field. He approaches the banc, adjusting his sash. When he was coming up through the ranks, Herse bore a kopis under his arm and his sash was as bedazzled as Ject's. Now he goes unarmed—the army is his sword—and his sash sports only one honor, the crossed spear and sword for basic weaponry, the first all soldiers receive and the one, Herse has explained, that binds them together in common cause for the city.

By declaring that Ayden, not a dragon, destroyed the wolf pack, that cause would be war.

Could Herse have been lying? Could he know about the dragon attacks too? A double dragon attack does seem less likely than an attack by privateers, especially with Solet coming up empty of late. As for other survivors, would Herse's forces silence them? Would he just pretend there were no survivors until it's too late to halt the war?

Livion knows the Shield has to make hard choices when it comes to protecting itself, like a captain has to when protecting his ship. Everyone, from Eles to the night soil man, knows the risks of impeding profit. It's business, not personal, just as someone has to supply the building materials in the wake of catastrophe. But to take a life, to start a war, to create the catastrophe; that Livion can't believe of them. He's worked beside them. He's taken their pay. He's devoted himself to them. And for all Herse's posturing, when Livion looks right at him, this man he's cheered on the hip-ball pitch seems trustworthy.

Who is he, a junior, to overrule them, regardless of what he may or may not know?

Ject opens his mouth to continue, but Eles recognizes Herse.

After checking that the rumor about the shipment of cinnamon was true and the cargo was awaiting liberation, Omer heads for Livion's office. In the Round Square, he looks at the poor sods selling their junk and thinks, *Am I any better? Every day I unroll my own blanket and lay out the latest rumors. Sure I have a contract with the Shield, but that won't last. Maybe this cinnamon is my chance*. He consciously avoids touching the pouch with his monthly and perk. *I have my stake. I could cover the harbor fees and buy the spice myself. Why shouldn't I get a taste for once? I could sell it to the Shield myself and double, triple, my money. When I put it like that*, he thinks, *I have to*.

To lift some other boats with his rising wave, Omer tosses pennies into several containers. Their merchants thank him with whispers. One battered and broken old drunk, having seen such gestures before, offers him for a penny more a shark's tooth engraved and inked with what could be a hook. He says, "With this you'll always have a fish in your net and a boy in your partner's belly. I'd bet a penny on it." Omer declines, the drunk himself proof of its uselessness, and looks around. Where is the man with the huge blue shells? He would have liked one. What pearls must have come out of them!

Omer takes a shortcut to the docks, worried that someone may beat him to the deal. He darts through alleys, dodging teamsters and drunks, fishwives and brats, relieved to come around a corner and see the docks at the end of the way. Then a man blocks out the light. Two more rush up behind him. The man in front digs his middle finger into the corner of his half-red eye.

"Members of the Council," Herse says, "I'm late because Ayden has again reached inside our walls."

"Not unlike yourself," Ject says. "Your trespasses—"

"Take your seat, General," Eles says. Ject complies, stiffly.

"Members of the Council," Herse says again. "Bandits supplied by Ayden have robbed and murdered our traders on the road, and their privateers have savaged our shipping. They've put our border towns to the torch for not sharing the spoils of our markets with them. Company agents in Ayden have been detained and valuable secrets about company operations have been revealed. And a quarter hour ago my men arrested an Aydeni for entrapping one of our own soldiers."

"Is this your news, General?" Eles says. "Another Aydeni detained?"

"No, but it shows the pattern of escalation that leads to my news. And I bring terrible news." He raises his voice. "We haven't struck back because proof was tenuous and the costs of responding far outweighed the losses suffered. But they've struck at our wallets now. And our hearts."

He pauses for effect—and to cue Rego to enter. The wispy man stops on the threshold so the guard can't close the door, and Herse says, "The Shield's wolf pack was attacked and destroyed by Ayden. They murdered two owners from the Shield, Mulcent and Sumpt, as well as Solet, a Hero of Hanosh."

His words carry into the waiting area. Livion hears gasps, jabbering, and then footsteps as many leave to spread the word. Eles is about to tell the guard to stop them when the chairs and tables scraping in the chamber make him hold up his hand to keep the company representatives in place. They squirm and pout, worried someone else is already taking advantage of the news. Rego walks to the seat beside Livion, and the guard closes the door.

"This accusation," Eles says, "should have been conveyed in private."

"It isn't an accusation," Herse says.

"Your proof?" Ject says.

"One of my patrols was told about two galleys wrecked on a beach near the Ynessi border. They investigated. At first they thought it was a dragon attack. However," Herse pulls a folded piece of paper from his pocket, "I received word not two hours ago that my men captured one of the attackers. He was Aydeni, badly injured, and hiding in the woods, abandoned as lost. He was questioned, and he revealed their orders: destroy Hanoshi shipping."

"Where is this man?" Eles said.

"The man didn't survive the questioning," Herse says. "His wounds were considerable. We were lucky to find him alive."

Ject says, "As much as I appreciate the general's yeoman investigative work, we must give careful consideration to any response."

"I share the general's concerns," Herse says. "Our evidence, however alarming, is scanty. I would be happy to seek further proof, as well as indications of future Aydeni attacks, but I thought it better to address the Council now, with facts that are likely accurate when we might do something about them rather than later, when the facts may be more solid, but obsolete."

Eles can't decide if he's looking at feed or feces. He says, "Let's hear from our sea general."

Prieve stands. He is the third of the city's three generals, commanding the sea guard and the piers in the Harbor, that is, anything touching water.

As old as Eles but more robust, Prieve maintains a pre-League bearing. Livion's even heard him use the old courtesy words, such as "please." He knows everyone who has ever docked in the Harbor by name, and he's been tested. He's arbitrated countless disputes because no one disputes his fairness. Since the rowers' guild was broken, he has even tried to improve the prisoners' lot. This has made him few friends among the shipowners and low people, who see a hard bench as a criminal's due, but every sailor and petty trader respects him, and he can collaborate with Herse and Ject, whom the Council keeps otherwise at odds.

Prieve says, "My patrols have made no reports about privateers or wrecks between here and Yness."

Herse says, "How many ships traveling that route have not arrived as scheduled?"

"Five," Prieve says. "Solet's three. The Shield's *Hopper*, four days late. And City United's *Harbourcoat*, two days overdue."

Eles recognizes a representative from City United standing near the wall. "We give our captains three days' leeway," the woman says.

"That's why you're a minor company," someone says.

"You're just petty," she says.

Eles's glare peels smiles off a dozen faces. "Noted. Can the councilors from the Shield explain the absence of the *Hopper*?"

"Our junior will address this question," Chelson says. He nods to Livion.

Before he can stand, Ject says, "Is the general insinuating that Ayden sank these other boats as well? Two days is hardly a delay. Nor is four. Ships serve at the mercy of the sea and storm and trade. They aren't public carts traveling upcity."

"We have to be on our guard," Herse says. "The general for the Guard hasn't seen what I've seen in the field. I mean to stop any threat long before he has to buckle his boots."

Eles says, "The Council recognizes the junior from the Shield."

Livion stands. As he does, Rego whispers to him through his hand, "Two heroes lost already. A third would galvanize any city."

I'm no hero, Livion thinks. *But could I be one?*

Omer has no idea who owns the men surrounding him, but that's irrelevant. He lowers his shoulder and charges. If he can get out of the alley, he'll have some room to fight. Red Eye gets lower than him, though, which enables the two men behind the rider to knock Omer over Red Eye. Omer knees Red Eye in his good eye, crawls free, and he gives Crooked Nose a heel to the mouth. He stands, but they get his ankles and, as he takes a step to run, they jerk him flat as a rug. His tooth cracks when his jaw hits a cobblestone.

Omer tries to climb the stones. He can't get a grip. A blade dives into his back. A boot plows into his ear. The Harbor becomes foggy. His limbs get heavy. Red Eye says, "Flip him. Let him watch." He's rolled over, Red Eye draws his hatchet, and the hacking begins.

5

Livion concludes his statement to the Council by addressing Chelson directly: "I had no chance to tell you earlier. I came straight here after hearing the news. Out of respect for Mulcent's and Sumpt's estates, I wouldn't have said anything to the Council before they were informed unless it was necessary."

"The company appreciates their contributions and regrets their loss," Chelson says.

Ject says, "Solet was hunting dragons in the area, which does make the junior's story more likely than the general's."

"What I find likely," Herse says, "is someone taking a chance to relive old glories."

"You would," Ject says.

Livion's feet swim in his boots, but he can't back down. "My trade rider's information has always been reliable."

"I would like to test that assertion," Eles says. "Is this Omer still in the city?"

"I know this rider," Ject says, "and if he is, he'll be at the Tripple in the Harbor. I'll have him collected."

Ject motions to Ravis, first guard of his personal retinue, whose bronze helmets and muscle cuirasses distinguish them from regular guards' plain leather caps and composite cuirasses. The man tasks two other guards to join him, and they leave to find the trade rider.

"What is certain at least," Eles says, turning to Chelson, "is that something did happen to your wolf pack. Always thought that was a foolish idea. Of course, if this was an act of war instead of misadventure, your insurers may reimburse you." Chelson's face doesn't move an inch.

"And the prison," Ject says, "may forgive the loss of its assets. I'll also have the families and associates of the Shield's rowers contacted to see if any have returned home. The Shield might do the same with its sailors. Another survivor would provide valuable testimony."

Chelson waves his hand abstractly. Livion says, "I'll have that done."

"Until the Shield's informant is produced," Eles says, "I move to postpone this portion of Council and, after a quarter-hour break, proceed with the public pleading." Blue Island seconds. Eles raises his ivory gavel, carved in the shape of an hourglass. "I would have moved that we keep this situation quiet lest the Shield suffer financially from uncertainty and baseless speculation, but, once opened, that door can't be closed, can it?" He sounds his gavel. The chamber empties as if on fire.

If Livion's created financial problems for the Shield, and that's likely, Eles will be the first to offer solutions. There's a reason his company is called Hanosh Consolidated.

At dusk Livion stands at his office window, wishing Solet or Tuse would row in and settle matters.

The Council was not pleased that Omer couldn't be found, especially after the first hour of pleading was taken up by complaints regarding the war with Ayden, and the second, as rumors spread, by those regarding the war with Ayden and their dragons.

Eles's fury had hardly matched that of Chelson. After Council, Livion followed him and Herse to the Shield's offices in the Blue Tower. They were trailed by various clerks and assistants, the mood funereal, the only sound the paradiddle of their footfalls on the iron stairs. One girl, Kathi, he thinks, gave him a look he thought was encouraging until she ducked her eyes and revealed it as pitying. She knew this march was his drumming out.

Felic knocks on his doorframe. "Do you need me?"

"Still no word of Omer?" Livion says.

"No," Felic says. "I went to the Tripple myself. He had a drink, he met a man, and he left, but he never took a room. He hasn't returned, nor has he been seen at his other haunts. We've promised perks to a few dozen people to let us know if they see him."

"Good," Livion says.

"Should I send to the Round for some dinner?" Felic says.

"No," Livion says. Felic slips away.

Livion sees Prieve below. Considering how he's been treated today, he wishes Hanosh retained some of its pre-League sensibilities. Even the little things might help, however much breath they waste. He runs to his door and calls down the corridor, "Felic."

The young man returns, wearing a light cloak and short-billed cap. "Yes?"

"Thank you," Livion says.

Felic gives a little bow, touches the bad side of his face, and leaves.

In the Shield's offices, Chelson led the party into the small hall and shut the door on the underlings so slowly Livion thought he was savoring the latch's click. "I don't know what you're playing at," he said, "or whom you're playing for, but the stakes are too high for you to sit at this table anymore. Here's what you're going to do." Herse stood behind him as Chelson jabbed his finger at Livion's chest to make each point. "You will see if this dragon nonsense is true. You will employ every resource at our disposal. And you will fail. In a few days you'll say that Ayden must have been behind the attack. You'll admit that delaying our response put the city at risk. You'll request an extended leave. The company will oblige." As an afterthought Chelson said, "And you will return those boots."

"What if I find out Omer was right?" Livion said.

"You won't," Herse said, putting a hand on Livion's shoulder. "Ayden attacked us. The city will believe us. Why can't you? Do you trust a trade rider more than us? A rat, I bet, who wanted a full purse for his information and promptly vanished?"

Livion can still feel Herse's hand beside his neck as clocks around the Harbor chime nineteen: three quick sets of five and a four. At his office window, Livion watches men and women head home or to the Round, shaking off the day, while on the piers a boy traipses from crane to crane, lighting the lantern by each as it loads and unloads. No movement comes from the gibbets on the bay.

Someone coughs behind him and he jumps. His servant girl is

standing there. The letter in her hand bears a seal of the bright yellow wax Tristaban currently favors.

"She's spoken with her father?" Livion says. The girl nods. Livion points to his desk, she lays it on a clear space, and he unfolds it. He reads the note without surprise and looks at the couch in his office.

His father-in-law gave him the couch when he was made a junior and installed in this office. "It looks comfortable," Chelson had said, "but it's not. You don't want a guest to be easy. That gives you an edge."

"What if I want a guest to be comfortable?" Livion had asked.

"Take him to the Round." His father-in-law had patted the still-empty desk and said, "Don't you get too comfortable either."

Livion says to the girl, "Let me write a reply."

"One isn't required," she says.

Livion flicks his quill across some papers. "Then tell Trist 'Good night.'"

The girl leaves. Livion returns to the window.

After Livion left the Shield's offices, practically sliding down the stairs, Ject met him in the tower's entry hall with his personal guard.

"You did well to speak up," Ject said, "however wild your story. Two dragons! And Chalfin. I remember him. Nasty business. You're going to the Castle?" Livion nodded. "Good. I'll go with you. We can compare notes."

A clanking on the stairs lifted their eyes to Herse coming down.

"What notes do you have to compare?" Herse says. "For one so concerned about jurisdiction, the battlefield is as far from yours as Ayden."

"That it was a battlefield remains in doubt," Ject said, "but the battle, thanks to your stunt, is in our streets."

"If you're looking for advice on combat—"

"I'm looking for peace."

"So am I," Herse said, "but I'm willing to fight for it." Herse pushed past them and left the tower.

"I'll find Omer," Ject said. "And we will prove him wrong."

Ject didn't say anything else on the way downhill, tapping the pocket with his paper instead, until they found the street blocked by a group of tanners. They were arguing loudly about the best way to give Ayden its due. They reeked of urine. One said to Livion, "Hey, hero, if you don't want to fight, why don't you leave?"

"Ravis," Ject said, pointing at him. Ravis pinned the tanner's arms and marched him to the general. Ject said, "You're Strig."

The man said nothing.

"Of course you are," Ject said. "I can't forget a face, and how could anyone forget yours, however much you've damaged it? What was it, ten years ago, you thought you could outrun me? No, eleven. How's your sister?"

Strig continued to say nothing.

"I hear of her from time to time," Ject said. "Nice girl. Hard worker. It'd be a shame if she was brought in because of something you did."

This got the man's attention.

Ject opened his hand. Ravis released Strig. "When you see her, let her know I'm thinking of her," Ject said.

"I'll be thinking of you," Strig said. "You're as bad as the hero here. Waves fall, though, when others rise." His friends dragged him away before he could say more.

The people looking on might have approved Ject's actions, except they were too afraid to be seen looking on.

Past the boulevard leading to Brimurray, Livion noticed his okono vendor's cart was gone, despite it being lunchtime. Near its place a cart full of apples had gotten one wheel wedged in the gutter. The driver asked several people passing by for help, but none had the time.

Ject ordered his men to pull the cart free. They made short work of it. Then they perked themselves with several bags of fruit. Ject chose his own apple, fat and pink, crispy and sweet. "This is what I'm fighting for," he said. "The simple give-and-take of public service. Why disrupt a perfect system?"

Night has the horizon in its clutches. Livion would get a room at the Round if he could bear the eyes and unspoken questions. Instead he bars the door, sits on the couch, and flops his head back.

A scream wakes him up.

6

A scream in the Harbor at night is not unusual, nor is a person yelling at the screamer to shut up. When he hears guards blowing horns, he gets up, closes his windows, and lies on the floor. The rug is more comfortable than the couch. He falls back asleep.

Felic rings the ship's bell Livion keeps on a shelf to announce the morning. He brings in a basin of water, a cloth, and a small pot of soap, then leaves to get him some breakfast. This isn't the first time Livion's spent the night in his office, although usually it's paperwork that keeps him and he wakes at his desk. Felic returns with a green stirrup of coffee from the Round, an okono, and Ravis.

Ravis says, "It's urgent."

"So I brought him straight up," Felic says.

Livion, having washed up and tucked himself together, pours coffee into a bowl. "Have you found Omer?" he says.

Felic shakes his head.

Ravis says, "The general wants you at South." The wall around the Upper City has five sides; four named after the directions they roughly face and "Gate" in the middle, named after its centerpiece. The city guard's headquarters buttress the south wall.

Livion unwraps his okono. Crab. "Why?" he says, and takes a healthy bite for appearances.

Ravis says, "I'll take you. He'll explain."

Livion puts down his okono and drains his bowl. The coffee doesn't wash away the crab. He follows Ravis past Felic, realizing that the casual observer might think he'd abandoned the Shield. Given the threat he felt yesterday, he's grateful for the xiphos hanging beneath Ravis's arm.

Unlike most of the buildings uphill in Hanosh, which are faced with stucco, whitewashed, and roofed with blue tile, South is a broad stone structure built out of the gray granite wall itself. Ravis leads Livion to a side door. Two guards outside recognize him and knock. A guard inside looks through a wicket, bars are removed on both sides, and the door is opened. Beyond an antechamber and a door made of iron bars, stone stairs plunge beneath the Upper City. Livion follows Ravis. The door guard locks and bars the exterior door, then unlocks the inside door. Ravis takes a lantern from the wall and starts down.

Livion doesn't. He says, "Why aren't we going in the front?"

"The general will meet us at the cells," Ravis says.

"Keep moving," the door guard says. "Can't keep the door open all day."

This doesn't feel right.

"Afraid of the stench?" the door guard says. "It'll get worse below, but after a few minutes you won't even smell it. Your partner will, though. Tougher to get out of your clothes than blood." He laughs. "Go."

Livion can't see how he could refuse. He descends.

The stairs turn twice before entering a vaulted room with a damp flagstone floor. Ravis says, "We'll wait here" and sets the lantern on a small table beside, unbelievably, the remnants of someone's breakfast. Boiled rat, which a live rat is gorging itself on. The lantern doesn't concern it. Livion is regretting that one bite of okono.

Ravis stands in front of a wooden door with a hang lock. Livion looks through the iron bars of two other doors in the room. They lead to barely lit passages lined with cells. The flag of Blue Island is painted on the wall at the end of each. These are holding cells, the least valuable investment in the complex because prisoners don't stay in them long enough to pay for board and sundries and the maintenance fees the city pays are minimal, although, like the other cells, Ject does guarantee that nine out of ten will be occupied.

Several minutes later, the general marches up one of the passages carrying a lantern. His mustache sags from lack of sleep; not a single fold of his uniform does. He produces two keys and hands them to Ravis, who uses the first to let Ject into the small room and the second to unlock the wooden door.

Ject says, "I need your experience."

"In what way?" Livion says.

"You'll see."

Ravis opens the door. Livion gags at the smell of fresh blood. The others don't. Around the walls of a large room are scarred chairs, split bamboo rods, coils of rope, heaps of chain, iron bars with pins, and other implements. Chains with hooks hang from the ceiling. In the middle of the room atop the drain are three bodies shrouded in bloody burlap.

"Let's start with the one on the left," Ject says.

Ravis unwraps a woman. Livion's seen men burned to death and drowned. He's seen limbs torn off and bodies horribly scarred, but he's never seen a person eviscerated. Her rib cage has been wrenched wide to get at her heart and lungs. A black chiton still dangles from her shoulders and covers her thighs demurely.

"She was found on the roof of a warehouse in the Harbor," Ject says, "spotted by someone farther up the Hill. There was no access to the roof from the warehouse. Now that one."

The middle bundle is roughly the same size as the first. The canvas is peeled away. Livion follows a barely crusting line of blood from a bare foot up to a scrawny knee and the hem of a black chiton. Blood pools in the fabric. Her neck is gouged halfway through. One side of her face blushes purple, grit embedded in the skin.

"She's our girl," Livion whispers. He realizes he doesn't know her name. She'd only been with them three months. Trist doesn't think it worth learning a girl's name until after she's served a year.

Ject is surprised. "When did you last see her?"

"Last night," Livion says. "Seven chimes. A little after. She brought me a note from my partner. Where did you find her?"

"Her dorm mother found her in a cut through between two Servants' lanes," Ject says. "The mother was out looking for our first victim, actually. She lived in the same dorm and hadn't come home after reportedly meeting some man. Did your girl go back to your house?"

"Yes," Livion says. "Maybe. My partner wasn't waiting for a response. She might have gone back to her dorm."

"When did you go home?"

"I didn't," Livion says. "I stayed in my office, waiting for word about Omer."

"Of course. Let's see the third."

The third body is a man's. His belly is ripped open, his viscera apparently gnashed to pieces. The rest of him is strangely untouched, but for a bruised chin and dried blood on his lip from a shattered tooth.

"And that's my rider," Livion says.

"He was found not far from the piers," Ject says, "tucked in an alcove in an alley. Curious, you knowing two of them. And you might have been the last to see each alive."

Livion edges toward the door. "I had nothing to do with—"

"Did I say you did?" Ject says. "Are you sure you don't know her?" He points to the first body.

Livion shakes his head.

"Come here. I want you to look at these wounds." Ject squats beside the hollowed girl and waves Livion to him. He says, "What happened here?"

"She looks . . . eaten. I've seen rats do this to galley cats."

"Pretty big rat, don't you think?" Ject pulls out his dirk and holds it over the wound. "Even if it took two bites to tear away the belly, its mouth would have to have been at least this wide."

"Where is this going?" Livion says.

"What has a mouth that wide that could also leave a body on top of a roof?"

Livion can't say it. It seems impossible. Ject does. "Your dragon's moved north."

"Dragons avoid cities."

"Maybe this one is too young to realize it should," Ject says. "Hanosh would look like a feeding trough."

"What really happened to them, though?" Livion says. "He does look devoured." Dragons, he saw during the first attack, savor the organs. "And our girl, maybe a knife did that. Maybe a claw."

Ject stands beside him and pats his back. "You've already done the right thing," he says, "by speaking. However tough that was, it'll be tougher to keep doing the right thing. But you've survived two dragon attacks. Few can make that claim. Your word, on top of what you said at Council, on top of your status, can stop this madness."

"What if I bring the madness down around me?" Livion says.

"You already have," Ject says. "I could easily say you're behind these deaths, couldn't I?"

Livion stops at his door to collect the breath he spent running from South. As he reaches for the latch, Trist's friend Asper opens the door.

She's dressed as usual in a white silk tokar and turban, from which descends a cloud of white veil. Her partner, Gaster, was killed by the plague before the *Comber* returned to Hanosh, and her outfit, worn decades after mourning ceased to be fashionable, has earned her the sobriquet the White Widow. Her inheritance made her extremely wealthy, which Livion considers some recompense. She's lately befriended Trist. Her relationship with Chelson is cool, given her attempts to make her silent shares in the Shield more vocal, and the scuttlebutt is that she hopes to influence him through his daughter. Livion's more concerned with her influence over Trist, who spends more time at her house than theirs.

"You're here early," Livion says.

"I spent the night," Asper says, stepping outside. "I can't approve of what you did at Council," she says, "but I do think Tabs feels more betrayed than she should. Why did you—"

A whistle's shriek from above cuts her off.

"Because it's true, whatever you heard," Livion says, "and possibly worse." He looks up. "She's on the sundeck?"

"Yes. Herse says—"

"I have to see her," Livion says and slips inside. He flips the door closed. The whistle echoes through the house.

A pergola keeps the sundeck cool with a drapery of grape vines and paper flowers. Tristaban stands at the railing with his whistle.

"That girl didn't show up this morning," she says. "And she won't come now." The whistle shrieks again.

Livion feels a pang that her fury at the girl has distracted her from being furious at him. "She's not coming," he says. "She's dead." He sits on a bench. "I saw her body. Several bodies. At South. It was horrible."

"How?" She actually sounds upset, not inconvenienced. "Why did you . . ."

"The Guard wanted to know what I thought."

"You?" And she's back, the daughter of a shipowner who married a lackey. "Ject is not a friend, Livion."

"I'm not sure anyone is at this point," he says. "And I'm worried about your safety."

Tristaban looks incredulous.

"The girl's wasn't the only body I saw. I saw my informant's too." He makes room on the bench.

She doesn't leave the railing. "The one who fed you that dragon nonsense?" Tristaban says. "I guess his lies caught up with him. You can't be the only one he sold them to. Father says Herse is furious. And Herse *is* our friend."

"There was another maid too," Livion says. "I saw her wounds. I saw theirs. I've seen them before. It was a dragon, a small one, like the one that attacked Solet."

"How convenient," she says. "Herse is right. You and dragons. You had your moment. Now you want more."

"I don't want anything," he says, "except for you to be safe." He gets up. "The maids were found nearby. One was ours. Something is hunting around here. And it's getting closer and closer to you. Ject is organizing a search."

"During which I'm sure he'll go lane by lane, house by house, to say Ayden didn't attack our ships, it was this dragon." She pokes her finger at him the way her father did. "He's using you."

"I don't care," he says. "So's your father."

"That's why he pays you!" she says. "You're not Hanosh's hero. You're his."

"I saw what I saw," he says. He stands in front of her by the railing. "Look," he says, "I'm scared. Maybe I didn't see what I saw. But I know what could happen if there is a dragon here." He reaches for her wrist, which doesn't move an inch. "Do me a favor: Stay home today."

He does look worried, the way he did when they snuck around behind her father's back. She remembers finding that endearing.

"I have appointments," she says. "Business. Do you know how that will look?"

"Like you trust me," Livion says, "the way I trusted you so your father wouldn't catch us."

"I can't just think about you," she said. "I have to think about him. And the Shield. And the future. And so do you. It's what you chose when you chose me."

"Think about them inside today," he says. "I wouldn't even stay on this deck." He would say "please," but she would consider that absurd.

Tristaban looks through the pergola. "What happened to the girl?"

"She had her throat torn open. The other maid was scooped out like an avocado."

Her wrist shifts against his hand. "I'll rearrange some things," she says. "I'm tired anyway. I didn't sleep."

He kisses her knuckles.

"You're going out."

"To help the search," Livion says.

"When will you be home?" she says.

"Dusk. Maybe later."

"I'll see you then," she says and smiles at him. He feels refreshed and leaves.

Tristaban goes to her bedroom where a dozen dolls watch her from shelves around the room. There's one appointment she can't miss and now she has more time than she thought she would. She holds up two peploi, one bright green, one a silvery perse, and asks the dolls what they think.

Livion likes the green too much, they say.

She tosses it aside. At a basin she washes the scent of yesterday's vanilla from her neck and puts on some shega oil. She's never worn it around Livion. It's not for him. It makes her feel weightless, no, unencumbered. And sparkly.

Between two houses across the lane a man in a beard and black shift watches Livion leave the sundeck. Then his attention goes to Tristaban's window.

7

By noon the guards are spreading across the city, searching district by district. They start in the Harbor, which runs along the base of the

Hill. One group continues up the West Hill to Servants, then to Lesser Silk, where Livion lives amid other juniors, deputies, and senior clerks, and Greater Silk above it. A second group climbs the East Side, from the poorest section, the Rookery, through the workers' lanes to the workshops, artisans, and petty trading outlets just beneath the Crest. That section is handled by an elite squad of guards drilled in diplomacy while guards search the Upper City clockwise around the Blue Tower.

Workhouse denizens are impressed upon to help, and many workers also join in, trading a day of labor and possibly tomorrow's employment for the golden ticket of a share of renderings. Armed with kitchen knives and craftsman's tools, armored in undyed cotton and bellies full of wine, they make so much noise that the guards send them ahead like beaters. And bait. Nothing is biting, though.

By midafternoon, the wine has soured in the workers' bellies, the temperature has risen, and the guards are quelling fights more than they are searching likely lairs: old buildings, cellars, obscure alleys and nooks, anyplace big enough a cow could crawl into. By dusk, even the guards, anxious to prove themselves every bit the warriors that Herse's soldiers are, grow discouraged. They and the workers agree that perhaps the search is some grand Aydeni joke.

At the Harbor, Prieve's men search under the docks and crawl up runoff pipes without any luck. He also has galleys searched, which does more to turn up contraband than any dragon. His patrols return with reports of clear skies and no wreckage from any ship that might have been attacked.

After being shown the bodies, Herse volunteers his force to help the search. Ject refuses them, saying it will be an inside operation. So Herse searches outside his walls, starting with Hanoshi Town, which spreads around the city like beggars around a trash fire. His soldiers take the opportunity to see who is supportive, while Herse sees no downside in finding a dragon. A prize is a prize, and he could make a great deal by killing a dragon. The day brings him no luck either, however.

Only Rego, Herse's adjutant, finds something intriguing.

He goes to the alley where Omer's body was found, then to the nearest pier, where three galleys are berthed.

He's trespassing in Prieve's jurisdiction, but he won't wait for official leave to investigate. It's stupid, having three security districts answerable to the Council, not an overall leader. Herse will change that.

The crew of two of the galleys, *Swan Two* and *Heron House*, both out of Meres, haven't seen Omer, but the first mate of *King of Birds*, a spicer from the Dawn Lands, might have. His fingers flex. Rego remarks on the number of Aydeni being questioned as spies and how a broader net might need to be cast. The mate indicates that Omer was brokering the sale of some cinnamon with a shipping company so they could pay their port fees, but he never returned with the money. Rego asks which company. The mate's memory goes slack. Rego points out that paperwork, like receipts for fees and records of people in the system, appears and disappears mysteriously. The mate says, "It sounded like 'wield.'"

Livion returns home at dusk. His neighbors are gathered on the lane. Most belong to shipowners and trading companies, and none are happy to see him. They didn't appreciate being questioned by guards or having a rabble of workers searching their lane.

A man from Blue Island, Eles's greatest ally and the Shield's greatest rival, says, "Getting too big for your boots? Hoping to bag another pair?" His neighbors chuckle. Fortune is a zero-sum game.

Livion unlocks the door and notices Tristaban's beaded hamondey is not on the shelf by the door. She never leaves home without her bag.

He calls her name. No answer. He calls again as he runs from room to room on the lower floor. He checks the second and the sundeck. She's gone.

Livion leans over the railing and asks his neighbors, "Did any of you see Trist leave?"

The Blue Islander says, "First he can't find a dragon. Now he can't find his partner. Don't lift your feet, Livion. Your house might disappear." This gets a bigger laugh than before. Apparently not just the rabble was into the wine today.

The Blue Islander's partner, exactly the person he deserves, says, "Maybe the dragon got her."

"That's not funny," Livion says. "I don't think that's funny at all." They laugh harder.

Why is he so worried? The city was searched. No dragon was found.

Then again, if a dragon wasn't found, neither was the person who might have slit his girl's throat and disemboweled the other maid.

A quarter hour later he knocks on the wicket in Asper's gates in the Crest. A house guard hands him off to a footman, who leads him into a treelined and torchlit courtyard. Livion's entire house would fit into it. The courtyard surrounds a black-bottomed pool that reflects the house. The footman installs him in a corner with granite benches where he can watch a school of bronze orfe dart through second-story windows.

It would be a pleasant retreat but for the figures of emperor snakes worked discreetly into the tiles and torch holders surrounding the pool.

Asper flows in and greets him warmly. She says, "I spoke sharply to you this morning. I hope you understand: I had a long night."

"I'm looking for Trist."

"I haven't seen her all day," Asper says. "Maybe she's at her father's."

"I was going to check there next," he says and stands, a little wobbly. "If she were here, it'd mean she hadn't left me. If she's there—"

"Here. Sit," Asper says. "This can't have been an easy day for either of you." She sits on the bench.

Livion doesn't know what to make of this. He sits anyway. She gestures for her footman to leave.

"You're not alone," she says. "I believe you about the dragon. It makes sense. And we're not alone. Other owners, in the Shield and out, they believe too." She laughs. "I heard it from their wives. They'd like to say publicly that war is bad for business, but they don't want to look soft, which is also bad for business." She touches his arm. "Will there be war? Chelson won't tell me anything. I need to know."

Livion thinks of Herse's hand on his shoulder. Maybe she and these silent owners could protect him if he helped them find their voice. "Yes," he says.

She compresses her mouth. "I thought so," she says. "Tabs is special to me. I hope we can be friends too."

Livion says, "Me too."

"Go," she says. "And when you find her send me word so I know she's all right."

Outside Livion watches the people on the street ignore him: Asper's neighbors, servants, peddlers. It's a ghost night, the Dawn Landers would call it. When you feel lost in sight of all.

Once Asper hears the wicket close behind Livion, she goes through the main hall to the stairs. In a guest room Tristaban is lying on a couch, soft and half-asleep. "You should have been home hours ago, Tabs," Asper says. "At least in the dark no one will see you leave."

Chelson lives on a higher street than Asper and in the tonier West Crest. His lane is more a promenade: gated, tree lined, and far wider than most because the tenants on the uphill side bought and razed the homes across from them to increase their views. Led there by a footman, Herse finds the lane indulgent in such a crowded and, for the most part, impoverished city.

His first home was a one-room shack his father built on scavenged beams over an alley in the Harbor. Loosely moored, it rocked like a galley until shacks were built around it and, in time, above it. He and his siblings had endless hours of fun dashing across rooftops. The summer he was six, he never touched the street, doing his piecework on high, playing hip ball on a slant, and drenching the unsuspecting with their communal bucket from increasingly clever blinds. Eventually the Council declared the shacks a blight and tore them down. His family moved to Hanoshi Town, but his father returned to the site every day for a year to build a warehouse complex. "Job's a job," he told his furious son, "system's the system." From the start his father called the complex the Castle.

Herse and Rego are admitted into Chelson's courtyard by one of his personal guards. The fineness of the man's uniform can't hide the brutality advertised by his half-red eye and hatchet.

The courtyard's no less brutal: shadowy, seatless, faced with unfinished gray stone, and decorated with six pedestals displaying nothing. Passed to a footman, Herse and Rego are installed in a small room with a stone bench and an iron brazier that offers little heat.

"Try out the bench," Herse says. "I want to see something."

Rego sits, back upright, head held high. He shrugs and is about to say, "I don't understand," when his butt shifts. He shifts it back, and it shifts again. Herse smiles. Rego says, "I can't quite get comfortable."

"The little trick of little men," Herse says. "You can't tell in this light, but the seat is deformed. And there's only one, which Chelson will insist we take, so he can loom over us."

Chelson slides through the doorway followed by Red Eye. He says, "My footman should have invited you to sit. If you will." He holds out his arm.

Herse says, "We're fine." Rego can feel the tension in Herse's chin as Chelson looks up at it. Herse says, "I think we can solve our mutual problem. Rego."

Rego describes the cinnamon deal. "Omer probably dealt with Livion."

Herse says, "Do you know anything about this?"

"No," Chelson says, "but such deals aren't uncommon. The rider would get a finder's fee."

"What if Livion planned to cut you out of the deal?" Herse says.

"He wouldn't do that," Chelson says.

"You said something similar before Council," Herse says. "And this deal was nothing for the Shield, but it might mean twenty purses to Livion, a nice sum for a junior with a new home and a partner with aspirations."

"Indeed," Chelson says.

"What if," Herse says, "Omer cut Livion in, and Livion decided to cut him out? I saw the rider's wounds. No dragon made them. Nor did a dragon kill his servant, who might have stumbled into the middle of things. He was the last to see both."

"Are you saying he killed them?" Chelson says. "Over some cinnamon?"

"I'm just drawing a picture," Herse says. He glances at Red Eye's hatchet. "One man's cinnamon is another's city."

Chelson's face darkens to Herse's satisfaction. Mystery solved.

"So why didn't he complete the deal?" Chelson says. "What happened to that other maid?"

"He had no chance," Rego says, "given what happened at Council. And she wouldn't be the first person to fall prey to the night, then to the rats."

"Do you have any proof?" Chelson asks.

"Proof is in the eyes of the Council," Herse says. "Ject's search for the dragon may have been fruitless, but it's left the city confused. Once you say there's a dragon, there's a dragon. If we say Livion's story was meant to cover up murders, that will discredit him, and we can get on with business."

"Ject would never go for it," Chelson says. "However compromised he is."

"If Livion's lies distracted Hanosh from defending itself," Herse says, "then it's an army matter. We can argue jurisdiction later. Call another special council. And I'll have the material brought in to sweeten the pot."

The footman appears. "Your son-in-law is here," he says.

"Bring him in," Chelson says, deciding something. To Red Eye he adds, "Holestar, have your men join us. And fetch a head sack."

8

Tristaban winds her way down through Artisans. She hasn't decided what she'll tell Livion, if anything. She doesn't need a chance encounter to complicate matters.

She doesn't know the district as well as she imagined, and finds herself in Workers with its streets missing half their cobbles and alleys full of eyes. She tries to get to a Hill street, but the lack of streetlamps and the bizarre layout of the houses drains her nearly to the Rookery before spilling her out across from Servants.

She crosses the street, sees her horrible neighbors from Blue Island wobbling out of a quick nip, and ducks into a lane running behind a dormitory. It's barely better lit than those across the street, but at least she knows the way up.

Two stairways, a lane, and an alley later, she stands beneath a dim streetlamp and realizes she's lost. She decides to make her way to the Quiet Tower. Surely a guard would escort her home.

It's oddly quiet here. Most day servants should be home or coming home. Or is she beyond their quarters? Surely they can't be hiding from a dragon. It hits her: She's done with Livion. How can she stay with the Boy Who Cried Dragon? She'll be a laughingstock. No one would blame her for dissolving their partnership. Her father would make it simple.

She descends a long flight of stairs into darkness and finds herself behind a warehouse. She turns west and after a few dozen yards finds another stairway switchbacking up. The Quiet Tower looms not far above its top.

At the first turn a shoe scuffs behind her. In the dim light seeping around a nearby shutter she sees shadow sliding against shadow. She would call out, but she doesn't want to draw attention to herself. Another scuff. She eases onto the next stair. It could be anyone behind her, a guard, a worker, a maid. Scuff. Two more steps. Three quick scuffs and Tristaban runs. She doesn't see the next switchback, trips and sprawls, smacking her jaw. It splits and blood runs down her neck.

The shadow falls over her. Its hands work their way up her body to grab her hair and yank her head back. Fingers scuttle over her lips and clamp themselves across her mouth. The shadow straddles her waist and pins her.

It whispers, "Be quiet, and we won't hurt you. Understand?"

She nods against his hands. Its fingers are rough on her lips. She wishes she'd brought Livion's whistle.

"Good," it says. "You don't want to end up like that maid. We had to remove her throat to show her we meant business."

Tristaban nods again. It releases her hair to rummage in a pocket. A cork pops, and a sickly sweet smell wafts over her. It's like burnt apple wine, but she can't place it. A small bottle clinks on a step above her head, then she hears a cloth set beside it, and she knows what it's going to do.

She bites his fingers deep enough to grind a knuckle. It yanks the hand free, cursing, and she howls for all she's worth. Shocked by her resistance, it stands slightly as if it might run. She launches herself upward, knocking it backward down the stairs. Shutters creak open. Candles are held out of a dozen windows. Voices call out to her. She doesn't answer and flies up the stairs, kicking the bottle so hard it shatters.

Two alleys and another stairway and she's on Brimurray, huffing, her dress soiled, her face a mass of sweat. She's smiling, though. She fought him off. She'll be scared later. For now, she's won. The light from the freshly lit street lanterns feels like a dusting of gold.

Tristaban rifles through her hamondey for her key and strides to her door. A bearded man pushes a black wooden barrow toward her. It's two-wheeled and deep, with a sagging canvas cover. She thinks it's early for the night soil man, and then realizes that without the girl she'll have to deal with their private matters herself. Maybe for a penny he will. His sandals are old and oft-repaired, but clean enough to come inside. Yes, she deserves that after what she just did. She's gotten her hands dirty enough today.

Tristaban waves the man over and says, "I need your help. Will you bring out for me . . ." She points to the barrow.

"Of course," the man in the black shift says.

She rummages in her bag for her key, unlocks the door, and steps back. They stand together a moment before Tristaban nods at the latch. The man says, "Yes," and opens the door for her. As he does, she looks at the barrow. It seems empty. It barely reeks.

"First stop of the night?" she says, feeling magnanimous. She enters and lights a wall sconce. "It must smell terrible by the last."

"It's not too bad," he says, stepping inside. "With that canvas covering the barrow, I can imagine I'm carrying anything. Honestly, so does everyone I pass." He presses the door closed.

CHAPTER NINE

The Generals

1

Once Livion is grabbed, bagged, and dragged away to Gate, Chelson sends the footman to bring his daughter to him as soon as she arrives home.

As he hurries downhill, Ophardt dreams of up-partnering. Livion will lose his home and place, given what he overheard his master and the general discussing. It would be a difficult match, but he wouldn't be the first footman to leap a few rungs to an owner's daughter. And Tristaban does flirt with him whenever he escorts her. She even uses his name now.

Ophardt turns the corner into Brimurray and bounces off a heavy barrow. He brushes at his stiff uniform in case any filth clung to it. Tristaban despises dirt. He tells the barrowman, "Watch where you're going." The barrowman swiftly replaces the cover dragged off a corner of the cart then bows his head in apology, eyes wide with concern. *Good*, Ophardt thinks. *He should know when he's offended someone from a Crest house. He should be afraid.*

The footman knocks at Tris's door. As he expected, there's no answer and no light inside. The door is locked. He leans against the door to wait. He likes finding her at home, especially when she pokes through the curtain of flowers on her sundeck to gaze down at him. A minute passes. He bucks himself up and knocks harder. No answer. He looks through the small window beside the door, and what he sees in the glow from the streetlights sends him loping uphill.

Chelson, followed by his three personal guards, storms into Brimurray. The one with the crooked nose pounds on the door. He reaches for the latch. Chelson jabs at the door. Crooked Nose breaks it open on the third slam.

The foyer is disarrayed. A small bench lies on its side. The decorative tray for Livion's boots has been overturned and kicked halfway into the hall. Oddments from shelves are scattered, the wall sconce is shattered, and blood splotches one wall.

Holestar yanks out his hatchet, the two others their dirks, and he leads Crooked Nose through the house while the third guard stays outside with Chelson.

He's stolen my daughter's life, Chelson thinks.

No, Chelson counters himself. *He couldn't have*. He was definitely worried when he came to Chelson's house. A trader's first skill is reading minds. Livion's too stupidly open to fool him. Had he just killed Tristaban, Chelson would have known.

Besides, Livion's incapable of murder. Personally, Chelson likes the boy. He's perfect for his daughter, happy to be imposed upon, and willing to watch her drama instead of staging a competing show. If Livion didn't drain away her craziness, he'd have to deal with it.

Despite all that's happened, he has to admit he was lucky his daughter had accepted Livion. The junior wasn't his first choice. He'd planned to partner Tristaban with his old captain Jeryon, another person dependably meek and meekly dependable, before he got himself killed and Livion showed his quality. *Sometimes the best man does win*, he thinks.

Whoever did do this will find that out himself, and what it's like to lose to Chelson.

The guards emerge. Holestar shakes his head. "Nobody," he says, "and no body."

Ophardt runs down Brimurray with a squad of city guards carrying lanterns. Chelson greets them solemnly and points the sergeant to the foyer.

As the sergeant holds up a lantern to examine the debris and the city guards fan out to keep the gathering neighbors back, Chelson gives the footman a ferocious look. "Why did you bring the guards?" he whispers. "We handle house matters in-house. You should know that by now."

Ophardt shrinks, hoping he will at least be kept on as a soil boy.

The sergeant touches the blood on the wall, slides outside, and closes the door to prevent gawking. He questions the footman, who tells him when he came, why, and what he saw. The sergeant asks if he saw anyone else on the lane; the blood is fresh so the killer might have been nearby. The footman scans the neighbors. They shrink back. Doors and windows close. Ophardt says he didn't see anyone suspicious.

Chelson is about to say that he fears his son-in-law was involved when the sergeant bends and holds the lantern near the footman's waist. It reveals a thin red smudge across his uniform. "Oh," Ophardt says, "there was the barrowman."

2

Near midnight Ject bars the door to his office and steps to a darkwood counter mounted on the wall. He dons a crisp white sleeveless tunic, lights several beeswax candles on the counter with a straw from his grate, and unrolls a red woven mat between them. Onto it he sets a white ceramic pot filled with clean water and covered with a white cloth. Next to this he arrays several objects removed from a finely carved box: an unhoned snow-white blade of deer bone, a tin with yellow paste, another with black, two more white cloths, rolled, and a horsehair brush with a black oak handle. He stretches and looks out the window above the counter, but the candles have snuffed his view of the lamplit Upper City. He pulls off his boots, stands one on the mat, dips a cloth in the water, and cleans it while considering what he knows.

There have been at least three murders in two days. The trade rider, stabbed in the East Harbor. A maid, horribly mutilated, found atop a warehouse in the West Harbor. Another maid, with her throat slit or torn open, found in Servants. Plus Chelson's daughter, badly injured at least, taken from Lesser Silk.

She may be alive. Why would the killer take the body? Chelson, though, took the more pessimistic view, and, not wanting to involve Ject, said that his men would investigate. A second citywide search, which an owner's daughter would merit, would indeed be very embarrassing, but Ject won't miss an opportunity to indebt Chelson to him, so he's ordered his men to make inquiries too.

Ject scrapes off some persistent splatter with the blade then washes off its residue. He shakes out a rolled rag, wraps it around two fingers, and digs out some yellow paste, a traditional dubbin of wax, soda ash, and tallow. This is one of his better batches, but the secret is in his black polish. He rubs it into the leather.

Ject considers the city guard from Quiet who is also missing. No one has seen him since he went on watch two nights ago—or no one's said so out of fear of dismissal. He was in the same area as the two maids. If he were murdered, how would he fit with the rest?

And now he's gotten a report of a man who assaulted a woman in Servants. He fled after she fought him off, leaving behind a substantial knife. He wore a long-sleeve black tunic and pants, and, from what little the witnesses saw of her, she resembled Chelson's daughter. Why would she have been there? Did the same person catch her at home?

Could he have also been this barrowman? Black is the color mandated for night workers, though.

Ject owes that footman for calling the guards. He wouldn't have heard about the barrowman otherwise. He'll find a place for him if Chelson finishes or diminishes him.

Ject works the yellow paste methodically up the shaft of his boot as he matches victims to the most likely suspects. Tristaban—Barrowman. Tristaban's girl—the unidentified assailant or Livion. The rider—Livion. Livion doesn't strike him as violent, but he can't deny Livion had the opportunity to kill the girl and he could imagine a motive, nor can he deny Livion had the chance and a possible motive for killing the rider.

They died so differently, though. The girl was probably killed from behind then her body was left in plain sight. The rider was stabbed or slashed many times in the abdomen, as if the killer were enraged or more than one were involved, then his body was hidden. Ject's seen meek men like Livion go wild and kill, and he's seen the meek kill methodically, but the same man wouldn't kill both ways alternately. And the wild don't hide a body, while the meek don't leave them out in the open. If Livion killed one, he didn't kill the other. He'll put Livion down for the rider.

Perhaps the person who killed the maid was interrupted when killing the girl, the way he was interrupted tonight. That seems a reach. No one's so bold twice.

Ject trades his cloth for the clean one and scoops up some black, a mixture of bone black and wool grease that will restore his boot's color and give it an unusual shine. As he starts at the toe again, he realizes the guard, Bern, and the maid have something in common. She was left on a rooftop inaccessible without a ladder. He was stationed atop Quiet, also inaccessible except by the tower stairs. If he didn't sneak away, what if he were taken while on Quiet? All a person would have to do is fly.

Could he have actually been right about the dragon story?

Too bad the story's in ruins. Livion's compromised. He's compromised. Herse's story, the only one still standing, however improbable, must command the truth, and Herse will again make the case for war at a special session of Council at seven hours tomorrow. Ject checks his clock. It's almost midnight.

If the Council submits to his story, half the city could be burned the way it was in the last war. Hundreds, probably thousands, will die before starvation and disease set in. And worst of all Ject, as is traditional and necessary in time of war, will be put under Herse's command along with Prieve, then likely relieved.

That can't happen. All he needs to do is produce a dragon.

Or a dragon of sentiment—a roaring fear, a monstrous rage—one that could sway or at least delay the vote.

He twists some black into the tips of his mustache as he decides what to do, curls them while he shapes his plan, and, feeling as revitalized as his mustache, pulls a bell cord to summon Ravis. He unbars the door and gets to work on his other boot. This will be a long night, but by dusk tomorrow Herse may feel like Ject's boots have been driven deep into his throat.

From atop the city's exterior gate, Herse and Rego look down Gate Street, one of the few roads winding through Hanoshi Town that's cobbled and lamplit.

Rego faces Thuban, the pole star, and tilts his head straight up. The star Tarf is nearly overhead. "It's almost midnight," he says.

A soldier on the gate tower to their left blows a curling brass horn: the gates will close in ten minutes. They won't be opened until six hours. In a tavern just outside the gate, someone says, "Last call!"

Rego looks concerned.

"He'll be here," Herse says.

Three men, two carters and a stevedore just off shift, hurry out the gate and head for the tavern. They nearly run into a woman stumbling from an adjacent alley. She curses them and smoothes her clothes, which weren't smooth to start. As the carters go inside, the stevedore asks her something. She shakes her head. He shakes his purse. She looks at the gate then shows him ten spread fingers. He asks something else. Ten fingers again. She's stunned when he accepts and grudgingly follows her into the alley.

"Ten pennies for ten minutes?" Rego says. "Good work if you can get it."

Herse says, "If Ject could get half a coin for the women he jails, he'd be on the Council himself. Ah, there we are."

Three large wagons crawl up the street. The canvas covering their cargo mounds reveals fragments of the Shield's logo on blond crates of various sizes. The soldiers at the gate normally stop wagons and ask about their cargo. These they wave through.

The horn sounds twice. People leave the tavern, many furious. A carpenter heads for the gate.

The lead driver appears on top of the tower.

Rego says, "Any trouble, Sergeant?"

"No," he says. "We brought all the weapons. Had to leave behind some shields. We didn't have another wagon."

"We'll manage," Herse says.

Rego says, "From what I saw when spreading the word, most supporters are already armed in a makeshift way."

Now the carpenter appears.

"Corporal," Rego says.

"The two men who just entered the tavern, they said if there's a war, wages will be docked eight pennies for every whole coin to pay for it. People are outraged."

"That can't be true," Rego says. "It'd be two at most."

"One to start," Herse says.

The horn sounds three times. Patrons are pushed out of the tavern, which has to close. They continue arguing in the street.

Herse says, "Fortunately, we have a more encouraging message. Birming, you brought the blue chest?"

"First thing loaded, as you requested," the sergeant says.

"Then we have the only weapon we really need."

The gates creak closed. The bars slide into place. The woman bounds from the alley. The stevedore laughs as she pounds on the gate, trying to get inside the city. She looks up at Herse pleadingly.

He shakes his head and turns away. She curses him with an athlete's creativity.

"Someday soon," Herse says to Rego. "Very soon."

Chelson pushes between two soft pink drapes into his daughter's inner room. The walls are lined with wardrobes, mirrors, and scores of shelves on which sit hundreds of tiny dolls. Each has been carefully ranked by Tristaban since she was a child, and she still moves them around occasionally as great or terrible things happen in their complex lives. Their heads swivel as one and look at him, it seems.

"My men will find the barrowman," he tells them, "and whoever hired him." Was it Eles or Blue Island? Thick as thieves, those two. No interest in war, only in rents and fees and regular routes. They did not claim. They collected. Would they really go so far to sway him and his allies on the Council to not call for war? If so, they miscalculated. War must have its sacrifices. And he must cut his losses.

The doll Chelson had made to resemble his daughter is not on top. It never is. He admires that. She's a striver. She wouldn't lose her will to climb like so many of the dolls on the middle shelves. The doll's currently third after two others. He can't remember their names.

He picks up the top doll. He ordered it for her from the Dawn Lands. Its face is red porcelain with a tiny black smile. Its dress is silk, the colors obeying no Hanoshi code. He smashes it on the tile floor between two rugs.

Whoever took Tristaban will pay, he thinks. No one steals from him.

The new number one is made of fine gray wool wrapped around cotton wadding and wood. The eyes are coming loose. *She used to sleep with this one*, he thinks. He rips off an eye, worms a finger into the torn wool beneath, and tears the fabric open. He strips off the wool like a glove from a finger, plucks away the cotton, and drops the remains. The bones clatter on the tiles.

The barrowman will be lucky to get off as easy as this doll after Holestar finds him.

Chelson picks up the Tristaban doll. She was seven when it was made. An engineer came, measured her features with calipers, and sketched her from every angle. She loves the doll, but hated standing naked and cold for so long. He shakes the doll's head. Something rattles inside. He reaches under its dress to grab its skinny thighs and whacks the head against a wardrobe. The articulated body sways, its arms flail, until the head shatters. A penny falls out.

By the time he's finished with all the dolls, the clocks are chiming four. Servants have come and gone from Tristaban's outer room, they've come and gone again, and now they're hiding in petty tasks, waiting to be told to retire.

Chelson leaves the room. He closes the drapes and presses their ends together. *Sometimes ventures fail*, he thinks. *You just have to start again*. So he'll make a new one. He's making a war. He's making an army. But why do all that to make a fortune if no one will maintain it after he's gone?

He remembers something. Back in her inner room, down on his knees, Chelson claws through broken bodies and scrapes away tattered clothes until he finds it. The penny. He pockets it.

An hour before dawn, Livion hears footsteps outside his hell. He flattens himself against the thick wooden door. A shadow blocks the knife-edge of light slipping between the wicket's hinges. He bangs on the door. "Just tell me if she's safe."

The shadow passes.

Deep beneath the Upper City, he doesn't hear a screeching come across the sky. It envelops the city and skitters the horses, but no one can pinpoint its origin.

3

By the third hour, Chelson's personal guards have questioned the foremen of the three companies that handle most of Hanosh's night soil, starting with the one owned by the Shield. None had serviced Brimurray yet. It's too far down Lesser Silk to have received such early service.

They then returned to Brimurray to question Tristaban's neighbors, who didn't appreciate being woken up, especially after their earlier inconveniences. Although most didn't like Tristaban or her partner, they helped because they feared Chelson more. Only one had something promising to report.

A junior assistant from Blue Island and his partner, both drunk, said that after Livion had come and gone, they had gone downhill a few blocks for a glass. As they left the lane, they saw a barrowman loitering in the boulevard. They didn't like the looks of him and told him so. His beard was trimmed with a carving knife, the woman said, and he wore a black shift her girl wouldn't have used to wipe a floor. His pants were the strangest leather, the man said. And he smelled, his partner said, like nothing she'd ever smelled before.

The barrowman said his looks were his own, as was his business, and the boulevard belonged to everyone. He spoke more directly than they would have imagined, and he spoke well too, almost like a junior, which only made his impudence more aggravating. They reported him to a guard outside the Quick Nip, who said he would look out for the man.

The guard told Chelson's men that when he patrolled uphill, he didn't see the barrowman, but he admitted he wasn't looking very hard. He wished he could've spoken to the couple with such impudence.

Hanosh has no end of freelancers in every trade, however despicable, which leaves Chelson's guards with the unenviable task of looking into them. To speak with the person who can probably tell them where to start, they repair to an after-hours in Workers called the Salty Dog.

The tunnel entrance extends so far into the Hill that the Dog is rumored to have a door directly into Gate's dungeons so prisoners can come out for a glass. And the ceilings are so low that some patrons flee the place, too strongly reminded of their time on the benches. Smoke collects between the beams, letting the meanest men stand to get a snort they couldn't otherwise afford.

Holestar, the man with the half-red eye, spins his pint between his hands. Skite of the Crooked Nose works on his second. The third man, Derc, who has no distinguishing features beyond his size, considers a man at the bar.

The man, a tanner by his reek, says to a corner full of cronies, "We found out where he stored his cart and waited for him. The Aydeni walks right up to us, like we're customers. Hah! First we let him watch us smash his cart, then we smashed him with the pieces. I never knew a wheel could do so much wrong to a man's face."

The men laugh. The tanner says, "One more round, then we'll get back to drafting folks for the morning." Ayes are said. Beers are brought.

Derc says, "You volunteering, Strig?"

"When Ayden gets here, I'll volunteer," he says. "In the meantime, we'll give a slap to anyone who doesn't want anyone volunteering. General orders, as it were."

Derc says, "So you'd rather fight Hanoshi than for Hanosh?"

"They aren't Hanoshi," Strig says. "And anyone fighting for Hanosh is just fighting for some company. Useless drones."

Derc says, "I fought, and I'll fight again. Hundreds will. Good men." He stands up. "Am I a fool? Are they?"

Strig looks at his cronies, and reluctantly stands. His cronies don't. Holestar hisses sharply. Derc sits down.

Strig says, "That all he has to do to pull your leash?"

All talk ceases. The smoke stands still.

"I'm going to make you a bet," Holestar says. He takes a silver coin out of his pocket and holds it up. "This whole coin says you can't beat me senseless."

Strig says, "I don't have a whole coin."

"What do you have?"

The tanner fumbles in his pockets. He finds ten pennies. "Half." He drops several pennies, which other patrons corral and return, a fair price for their amusement.

Holestar says, "That'll do." He puts the silver between his teeth and gnashes the coin in half. He drops one shard on the barrel he's drinking around and pockets the other. "Now, you could concede our bet, pay me my ten pennies, and leave, or we can play this out."

Strig hesitates. A broken old tar in the corner fondles a shark's tooth and says, "I'll bet a penny he pisses himself before he can answer."

Strig rubs the pennies off his sweaty palm onto the plank and runs from the Dog. His cronies follow sheepishly. Holestar gives the pennies to the tapman, who raises one in appreciation.

A woman comes in. Her face has the skin of a much larger face. The veins ridging her arms and hands are almost as thick as her bones. She says to the tapman so everyone can hear, "What's the story of that guy who left? I swear he pissed himself just looking at me." The after-hours patrons laugh. "Fakkin Tawmy," one says, shaking his head.

She grabs a pint, spots Holestar's crew, and comes over. "Need some help," Holestar says. He pushes the half coin to her with his cup.

"So generous," Fakkin Tawmy says, pocketing the shard. "Must be company business. No receipt, of course."

Holestar says, "I need a barrow: black, deep, two-wheeled, probably wood, possibly used for night soil, possibly not by someone formally associated with that trade. Who would I want to find?"

"You interested in the barrow or the man?"

"The barrow, to start."

"I can think of a dozen barrows like that. One stands out. It was stolen this afternoon in Servants, and found not long ago."

"Where?" Holestar says.

"Alley in the Upper City. Near the tower."

"Where is it now?"

"Back with its owner."

"Know who stole it?"

"No," Fakkin Tawmy says. "And it was empty when it was found. Someone probably needed to move something uphill and didn't want to pay a carter."

"Something, yes," Holestar says. He drains his beer. "So who's the lucky owner?"

A quarter hour later the crew watches a woman scramble out of a cesspit. She spits filth off her lips and points to a barrow, which is half-full. Holestar points at Derc.

Derc says, "Why me?"

"For spouting off in the Dog," Holestar says.

Derc takes a deep breath and squats beside the barrow with a candle. He runs his finger along the top strake. Nothing. He scratches at the residue there. He holds his palm to the light. Flakes of dried blood.

"Tell me," Holestar says to the woman, "exactly where the barrow was found."

Standing in the mouth of a pitch-black alley, the tower looming above them at its far end, Chelson's guards consider where the barrowman might have gone. The lamplit street has a dozen shops that service the tower, all closed, as are the offices of petty merchants above them. The city gates don't open for another two hours, so the shops won't open until then at the earliest.

"Not a bad place to dump a body," Skite says. "Quiet."

"I'd carry her off in the canvas," Derc says. "Like the rug that time."

"He could have put her in another barrow," Skite says, "or a carriage. She could be out of the city."

"We can't be sure she's dead," Holestar says.

"She's dead," Skite says. "No ransom note." They'd stopped at Chelson's house on the way uphill to check. "Why keep her alive? And if a company took her, would they really bring her to the tower?"

Derc says, "Maybe they want Chelson to worry all night, then speak with him right before Council when he's exhausted."

"They should be the ones worrying," Holestar says. He surveys the street and alley. "How far could he have carried her body?"

Two tower guards in their blue leather caps come around the end of the block, footfalls echoing, their shadows splattered by the streetlamps. "You three," one says. "Step out of the alley." Holestar slaps Derc's arm, which has been catching the light.

Chelson's men oblige. "What's your business?" the other guard says.

"None of yours," Holestar says. He produces a Shield badge.

The first guard says, "Not the best badge to have come morning."

"Why's that?" Holestar asks.

"Word's spreading that a war would be paid for by all our monthlies."

"Owners excluded, of course," the second says, "on account of all they do for us already with their owning."

"Who's spreading this word? Besides yourselves?"

"Talk to the people in front of the tower," the first guard says. "Give you a place to move along to."

"We'll move when we move," Holestar says.

"You'll move along now," the first guard says. He sits his hand on his pommel.

"The army could use two stalwart boys like yourself," Holestar says. "Shall I spread the word you're interested? Or would you like to keep patrolling empty streets far from any front?

"You have a nice night," the second guard says. They move along.

"Let's check this alley," Holestar says. "Give me a candle."

With flint and steel Skite sparks a piece of char cloth, with which he lights a spunk and, in turn, three candles. He passes them around and repacks his battered little tinderbox.

The alley is wagon-wide and separates two buildings whose side doors are locked. One, the dormitory for tower staff, has a fenced-in yard with a locked gate. It's shut too tightly for someone to squeeze himself or a body through, and the fence is too high to pitch a body over.

The alley opens onto a yard that wraps around a back quarter of the tower. Its windows are dark too. The crew doesn't need to be told to keep quiet as they approach the tower's service door: broad, double, made of thick wood, and standing atop a brick loading dock. It's locked. Holestar gently rattles the latch in frustration. "Who is this guy?" he says. "What's his game? Where did he go?"

Derc, seeing a glint in the candlelight, taps the side of the loading dock with his dirk. Metal. Holestar holds his candle down. Set into the side of the stoop is an iron grate painted black. A fresh scrape on the cobbles indicates it's been opened recently. Derc tests the rivets holding it in place. One falls off in his hand.

"Must be an old way to move stuff straight into the basement," Derc says. "Big enough for a man."

"A little man," Skite says.

"You have the honors, Derc," Holestar says.

Derc grumbles. He's hardly little compared to most men.

"Go," Holestar says. "We have maybe an hour and a half until dawn, two until we have to escort Herse to Council. Be nice to grab some sleep first." He wishes Chelson would let them use powder.

4

An hour before dawn and riding a double high tide, a Shield galley called *Blue Belong* approaches Hanosh at double-time and under full sail. A dinghy with a customs official named Mags, a scrivener, and three sea guards is rowed out to meet them just beyond the gibbets. The galley lowers her sail and draws in her oars. The official declares himself and requests permission to come aboard. The captain, Sivarts, grants it, the dinghy ties on, and the party climbs aboard. The two rowers, employed in one of the last positions available to guild members, stay with the dinghy.

Sivarts has never given Mags problems before, and his paperwork is always neat and accurate, so Mags's little visits are usually quick and uncomplicated. In the cant of his profession, they are enjoyable.

Sivarts presents his manifest. As he examines it, the scrivener looks over his arm to calculate the harbor fees. Mags hands it to him, then he takes some records from the satchel the scrivener wears on his back. He compares them to the manifest. Mags says, "Your load looks light compared to previous ones. And you're three days early."

"Our enterprise wasn't paying out," Sivarts says. "No sense in staying in Yness." He knows questions like these are within Mags's purview, but it's always felt like prying to him. Fortunately the Shield's informants say Mags isn't an informant for their competitors.

"Why the rush?"

"Time. Tide."

Mags checks the crew roster again and digs out more records. He says, "Why do you have three cabin boys? On your previous voyage you had two. I thought that was the standard Shield complement now."

Sivarts says, "One fell ill in Yness. We took on a new boy to handle his duties."

"Ynessi?"

"No, Hanoshi," Sivarts says. "And a Shield boy. He'd been left behind by an earlier ship. Got a long-deserved whipping for tardiness."

"You're lacking two rowers."

"Powder burn."

"That why you took on a healer?"

"Yes," Sivarts says. "My rowers' boy has a heavy hand. That's why he took ill, too." Sivarts shakes his head. "Shame to lash someone so sick. He really couldn't appreciate it."

"This healer a Shield orphan too?"

"No," Sivarts says, "but she's Hanoshi. Traded her craft for passage home."

"Good," Mags says. "Let's take a look at your cargo."

"Is anything out of order?"

"Not that I can see," Mags says, glancing at the paperwork. "But, security's been tightened. We could be at war with Ayden in a few hours."

"War? What's changed in the last week?"

"Time. Tide," Mags says. He turns to a guard. "You come with us."

"You realize this is a Shield galley?"

"Entirely, Captain."

Sivarts smiles with clenched teeth. So that's the way of it. They need better informants. "Let's go below." He ushers the agent and reduced party forward.

The search is perfunctory, Mags's point made. In twenty minutes the dinghy is leading the galley to the pier, where the cranes go to work immediately. Once Mags has moved off, a wagon is brought up. Two sailors carry a stretcher out of a stern cabin. On it an unconscious figure is wrapped to the chin in clean white sheets. What's visible of her face is badly burned.

The new cabin boy, Rowan, walks with the stretcher to the wagon. He helps load her, then climbs aboard himself.

Sivarts says, "They'll take her to the Castle. You'll come with me to see an owner."

"She'll be taken care of?" Rowan says.

"Yes."

The boy squeezes Everlyn's hand and climbs out of the wagon. He and the captain walk uphill.

The wagon rumbles through the Harbor, nearly overwhelming the screeching that comes across the sky. The poth stirs, but can't sit up. The straps beneath the sheets are too tight.

Before the lowest gates of the West Crest a crowd of workers has gathered. A few are half-drunk from earlier that evening. Most are sober and well behaved. No one says anything as Sivarts passes through them, but they barely part, forcing him to rub his pristine silk against their dingy leathers and sagging cottons. Rowan nods at them, but their faces don't unscowl.

Sivarts says to a Crest guard corporal, "Who's let these people gather?"

"That's Quiet's business," he says. "Ours ends at the gates."

"And where are they?"

The corporal has no response.

"Open the gates, then," Sivarts says. "I have company business with Chelson. Sivarts, captain of *Blue Belong*."

A guard in a lamplit guard box checks some papers. He shakes his head. The corporal says, "I'll have to send for confirmation."

"Has this city gone mad?" Sivarts says.

"Just doing our duty," the corporal says. A glance sends a private walking toward Chelson's house.

The crowd stares at the captain. Their faces are flashes of beard and bitter flesh in the lamplight. Their eyes are holes. Tiny shuffles and slow shifts press them closer to the captain, who puts an arm in front of the cabin boy and reaches for his sword.

Rowan says, "Why are you here?"

A woman in a worn tunic carefully repaired and soft leather pants that have been severely brushed says, "I will not pay for their war." People shake their heads. "None of us will. Whatever Ayden did."

"If they did anything," a painter says.

"What did they do?" Rowan says. "Did they attack us?" He asked Sivarts for permission to go home, but the captain refused. Now he really wants to go. His father, as a sergeant in the army, would know what's happening.

One of Chelson's footmen approaches. "I'll take them," he says to the corporal.

The corporal opens the gate just wide enough to admit Sivarts and Rowan. Still, the woman in the tunic tries to slip in. The corporal gives her the back of his hand and sends her sprawling. Fish that had been hidden under her tunic spill onto the cobbles. The guards laugh, which makes the crowd grumble. This quiets the guards, and the sound of steel sliding from the guard's scabbards quiets the crowd in turn. The painter helps the woman up.

Sivarts can't imagine Chelson sleeping. His face is a shell, his eyes glassy and unblinking, black as a doll's, his body, like his will, unbending. He seems particularly stiff when he meets them in a room off his courtyard. It's lit by a brazier so tepid it sucks light from the air rather than casts it. The servants look as wan. Only the footman who fetched them has a spring in his step.

"This is Rowan," Sivarts says, "the *Hopper*'s boy and its only survivor."

At the name of the ship Chelson's eyes clench. Sivarts figures he knows something of the story already. He proceeds as if it's new, though.

"Three days ago," he says, "he showed up at our agent's in Yness with a woman and a remarkable tale."

"Where is the woman?"

"The Castle," Sivarts says. "She's injured and uncooperative."

"Who have you told this story to, boy?"

Rowan says, "The captain and the agent."

"And the woman, who has she?"

"No one," the boy says. "I brought her straight to the agent's."

"She's barely told us anything," Sivarts says. "She had no contact with anyone except Rowan, and he never left her side."

"Summarize."

"Four days before Rowan came to us and not long after the *Hopper* made the turn east, the galley was attacked and badly damaged by a small dragon—a dragon that was being ridden. It carried off the captain."

"Where did the woman come from?"

Why would Chelson be more interested in a stranger's history, Sivarts thinks, *than his captain's fate?* "The *Hopper* followed the dragon and found an island in the ocean. Possibly Gladsend."

"It doesn't exist."

"Or maybe not. The woman, Vel, was living there. She had a sword. She defended her land."

"Admirable. Why was she there?"

"She wouldn't say. Right after the galley landed, the rowers, led by one called Bearclaw, attacked the crew."

"While chained?"

Rowan says, "Before he was taken Tuse made sure they would be freed so they wouldn't burn alive."

Chelson scowls. "Go on."

"The battle took to the woods," Sivarts says. "The woman took the crew's side, apparently. She saved Rowan from Bearclaw, their last man standing, after he killed ours, a harpooner named Igen. She was badly injured, so he sailed her to Yness in the galley's dinghy."

"What about the dragon and its rider?"

"No sign was found of them. The cabin where the woman lived, though, had a second bed. It could have been his. She said it was a man's. Said his name was Jon."

"And Tuse?"

"No sign of him either. The woman said she didn't know anything about him or a dragon, ridden or not."

"Is all this true, boy?"

"Yes."

"A boy sailed to Yness in a dinghy from an island in the ocean, and he kept a woman alive?"

"We had the wind," Rowan says, "and supplies from the island. The woman kept herself alive. She knows medicine."

"Probably how she stayed alive on the island," Sivarts says. "She was horribly burned at some point."

"Was the rider Aydeni?" Chelson asks.

"I couldn't tell," Rowan says. "He was flying very fast. He had a beard. But his skin looked as dark as ours."

"But could he have been?"

"Possibly."

Sivarts says, "The woman is Hanoshi. In fact, she's wearing an old Shield captain's blouse."

Chelson has half a thought then pushes it aside. "Probably some ragpicker's prize," he says. "What matters is, you must be sure."

"How?"

Chelson brushes a fleck from Rowan's shoulder. "What will you be, boy, when you grow up?"

"A captain."

"No," Chelson says. "You will be what I say you will be. Isn't that right, Captain?"

Sivarts says, "Yes."

Rowan looks at Sivarts. *No matter what you wear, you're never not a cabin boy*, he thinks.

"So was the rider Aydeni?"

Rowan's father always reminds him, "It's not your lie if they make you tell it." So he says, "Yes."

"Good," Chelson says. "At Council this morning, you will repeat that. In the meantime, Sivarts, you stay with the woman."

"She needs a surgeon more than me."

Rowan brightens at this. *Boys and their attachments*, Chelson thinks. Nonetheless, if it will grease his compliance, Chelson says, "Of course. The Shield takes care of its own. I'll have our best surgeon attend to her, not one of those bloodletters or useless herbwives."

Rowan relaxes. Sivarts departs. Chelson gestures to his footman. "Have they arrived?"

The footman shakes his head.

Chelson's expression suggests he doesn't know if this is a good sign or a bad one. "Tell my house guard to assemble. They'll escort us to Council. And see that the palanquin is readied. I will give you a note for the surgeon before we leave." The footman bows and leaves. "Have you ever ridden in a palanquin, boy?"

Rowan says, "No."

"You won't today either," Chelson says. "Always provide a diversion. By the time people realize you're not where they think, they may have run out of fish and rocks to throw at you."

5

Derc slides into an improvised pantry. Shelves wall it off from the rest of the kitchen that fills much of the tower's basement. He feels his way around, listening, but no sounds come from the darkness.

"Give me the candles," he says. They're passed down and he paces the kitchen's perimeter. Their quarry isn't here, and the sculleries must sleep in the nearby dorm. They'll be arriving soon, though, probably in less than an hour, to light the fireplaces and ovens. The kitchen serves all the companies in the tower, and the slightest fault in service is considered a great slight.

Derc goes back to the grate and slips in a pool of something on the floor.

Holestar calls down, "What's the problem?"

Derc checks the ground. Olive oil. He looks around. A jar of peppers is smashed on the floor, and jars don't leap from shelves by themselves.

"He's been through here," Derc says.

"That clinches it," Skite says. "He's Aydeni. If he'd been working for a company, he'd have had a key to the door."

"Let us in the back door," Holestar says. "We can't fit through the grate like you, Little Man."

Derc grits his teeth.

Holestar watches the candleglow fade as Derc heads upstairs.

While they wait they put the grate back into place. No sense in letting anyone else know there's a secret way into the tower. They might need it themselves some day.

Several minutes pass. Skite works the door latch absently. Holestar hisses. "Let's go in and see what's happened to him," Holestar says.

The men reopen the grate and squeeze into the basement, nearly shattering several more jars, and replace the grate behind them as best they can in the dark. They feel their way to the stairwell whose stone steps end in a door ajar. Candleglow seeps past it.

Holestar peers through. The candles are scattered on the flagstone floor. One remains lit. Holestar doesn't hear anything, so he and Skite draw their weapons and enter the arched service hallway beyond.

It circles the tower beneath the council chamber. Doors lead to cloakrooms, janitorial closets, night closets, and a small armory. At each end a door leads to the tower's entry hall and in the middle is a spiral servants' stair leading to the top of the tower.

Holestar sees Derc's weapon on the flagstones. It sits in a smear of blood and points toward a closed door. Skite listens at the door. He hears a steady sound, like someone tapping his foot unconsciously, and he smells excrement. He checks the door. It's unlocked. They relight the candles and stand them on the floor. Holestar counts to three and flings open the door.

Derc sits on a circle of wood atop a brick-lined cesspit, his throat slashed, blood dripping between his legs through a hole into the pool of waste below.

Skite says, "Was he lying in wait for us?"

"Maybe he saw us approaching," Holestar says. He closes Derc's dumbfounded eyes and says, "We'll come back for you." He closes the door.

They hear two whistles from around the dark curve of the hallway. A hinge creaks. Holestar whispers into Skite's ear, "Take the candles. I'll circle around through the entry hall and come down the other side of the hallway. In a minute move up slowly. He'll think I'm still here, and I'll catch him from behind." Skite nods and picks up the candles. He holds two in one hand, one in the other, and spreads them far apart to make it look like two people are advancing.

Holestar takes Derc's weapon and passes into the entry hall. He sees the vaulted space in his mind. The creamy granite walls that give off a rose aura in the right light. The huge brass doors, twenty feet high. The two black-iron spiral staircases, one for the public, one for owners, that lead all the way to the top of the tower. The broad sweep of marble stairs leading to the half floor where Council is held. And on the far side the other door to the service hallway.

Through tall windows, skinny as arrow slits, Holestar sees pinpricks of light, the torches and lanterns of cowards and sympathizers, defeatists and capital saboteurs. *They might as well be fireflies trying to raze a barn*, he thinks.

Holestar enters the hallway. He creeps forward. By his count Skite will be moving too. He can't see the candlelight yet. He flexes his fingers around his hatchet and the dirk. His palms are dry as stone.

Chelson wants the barrowman questioned before he's killed so he can know why his daughter was taken. Holestar thought it would be a waste of time, but the chase has him looking forward to it. He wants to chew off the man's fingertips for killing Derc.

Candleglow seeps around the corner. Holestar tenses. The door to the servants' stair is ahead. It's ajar. The candles advance. He edges toward the door. Skite gives a slight bob of his head to indicate he sees Holestar, but doesn't move to alert their quarry behind the door. When the light touches his feet, Holestar rips open the door.

There's no one there, just a dark wood panel in a frame where a painting might once have been set.

Two whistles echo down the stone steps. They bolt upstairs. Skite shakes the candles out so they can't be targeted in the dark.

There's nothing more intimate than a blind fight, sensing your partner's movements, reaching out deftly, wanting the fatal touch.

Their quarry scurries away.

"Headed for the first chambers," Holestar says. Skite grunts, too winded for speech.

At the top of the stairs, they fold over, gasping, waving their dirks before them to stave off any attack. They hear a clanking in the darkness. More stairs. The original council chamber is ringed with broad windows, the walls far thinner up here than they have to be at the bottom. They can see the first brush of dawn on the horizon, but that does little for the vaulted room.

Skite says, "We've got him trapped up here. Let's get some more men and make sure he doesn't get away."

"No," Holestar says. "We've come this far. And it's nearly six. This place will be swarming with people soon, and Chelson doesn't want outside interference."

Skite exhales long, inhales slowly, and stands up, ready. Holestar claps him on the back.

"There's a door onto the widow's walk to our right," Holestar says. They inch along the wall. Skite bumps into the door, which is barred. "He couldn't have gone this way."

Holestar, nodding in the dark, says, "He's on top of the dome. Follow me."

"I can't," Skite says. "I have to get my bearings. Let's light a candle. He probably knows where we are. If he's waiting nearby we'll see him."

"I don't like it," Holestar says, but he lets Skite light his candle.

They're behind the banc. Sailcloth covers it and the pews and desks arrayed before it. Dust covers the rest. There are faint footprints and drag marks on the thick red runner that circles the room. They end at skinny decorative iron stairs that run up around the back of the dome. A catwalk then leads to a ladder rising to a trapdoor in the center of the dome.

"Of all the places in the city to hide, why this one?" Skite says. "Why not get lost in the Rookery?"

"Who would look here?"

"He'd have to be strong to get the girl up here, if he has," Skite says. "I hope we're after the right guy."

"He's the right guy now," Holestar says. He peers at the trapdoor. He could swear it was open just enough for someone to look through.

"How do you want to go through?"

"He'll take off any head as soon as it pokes through," Holestar says. He points across the room. Behind the banc stand several short flagpoles for displaying the councilors' company colors during sessions. "That's what we need. I'll go first. You push open the trapdoor with a pole and stir it around. That'll distract him enough for me to get through and take a swipe."

"I'll mop up. As usual."

Skite admires Holestar's courage. Holestar admires Skite's optimism.

The iron stair was not made for such large men. It creaks and pulls at the arches in the dome. They get into position on the ladder, Skite holding the candle against the pole. Holestar checks the trapdoor. It

doesn't give. Something heavy blocks it. Then it slides aside with heavy footsteps and the door loosens.

Skite gives Holestar the wide eye. Holestar gives the signal. Skite pushes the trapdoor and rams the pole through. Holestar and his hatchet follow. Three whistles, a snap of wood, a snap of bone, and the top of the pole falls through the door, followed by Holestar's hand with the hatchet. They thunk onto the catwalk. Holestar hisses and tries to slide down the ladder. Skite, frozen, blocks him. Holestar looks up and ducks his head.

Not far enough. Skite hears three whistles again and sees what looks like a great gray shark head dive through the trapdoor to clamp Holestar's head, twisting it as he screams, then wrenches it off.

Holestar's other hand releases the ladder. His body drops on Skite, who holds it above him like a shield as he drops to the catwalk. The head lashes out and grabs Holestar's body. It smashes him against the sides of the trapdoor repeatedly until enough bones are shattered for him to fold in half and squeeze through. Between smashes, Skite dives backward. He drops the candle through the grate. He watches the flame get very small before puffing out.

The trapdoor, this high up, lets a touch of dawn glitter on the falling plaster. *Like snow*, Skite thinks. He hears an awful screech. At first he thinks the creature made it, then he realizes it's a female voice, terror, agony, and confusion compressed into a single withering note. The light vanishes as the creature pushes through the trapdoor again. The screech is damped.

Skite puts one knee forward. He has to move. He slides his hand along the iron. He moves his knee. The creature snaps at him, and its snout knocks him half off. He hangs in the darkness, swinging his legs, trying to find the catwalk with his foot.

The creature watches him.

Skite's foot catches the catwalk. He pulls himself back up. He crawls halfway to the stairs. Somehow he can see in the dark. He's almost there.

The creature hammers its head against the ladder. The shock cascades through the iron to the catwalk, dislodging Skite's hand. The creature's breath sounds like a chuckle. It hammers the ladder and bounces Skite off again. He dangles, twisting, by one hand. He reaches for the catwalk. His fingertips graze the iron. *It's always rougher than it looks*, he thinks. The creature hammers one more time. The iron buzzes, his fingers leap off it as if stung, and he falls.

CHAPTER TEN

The Tower

1

The city gates open at six hours. Farmers from the garden villages with wagons full of produce, caravans from other cities, and traders on foot and horseback start to line up before sunrise, hoping to get a jump on the competition. They're usually met by carts selling okono and coffee, and a squad of Hanoshi Town guards who keep the peace and a portion of everyone's wares.

Workers normally appear just before the gates open, but today they've already formed a column of their own, five shoulders wide, longer than usual and so unruly that several platoons from the camp march along either side with tower shields to contain them. Many want to attack Ayden, and they cheer as soldiers drag away those who say they don't. When some of the silent are also taken away, the rest become more vocal supporters as a matter of disguise.

The traders bet on who will be pulled out of line next while others laugh that they might as well be betting on raindrops wandering down a window. When one decides this might not be the best day to trade in the city and turns out of the line, the soldiers descend on him, yank him from his horse as a possible spy, and arrest him. Before the town guards can confiscate his bags and mount, the soldiers take that as well. From that point on the traders express their hope for a speedy victory.

A quarter hour before six Rego emerges from an interior tower with a Sergeant Pashing and two soldiers, who carry a blue chest between them. In the gate plaza they link up with the other ten men in Pashing's squad. Like the two bearers, they wear brass helms, plain cuirasses, bracers and greaves, and their tower shields create a wall around a horse-drawn cart. Two turn their shields like a double door, and the chest is put in the bed of the cart. Rego checks the lock again and tries not to touch the pocket where he put the key.

Then he confers with the gate sergeant, who's inspecting his own squads. The sergeant says his men have noted who should be let in and who should not. Rego doesn't want any trouble he doesn't expect.

Birming runs up. The sergeant is in uniform now, that of a supply master, but it's as rumpled as his ashen face. He looks more exhausted than Rego. Pashing is disgusted, but Rego sees no point in chewing him out.

"Are you sick?" Rego says.

"No, I'm ready."

Rego has heard rumors about Birming's problems with his partner, but you don't ask after another's house. Birming's not the type to speak about his family anyway. Nor is Rego.

Birming climbs onto the wagon and takes the reins, Rego sits beside him, and Pashing's squad escorts the wagon to the Blue Tower.

From some windows they receive cheers. From others, the splatter from upturned pots of excrement. Rego nods to them all. He understands why Herse has craved his influence since they were boys. Nobody hates a nobody.

Rego hears a crowd in the tower plaza, the largest in the city, when they're still several blocks away. It sounds like the sea crashing against a cliff. Throughout his sleepless night, Gate had received reports of people gathering there in defiance of the law, but apparently with the blessing of the guard. *They can't quail now*, Rego thinks. *This is where it begins*. Herse once confided in him that a war wouldn't start with Ayden, it would start with Hanosh, and this wagon is the van. They have to show themselves.

As they come around the corner into the din, Rego sees that people have flooded the south half of the plaza in front of the tower and more are surging in from surrounding lanes. Too few demand the war. Laborers, fishermen and seamen, foremen, traders and shopkeeps, barkeeps and night folk, the vomit of prisons and workhouses, artists and other wastrels, a motley of the undyed, the white, the black, and even a few silk. Whole factories and offices must be empty. Rego reads the simple declaration in their numbers: *You can't fire us all or fit us in your dungeons*.

Many, unable to wait for Council to begin, are throwing dead fish at the tower's massive doors while the four guards flanking them maintain their stiff posture. There are nearly as many children as adults in the crowd, and they've taken to the chanting with a passion and a pitch all their own, especially those armed with sacks of minnows. A majority has strips of bleached cotton tied around their heads like whitecapped waves. Women are tearing off the hems of their skirts to make more.

This is not good. These should be their people. He has to hand it to Ject. His rumor was an effective counter, and his guards are letting it simmer. A couple dozen arrayed in pairs around the plaza are doing less than the tower guards and with worse posture. Their commanding sergeant, Husting, meets the wagon as it enters. Pashing says to him, "Break up this demonstration. It's illegal."

Husting says, "Why, as a restraint of trade? Ask the owners of those grill carts and coffee carts. They've never done so much business this early. It's a flash market, not a demonstration."

A pig-tailed little girl in a darling blue-check dress made of feed sacks sees them and yells, "Pa, there they are! Let's get them." Part of the crowd breaks toward the wagon.

A man with six fingers and a stub says, "If there's a war, it won't come out of our pockets!" The others shout in agreement. Another holds up his bony son and says, "You want him to starve?" The boy cries in terror, which infuriates the crowd more.

Rego has never fought in a battle or wanted to. His blade is slow, and he'd be washed away on a battlefield like crops in a flood. But he would follow Herse anywhere, just as he did when they were growing up, Rego younger and smaller, Herse including him in all his escapades and making sure Rego ate. Herse always said he would shine in his own way sometime. This is his moment.

Rego and Birming take the chest from the bed and put it between them on the seat. It lands with a distinctive jingle and clink. He stands and with a flourish takes the key from his pocket. The crowd's anger shifts momentarily to curiosity. Rego unlocks the chest with a happy snap. He pockets the key and turns to the crowd, one hand on the chest lid. He flips it open. The chest is stuffed with the small raw cloth bags he spent the night filling while Herse was out rallying the troops.

He opens one and tips silver into his hand. "If there's a war, those good Hanoshi who volunteer will receive an immediate bonus of four whole coins."

That's the monthly for many. A discord resonates throughout the crowd. One man calls out, "I'll do it for three!"

The six-fingered man says, "You fool! They'd pay you with your own money."

"No," says the father, "they'd pay you with my money." He lowers the boy and confronts the bargainer.

Arguments break out across the plaza. Scores of people surge at the wagon when they hear the army is giving away coin.

"You can't perform army business in the city," Husting says.

"Except for recruitment," Rego says.

The crowd bores in. The soldiers' shield wall expands to collect

Husting and Pashing, then condenses again and stiffens. A fish flies past Rego's head. Rego sees the man who threw it knocked down. The arguments are turning physical. Rego says, "Unless there is order, there will be no bonuses." This only confuses people, who surge against the shields. Rego feels like he's on an island.

Pashing says, "Either the guard moves these people back or we do."

"You move back. Get this wagon out of the plaza. And the city," Husting says.

A roar erupts from a street east of the plaza and a large band of workers, armed with hammers, awls, and fury, appears. A moment later the gate horn blows three times. Their sympathizers outside will soon arrive and with those already here clamp down like a crab claw on the antiwar faction.

Chelson and Rowan approach the plaza from the east on Hill Street, surrounded by Chelson's house guards. They hear the singing before they see the band of workers emerge from alleys and lanes behind them. The house guards half draw their weapons at their approach, but when the band sees their badges they cheer.

A tanner shakes a poker like a mad conductor. "Up with the Shield!" he shouts. "Down with Ayden! It's time they pay." Some are wearing bits of kit from previous service. Wannabes wear scraps of salvaged uniforms. All carry tools yearning to be weapons.

They part to reveal Herse in full uniform, his sash perfectly ordered for once. He says, "What do you think of my own guard?"

Chelson thinks, *These people should be the making of my army, not his*. And at least two of the men are the Shield's. He wonders what work is not getting done.

He says, "We have to speak."

"Of course." Herse leaps onto a nearby barrel so he can be seen, holds up his arms, and says to the crowd, "I'll meet you at the tower in a few minutes. And in a few weeks we'll meet in Ayden!"

The crowd thrusts their weapons in the air and continues on. Herse jumps down and the guards create a wall around him and their master.

"A dragon did attack the *Hopper*," Chelson says. "This powder boy is the only survivor."

Herse grimaces.

"He can turn it to our advantage, though," Chelson says. "The dragon was ridden—"

"Ridden?" Herse says. "Mounted-on-its-back ridden?" He holds his hands as if gripping reins. "And flying?"

"Yes," Rowan says.

"What I could do with that," Herse says.

Finally, Rowan thinks, *someone who's amazed*.

"The boy will tell the Council the rider was Aydeni."

Herse smiles. "Ayden armed with a dragon," he says. "That'll put the fear of night into people."

A roar erupts far ahead. "If our soldiers haven't already," Chelson says.

Eles, the other councilors, and their remora—assistants, accountants, and adjutants—are escorted to South by city guards, then led as a unit to the Blue Tower. Why pay for personal guards when you can use the city's? And it's so much more impressive.

Ject, Ravis, and the rest of his own guard take the van. Eles says, "I've gotten reports of disturbances all night and people gathering, and I don't like the way that person is looking at us."

A scrawny old cabbage dealer with a green headwrap and a thin gray beard peers at them from behind a wagonload of crop. Ject snaps his fingers. Ravis knocks a wave of cabbages over him. The man ducks, crying, "My cabbages!"

"They're worried about the war," Ject says. "They haven't caused any trouble."

"What business is it of theirs?" Eles say. "They have no skin in the game."

As they turn into the plaza, a roar erupts on the other side and chants bleed together into a muddle.

Ject doesn't see anyone from the offices in the tower. That is not a good sign. They're tougher to scare off than squirrels.

"This is outrageous," Eles says. "The city will grind to a halt."

"Sometimes," Ject says, "it's better to let a person rage for a few minutes than beat him into raving for a day."

"And whose minutes are they using?" Eles says. "Ours." The others, huddled together, nod. "I want these people at their jobs by seven."

Ject says, "Of course."

"And arrest those with no better employment," Eles says. "If there is war, we'll need the troops."

Ject looks up to avoid looking exasperated.

A guard stumbles out of the crowd. He pulls himself to attention before his general. Ject says, "Report."

"A mob for the war just arrived," the guard says. "They're armed. Those against it are not."

"Except for fish," Eles says. "Let's see them defend themselves with those."

"And at the top of the plaza," the guard points toward Rego's wagon, "the army is stirring up trouble. They've offered a bonus to volunteers."

Eles sucks at a hard bony lip and says to himself, *I will not be provoked*.

Ject is silently triumphant. Herse has overplayed his hand, and Ject will take the pot, starting with the money the soldiers are giving away.

For the moment, though, he has to bring some order to the current situation. Chaos is no longer necessary. He tells Ravis, "Blow the general alarm. Then we'll bring the councilors back to South until the plaza is safe."

Ravis blows. Horns respond from around the plaza. It's a sad scattered sound. The crowd's energy hardly abates.

A riot will still be worth it, Ject thinks, *even if we take no prisoners*.

To avoid the tower plaza, Chelson's party approaches the tower from the rear. "Only fools take the front door," he says.

Chelson leads them down an alley to a small courtyard where several carts are making deliveries at a wide stoop. A cook complains about the filth on some cabbages. When she sees Chelson approach, she stands aside. The cabbage dealer doesn't realize he's there until Chelson is breathing on his shoulder, astounded that someone is in his way.

Chelson tells the cook, "Buy no more from him," and goes inside.

The cabbage dealer apologizes to no avail. Herse waits until Chelson disappears and says, "Speak to Birming, one of my supply masters. He'll need your cabbages." The man glows.

The cook approves, but warns him, "Tell your man to make sure there's no filth on them."

Eles elevates his nose and says, "We will not go back to South or back to anywhere. We will go to the tower." He cuts between Ject and Ravis and stalks across the plaza. The guards hurry to catch up, and the rest hurry to stay within their circle. Ject reluctantly follows.

Near the steps to the wide porch in front of the tower they're seen. The tide turns and tips toward them.

Eles mounts the porch as workers lap against Ject's men and are pushed back. The tower guards knock, the doors are unbarred, and as they open Eles says to the crowd, "Get to work, you useless eaters."

Ject watches a small silver fish—a boops, he thinks—arc, glistening, and hit him squarely in the eye.

The crowd on each side of the issue laughs as Eles wipes fish smear from his face. They laugh harder as he wheels around and leads his party to the brass doors. Eles surveys the crowd as the Council enters. His expression suggests the crowd has overplayed its hand.

As Ject enters, Eles says, "We won't require your testimony today, General." And he signals for the tower guards to shut the door behind him, leaving Ject outside.

Ject looks up now in total exasperation. He notices the huge Hanoshi ravens aren't circling the dome or perched on the edge. That can't be a good sign either. Nothing drives them off. He wonders what might have and realizes something.

"Ject?" Ravis says.

"When we looked for the dragon," Ject says, "we didn't search the cupola."

2

Herse and Rowan stand in the waiting area outside the council chamber while the Council conducts some last-minute horse-trading over who will get what shares of the army contracts. After seeing Eles close the door on Ject, Herse is feeling confident. Rowan looks less so.

"You'll do fine, son," Herse says.

"It's not that," Rowan says. He's reluctant to be too familiar with the general, but he's Herse. Rowan was raised on stories of his exploits on the ballcourt and how he used to go into the crowd after big wins, especially against Aydeni teams. His interest in a ship's boy is encouraging.

"It's my father. He's a supply master. Birming."

"I thought I recognized you. You used to wait for him outside camp." The boy nods. "Steady man, your father," he says. "Like yourself, I understand."

Rowan's spine stiffens.

Herse got the basics of Rowan's story from Chelson as they walked to the tower. The boy saw scores of men die horribly. Herse knows what that's like from fighting bandits. You can't get the images out of your eyes, like the glare that persists after you look at the sun. As much as Herse wants to ask about the dragon and how Rowan survived, he'll wait until after Council. When they grill him on this, he needs Rowan's emotions to be fresh and raw.

"Have you seen him yet?" Herse says. "Or your family? You have a sister, right?"

"A sister, yes," Rowan says, "and no. There's been no time."

"I've kept him busy the last couple days too. Right after Council, we'll change that."

"It's not that either," Rowan says. "When we go to war, what will happen to him?"

"He'll do his job," Herse says. "I've always counted on him."

"Will he die? Like Tuse?"

Herse says, "I was younger than you during the last war. Do you know why it was fought?" Rowan shakes his head. "Tolls. Tolls. My father went, though. Many fathers did. Not for the owners. For their neighbors."

"What happened to him?"

"He fought," Herse says. "He was no soldier. But a sword's a tool, and he knew tools. He could make anything. Build anything. He showed me the sword he made. It was nearly as impressive as his saws. Or his uniform." Herse listens at the chamber doors for a moment. "He looked taller in it, more solid. Nicest clothes he ever had. Same's true for most of our men. You should have seen them on parade."

"What's parade?" Rowan asks.

Herse looks sad. "I don't imagine you'd know. Parades were like parties the city threw itself, some people marching, some watching them march, and everyone in fancy or fantastic clothes. Sugar cakes and salted knots sold on every corner. A hundred songs blooming across the city. My mother nearly swooned when Papa marched by. I thought she was scared of what would happen to him. I was scared myself, but when I got older and put on my first military uniform, I realized she'd swooned because he'd looked so good."

Rowan can't imagine his parents looking at each other like that. They don't hold hands. They don't hug. That's why his father sent him away. That's why he happily went.

"A war will bring that back," Herse says. "We'll have parades again."

"Did your father die?"

"Yes." At Rowan's expression he adds, "Many years later with a beer in his hand and a pipe between his lips."

They smile. The chamber door opens. The tower guard says, "They'll have the boy now." Herse pats Rowan on the shoulder and gives him a gentle shove toward the arc of cold faces.

At this point Ject can't recall if he really believed the dragon story. "We have to check the cupola," he says.

Ravis looks dubious, but that's as far as he'll go.

They stride off the porch with as much dignity as possible with the crowd jeering Ject. At the edge of the plaza he stops a half squad of guards just arriving. They're from Quiet, not the best men, certainly not as capable as those from their opposite tower, Riot, and more used to soothing silk than wading into a seething mob of drunks in the Rookery. He relieves them of their crossbows and hip quivers and sends them to South to help with processing.

One, Isco, looks too relieved. *He will profit from a post in the dungeon,* Ject thinks.

The general gives the weapons to his own men. "We're going up top."

Oftly, the newest member of the detail, looks dismayed. "Will we still get a share of the arrested?"

"If we bag what's up there," Ject says, "the boys down here will want to share with us."

Ravis holds up a hand. He presses his middle three fingers together and flaps his pinky and thumb. The men stand a bit taller. They'll get new boots from this.

Ject quickly directs several sergeants to form up two ranks like plows along the west side of the plaza, then he leads his own men to the tower's rear entrance. A huntsman with a bag of turkeys nearly leaps off the stoop, having seen how Chelson treated the cabbage dealer.

Inside Ject pushes past the cook and says, "We're going up top." He spies a scullery looking out the door to the kitchen stairs. "Keep your people down here."

"What's the—"

"Guard business." Ject and his men march into the entry hall, where several tower guards stand behind the brass doors. Several more stand before the outer doors to the council chamber's waiting area. They look through the windows, hands on their pommels. Their sergeant, Chevron, brings them to attention.

Ject says, "Put two men on the back door. Keep the main ones closed."

"Yes," Chevron says. "Can we assist—"

"If you hear our horns, come running. That'll make up for your men locking me out."

Herse listens at the chamber doors, but can't make anything out. He paces the waiting area. He never realized how tight it is, the long room locked between two sets of doors with two lines of iron benches, the dim light letting the walls teeter over him. He could use some air. His job's done anyway.

He knocks on the outer doors. A tower guard opens one just in time for Herse to see Ject and his men disappear up the public stairs. He notes crossbows, and he wonders where they are going in such a hurry, especially with a confrontation heating up outside and Ject the one who threw the soup together and put it on the fire. Certainly he can't be thinking of shooting down into the crowd. Herse has to see what the city general is up to. Besides, he can't go back into the waiting area.

Taking the owners' stairs would expose him as much as following Ject up the public stairs, so he descends to the entry hall and heads for the service hallway. The tower guards give him dirty looks. As Ject goes, so do they. There's no point in reminding them that the city expects they will do their duty. He looks forward to the moment when they, like the rest of the guards, are under his command.

Herse closes the door behind him and, using a key copied long ago, enters the closet that serves as the tower's armory. He selects a dirk, a crossbow, and a half-dozen bolts, makes sure the hallway's clear, relocks the door, and runs to the servants' stair.

Above the company floors Ject finds a locked door. He sends Oftly to the cook, who sends him to the tower seneschal, who has much to do, so much to do.

"I have much to do," the seneschal says as Oftly releases him in front of Ject like a cat presenting a rat.

"The door," Ject says. "And any above."

"Why?"

"Guard business."

The man produces an enormous key ring with dozens of keys. He considers each slowly then flips it over the top of the ring. He says, "I thought you'd come to investigate the thefts we've suffered."

"What thefts?" Ject says.

"Meat. Drink. Two nights ago. I had to beat a scullery. Do you know what our tower contract costs? How are we to make a profit—"

"How much meat?"

"Two roasts. A belly." Another key flips over. "The meat was shifted to disguise their disappearance, but I knew."

Is that enough for a dragon? Ject thinks. *Do dragons steal? Could the dragon have an ally, some misguided girl who thinks it's her friend?* He should speak with the scullery. For the moment: "Open the door, and I'll look into it."

"What assurance do I have?" Another key flips.

"What assurance do your ledgers provide that you didn't steal the meat yourself?"

"Perfect assurance," the seneschal says. "Ah, here it is." He fits a key into the lock.

Herse reaches the door leading to the unused portions of the tower. The lock's already been forced, then rigged to appear not so. It opens on darkness. He's pulling a candle from a sconce on the wall when a face appears below.

"You can't go up there," the scullery says.

Herse can see down her ratty tunic. Her bony chest is covered with bruises. He says, "The cook beat you?"

"That's the seneschal's privilege. He said I was a thief."

"Are you?"

"Does it matter?" the scullery says. "If you go up there he'll blame me. And for the lock."

"Did you break it?"

"No," she says. "I found it that way two days ago. He'll send me to a whorehouse to work off the damages."

There will come a time very soon . . . how often has he thought that? He would ask her why a scullery was all the way up here, but her puffy eyes tell that story. In the meantime, he can do something to help her.

He takes the crossbow from the shadows and smashes the lock with the butt of the stock until something snaps inside and the door swings free. "There, I did it."

The scullery smiles with her remaining teeth. She's never had a hero before.

Herse says, "Do you have a candle I could borrow?"

The scullery rummages through the pockets of her apron and comes up with a tallow stub. She lights it with a sconce and hands it, quivering, to him. He makes sure to touch her finger lightly as he takes it. Her hand shakes more.

"I'll return this soon," Herse says. "Don't let anyone know I'm up here."

The public stairs twist through ten stories of musty spaces filled with forgotten storage and touched for years only by the yellow glow seeping through the canvas-covered windows and the rats peering out of every corner. These would make wonderful apartments if the councilors and shipowners would allow someone above them.

Near the top Ject realizes the rats are keeping to the lower floors. Ravis notices this too. "That's a good sign, I suppose."

Ject says, "It's a bad day when finding a dragon is good."

"A what?" the seneschal says. "So much to do. So much. You can find your own way." He bobs down the stairs.

Indeed, how dramatic it would be to find the dragon here, Ject thinks. *They'd call it the Dragon Tower ever after, and war would be forestalled.*

Of course he would have to do something about the dragon before it did something about them, and that would be dramatic enough to elevate him above Herse. How could a nimble hip compete with a dragon slayer? How could a liar compete with a new Hero of Hanosh? And Herse would have been so close to getting his war too. The wave rises, the wave falls.

"Load your weapons," Ject says. The crossbows make an eerie straining in the echoing stairs.

The stairs open at last on a foyer outside the old council chamber. The bare windows are wider here because the walls are thinner than below, and, being higher, they're letting in more of the morning. The stained glass, red, gold, and blue, burnishes the room. Dark wooden benches blanketed in dust warm themselves in the sunlight. Between the spiral staircases, a door leads to a widow's walk. Opposite it, the brass doors to the council chamber have bas reliefs that, like the mosaics in the tile floor, depict images of Hanosh at the founding of the League, the ruins of war rebuilt with the promise of prosperity for all.

"You don't see its like anymore," Ject says, "that art. Too many flourishes. Too much light." Too many smiles, Eles once said of the style. No market for it now. Art should be plain and prudent, properly flat. The doors and floor do feel aggressively showy to Ject, like a naïf made up to seem older.

Ravis unlocks the chamber doors, but the hinges are frozen. It takes four guards to pull the doors wide enough for Ject to look in. Canvas shrouds the banc and the pews and tables arrayed before it. They're covered with droppings and littered with dried rat guts and bones. Dust sparkles in the light coming through the stained glass.

Ject hears a tap from the center of the room, an area walled off by canvas. He holds his hand up. The guards form two lines behind him. The tap comes again. Ject points and stands aside. His men enter with crossbows drawn, one line curling left, the other right. At the head of the left line Ravis sights his crossbow over the pew nearest the sound, then waves Ject to him.

A body lies in a pool of blood, its legs bent along new joints, its face smashed. Nonetheless, Ject says, "That's Skite." He carefully digs a house shield from the body's pocket to confirm this. "Why was he up here?"

"Up there," Ravis says, pointing. "He must have fallen."

Ject looks at the top of the dome and notes the dark stain outlining the trapdoor to the cupola. A drop of blood falls from it and taps the pool around Skite.

"I think I know where we'll find Chelson's other men," Ject says.

Last night, Ject thinks, *their only mission would have been finding Chelson's daughter. Could they have tracked her here? Was her abductor also the tower thief? Did he drive off the ravens? He couldn't have come through the main doors, though. They were locked and stiff.* He looks toward the servants' stairs and notices the door is slightly ajar. That's how he came and went. Ject's heart sinks. Well, he thinks, if there's no dragon, at least he can catch the bad guy and maybe rescue the princess.

"Let's take a less direct route," Ject says. "The widow's walk." Ject looks from the door outside near the servants' stairs toward the one leading outside from the foyer, and that's when he sees the shadowy face staring at them through a window near the latter.

Peeking through the cracked door from the servants' stairs, Herse watches Ject's men open the brass doors across the old council chamber. They check the body as he had been doing a moment ago before hearing them approach and hiding.

He was not surprised it's Skite. Herse heard about Tristaban's abduction last night from a friend in the guard. Chelson's men must have tracked the abductor here. He can't imagine why here, but why he fell is obvious. The stairs and catwalk are very defensible. And it would be easy to slip in the dark, especially if pushed from above.

Ject looks at the servants' stairs, Herse slides into the darkness, then Ject races with his men back to the foyer. Herse would have been leery of climbing to the trapdoor, but as the guards pour onto the widow's walk, their distraction makes that approach less complicated. He loads his crossbow and holds the dirk along the stock. If the girl is up there, he could save the day.

As he slips past the servants' stairs door, he notices that the bar for the door beside it, which leads to the widow's walk, is lying on the floor. Wanting to protect his rear, Herse replaces the bar.

3

Earlier, after Skite fell, Jeryon flew down the servants' stairs to hide Derc's body more thoroughly. By candlelight he stuffed him into the cesspit with a broom and replaced the seat.

He wiped up the blood in the hallway with a rag and water from the kitchen then cleaned up the broken jar and dried the floor. Having covered his tracks, he browsed the pantries for some breakfast. As famished as he was he knew he was really just killing time. He couldn't bring himself to return to the cupola. He only admitted this to himself when he heard footsteps on the stoop. He doused the candle and went up the kitchen stairs, but as he reached the door to the service hallway, the tower's backdoor was unlocked.

Jeryon peeked out. A scullery in a ratty tunic entered from the back stoop. She cradled a stub of candle to light her way. Jeryon drew his knife. He didn't want to kill her, but others would arrive soon, and she was between him and the servants' stairs. She was so scrawny he wouldn't need the broom to get her into the cesspit.

The scullery closed the back door and walked toward the kitchen stairs. Jeryon moved the knife to his left hand so he could take her without exposing himself. She stopped. He bent his legs and waited to spring. She hung her head and tears fell into her hands, so many they nearly put the candle out.

Is this how all her mornings began? What had she done? The men upstairs, he'd recognized them as Chelson's guards. He'd known what they were and what they would have done to him. Tuse and Solet, their crews, they were all soldiers in a war the Shield had started. The girl with the knife he'd dumped in the sea, he probably shouldn't have let her live. Who knows how she'd come back to haunt him. Foolish sympathy. But this scullery, she was no one. She might have welcomed his knife, but she hadn't earned it.

Jeryon tiptoed down the stairs and hid in a corner. Is this how all his mornings would begin? Hiding and waiting and making excuses the poth couldn't hear? He was so close to what he wanted, but it felt further away than her.

The girl came down a moment later, and as she kindled the stoves and ovens he tiptoed up and ran down the hallway to the servants' stairs. At the door to the empty stories he put his candle back in its sconce and rigged the door to make it appear locked.

In the old council chamber Jeryon stood over Skite until dawn illuminated the stained glass and the trapdoor above stopped thumping. Gray isn't gentle with her food, especially long pig, which she's favored since Tuse. She barely nibbled the meat he stole.

Jeryon hoped the girl stopped screaming because she'd been obedient.

When the thumping started again, Jeryon decided he needed some fresh air.

The door in the council chamber to the widow's walk was locked and barred, but he found a dusty key hidden atop its arch. He crawled outside so he wouldn't be seen from below, and closed the door behind him. He heard chanting and arguing in the plaza, so he looked through an iron balustrade painted cream to match the tower. He was astounded by its size and the fact that the guards weren't arresting anyone.

Jeryon considered how he could work the crowd into his plans. Being discovered by Chelson's men meant he would have to accelerate matters. Surely others knew where they went. If he were to expose Livion and the Shield for what they'd done, simply flying into the plaza might have made his case. Of course, he might have also caused a panic and caught a dozen crossbow bolts before he reached the ground.

He could make his case directly to Ject, but Jeryon can estimate his price: the dragon.

While he waited in the Round Square to see Livion yesterday, Prieve walked by, and Jeryon thought about making his case to him. The old man would have been sympathetic; their interactions had always been enjoyable, but unlike Ject Prieve couldn't have overlooked the guard and maid that Gray plucked off Quiet Tower.

The crowd roared, and Jeryon crawled to the north side of the tower for a better view. The people swirled and clashed. Soldiers entered the plaza, but few and in danger of being overrun. Jeryon doesn't know this city anymore.

And they didn't know him. He must have seen a dozen acquaintances in the square and none recognized him. He was glad at first, not wanting his plan disrupted, then increasingly sad. When his father appeared and put a few poorly made pieces of scrimshaw on the cobbles, he stood up so his father could get a good look at him. Nothing. His eyes were blank.

The sun crowned on the horizon. The glare reminded him of how his father's eyes used to be and what drove him to the tower when he was a boy.

His father had been reduced to making penny bets to pay for his beer, bets he always lost for pennies he never had, which saw him paying off his debts with scars and bruises. People would bet him just to beat him after he lost. One day someone in the Salty Dog with rare pity slipped Jeryon some pennies. His father noticed and told him to turn them over. Jeryon refused. So his father went after him with a knife and glass. A man doesn't get in the way of another's business, plus the betting favored Jeryon, so no one stepped in. Jeryon couldn't do what had to be done. He flung the pennies at his father and fled to the tower. If he hadn't been lured by the sea he might have jumped.

The thumping in the cupola diminished. He decided to give Gray a few more minutes to digest before going up. In the meantime, he watched the crowd. He pillowed his head on his arms. He hadn't had a decent hour's sleep in weeks. His legs were full of sand. His head was too. The walk was cool. The breeze was soft. He'd deal with Skite later.

Jeryon's startled awake by a sound inside. So used to worrying about the blue crabs, he leaps up, draws his knife, peers through the stained glass beside another door, and finds several shadows peering back.

4

Ravis unbars and unlocks the door to the widow's walk from the foyer and Ject's detail surges through. Two run left around the northwest arc of the tower, and two run right. Ravis and Oftly turn and scan the dome, the short eave two feet above their heads. Both spy the man crawling toward the cupola. "Got him," Ravis says. "You. Stop."

Ject shouts so all his men can hear, "You. Stop. You're surrounded." The man looks back through goggled eyes and a scraggly beard, but keeps climbing. "Wing him," Ject says.

Ravis leans back over the balustrade, aims, and lets fly. The bolt hits the man on the side of his buttocks, but it skips off his odd black leather pants and clatters over the dome.

Oftly aims for the man's sandaled foot. The bolt hits him in the heel with a clank and bounces away.

Ject says, "What the—"

The man whistles. In the cupola, a sinuous silhouette rises over the chest-high walls stretching between its pillars. Ravis and Oftly reload, trying not to look.

Who is this man who can command a dragon? Ject thinks. How is that possible? He could try to capture them, but generals who overreach generally fall.

Bolts twang from around the walk. Two hit the cupola, one chips off some cream-colored marble, the other lodges in its tiny blue dome. Two others sail through the cupola, past the shadow, and disappear into the city. Ject doesn't want to know where they land.

A gray head emerges, flecked with golden light and gore. A long neck follows it then two little claws pull two wings over the wall.

"Tiny," says Ravis, "as dragons go."

"Big enough for me," Oftly says.

"Is that a pack on its back," Ject says, "or a saddle?"

The rest of the dragon pushes out of the cupola, and it picks its way toward the man, tail waving for balance, claws grating on the dome's tiles. Clay scree showers the guards. The man mounts the dragon and faces Ject.

Ject sees through the beard, the goggles, and time. "Impossible," he says.

As the shadows of Ject's detail dance across the stained glass windows, Herse mounts the iron stairs. Halfway up, he grabs the railing as they're rattled by something heavy banging on the dome. Several different thoughts assemble into an unexpected whole.

Was that feet? The person who snatched Chelson's daughter must be hiding above. What creature that large could get on top of the tower? Someone riding a dragon destroyed Tuse's ship. Solet's wolf pack was destroyed by a dragon. Is there a dragon up there? Is the abductor its rider? Could he be responsible for all three attacks and the body here? If so, Herse doesn't care what the rider must have against the Heroes of Hanosh. He wants the dragon.

He crawls along the catwalk lest he be shaken off. He doesn't touch the severed hand resting there. He climbs the ladder, which smears his hands and clothes with blood, which can't all be Skite's. Holestar and Derc must be above. That would explain the stain around the trapdoor.

Footsteps move down the dome toward the widow's walk. Ject is standing tough, Herse will give him that.

He pushes the trapdoor. Blood rains down his arm and over his face. Something's blocking the door. He climbs higher and rams it open with his shoulder. A weight slides off it; he whips his crossbow up and points the bolt at the wide, icy eye of Tristaban.

Ravis steps in front of his general and raises his crossbow, but he can't bring himself to fire. His face loses all color; his eyes, all focus; his heart, all warmth. He wishes the eave offered more cover. The dragon's teeth are so white.

Ject looks into the dragon's lacy eyes and sees the future: the creature biting off Ravis's face, grabbing Ject's head, tossing him over the balustrade. This is not the victory he imagined by discovering the dragon.

"Hold your fire!" he yells. He puts his hand on Ravis's shoulder, and the first guard dips his crossbow. Oftly does too. Then Ject says to the man, "I remember you. Before the beard."

The man guides the dragon to the lip of the dome. It's ungainly on all fours, head bobbing, tail swishing, like a horse whose legs were cut off at the knees. Ject is terrified it will slip and fall and carry them to the plaza. The dragon sniffs Ject and Ravis. Its breath is a miasma of fish and fresh meat.

"I don't want to hurt you," he says.

"I don't want to hurt you either," Ject says. "I need your help. To save the city. Again."

"You can help me too."

"I'll do what I can. You can trust me, Jeryon."

The cupola is disturbingly well organized. On one side a canvas tarp, rolled and tied, sits beside crude woven baskets of food and black skins full of water or wine. On the other, a neatly collected pile of scat, bones, and the remains of a city guard, probably the missing man from Quiet. The floor glistens as if recently mopped. In the middle lies Tristaban, wrists bound behind her, mouth gagged, body bruised and bloody. Holestar's head sits nearby, as does his body, the belly torn open.

Herse smiles, lowers the crossbow, and puts a finger to his lips. Tristaban shivers a nod. He climbs all the way into the cupola, keeping his head below its low walls. He lifts her onto her knees, pulls her gag loose then plucks a ball of dirty cloth from her mouth. She coughs and spits. He shushes her soothingly, and she remembers how to act alive.

"Are you all right?" he says, pointing at several aloe leaves tied on like bandages with thread.

"It ate him," she says. "I watched it eat him."

"Listen." Herse holds her cheek. "Who's he with?"

"What? A company?" Tristaban says. "None. It's Jeryon."

"Who?"

"The captain of the *Comber*."

So the rumors are true. Jeryon was given the captain's chance. Herse should have known. Chelson had to have seen something in Livion.

"He was going to trade me for their confessions," Tristaban says. "Livion's. And my father's. He'd ruin us." Her eyes dart to the crossbow. "You have to do something."

"Of course," he says. "We're partners."

His hand is still on her cheek. She smiles. "I like the sound of that word when you say it."

He pats her cheek and crouch-walks to the wall.

She twists to watch him. "Cut me loose," she says.

He shushes her and peeks over.

"I have to ask," Ject says. "Did you take Chelson's daughter?"

"Yes."

"Is she all right?"

"Yes."

"Up there?"

Jeryon nods.

"Good." Two fish, one hook. "Why don't you come down from there? My neck's getting a crick looking up like this."

Jeryon stiffens. He says, "With your men waiting to take me?" He plies the reins. The dragon swings its head to watch Ravis and Oftly.

"I'll call them off. Stand down! To me!"

This breaks the spell cast over his first guard. Ravis reluctantly lowers his crossbow to his side.

Ject's guards edge around the tower, crossbows half-raised, confused. The general says, "At ease. We're all friends here."

"Is that everyone?" Jeryon says. Ject nods. "Put the weapons down."

"Let's go one better," Ject says. "Ravis, lead the detail inside so the captain and I can talk."

"They'll stay out here where I can see them."

Ject shrugs and flutters his hand. His men lay their weapons on the walk.

Ravis turns away from the dragon to put his down, and with his eyes directs Oftly's to the cave. The first guard slashes a finger toward himself and to the dragon as he turns back. Oftly understands. They couldn't climb onto the dome before being attacked, and even if they could the rider is far enough from them that he could take off before they could attack. If Ravis struck at the dragon's neck, that might distract the rider enough for Oftly to get to him.

Keeping the detail in view, Jeryon backs the dragon up the dome and edges east and west to make sure no one is on the walk. A shadow shifts in the corner of his eye. He glances at the cupola. The girl isn't watching him. He's not surprised. He left her half-catatonic. She's probably seen enough in the dome to put her off meat for life. Satisfied, he returns to Ject.

"At least someone in this city isn't a liar," Jeryon says. He gives a little downward tug on the dragon's halter, and it rests on its elbows, which causes the crossbow bolt whistling toward the back of his head to only graze his scalp.

5

As the city guards assemble in ranks on one side of the plaza and the tanner stirs up his cohorts on the other, some in the crowd sink back into the city, but the pressure pushes the rest near boiling.

In front of Rego the six-fingered man, the pig-tailed girl, the father and his son surround the man who would take three coins. Several come to his defense, while others offer themselves up for two. Jostling turns into shoving. The boy starts crying and his father tells him to shut up, which makes him cry louder and makes the girl tell the boy to shut up. Now the father turns on the six-fingered man, who says he has no idea who the girl is. Meanwhile the girl picks both their pockets, and the bidding drops to thirty pennies.

In the middle of the plaza a woman in an old tunic and well-tended leather pants screams. The crowd parts, repelled by the realization that the man standing beside her has a crossbow bolt plunged through his eye and out the base of his skull. He blinks his good eye and collapses. The crowd turns on the guard while Rego traces the bolt's trajectory back to the dome and sees a man falling from the widow's walk, trailing fire.

Herse ducks behind the wall as quickly as he looked over it to fire and pulls a new bolt from his quiver. Tristaban says, "Did you get him?"

He shakes his head.

"You have to," she says, "but free me first."

"You're safer tied up," he says, and sits down so he can put his foot in the crossbow's stirrup.

"I can't stand this place."

"Stay put," he says. Herse leans back and cocks the crossbow. "No, sit on that trapdoor. Make sure no one gets up here."

Herse loads a bolt, but he can't risk another shot yet.

Jeryon watches the bolt kill a man in the crowd, glances back to find no one behind him, then glares at Ject and whistles three times. Ject throws up his hands, yelling, "Wait, wait!" The dragon lunges. Ravis's sword leaps from his baldric and arcs toward the dragon's reaching neck. Oftly grabs his sword, grabs the eave, jumps, and presses himself onto the dome. The other guards dive for their crossbows. Ravis's leaf-shaped blade sticks in a plate from which one of the dragon's spines grows as the dragon snaps a medal off the general's chest. Oftly charges Jeryon, who sweeps his knife at him and delays Oftly just long enough for the dragon to whip its head around to face the guard. The sword falls off its neck and clatters to the walk. It spits the medal onto the dome at Oftly's feet. The guard screams. Jeryon says, "Comber."

The flames envelop Oftly and chase him as he stumbles off the dome. Ravis throws himself and Ject aside, but the rest of the guards are caught. Oftly bounces off the balustrade and plummets to the terrace while the rest beat at their flaming bodies with flaming hands.

Jeryon yells at Ject, fire dancing in the lenses of his goggles, "Why did you do that? Why?"

"Whoever fired that bolt," Ject says, "that wasn't my man."

"This one is," Jeryon says. The dragon turns on Ravis.

Ravis crawls to his sword. It was a mistake to strike the top of the neck. One good sweep to the throat and the dragon will be finished. He grabs the sword and starts to roll, and a massive weight lands on his back. The gnashing heat of the dragon's fire envelops him. The cries and commotion of the city dissolve into the simmer of waves receding. He feels weightless. Over the balustrade he floats and over the plaza, and when the dragon lets go he feels like he's rising away with it.

When the first body splashes on the terrace, the plaza goes silent. Hundreds of faces look up and see the dragon. Differences are forgotten. A few say what many think, "There was a dragon. There will be no war." When the dragon grabs a second man, dives, and flings him at the plaza, everyone thinks, *There is a dragon, and it's coming for me.*

The crowd tries to drain into the nearby streets, but they're blocked by the guard and the tanner's cohorts. In the center, many people stand like rocks amid the breakers, and that's where the trampling begins.

At the north end, people crash against the shields of Pashing's squad, which drives the soldiers against the wagon. The horse whickers and dances, alarmed. As Birming tries to control her, Pashing says, "We have to get the money out of the plaza."

Rego, standing on the seat, watches the woman in the old tunic crouch over the dead painter, protecting him from the dragon and the crowd.

"No," he says. "We have to let these people out. Sergeant, your horn. Order the Guard to fall back and open up those streets."

Husting puts his hand over the horn hanging from his belt and says, "No. The Guard doesn't retreat."

As if in agreement, several guards fire, but in haste. The dragon kicks right and up, avoiding them. Rego sees the man on its back, but his brain rejects the notion, and after the dragon circles out of sight east around the tower all he remembers is gray hide, spikes, and teeth.

"Pashing," Rego says, "take half your men and break up that clot on the east side. Focus on the tanner. He's the ringleader."

"But they're for us," Pashing says.

"And you'll expose us," Husting says.

"This city has too many uses," Rego says.

The dragon rises over the dome, a shimmering fleck of sun, and Husting realizes they're trapped by the masses flowing around them. He jumps onto the wagon so he can be seen and blows the command to pull back.

As Jeryon circles the cupola, apparently aggravated at not finding what he figured he must, Ject wonders who fired the bolt. The girl? Jeryon wouldn't have left her armed. Or untied. From what little he knows of him, Jeryon would be too scrupulous for that.

Ject figures the tower guards must be on their way—a falling body's worth a dozen horns—but they can't have run up here so quickly. It would take five minutes at least. He'll have to do for himself or play for time.

Jeryon circles the walk, looking through the windows, remaining frustrated, and the look he gives Ject says the general won't be passed by again.

Ject can't go back the way he came. The door to the foyer is on fire, so is the doorway, and both are blocked by the roasting remains of his detail. So he waits until the dragon disappears around the east side of the tower, grabs a fallen crossbow, and runs to the door to the council chamber. It had been unbarred. That must have been how Jeryon got out here. He presses the latch. The door is unlocked, as he had hoped.

Ject hears the dragon coming back around. He gets down on one knee and presses himself against the tower so he has cover from the eave and balustrade. Forget the door. He'll deal with Jeryon directly. He has one shot. And Jeryon is just a man. Ject lifts the crossbow to his shoulder.

The dragon's wing appears. Ject's finger tightens on the trigger. And the dragon tightens its turn, rises, and lands somewhere above him on the dome. Now the eave gives Jeryon cover. Ject will have to move out to the balustrade to have a shot at him, but revealed, he might be dead before he can fire.

Roof tiles shatter. Shards slide onto the walk, falling in a line that moves away from Ject, then comes back. The dragon must be coming back too. He hears it breathing. He smells its breath.

Ject aims at the sky in front of the eave. He listens for the whistle. As soon as the head appears he'll fire. If he misses he should still hit the neck, a point-blank shot, and that might be fatal. The roof falls silent. Ject waits. The point of his bolt bobs with his breath. He can't slow it. Skittering above him. Can Jeryon command the dragon to attack silently? More skittering, like a faulty step. A shield-sized expanse of tiles smashes onto the walk. Ject, startled, nearly fires. The dragon moves away south.

Ject exhales and his ears open to the din of the plaza. The walk blocks most of his view, but what he can see looks like a riot. Soldiers are plowing into a group of workers and driving them out of the plaza, while others flow to the west. They keep looking up to make sure they're escaping the dragon. Where are his men? What a terrible day for the Guard.

Ject pivots to the south, aims again, and hears the thud of sandaled feet landing on the walk. So that's his game: while the dragon waits on the dome, Jeryon will flank him. Ject will get the drop on him instead. He crouch-walks a couple steps and listens: sandals scraping on the stone. Another step: The scraping is just beyond the turn of the tower. Ject charges the last few steps and he can't help himself, he can't risk not doing it, he fires.

There's no one there, just two sandals tied to a cord that extends up and onto the dome.

Ject hears three whistles behind him and after the first he's running for the door. After the second, as quickly as they come, he has the door latch. At the third he pushes in. The door chunks solid against its bar. *Why?* Ject thinks. He watches the shadow of the dragon's head and neck slither over the wall toward him. He's wheeling around to brain it with the crossbow when his left shoulder explodes in pain.

The dragon shakes him until his weapon is flung away, then it lifts him half over the balustrade. Ject's fingers briefly find a hold, which lets him jam his legs through the balusters and wrap his feet around them. The dragon shakes him more violently. He won't be able to hold on for long, but the guards should arrive soon.

More tiles give way beneath the dragon, and it releases Ject before it tumbles off the dome. The general sits down hard on the balustrade. His sash, bitten through, plunges into the city, weighted down by so many medals. Ject tips backward, but catches his feet in the balusters and hauls himself back up as the dragon regains its footing.

"I only wanted justice," Jeryon says. "I only wanted my due. Is that too much to ask?"

"I can get you that," Ject says.

"Not after all this."

The dragon snaps at Ject, but he's just out of reach, so it rears its head in anticipation and glances at Jeryon.

Ject loosens one foot from a baluster. If he could get to the foyer door he could dive through the flames into the tower. With a wince, though, he realizes that his ankle's broken. He can't run. So he considers letting himself fall. He might survive. There's a precedent.

Decades ago, after the tower was heightened and the blue dome built, the widow's walk was open to all. People came from every city in the League and every town in between. Lines wrapped all through the plaza, whatever the weather. Couples signed partner agreements on the walk. Owners signed contracts. People picnicked and shouted. They dreamed and escaped. Then they started to jump.

One a month, five, ten. Leathers and silk. Rookery, Harbor, and Crest. The walk drew so many visitors the Council didn't want to close it, so guards were stationed on the walk and trained to identify jumpers. One of those guards eventually jumped. Some jumpers had been ruined. Many saw no way to fortune. A few were successful and apparently content. Countless were the couples that couldn't afford to partner. And one man tossed his three sedated children into the plaza; he didn't jump himself. The terrace became a death trap.

A woman named Uly was the person who lived. A huge councilor broke her fall. He died, and as a result the walk was closed, the doors above the offices were locked, and Uly, still in a coma, was put in a gibbet with her shattered legs and hips.

The smallest chance is better than none, Ject thinks. *Just tip back and let go*.

He can't. He says, "But the girl's all right. We could find a way to make things work out."

"I'm done trusting this city."

"You could rule it. You have a dragon. And you could confiscate . . ."

"I only wanted to serve. Look where it's gotten us."

Ject can't look at the dragon, so he looks past Jeryon and sees a shadow appear above the wall of the cupola. It's Herse with a loaded crossbow.

6

As Jeryon circles the cupola Tristaban squeezes her eyes shut. She's grateful Herse had the foresight to leave her bound. Otherwise, Jeryon might have had the dragon eat her before she got away. And if she had escaped, who knows what he might have done in retaliation. He knows where she lives. He knows where her father lives. He might have burned them out.

Herse thinks of everything. He's played the Council as perfectly as she played her father when it came to partnering with Livion. What they could do together. Yes, he was born in the gutter, but look how he's risen. And once he plunders Ayden, his wave will crest. She should ride it. His share could make him nearly as powerful as her father, maybe more so. What's Livion in comparison? A pair of boots. Herse is the whole uniform.

Why did those boots make her so foolish? At least Livion was the bigger fool. His feelings made him blind to their contract's bottom line. She severs it, and he'll be due just a small dowry. She could, in fact, pay it herself. She will, she decides, and she'll arrange her next partnership herself. The way Herse touched her cheek: She can make him sign just like Livion did. And let her father squawk if he doesn't like it. She's won't be his Little Doll anymore. It's time to put herself on the top shelf.

When she hears it land on the dome below the cupola, she rolls aside and thumps the trapdoor with her heels. Herse opens it from below, having had the foresight to hide on the ladder when the dragon started circling in order to find whoever fired the bolt. He climbs up with the crossbow. She says, "He's down there."

"I knew you were tough," he says, and returns to the wall. Before hiding, he'd seen how Jeryon maneuvered the dragon, making it move and turn, dive and rise, with a combination of whistles, reins, and knees. It shouldn't take him long to master. Herse aims the crossbow at Jeryon's back.

Jeryon removes his sandals and ties them to a cord he takes from a saddlebag. He casts them over the edge of the dome to his right like a fishing line, plays it a bit, then whistles three times. The dragon's head lashes out. It catches something and rises. Ject's face appears. The dragon shakes him ruthlessly, but Ject can't be thrown over the balustrade. The dragon lets go.

Ject bargains with Jeryon. Herse can barely hear what they're saying, but Jeryon's posture is unmoved and Ject looks resigned. Then Ject meets Herse's gaze. For a second the thought flares in Ject's eyes to tell Jeryon where Herse is. Surely he's complained that one of his men didn't fire on Jeryon. Ject knows Jeryon wouldn't buy it, though, so he pleads with his eyes, "Shoot him, Herse. Shoot him now."

Ject watches Herse rest his arms on top of the low cupola wall to steady the crossbow. He takes careful aim, then looks at Ject and shakes his head.

"Comber," Jeryon says.

No one can doubt, Ject thinks, *that a dragon, this dragon, not Ayden, destroyed the wolf pack*. Jeryon's wearing the goggles Solet had specially commissioned. Herse's lies will come out. He'll be ruined. Chelson will be too. As the flames envelop him, Ject thinks, *I've won*.

As the heat from Gray's breath flows back over him, Jeryon looks across the bay. The sun is perfect; the water so blue the fishing boats and galleys look like they're flying. Eryn Point gleams, and the sea beyond sparkles. It still draws him as strongly as it did when he was a boy. Tuse was right. He should have taken Everlyn into the dawn.

He'll go to Yness. Not many people know him beyond the beaches, and he isn't the man they knew. If the poth made it to land, she likely passed through the area. At the very least he could send out agents from there to find her. He has a fortune in render. He could hire the best.

His focus pulls to the Castle. He could light it on fire as he leaves, a parting shot. Why bother, though? He'll leave the girl too. Let her be a reminder to Livion and her father every day that he's out there and he can get to them. Maybe that's the best revenge, the constant threat of revenge.

Jeryon feels relieved. He's won.

The last drops of fire sputter from the dragon's mouth, and Herse shoots. The bolt goes clean through Jeryon's neck, and blood fountains over the dragon and the dome. He drops the reins and grabs his throat, curious what happened.

The dragon doesn't notice. It's watching Ject burn the way children stare at candles.

Herse kicks off his sandals, vaults the cupola wall, and walks gingerly down the dome to the dragon. The tiles are cool on his feet and easier to grip than he would have thought, being rough with the barnacles of old raven droppings.

Jeryon sways in the saddle. He puckers, but his whistle is a froth of blood. As Herse reaches him, he flails his knife until Herse catches his wrist. Jeryon flops onto him. Herse reaches into Jeryon's lap to undo the strap securing him to the saddle, slides him off, and lays him on the dome.

Jeryon's eyes struggle to focus. He lays his hand across Herse's cheek.

"I know what they must have done," Herse says. "I know how you must have suffered and wanted and waited for vengeance. I know. I understand. You will have it. We will have it. I promise."

Jeryon squeezes Herse's cheek and mouths, "Ev." His hand drops to his chest. His head rolls slightly, and the sun flares his goggle lenses pure white.

Herse stands up and finds the dragon staring at him. Its eyes slit. Its head rears. Its jaw drops.

The plaza has emptied considerably. Rego stayed with Husting while Birming got the wagon back to Gate.

"It's odd," Rego says, "working on this side of the wall."

"Don't make a habit of it," Husting says. He looks at those who've remained to watch the drama on the dome and those who've returned, wanting a better view than the side streets offer. They're dead silent like at the end of a close hip-ball match.

"Maybe we should round up the stragglers," Husting says. "The general would want to salvage something."

"Doesn't matter. Look."

They can tell Ject by his clothes as the dragon snatches him from cover and shakes him and sets him like a potted plant on the balustrade. When the flames engulf him a few people applaud. Most cry out in horror and fury. Ject was a bastard, but he was their bastard.

Husting points two guards at the clappers. There will be some profit in this day yet.

When the rider arches and grabs his throat, the plaza is confused until Herse walks down the dome, and they cheer as if he'd just scored the winning goal. When he dismounts the rider they roar.

Rego clenches his whole body. If Herse can take the dragon, everything they've ever whispered about since they were children becomes more possible. If he can't, Rego won't know what to do with himself. So when Herse faces the creature and it rears its head Rego feels like he's strangling his own heart.

Before he can question his sanity, Herse grabs the dragon's halter, nearly slipping on the dome, and whistles twice. The dragon pulls back, closing its mouth. Herse holds on tighter and whistles again. The dragon, incredibly, sits. He makes sure of his footing then rubs its neck. It pushes against his hand. He rubs more aggressively.

If this were a horse he were trying to break, he'd give it an apple or carrot. If it were a dog, a piece of meat. Herse points the dragon's head at Jeryon's body and whistles three times. He'd been wondering what he'd do about this evidence against Chelson and, by extension, him.

The dragon sniffs Jeryon, looks at Herse, and tilts its head. Herse whistles three times. The dragon shrugs and gnaws its way into Jeryon's belly.

Herse mounts the dragon. He's not particularly comfortable, but the saddle is cleverly designed; his saddlers will enjoy making something better. He holds the reins loosely so the dragon can keep eating. It burrows its whole snout under Jeryon's rib cage to tear out his heart. The dragon tosses it back then goes to work on Jeryon's face. The glass and leather goggles don't slow it down.

It occurs to him there's another loose end he should trim, one he should have dealt with before he shot Jeryon. He looks at the cupola. Tristaban kneels at the wall, smirking, as if knowing too much is an asset. Herse winks.

Once the dragon's eaten its fill he walks it up the dome to her. She stands up against her pain, her arms behind her back, her mouth half-open, her chest and neck aflush. A bandage slips off, and Herse feels a little sorry for her.

When he's halfway there, though, the tower guards burst onto the walk, Chevron calling orders, and the distraction opens his ears to the crowd.

He turns the dragon around. She'll have to wait. The plaza is filling again. All the streets around the tower are filling. Everyone is looking up at him and cheering. He's a parade of one, triumphant. He lifts an arm. The city roars. He can see them in the Harbor. He can see them on the roofs of Hanoshi Town. On the lanes and streets and boulevards up and down the Hill. Only the Crest is quiet. This is his city. This is his real army. He will give them the war they need to mold them into a people again.

For too long Hanosh has followed the sail of the sea. Now they will follow the sail of the sky. And knowing what his people want, Herse snaps the reins. The dragon's wings clap above his head, and Herse holds on for his life as the dragon screeches and takes flight.

EPILOGUE

In the highest room of the Castle's highest tower, Sivarts scans the city from a tall paned window. He can't imagine what's taking the surgeon so long. He has to get back to his galley. He's on the verge of having Felic find the man and escort him there directly when a woman on the street below grabs her companion's shoulder and points at the tower.

Something circles the cupola. "That's the biggest raven I've ever seen," Sivarts says. The creature lands on the dome, perfectly profiled, shining silver in the sun. "Or is it an albatross? Immense." It snaps at something on the walk, shakes it and releases it then the creature vomits fire. Flames shower the east side of the tower, dissipating halfway down.

"That's no bird," Sivarts says. "That's a dragon. And—" A figure rises on the dragon's back and, despite the distance, looks straight through Sivarts. "That's a man," he says. "Can you believe it?"

Sivarts looks over his shoulder at Vel. She's still gagged and fixed to the stretcher set on the floor. She's been watching too. Her eyes grow wet, then huge. Sivarts turns to see the man arch as if shot. Another man climbs out of the cupola and walks with incredible ease down to the dragon. He takes the rider in his arms and lays him on the dome. Strangely his eyes reflect the dawn like two white diamonds. A moment later the second man climbs into the saddle.

When the dragon bites into its former rider, Sivarts chokes on his gorge and the woman moans. He wants to back away. Instead, he fills the window so the woman can't see anymore. He suspects who it must have been, her Jon.

Her expression confirms his suspicions. Her eyes have dried as hard as flint. The burned flesh on her face can't hide such vital fury.

The steps outside creak. Felic opens the door to let the surgeon in. He's wearing the outfit of his profession: loose cotton pants and a long-sleeve tunic with a hood, both black to better hide blood and other errant fluids. Even the bandage around his hand is black. He crouches beside the woman and sets his leather satchel down.

"So, this is our patient," the surgeon says. He notes how she's biting the gag and lifts the covers to see the straps. "What's all this for? Is she dangerous?"

"Possibly."

"We'll take care of that," the surgeon says. "Now leave us. Our examination requires privacy."

"I'll post a guard outside," Sivarts says.

"At the bottom of the stairs, if you must. Stamping and snorting is terribly distracting."

The surgeon locks the door behind Sivarts and removes a small bottle and a black rag from his satchel. He uncorks the bottle. A sickly sweet odor fills the room. He dabs some onto the rag.

The woman's brow furrows. She protests through her gag.

"Oh, no," he says. "This isn't for you. It's for us. We've had a very trying night." He huffs his rag, sighs, and tucks it in his collar. He puts the bottle away and pulls out a scalpel and a pair of pliers. "These are for you. To cure you of your reticence. We want to know everything you know. Things you don't yet realize you know. Let's start with where you got that blouse."

As the surgeon huffs his rag, Everlyn looks out the window. Gray makes another circuit of the tower. The new rider waves. To check her feelings, she concentrates on the placket of Jeryon's captain's blouse. She slides her arm slowly between a strap and her belly to run her thumbnail along one edge of the placket until it catches on a tiny hard surface inside. She presses. Having taken a cue from the pant cuffs of Jeryon's uniform, she pokes a long, needle-thin, but single-edged dragonbone blade through the cloth.

Also released, or maybe it's just her mind playing tricks, is the last faint whisper of how he smelled. Her hands shake. She thinks of his beard and how nice it made him look, how rough it felt at first, then how soft. Her hands settle.

Everlyn slides the blade free one finger push at a time and palms it.

She will escape this monster, escape this place, and then she will get their dragon back.

In the highest room of her compound, the White Widow looks up through tall windows at the dragon circling the tower. The flames on the dome are dying down. The cheers are not. She gongs for one of her maids.

The young woman has rough hands like most maids, but her calluses didn't come from churning a lye pot. She's better fed too, and her arms and legs are taut as drumheads.

"Dress like a trade rider this time," Asper tells her, "and bring word to my father immediately. They may close the gates. Hanosh has a dragon." It swoops low over the compound, and Asper realizes who the rider is. "No, tell him Herse has a dragon. And whether or not we're at war already, Ayden must take it. Or kill it."

Acknowledgments

Nobody makes a book alone.

I'd like to thank:

My first readers: David Fantini, Brian Hopper, Eric B. Lass, and Nathan Ophardt, for their excellent advice and much-appreciated encouragement.

My team at Simon451, especially my editor, Brit Hvide. Her editorial vision and enthusiasm is why I signed with them. Her pointed notes and unflagging desire to get the book right demonstrated that I'd made a good decision. Elina Vaysbeyn, my online marketer, gave me extensive notes on my website. Tornstein Nordstrand painted the perfect cover image. Jonathan Evans and Dominick Montalto made sure that every comma was in its place.

My former employer, John Wiley & Sons, which, by laying me off and giving me a generous severance package, thereby provided both the impetus and the means to write this book.

My wife, Chris Condry, and our daughter, Alice Hope Condry-Power, for many things, but in particular for their forgiveness. I can get testy when I'm writing. The same is true when I'm hungry, but that's not important here.

And finally my agent, Eric Nelson, who found the book a wonderful home, who gave me critical advice along the way, and who inspired it in the first place. One day he said, "Why would someone write a book for kids without a dragon?" and I thought, "Why would someone write a book for anyone without a dragon?"